M000020792

THE
CASTLE

THE
CASTLE

**A
NOVEL**

JASON
PINTER

The following is a work of fiction. Names, characters, places, events and incidents are either the product of the author's imagination or used in an entirely fictitious manner. Any resemblance to actual persons, living or dead, is entirely coincidental.

Copyright © 2017 by Jason Pinter
Published by Armina Press

Cover and jacket design by 2Faced Design
Interior designed and formatted by E.M. Tippetts Book Designs

ISBN 978-1-943818-99-0

Library of Congress Control Number: 2017907545

Also by
JASON PINTER

The Henry Parker series
The Mark
The Guilty
The Stolen
The Fury
The Hunters (novella)
The Darkness

For Children
Zeke Bartholomew: Superspy!

For Dana and Ava
My Queens

"*I am not afraid of an army of lions led by a sheep.*
I am afraid of an army of sheep led by a lion."
—*Alexander the Great*

"*Revolution is not a dinner party, not an essay, nor a painting, nor a piece of embroidery; it cannot be advanced softly, gradually, carefully, considerately, respectfully, politely, plainly, and modestly.*"
—*Mao Zedong*

"*There is a savage beast in every man, and when you hand that man a sword or a spear and send him forth to war, that beast stirs.*"
—*A Storm of Swords, George R. R. Martin*

SUMMER

"He knows. I don't know how, but he knows."

"That's impossible. We've been careful. The burners. The secure server."

"Not careful enough, obviously. He banned me from the meetings. He's going to officially announce it in the next few weeks. The bastard is really going through with it. He wouldn't have banned me if he didn't think I was dangerous."

"Shit."

"You see? He knows."

"You can stop right now. We never have to speak again. You've given us more than enough to go after him if he really goes through with it. And Paul? The senator can protect you."

"No, she can't. You don't know Rawson Griggs the way I do. And if I'm right, if this is all true, then he's in deeper than you can imagine."

"You need to take precautions. You might be in danger."

"You don't think that keeps me awake every single night? I haven't slept in months. Just...stop him."

"How?"

"I don't know. Somehow. Because if he runs, and he wins, nothing will ever be the same."

CHAPTER 1

Had Remy Stanton known his life would change that night, that the next time he woke up there would be a bullet hole in his chest and the world at his fingertips, he would have chosen a better beer than Miller Lite to drink before it all went down.

A fine, aged scotch. Or perhaps a craft beer, the kind brewed by men in thick flannel shirts and rumpled overalls, suds dripping from their frizzled beards as they stood approvingly over massive stainless steel vats.

But nope. Brand new bullet hole, the world within his grasp. And he chose Miller Lite, a.k.a. the Styrofoam of beers.

He'd been stuck in the office until 9 p.m. Kevin McCarty, his direct supervisor at Pulaski & Associates, informed Remy on his way out—at 5:30, the lazy prick—that he was needed in the office at 7:30 the next morning, a Saturday, for a briefing on a new client, some app developer flush with thirty million in VC funding who would likely burn through it within two years.

There was no reason the meeting needed to be held on a Saturday. Yet Remy had realized early on at Pulaski that most of the senior male consultants enjoyed being at home with their families about as much as they enjoyed getting a heat rash. And younger consultants like Remy, most of whom didn't yet have families to avoid, had no excuse.

Pulaski & Associates was an international strategic planning firm. Travel was constant. Remy logged more miles than most sports teams. Seattle one week. London the next. Dallas. Amsterdam. St. Louis. Munich. Phoenix. Vancouver. His blood type was airport coffee and mini pretzels, and he racked up miles like George Clooney in that movie where he was paid to fire people and ended up fifty and single with nothing but an empty backpack and nobody to talk to but Sam Elliott's mustache. There were months where Remy spent more time in hotel beds than his own. And the worst part: most hotel bars closed at eleven.

He consulted with wealthy CEOs and CFOs, clients a generation or two older than him. Businessmen and women who gawked at this twenty-eight-year-old and wondered whether they'd just lit tens of thousands of dollars on fire.

Yet once the job was complete, they knew Remy was worth it. He could size up companies, situations, and employees like a scout evaluating athletes. Ninety seconds with an executive and Remy would know that he was a pathological narcissist who drove company morale off a cliff. Or a half hour with a company's books, where Remy could add three percent right to their bottom line by cutting off employees who charged champagne room visits to their corporate AMEX.

And, of course, there were the layoffs. "Bloodletting," Pulaski called it. A company had to lance a wound to let the bacteria out. Pulaski was not what Remy would call a people person.

Remy had spent years traveling the globe making money for men like Pulaski. Driving himself towards exhaustion and madness.

So, after leaving the Pulaski offices on Madison Avenue and 53rd Street at nine, Remy decided he needed, no, *deserved* a drink. Maybe several. His tolerance wasn't what it used to be, so he had to be careful not to overdo it. Back in college, he could down a case of PBR and still wake up the next day with the dexterity to tie his shoelaces. Sleeping off a hangover until noon was no longer an option. Hence, the choice of the barely-alcoholic Miller Lite.

Remy wasn't really in the mood to have to wait for a barstool, and on Friday nights, most bars around Madison Avenue were packed with oily finance bros. He simply wanted a stool to sit on and a cold pint and maybe a ballgame to watch in peace. Thankfully, he had just the place in mind.

Remy hailed a cab and told the driver to take him to 85th and York. He tipped the cabbie well and entered Bailey's, a no-nonsense Irish pub with a glossy dark wood bar top, a well-worn dartboard, and a clientele that thankfully preferred to mind their own business. His kind of place.

Remy pulled out a stool and ordered a Miller Lite. The bartender, a ruddy-faced gent named Ian, with deep acne scars and wearing an Arsenal soccer jersey, poured the draft and sat it on the bar without once taking his eye off the television. The Yankees were losing. Ian made a sucking noise through his teeth as the Twins pitcher struck out the side to end the fourth. Then he poured himself a Jameson and slammed it.

"Haven't seen you in a spell," the bartender said. "Thought you might be cheating on us with another bar."

"Never. You're the only place in the city where the drafts are cold enough."

"Keep the beer colder than your heart," Ian said. "That's the key to a successful pub."

Remy took a healthy gulp of his beer, put his elbows on the bar, and relaxed. He'd been introduced to Bailey's a few years ago while dating a pretty redhead named Nicole. It was the perfect spot to make out in a cozy, dimly lit booth without being interrupted. After they broke up, she got a hedge fund manager and a house in the suburbs, and Remy got the bar.

Remy finished his beer and Ian brought him a new pint without asking. A dingy mirror ran along the back wall behind the liquor bottles. Remy checked himself out. He was still young, having turned twenty-eight in February, but felt like he'd been aging faster than an open milk carton.

A few months back, Remy had found his first gray hair. Since then, they'd invited friends. His light brown hair hid the grays for the most part, but the ten pounds he gained since college was evident every time he loosened the belt buckle on his size thirty-fours or found himself breathing a little too hard after a 5k. He was on the slender side, still made time to go to the gym four times a week, and forced himself to get in fifty push-ups and sit-ups on days when he couldn't make time. Most importantly, he occasionally mustered up the willpower to pass on nachos.

After graduating summa cum laude from Yale with a degree in political science, Pulaski had offered Remy eighty-five grand a year, which would help pay off his rather massive student loan debt. Pulaski wasn't McKinsey, but it was a steppingstone. Six years in and he was making a hundred and ten grand. He could pay his rent, barely, pay his bills, barely, and was chipping away at his loans. Vacations were out of the question. And dating in Manhattan was hell on his credit card statement.

Lottery tickets were cheap. Lychee martinis were not.

All in all, Remy knew he was just starting his life. His career was on the upswing, if not quite yet at the apex, but it was heading that way. Despite it all, something was missing. Remy couldn't quite put a finger on it. McKinsey hadn't come calling. He could go to the grave accumulating five percent annual raises.

At some point, Remy wanted the world to open up to him.

"You believe this?" Ian said, pointing at the television and speaking to nobody in particular. "Bum gets paid sixteen million a year and can't hit a curveball. Hell, I can't hit a curveball either and I'd play for *half* that."

"I'm pretty sure we could field a team of everyone in this bar," Remy said, "play for a whole lot less money, and score just as many runs."

Ian surveyed the drinkers. Two women in their late fifties were bonding over pints of Guinness. One man, fortyish and sweaty, nursed a glass of something amber in a highball glass while tapping out something on his phone with the concentration of a nuclear engineer. Two girls and two guys in their early twenties held court in a booth, taking selfies and downing shots of chilled vodka. An older black man stroked the leg of a purring woman wearing too much eye shadow on the next stool.

Remy eyed a cute brunette sitting at the end of the bar wearing a green spaghetti strap tank top that showed off tanned shoulders and glistening curves. She was sipping a glass of white wine and looked bored. Remy smiled at her. She smiled back. He was about to get up and introduce himself when another man walked past Remy, went up to the girl, and kissed her on the lips.

Well, shit.

"Tell me this isn't the sorriest lot you've ever seen," Ian said. "No offense. I love whoever pays my bills."

"None taken. Proud to be a member of that sorry lot."

He looked Remy over.

"You're a young kid. Still got your hair. Remind me of my son a bit. Except for the suit. He's some sort of graphic designer, which I think is just an excuse for him to wear a t-shirt to the office. So why ya drinking alone? Where's your lady tonight?"

"Don't have a lady," Remy said, sipping his beer.

"Man friend?"

"Nope. Appreciate your political correctness though."

"Have to be these days. Say the wrong thing and you get a nasty review on that Yelp thing and three months later you're out of business. I liked it better when if people didn't like your bar, they just threw eggs. Eggs you could clean off. Now if someone doesn't like you, they think it's their duty to let the entire godforsaken world know. Heaven forbid people just suffer in silence."

"To suffering in silence," Remy said, holding up his beer. Ian poured out two shots of Jameson. He placed one in front of Remy and held the other one out.

"To suffering in silence," he said.

"I really shouldn't," Remy said.

"Making a man drink alone is the eighth deadly sin."

Remy picked up the shot. "I never really paid attention in Sunday school anyway. To suffering in silence."

They clinked glasses and Remy downed the liquor. He felt pleasant warmth spread through his body. Ian went back to the game.

After he finished his beer, Remy asked for the tab.

"Leaving us already?" Ian asked.

"Sadly, this member of the sorry lot has work tomorrow."

"That'll be eighteen for the beers. The Jame-O is on me."

Remy pulled out a twenty and a five, laid them on the bar, and told Ian to keep it.

He left the bar and walked to the corner with every intention of heading home. He lived in a studio on West 12th Street, just north of Abingdon Square Park. Remy breathed in the early summer air, the cool, fresh air welcome after a day in the cubicle farm.

He stepped to the corner, raised his hand, and a cab pulled up. Remy hesitated. The driver lowered his window and said, "Hey, man, you getting in or what?"

Remy felt the June air against his skin and looked east.

"Nah, sorry. I changed my mind."

The cabbie cursed in two different languages before driving off.

Remy hadn't walked the East River Promenade since Nicole. They used to make out on every park bench like they were checking off a list. Fond memories. It felt like a lifetime ago.

He missed that electricity and companionship, the way a woman sighed as their lips met, as they touched for the first time, then grew to know every patch of skin. Remy wasn't surprised when Nicole broke up with him. He returned calls and texts sporadically, at dinner he would check his email like the Pope could drop him a line at any moment, and when he stayed the night, he would more often than not leave before breakfast. Finally, after a pint at Bailey's one night, Nicole kissed him on the cheek and said, "I hope you find what you're looking for."

So far, he hadn't.

Remy checked his watch. It was ten thirty. Still enough time for a solid seven hours of sleep. But Remy didn't feel like sleeping. He felt like walking.

He headed east, felt a cool breeze skimming off the East River. Sodium lights from the Queensboro Bridge made the dark water shimmer like liquid glass. He walked north past Gracie Mansion, curled back around under the FDR Drive, and began to head back west on 89th Street towards York Avenue. The crisp air invigorated him.

He noticed a couple walking about twenty steps ahead of him, heading west on 89th Street as well. They were young, dressed smartly, and walking at a leisurely pace. The woman was blonde and trim. Her right arm was looped through the man's elbow, and her head rested gently against his shoulder. Remy could see the diamond on her left ring finger. And if the ring was visible from that far away, it must have cost a fortune. The husband was probably some hedge fund big shot, the kind of guy who bought a house in the Hamptons at thirty-five and was retired by fifty.

Remy watched them, not sure if he was contemptuous or envious. Maybe a bit of both. They seemed happy.

Two men walked swiftly past Remy, passing him on either side. One tall, one short. They seemed to be in a hurry. Both wore dark pants and black jackets. Remy didn't think too much of it until he noticed they were both wearing gloves. There was a slight chill from the wind coming off the river, but it wasn't near cold enough to be wearing gloves. Two men, wearing gloves and matching outfits, following an unsuspecting couple.

Remy immediately knew they had bad intentions.

He walked faster, trying to keep pace with the men. Remy could tell something very bad was about to happen. Based on their clothes, Remy could tell the couple had money. They were easy targets.

He took out his cell phone and opened the phone app. Just in case his instincts were correct. He wondered, for a moment, if he was jumping to conclusions. A few drinks and a wandering mind leading him to assume the worst.

He felt silly. Slipped the phone back into his pocket.

And that was when the light fixture atop an awning illuminated the taller man's hand, and Remy saw that he was holding a gun.

It was palm sized. Barely noticeable.

Remy's eyes went wide. His breath shortened. Heart hammered. He sped up.

The next few seconds felt like hours.

Remy heard a click and knew the tall man had taken the safety off. Then he raised the gun.

This wasn't a mugging.

The couple was completely oblivious to what was happening behind them. The woman's head was still nestled on her husband's shoulder. Their arms were intertwined. Just moments from absolute horror. And Remy was the only one who could stop it.

Without thinking, Remy charged forward and shouted, "Gun!" The couple turned around. The husband's eyes widened and his mouth opened but no noise came out. The woman screamed and pulled her husband down to the ground.

The taller man brought the gun to point directly at the husband's head, and that was when Remy launched himself forward and drove his shoulder into the gunman's back.

He heard a *whump* sound, breath leaving the gunman's lungs. There was a deafening crack, and Remy knew the gun had gone off. They toppled to the ground in a heap, the man's head bouncing off the pavement with a crunch.

Remy could hear the woman screaming, but it was a far-off noise, like he was wearing headphones. Remy leapt on top of the downed gunman. He still held the gun, brought it up, trying to aim it at Remy's head.

Remy grabbed the man's wrist with both hands and slammed it against the pavement. Two more times and the man dropped the gun. Remy then brought his right fist crashing down into the man's face.

Then his left. When the second punch connected, he heard two cracks. The first was the man's nose. The second was Remy's hand. A sharp bolt of pain shot up his arm, and Remy knew his left hand was broken.

The man under him had gone limp. His gun was on the sidewalk. Remy went for it, but saw another hand reach down and grab it. Remy looked up. It was the husband. He was shaking, his face pale, eyes large and terrified. The husband held the gun, fingers pinching the grip like it was a poisonous snake. The barrel hung downward towards the sidewalk.

The man underneath him stirred. Remy raised his fist to deliver one more blow, hopefully knock him out cold.

Then something occurred to Remy. The other gunman. Where was he?

The question was answered as another crack of thunder broke the air. Remy felt a burning sensation tear through his upper body near his left shoulder. He looked up at the terrified husband and saw flecks of red spattered against his face.

Remy thought, *So that's what it looks like when someone else is covered in your blood.*

The husband whipped around, gun held out with a wobbly arm, and Remy could see the other man running away. He could not see the man's face. A glint of light from a streetlamp illuminated him for a moment. Before he disappeared, Remy saw that he had an earlobe gouge with a large silver ring embedded in the hole.

Remy heard another loud noise, a car horn, somewhere close. Then a man's voice yelled a word that sounded like *stani!* Then the street went silent.

A moment passed. No more gunshots. Nobody moved.

Remy tried to stand up, but a wave of dizziness and nausea suddenly overwhelmed him. He fell back on the ground. His breathing was labored. He splayed out next to the first gunman. The man's nose was crooked, his face covered in blood. Remy wondered whose blood made up the bulk of the mess. He couldn't be sure.

Remy managed to prop himself up on his elbow, but saw something that caused panic and terror to surge through him.

Blood was pooling on the pavement. Not a drop here and there. A steady stream that was quickly spreading into a small puddle.

Remy felt his chest. His hand came away wet.

He felt his arm begin to tremble. His elbow could no longer hold his weight. Remy fell to the ground. The sounds around him seemed to fade out. The husband stood above him, petrified. His mouth was moving. Remy could barely hear the words he spoke: "What should I do?"

Remy turned his head. Saw the wife on her phone, talking animatedly. She was staring at Remy. He heard her say, "Oh god, please send an ambulance quick, he's been shot and there's blood everywhere. Please just come!"

She dropped the phone into her purse and ran towards Remy, the best she could in her heels, and knelt down next to him. She took his hand and stared at him. The fear in her eyes terrified Remy more than the blood.

"It'll be okay," she said, softly, her voice quivering. "It'll be just fine."

Her eyes told Remy that she was probably lying. She put her hands against Remy's chest and pressed down, hard. He felt a distant pain, but the numbness spreading through his body drowned it out.

Remy felt like he recognized the woman from somewhere. Probably just his brain beginning to short circuit. Remy began to shiver.

"Stay with me," the woman said. "Stay with me. Just stay with me."

Then the shivering stopped and darkness consumed him.

CHAPTER 2

The first sliver of light peeked through Remy's eyelids softly, like morning sun filtered through thin curtains. It took a moment for him to realize he was awake, and even then, he was disoriented. It felt like there was Vaseline smeared over his eyes, grease swirling around his brain. He could feel his eyelids fluttering, but he had trouble focusing. Everything was blurry. There was a consistent *thump thump* on his left side, like a second heart had been transplanted somewhere under his armpit. A dull but solid pain radiated throughout the left half of his body and down to his hand.

Remy's mouth was dry. He eased his eyes open, adjusting to the light. The blurriness began to clear.

The first thing he noticed was that he was in a hospital room. Clean white walls. An antiseptic smell. An IV ran from his left arm up to a bag of fluid that dripped continuously. Oxygen tubes were hooked into his nostrils. The oxygen was cool.

He tried to sit up, but realized his left arm was tucked across his body in a sling. His left hand was in a splint and padded. He could see speckles of blood seeping through a bandage wrapped around his shoulder and upper chest.

I'm a goddamn mess, he thought.

At first, Remy felt panic.

He had been hospitalized twice in his life. The first time he was nine and learning how to ride a bike. He rode over a patch of sand near home, skidded as the wheels kicked out from under him, toppled over, smacked his head on the asphalt, and knocked himself unconscious. The second was how he got the faint white scar on his upper lip. Made kissy noises to the neighbor's ferocious eighteen-pound Lhasa Apso and ended up in the emergency room at eleven o'clock at night holding a bloody rag to his face, getting a rabies shot, and waiting for a plastic surgeon to be called in from dinner. He ended up with thirty stitches in his lip. It could have been worse, given that Remy could smell the brandy on the doctor's breath before he put his lip back together.

But he'd never woken up being given oxygen.

As he adjusted to being awake, the room came into better focus. Immediately, Remy could tell that a few things were very strange.

First off, the room was filled with flowers. Not a few flowers, or a couple of vases here and there, but literally filled nearly floor to ceiling with bouquets. They lined the windowsill, covered the floor, crowded against each other, seemingly fighting for space.

Roses and lilacs and chrysanthemums and flowers he couldn't even name. Remy managed to push himself into a seated position in his hospital bed and tried to figure out what the hell was going on. He didn't have nearly enough friends to explain all the flowers, and the folks at Pulaski weren't exactly the sentimental type.

But an even stranger sight than the greenhouse of plants choking his hospital room was the woman sitting in the chair next to the door.

Her eyes were closed. She appeared to be sleeping. Her blonde hair was tied back in a tight ponytail, but there were enough disparate, frizzy strands that Remy could tell she'd been there a while. She wore jeans and flat shoes and a lightweight leather jacket. Makeup appeared to have crusted slightly around her eyes. She was pretty, naturally so, a hint of contour and blush to outline her cheekbones. A smidge of concealer. Remy watched the rise and fall of her chest as she breathed in and out. He had no idea how long she'd been there. Or how long *he'd* been there.

Then Remy felt a glimmer of recognition. And it all came back to him.

The girl sleeping in his hospital room was the wife from the street. The one who'd called 911 and tried to stem his bleeding. And now she was asleep in his hospital room, which was covered in enough plant life to be rechristened the medical wing at Versailles.

The woman must have heard Remy stirring, because she shifted in her seat, opened her eyes, and stretched. She checked her watched and yawned. Then she locked eyes with Remy and smiled at him the way one might if they woke up presented with a gorgeous sunrise and a hot cup of coffee.

"Hey there," she said. Her voice was soft and pleasant.

"Um, hi," Remy replied, unsure if he was actually awake or having some sort of bizarre erotic botanical dream.

She stood up, bracing herself against her chair. Her muscles were stiff. She must have been there a while.

She walked over to Remy's bed and leaned over him. She gently placed her hand on his. She smelled good. Vanilla and deodorant. If such a combination could be appealing.

"Good morning," she said.

"It's you," Remy said. There was still a lag time between his brain and mouth, and neither was in perfect working condition at the moment. He looked at her left hand. He remembered seeing that massive wedding ring glimmering in the dark. Now, seeing it up close, it was even more impressive. The diamond looked flawless and close to four carats, in a channel set band filled with smaller gemstones. A setting like that must have run close to a hundred grand. This woman wasn't some random. She was *somebody*.

He looked into her face. And even through the drugged haze, he felt like he knew her, had seen her somewhere. She obviously sensed he was searching for answers.

"Don't worry," she said. "You're going to be fine. This time I mean it."

"Was I...not fine?" Remy asked.

She laughed softly. "I'll let the doctors fill you in. But we were worried for a while."

"We...were worried. We...who is we?"

"My husband and I. And, well, a lot of other people too."

"Other people?"

Remy searched his memory. The only people on the street that night were this woman, her husband, and the two gunmen. He doubted that the gunmen really gave two craps about his well-being, and generally speaking, "people" referred to a larger group than one couple.

"Your friend, Trevor Mayhew, was listed as your emergency contact. He came right away. Slept here for two nights. He said he had to teach a triple today, whatever that means, but to let him know when you woke up."

"Trevor," Remy said. "My best friend. Old roommate. He's a fitness instructor."

"Ah. I thought he might be your..."

"No. He's not my...whatever. But he is married. Not to me. To another guy, though. What's going on?"

Remy was missing something. And his mind wasn't functioning well enough to understand what the hell it was.

As Remy was trying to battle through the medicated fog, a doctor entered the room. He was in his mid-fifties, with a crown of thinning gray hair and a weathered face with kind eyes. He looked at Remy with a mixture of sympathy and relief.

"I see we're awake," the doctor said. He approached Remy's bed. The woman shook the doctor's hand.

"Thank you for everything, Dr. Kurzweil," she said. She took a few steps back, allowing the doctor access to Remy's beside. The doctor did not ask her for privacy, and seemed to have no hesitations about her being in the room at all. Remy felt even more confused.

"Mr. Stanton. Jeremy," the man said. "I'm Dr. Kurzweil. You're at

Lenox Hill Hospital. You've been here about forty eight hours. How are you feeling?"

"Remy."

"I'm sorry?"

"It's…Remy. Nobody calls me Jeremy."

The doctor laughed. "Apologies for the formalities. We're all playing a little catch up, Remy."

"Two days," Remy said. "I don't understand."

"I'll explain everything. But first off, how are you feeling?"

"Out of it," Remy said. "There's pain. It feels like it's on the inside. Here." He gestured towards his left shoulder area.

Kurzweil said, "What do you remember?"

Remy could see the blonde woman standing a few steps behind Kurzweil, listening to everything he said. Why was she allowed to be here?

Remy's left arm was immobile, but he gestured with his head towards the woman.

"She…she here?"

Kurzweil turned around. "Alena and her family were very concerned. They're very grateful and have taken an active role in your well-being. That's why…" Kurzweil spread his arms out, gesturing to Remy's hospital room greenhouse.

Remy had the room to himself. He knew you didn't get a solo room in a Manhattan hospital unless you paid extra. A *lot* extra. And his hospital room was bigger than his studio apartment. There was a decent size flat screen television mounted to the wall, and a small refrigerator in the corner.

"The fridge is pretty full," the woman now known as Alena said. "But I don't think the doctors will let you drink champagne just yet."

"Champagne?"

"At least three or four bottles. Good ones. From well-wishers. For when you're back on your feet."

Well-wishers?

Alena. Why did that name sound familiar? Who was this woman?

"What…" Remy said, then erupted in a coughing fit. His mouth felt like sandpaper, his lips were chapped, and his throat burned.

"That's from the intubation," Kurzweil said. "That scratchiness in your throat will go away in time."

Kurzweil went to the fridge and took out a bottle of water. He handed it to Remy, who sipped it slowly.

"Better?"

Remy swallowed, grimacing at the pain. He nodded.

"A little. Thanks. What happened?"

"You're very lucky," Kurzweil said. "One centimeter higher and we wouldn't be having this conversation."

Remy's eyes grew wide.

"What…what do you mean?"

"You suffered a traumatic gunshot wound," Kurzweil said. "If I may…" He motioned towards Remy's left arm. "May I?"

Remy nodded hesitantly, fear rising.

The doctor gently lifted Remy's left arm. Remy felt a dull pain. He was still heavily medicated, but there was a palpable tightness.

"Due to the angle of the wound, I believe your arm must have been raised at the time."

Remy nodded. He remembered punching the downed man in the face, and the thunderclap when he raised his hand for one more blow.

"The bullet entered your left deltoid at a slightly elevated angle. It then partially severed your axillary artery."

All that blood, Remy thought. He remembered the pool of blood spreading below him on the concrete. It came out so fast, so red. No wonder. It was arterial blood. Jesus.

He could see Alena standing behind Kurzweil, listening.

"Your hand isn't too bad. A fracture of the fourth metacarpal. We had to insert a screw to set the bones, but it should heal well. A clean break. We call it a boxer's fracture. Just don't get any ideas, Pacquiao."

Remy laughed at that. The first punch he'd thrown since a bar fight in college and he broke his hand. Fitting.

"Thankfully, Alena called 9-1-1 immediately. Several people

heard the gunshot from their apartments and did the same. Saved your life. Had that bullet shifted just a centimeter or two, it could have completely severed your axillary artery. And then, well…"

"I'm not in this bed," Remy replied.

"No," the doctor said. "Probably not."

"That's what I get for trying to be a good Samaritan," Remy said. He coughed, and a searing pain shot down the left side of his body that made him cry out. He heard Alena gasp. She took a step forward.

"That's alright," Kurzweil said. "You have both interior and exterior sutures from the surgery. We had to sew the artery itself, and then both the entrance and exit wound. You actually got double lucky. The bullet didn't touch any of the nerves in the brachial plexus, and didn't hit any bone. Clean entry and exit. You could have been looking at permanent nerve damage otherwise."

"Kind of hard to feel lucky when you're lying in a hospital bed unable to remember the last four days."

"I understand," Kurzweil said, "but you're going to make a full recovery. We'll go over the next steps, but for now your vitals are solid. You suffered significant blood loss, however, so we are going to keep you for a few days so you can rest and heal."

"Thank you, doctor."

"One thing," he said, "is there anyone else we can call? We contacted your friend, Trevor Mayhew. Parents? Your records state that your mother is deceased."

"That's right," Remy said.

"And your father…"

"I don't want anyone contacting him. That's my right as a patient, isn't it?"

Kurzweil nodded. "That is your prerogative. Is there anyone else we can call for you, then? We did inform your employer. Pulaski & Associates, correct?"

"That's right."

Alena said, "I spoke to Andrew Pulaski. He sent some chocolates. They're in the fridge."

Remy laughed, causing more pain to lance through his arm.

"Chocolates," he said. "Figures."

"They're not even especially good chocolates," Alena said with a mischievous smile. "We'll do better."

"We?" Remy said. "We'll do better?"

"My husband," she said. "My father. We owe you a debt that can never be repaid."

"Anybody in my situation would have done the same thing. There's no debt," Remy said, though he wasn't quite sure if that was true. All he knew at that point was he had a luxury private hospital room with enough overflowing bouquets to start his own flower shop and a fridge full of champagne, somehow because of this woman, Alena. She had money. There were clearly a lot of people who cared about her safety enough to send gifts to a complete stranger out of gratitude.

"Not everybody would have done the same thing," Alena said. "You saw a gun. You acted. You knew the risks. And you ignored them."

Remy shrugged. At least tried to.

The door opened, and a tall, slender man entered the room. He wore a black fleece zipped up all the way to his chin, with rimless glasses perched atop a sharp nose. His wavy black hair looked like it had been parted with a straight edge razor, and his eyes darted around the room. There was a hesitant, anxious look on his face, like he was waiting for a piano to fall on his head. This was a man who looked like he was born to carry worry.

He walked over to Alena and kissed her quickly on the lips. Then he approached Remy.

"Mr. Stanton," he said. "Paul Bracewell. Thank you for what you did for me."

For me? Remy thought. *Doesn't he mean us?*

"I'll leave you alone," Dr. Kurzweil said. "A nurse will be by soon to refresh the drip bag and check your levels. Take it easy, Remy. No marathons or boxing matches."

"No promises," Remy replied. He was starting to come out of the fog. He recognized Paul Bracewell, remembered him picking up the assailant's gun after Remy had knocked it away. Bracewell held it like he was handling a rattlesnake. Paul didn't strike Remy as the kind of person who would have intervened. He seemed nervous, shaky, literally teetering from foot to foot. Even in his medicated state, Remy could tell Bracewell was uneasy.

"How are you feeling, Mr. Stanton?" Bracewell asked.

"Call me Remy," he said. "I'm feeling okay, all things considered."

"Alena and her father spared no expense in your treatment and recovery," he said.

"The last time I got shot, nobody sent flowers," Remy said. Paul said nothing. "That was a joke."

Paul smiled weakly, then leaned towards his wife and whispered in her ear.

Alena responded audibly, "I texted him. He's on his way."

Paul nodded and Remy noticed him take a sharp breath. He didn't know who "him" was, and whether "him" coming was good or bad news.

"Who's coming?" Remy asked. "Are you talking about my friend Trevor?"

He couldn't think of who else might visit. He doubted Andrew Pulaski would bother; his secretary likely ordered the chocolates. Other than Trevor, he had few friends in the city, and couldn't imagine that Alena or Paul had gone through his contacts list.

"My father," Alena said. "He wanted me to let him know the moment you woke up. He wanted to meet you in person."

"Your father? I don't understand."

"You will," Alena said. "You saved our lives. My father always takes care of people who take care of his family."

"Do I know your father?" Remy asked. He could appreciate Alena and Paul looking out for him, but he just wanted to heal up and go home. He wanted to eat bad hospital food, sleep some more, then get the hell out of this place. It was a boss hospital room, but it was still a hospital room.

"I don't know if you've ever met him," Alena said, "but I'm sure you know him."

"That…doesn't make any sense," Remy said.

"It will," Alena said with a confidence that unnerved Remy. For a moment, he wondered if this was all some sort of cosmic joke. Taking down a gunman only to be subjected to some creepy family ritual like a Brooks Brothers version of the redneck cannibals from *Texas Chainsaw Massacre*.

"I have a stupid question," Remy said, raising his functioning arm. Alena laughed. "Are we back in grade school?"

Remy and Alena laughed. Paul did not. Remy registered this.

"Who are all these flowers from? I don't have this many friends, Andrew Pulaski isn't the sentimental type, and I don't remember owning any 1-800-Flowers stock. Would you mind checking the cards?"

"I know many of them were sent by my father's friends and associates," Alena said. She went over to a large crystal vase filled to the brim with red roses and yellow calla lilies. "This one reads, 'Mr. Stanton: the city thanks you for your heroism. You had our back. Now we'll have yours. Governor Emily Richardson.'"

Had there been any water in Remy's mouth, he would have spat it out.

"Emily Richardson. Governor Emily Richardson. Those flowers were sent by Governor Richardson. Seriously?"

"Seriously," Alena said.

"Um…why?"

Paul Bracewell looked at his wife, then back at Remy. He said, "What you did the other night was really brave. And the fallout has not happened in a vacuum."

"Fallout?" Remy said. "Did I prevent a nuclear war or something?"

Alena said, "Maybe not that far off. My father met Governor Richardson when she first ran for city council. She officiated my wedding. She was extraordinarily thankful you were there the other night. A lot of people were. And even more so that you pulled through. She said she plans to visit in person."

"Governor Richardson," Remy repeated. "I voted for her." Remy looked at Paul. "Hold on. Why did she officiated *your* wedding? And what do you mean by 'the fallout didn't happen in a vacuum'?"

"See for yourself." Paul picked up a remote control from the tray on Remy's bedside and turned the television on. He flipped through the channels but didn't have to go far to find what he was looking for.

Anderson Cooper was on CNN reporting live in studio. A chyron read UES HERO WAKES UP. Anderson cut to a live video feed and a reporter standing outside Lenox Hill Hospital.

"Wait," Remy said. "That's not about…"

Just then, a picture appeared in the upper right-hand corner of the screen. Remy recognized the photo. He remembered taking it. He'd gone out drinking the night before, came into work hungover beyond belief, and was horrified to learn he was required to take a new photo for his employee ID. He'd been pleasantly surprised at how it came out.

That photo was now being broadcast on CNN.

He was the UES hero.

"You've got to be shitting me," Remy said.

Anderson Cooper said, "We have word that Rawson Griggs himself is on his way to visit Jeremy Stanton at Lenox Hill Hospital. Mr. Griggs has not commented on the attack, other than releasing a brief statement thanking law enforcement for their swift action leading to the arrest of Dastan Nogoyev. Nogoyev was incapacitated by Jeremy Stanton following the incident on Manhattan's Upper East Side, in which Nogoyev and an unidentified accomplice pulled guns on Mrs. Griggs and Mr. Bracewell."

"Rawson Griggs," Remy said. "Your father is Rawson Griggs."

"That's right," Alena said.

"You're Alena Griggs, then."

She nodded, said, "That's right."

"These are some amazing drugs," Remy said. "Because otherwise you're like a quadrillionaire."

Alena smiled. "I don't think that's a real word. But yes. Rawson is my dad."

Now Remy knew why Alena said he would know her father. Everyone knew Rawson Griggs. The whole world knew Rawson Griggs. More people could pick him out of a lineup than the Pope.

And if this was true, if Alena really was the daughter of Rawson Griggs, she was one of the most revered young heiresses in the country, the only child of one the wealthiest, most powerful, and most influential men alive. Rawson was a business tycoon, a trendsetter, and an economic disrupter. And until she married Paul Bracewell, Alena Griggs was the most eligible bachelorette on the planet. Now here she was, standing in Remy's hospital room, laughing at his jokes.

"Dastan Nogoyev," Remy said. "Is that the man I hit?"

Alena nodded. "You broke his nose and fractured his cheekbone. He was unconscious when the police arrived. To be honest, I think a few of them were disappointed they didn't have to draw their weapons."

Remy noticed Paul Bracewell looking out the window, fidgeting.

"The other man," Remy said. "The one who shot me. Nogoyev's accomplice. What happened to him?"

"They haven't found him yet. The FBI told my father, quote, 'the investigation is ongoing.' But if I know how much this city loves my father, half the NYPD is looking for this asshole, and the second he pops up...."

"But he's still out there," Remy said.

Alena nodded. "We have security."

Remy saw Paul chewing a fingernail.

Remy turned back to the television. Anderson Cooper continued. "The Department of Homeland Security and FAA announced that they discovered a plane ticket purchased two weeks ago in Dastan Nogoyev's name. The flight was scheduled to depart JFK on Aeroflot Airlines, have a two-hour layover in Moscow, and then arrive in Bishkek, Kyrgyzstan, where Nogoyev was born. Sources within the FBI tell us that they believed the attack on Mrs. Griggs and Mr. Bracewell was premeditated, and that Nogoyev and his accomplice planned to leave the country in its wake."

"But they don't know who the other man is," Remy said. "So he could be halfway around the world right now."

"They *will* find him," Alena said. "My father spoke to NYPD commissioner Ragsdale and he assured us that before the week is out they'll know more about Dastan Nogoyev and his accomplice than their mothers do."

"As long as everyone is safe now," Remy said. He heard Paul make a noise like *hmph*. He seemed completely removed from the conversation, like there was something else on his mind.

Back on CNN, Anderson Cooper said, "We have word that Rawson Griggs is arriving at Lenox Hill Hospital as we speak, no doubt to pay thanks to the young man who saved his daughter's and her husband's lives."

The camera cut to a feed from a helicopter flying above Lenox Hill Hospital. A convoy of cars approached the hospital entrance: a massive black SUV, followed by a long black limousine, then backed up by another SUV. The three cars pulled up to the curb. Remy sat up to see the television better, then yelped as a searing pain shot through his body. He fell back into the bed, sweating.

Alena rushed over.

"Take it easy," she said, handing him more water.

Remy watched the screen, captivated, as several large, suited men exited the cars bracketing the limo. The helicopter camera zoomed in. The men wore sunglasses and earpieces. Security. No doubt Rawson Griggs never went anywhere without a cavalcade of protection, and the events of the other night surely made him even more cautious.

A crowd of onlookers had gathered in front of the hospital, held back behind police barricades. Four of the guards created a human funnel inside the barricade, leading into the hospital entrance. One of the guards spoke into a mouthpiece and then waved his hand as though signaling an all clear. Then the limousine door opened and a man stepped out. He waved briefly to the cheering crowd and entered the hospital.

Alena smiled. "My dad is here. He couldn't wait to meet you. Just a piece of advice: be yourself. He hates ass kissers."

Three minutes later, there was a knock at the door. Alena opened it.

Standing there was Rawson Griggs. He entered and said, "Mr. Stanton. I owe you a debt that can never be repaid. But I'll try."

Remy swallowed. The pain was gone. He knew at that moment that his life had irrevocably changed.

CHAPTER 3

R emy's first thought, to his own still somewhat-drugged
embarrassment, was, *Rawson Griggs is a big motherfucker. I'm
glad I didn't have to fight him the other night.*

Rawson Griggs was far larger than he appeared in his photographs.
Remy estimated he was around six three or six four, but a broad man
with shoulders the width of a sawhorse, chest as thick as a barbecue
grill, and a dark, Paul Bunyan-esque beard. Rawson was an oak of a
man who looked like he could swallow a punch whole, digest it, and
crap it back out. He wasn't trim, but he wasn't fat. His chest was thick,
his midsection ample. His suit jacket was tight around the arms, and
Remy was sure it was intentional. His brown hair was streaked with
gray, with a part down the left side that curled up like an ocean wave.
He clearly spent time at the gym, and though age had softened some
of the muscle, Rawson still looked like a man who could break a two-
by-four in half with his hands.

Remy had seen Rawson on television hundreds of times. He'd
graced the cover of nearly every magazine and newspaper in the world,
the billionaire maverick who had built one of the most recognizable
companies in the country, had more enemies than Batman, and

enjoyed a lifestyle so lavish that entire magazine spreads had been devoted his wardrobe.

Rawson embraced his daughter, enveloping Alena in his bear-like arms. Remy saw Griggs close his eyes as Alena disappeared into his bulk.

When they disentangled, Rawson turned to Paul and simply extended his hand, as though greeting a colleague he was not particularly fond of.

Paul shook Rawson's hand, the elder man's wrist as thick as his son-in-law's arm. Immediately Remy could tell there was a chill between Griggs and the man who had married into his family. Rawson was cordial, but nothing more. Remy watched those few seconds with fascination. You could read a million articles and see a million interviews with a man like Rawson Griggs, but few people had the chance to see how he acted up close, in private moments, while the cameras were off.

After he finished with Paul, Rawson said, "Alena, give us a moment."

"Of course." She said to Paul, "Let's get a cup of coffee."

As they left, Remy saw two security guards follow.

When the door closed, Griggs turned to Remy and said, almost wistfully, "She fights me, that one. If it were up to me, she'd have the National Guard protecting her every waking moment of her life. But she won't have it. Wants to lead a normal life, as she calls it. But desire and reality make awful bedfellows."

Rawson's voice was deep, baritone. He could have been on the radio. He wore a deep, black Brioni suit, so shiny it looked recently polished. It must have run ten grand. A bright red tie hung down below his leather belt. His shoes were polished, his hair fastened in place. If Remy didn't know better, he'd think Griggs was a funeral director.

Remy wasn't sure what to say. "She seems nice," he uttered, and immediately felt silly. He supposed it was a good thing he could chalk up any ridiculous statements to the injuries and medication.

Griggs ignored the comment and began inspecting the various

flower arrangements. He opened up the cards, which struck Remy as odd, given that they weren't for Rawson. He supposed Rawson was cataloguing which of his colleagues had sent well wishes. Those who hadn't would probably end up on some Griggs shit list, the notion of which was terrifying. Remy watched Rawson, transfixed, still trying to wrap his head around the fact that Rawson Griggs was in his hospital room.

Griggs then went to Remy's bed, towering over him. Remy did his best to turn and face the man, but his sutures prevented him from twisting. Griggs seemed to realize this, and repositioned himself at the foot of the bed.

"Better we can see each other man-to-man, wouldn't you agree?"

"Yes."

Rawson pointed at the sling on Remy's arm.

"Are you a righty or lefty?"

"Righty," Remy replied.

"Small favors," Rawson said. "At least you'll still be able to sign your own name."

"That was the first thing I thought when I woke up," Remy deadpanned. Rawson smiled. Remy figured that was a good thing.

"You know who I am," Griggs said, the smile disappearing, his voice turning deadly serious. It wasn't said with braggadocio, more to get it out of the way.

"I do," Remy said.

"Then you know why I'm here."

"Um…sort of?"

"I'm not a man who tends to take things lightly," Griggs said, watching the tube hooked up to Remy's arm. He watched the medication plink downwards as he talked. "I'm not overly sentimental. And I don't let my emotions control me."

Griggs looked at Remy, stared him right in the eyes. Remy saw every line etched on the man's face, every fleck of gray struggling for notice in that brown beard. Griggs made Remy shrink involuntarily.

"But you saved my daughter's life. And there is nothing in the world more serious to me than Alena's safety," Rawson said. "Emotions are tricky things. They can help you focus and discern what is and is not important. But if they overwhelm your senses, you can make terrible, irrational decisions. My emotions led me to make a terrible decision. I've fought for a long time with Alena over my insistence that she have protection twenty-four seven. She fought me on it. She's a smart, tough woman. Probably tougher than I was at her age. I'm proud that she never took her privilege for granted. She wants to lead a normal life with Paul. Bodyguards don't allow for that. So I relented. I let her go about her *normal* life. Not because it was the right thing to do, but because I wanted to make my daughter happy. Emotions, rather than intelligence, made that decision for me. And it was the wrong decision. And it nearly cost me my daughter."

Rawson came around to the side of Remy's bed. Remy could feel his heart jackhammering in his chest. Rawson placed his massive hand on Remy's right arm. His hand was rough and calloused, which surprised Remy. Remy had shaken hands with many wealthy men, and to a one their hands were soft, baby-like. Not Rawson Griggs. His hand felt like tree bark.

"You saved my daughter's life. You almost paid a price you never should have had to pay. But you didn't think twice. And because of that, my little girl is still on this earth. So, Jeremy, from the bottom of my heart. Thank you."

Remy's mouth felt parched. "You're welcome." He reached for the water bottle Dr. Kurzweil had left on the tray but couldn't reach it. Rawson handed it to him. Remy gulped it down. When he finished, Rawson took it to the sink, refilled it, and brought it back. "You can call me Remy."

"Remy," Griggs said, as if rolling the name over on his tongue. "Does everyone call you Remy?"

"People who know me do."

"And you like the name?"

"I guess. Been called it since I was a kid."

"Well, it is a child's name," Griggs said. Remy detected an ounce of patronization in his voice. "Not many people would do what you did, Jeremy, nearly die for a stranger. And I believe you would do it again."

"I would," Remy said.

"I think there's something special about you, Jeremy Stanton. And I believe the other night was the catalyst for something great."

"Thank you, sir," Remy said.

"I spoke to your doctors. Kurzweil. He's the best there is. I requested him specifically for you. They anticipate you'll be strong enough to leave here in about three days. Today is Sunday. That means you'll probably be discharged by Wednesday. I want to see you in my office at seven thirty Monday morning."

"Mr. Griggs, I appreciate this, but I have to be at my job Monday morning."

"You report to Richard McCarty. I've met McCarty before. Not an impressive man. Andrew Pulaski keeps him around for amusement. I'll talk to Andrew. He will excuse your absence."

"How do you..."

"I know far more about you than you think, Jeremy. As I was saying. Take the weekend to recover, to think. Then, Monday morning, be at my office."

"Your office?"

"Griggs Tower. I'm sure you're familiar with it."

"I am, I just...never really thought I'd ever have a meeting there."

Remy didn't know what to say. The lights in his head were dimming. He had no idea why Griggs wanted him at his office, nor could he fully believe what was even going on. But he replied with the first thing that popped into his head.

"I'll be there."

Griggs nodded. "Good."

"So do I, like, just ask for Rawson Griggs when I get there?"

"One of my staff will greet you," Rawson said.

A BREAKING NEWS chyron popped up on CNN. Anderson Cooper's face returned to the screen. Rawson noticed and turned to face the television.

It read, DASTAN NOGOYEV REPORTEDLY KILLED IN PRISON.

Remy's eyes popped open. Nogoyev was dead.

Anderson Cooper said, "We're getting reports from the NYPD that Dastan Nogoyev, one of two suspects in the Upper East Side attack on Alena Griggs and her husband, Paul Bracewell, has been murdered in prison. Nogoyev was being held in the Tombs detention center following his arraignment in Manhattan Criminal Court when the incident occurred. Federal authorities were hoping Nogoyev could provide information on the motive behind the attack, as well as the location of his accomplice, who is still at large. There is no word on whether Nogoyev provided any of that information before his death. Again, one of the two men responsible for the attempted murder of Rawson Griggs's daughter and son-in-law has been killed. We will update you with more information as it comes in."

Griggs turned back to Remy. There was no reaction evident on the man's face. If there was rage, Griggs hid it. If there was pleasure in the death of the man who tried to harm his daughter, it was buried deep down. It also meant any information Nogoyev had on the attempted murder, his accomplice, or any future attacks died with him.

Rawson Griggs took a single deep breath and said to Remy, calmly, "Next Monday. I never make an offer twice."

Then he left. And Alena Griggs opened the door.

She said, "Please. Be there."

As soon as the door closed, Remy nestled into the darkness.

CHAPTER 4

The only thing that gave Remy a clue as to the mob scene that awaited him was an offhand comment by the kind orderly who helped him into his wheelchair prior to being discharged.

"My goodness, I should get your autograph before the reporters outside tear you limb from limb."

Joking about patient dismemberment, to Remy, was subpar bedside manners.

Remy didn't think he needed the wheelchair. He'd been walking without assistance for much of the past two days, and other than a brief dizzy spell—"Your body is still recovering from the trauma of significant blood loss," Dr. Kurzweil said. "Don't push it."—he wanted to get back to a semblance of normalcy.

Two NYPD detectives had visited him the day after Rawson Griggs's visit. Remy told them everything he could remember about that night. Ian, the bartender at Bailey's, had confirmed Remy's timeline.

As Remy recounted, he'd seen Alena Griggs and Paul Bracewell walking west on 89th Street from East End towards York Avenue. He couldn't see their faces and didn't know who they were. Then he saw two men—Dastan Nogoyev and the other unidentified suspect—approach the couple. He saw Nogoyev brandish the gun, and that was when Remy acted.

He remembered knocking Nogoyev to the ground, and Paul Bracewell picking up the fallen gun. He remembered the gunshot and feeling the bullet tear into him. He did not get a good look at the other gunman, just a dark shape disappearing into the night. The next thing Remy knew, he woke up at Lenox Hill with a flower smorgasbord usually reserved for deceased heads of state or Easter at Martha Stewart's house.

Trevor Mayhew had come to the hospital to bring Remy home. Trevor was a hugely popular fitness instructor, teaching fifteen classes a week at a Flatiron spin studio called CyclePro. He also trained several dozen private clients who paid him two hundred bucks an hour to whip them into "Trevor shape." If anyone had told Remy that sitting on a stationary bike for twelve hours a week and yelling "pain is temporary!" at brides-to-be would earn him nearly a hundred and thirty grand a year, Remy would have thought twice before taking out enough student loans to place a down payment on a house.

Trevor lived above Trader Joe's in the Flatiron district, which he referred to as "the seventh circle of supermarket hell," married a client named Chris he met while teaching at CyclePro, and seemed to have it all figured out. His plan was to teach fitness classes until his skin started to sag, at which point he and Chris would move to the suburbs and open an animal sanctuary.

Remy had a hard time even making dinner plans.

Having a father who was employed once every leap year, Remy had grown up believing a steady nine-to-whenever job was necessary to make something of yourself. Stability and routine were keys to success. Sit at a desk, rack up frequent flier miles, and you were on your way.

As Remy was quickly learning, the road he'd taken hadn't quite taken him on the path he'd dreamed of. And the meeting with Rawson Griggs loomed.

When Trevor arrived at the hospital, he was dressed head-to-toe in CyclePro gear: track pants, a CyclePro t-shirt, and a Mayhew Fitness cap. Given the media ouroboros waiting outside, Remy had to admit that Trevor was a brilliant self-promoter.

Trevor wheeled Remy towards the hospital entrance. Remy felt like a boxer about to enter an arena. He said to Trevor, "You could have at least brought me a change of clothes. I smell like the inside of an armpit."

"That you do," Trevor said. "I can picture the *Post* headline tomorrow. 'Smell Ya Later: Funky-Smelling Hero Leaves Hospital.'"

"You know I hate you, right?"

"You hate me and you love me. Our relationship is very complicated."

An orderly opened the double doors. A phalanx of at least twenty photographers and reporters was packed outside the hospital entrance, barely kept at bay by a half dozen NYPD officers.

Suddenly the orderly's comment about Remy being ripped limb from limb didn't seem all that hyperbolic.

Remy was dressed in a loose-fitting hospital gown with a paisley blue pattern straight out of the nursing home grandmother collection. Trevor looked like he could run a marathon at a moment's notice.

Remy said to Trevor, "What do you think about switching places for the next ten minutes?

"And ride in the convalescent-mobile? Not a chance." Trevor clapped Remy gently on his good shoulder. "I wouldn't trade places with you right now for the exclusive rights to the fly zone surrounding Ryan Gosling's underwear."

"You're a good friend."

"Hey, we all have to make sacrifices. Besides, enjoy it. People love you."

Remy felt rivers of sweat dripping down his lower back. He had no idea how to handle this.

THE UPPER EAST SIDE HERO, *The New York Daily News* had called him. The photo splayed across the front page had been taken from a traffic camera. It showed a black-and-white image of the carnage.

In the photo, Dastan Nogoyev was on the ground, on his back. Remy was on top of him, fist raised in the air. Alena Griggs stood just a few feet away, her hand to her mouth, horrified. Paul Bracewell was leaning down, about to pick up Nogoyev's dropped gun. Another man, his face and features masked in the gloom, stood just a few feet away from his downed partner, gun raised and pointed right at Remy. A moment later, that gun would go off, and Remy's life would hang in the balance.

Seeing a literal picture of the moment when, if not for luck or poor aim, he could have left this mortal coil, made Remy shiver at what might have been if Dastan Nogovey's buddy had just aimed an inch or two to the left. The newspaper headlines would be very different.

"You ready for this?" Trevor asked. Remy could sense his enthusiasm.

"Geez, don't sound *too* excited," Remy said. "I bet CyclePro will be thrilled you're wearing their logo on your ass for all these cameras."

"Hey, I'm here for you, first and foremost, Remy. But you know how the saying goes: when life gives you lemons, you turn those lemons into cold, hard cash."

"I don't think that's how the saying goes."

"Well, that's how my saying goes. Once people see this face and this logo all over the news, you won't be able to book a bike in my class for months."

"Do I at least get a commission for all this free marketing?"

"No, but I'll reserve a bike for you. I've been trying to get you to come to my class for years."

"No, thanks," Remy said. "I already almost died once this year. I don't need to tempt fate a second time."

"You know, you *could* stand to lose a few pounds," Trevor said. "Especially since you now have paparazzi. You gotta look sharp."

"Christ. Can you take me home already?"

"You got it. Ready for this? There's a limo waiting just past the crowd. Courtesy of Mr. Rawson Griggs."

"He sent a limo?" Remy said.

"Not just any limo. A freaking stretch SUV limo. Even has the Griggs company logo on it."

Remy laughed. "Rawson's a better marketer than you."

"Tell me about it. Even *I'm* impressed."

"Okay," Remy said. He took a breath. "I'm ready."

"Hold onto your butt. Here we go."

Trevor began to roll Remy's wheelchair towards the entrance. Several doctors, nurses, and orderlies clapped as he passed by. Remy smiled and waved, like a smelly, robed Miss America.

Suddenly he was in the middle of a maelstrom of microphones and cameras. Men and women were shouting at him, shoving microphones into his face, screaming questions faster than he could understand them. He saw his face reflected in half a dozen cameras.

This was madness. He saw camera crews from CNN, NBC, Fox News, the BBC—why in the hell did the BBC care about him?—and a few local New York crews. The questions were shouted at him like he was a celebrity leaving rehab after a six-month bender.

"Mr. Stanton, how do you feel?"

"Mr. Stanton, did you know it was Alena Griggs and Paul Bracewell that night?"

"Mr. Stanton, is it true you met with Rawson Griggs?"

"Did you know Dastan Nogoyev?"

"Mr. Stanton, couldn't this have been avoided if you, Mrs. Griggs, or Mr. Bracewell had legally been carrying firearms for protection?"

"Mr. Stanton, who did you vote for last election?"

"Mr. Stanton, do you have a girlfriend?"

Remy's head was spinning. But deep down in the reptilian part of his brain, Remy *liked* the attention. A lot.

For the past five years he'd felt like nothing more than a small cog in a massive wheel. Finally, a new path had opened for him. Maybe embracing the attention—and even taking pleasure from it—wasn't such a bad thing.

Remy tapped Trevor on the arm.

"Stop for a sec," Remy said.

Trevor looked at him, slightly panicked. "You sure? We slow down and they might eat you alive."

"I'm sure."

Trevor eased the wheelchair to a halt. Remy raised his good hand. The press corps fell silent.

Remy braced himself and slowly stood up. The crowd stood there, rapt. Remy's arm was in a sling, his balance still slightly off. But he was able to stand firm.

"I just have one thing to say, and then I'd like to get home. I did what any other person would have done in that situation. I saw innocent people about to get hurt, and I believed I could help them. I'm just glad Mrs. Griggs and Mr. Bracewell are safe and sound. Thank you for being here and taking an interest in me and in their safety. Hopefully, if anything, this story will encourage other men and women to help when they see bad things about to happen to good people. That's all I have to say for now. Thank you."

The moment he stopped speaking, a thousand more questions were fired at him. Remy pushed the wheelchair backwards with his good arm, a signal that he didn't need it anymore. Trevor helped him to the limo. The driver came around and opened the passenger door. He was a hefty man wearing a navy tuxedo with the Griggs logo embroidered on the pocket. Remy slid in. Trevor followed and shut the door. The media horde was still hounding the car, inches from the windows, cameras recording him even as he sat inside the vehicle.

"This is insanity. Does anyone actually want to see footage of me sitting inside a car?"

"It's dramatic. You've seen *Law & Order*, right?" Trevor said as the limo pulled away from the hospital. "Hey, you think they got the CyclePro logo?"

Remy laughed. "I think the company should give you a raise." He turned to Trevor. "Thanks, man. Really. I appreciate it."

"Don't sweat it," Trevor said. "But if you think this shit is over, you got another thing coming. This is just the beginning. You saw that outside. You barely gave them anything. You're the story now, Remy. People are going to want more of you."

Remy smiled.

When they got to his apartment, Trevor helped Remy into bed and fell asleep on the couch. Remy took his pain medication and promptly fell asleep for ten hours.

He dreamt about that night. The pool of red spreading beneath him. Paul Bracewell's face covered in his blood. The terrified look on Alena Griggs's face as she called for help. His body shivering uncontrollably, sure he was going to die.

Remy woke up at four a.m., covered in sweat. He sat up on the edge of the bed until the shaking stopped. Then he got up, still a little dizzy, and got a glass of water. His stomach rumbled, and Remy realized he hadn't eaten anything other than hospital glop in nearly a week.

He checked the fridge. Embarrassing. Condiments, orange juice, and, yes, two slices of pizza he'd forgotten to wrap up that had grown moldy. He tossed the pizza and decided to order Fresh Direct in the morning. It was time to rejoin the human race.

Trevor was asleep on the pullout sofa, snoring softly. Remy smiled. Felt like old times. Remy remembered countless college nights where he and Trevor stumbled back to their apartment on Temple Street, blitzed on cheap beer and boxed wine. Remy felt fortunate that they both ended up in the city, though he found it somewhat hilarious that Trevor's degree in Renaissance studies had led to a burgeoning career in the spandex and Lycra-clad field of professional fitness.

Remy gulped down a glass of water, refilled it, and downed another. He'd been given a prescription for Oxycodone to help with the pain. His shoulder was throbbing and his hand itched. He'd have to wear the sling for another three weeks while his sutures healed. He took one pill and washed it down, making a mental note to try to kick the stuff as soon as possible. The medication made his brain feel fuzzy, unfocused. He didn't want to be in low gear when he met with Rawson.

Remy lived in a large alcove studio, generously listed at four hundred and fifty square feet, with a window overlooking a lovely brick wall that completely blocked natural sunlight for twenty-one hours a day. That's what three thousand dollars a month bought you in the West Village. His twin mattress barely fit into the alcove's nook. It was so close to the walls that Remy had to climb out of bed the long way every morning—a few dates had learned this the hard way. There was a kitchenette with a two-burner electric stove, a small but updated bathroom, and a security buzzer system that would deter, maybe, eight percent of blind, deaf, and legless burglars.

He'd furnished it with a pullout polyester couch and a round balsawood breakfast table that could fit two people, provided they didn't back up too far.

His walls were bare save a forty-eight-inch flat screen, his framed college diploma, a picture from Trevor and Chris's wedding that was thumb-tacked above his twenty-seven-inch iMac, and a Corgi wall calendar that was a gift from an aunt who had what Remy felt was an unhealthy Corgi obsession.

Remy was never much for decorating, but he began to feel a sense of sadness, remorse that he hadn't taken greater care in preserving the memories he'd earned, cherishing the friends he'd made and experiences he'd taken for granted. If he'd died the other night, what would be his legacy?

Remy got his iPad out and took it into bed, shifting his weight to avoid putting pressure on his arm. The pain was constant. A maddening itch just beneath the surface of his skin.

He propped a few pillows behind him and did a Google search on Rawson Griggs. Remy knew the basics. But he wanted to know everything he could about the man.

Rawson Griggs was born on March 30, 1949 in Bensonhurst, New York. He was orphaned at the age of fifteen after his parents, Emily and Horace Griggs, were killed in an automobile accident in the

Berkshires. After being drafted in 1969, Rawson Griggs fought in the 25th nfantry Division where he saw combat in Cambodia before being redeployed to the Schofield Barracks in Hawaii.

Upon returning to Brooklyn in 1972, Griggs managed to secure a thirty thousand dollar bank loan and proceeded to build his first low-income housing project in Sheepshead Bay. He sold it in 1975 for over half a million dollars. By 1981, Griggs was the single largest developer in the tri-state area. He continued to build and then spread his investments among several emerging energy and technology firms. According to *Forbes*, The Griggs Organization officially became valued at a billion dollars in 1986. And Rawson never looked back.

Rawson met Liliana Ricci, a magnificent bronze-skinned beauty, while overseeing the construction of a Griggs villa resort in Tuscany. It was his first European development, and like all his early ventures, he helped personally select the building materials and finishes. Liliana, a struggling model, had been hired by a marketing firm to give tours to prospective investors. Rawson took one tour, incognito, to ensure the villa was being promoted to his liking. According to an unauthorized biography of Griggs, Rawson was so smitten with the beautiful tour guide that he spent the entire presentation gathering up the courage to ask her to dinner. It was the last time Rawson Griggs ever questioned his own moxie.

Liliana swooned over the charismatic, charming American. They were engaged three months later, and married two months after in Lanai, Hawaii, on a gorgeous bluff overlooking the Pacific Ocean. Paparazzi flew overhead in helicopters, snapping photos with telescopic lenses.

Though Liliana was a model married to a billionaire, she seemed to shy away from the spotlight. As Rawson's empire grew, Liliana retreated to the relative privacy of their various homes, raising the young Alena, gardening, writing poetry that nobody else saw but that Rawson raved about in interviews. He said if she wanted to, she could have been the country's poet laureate. People fell in love with the woman who grounded the high-flying Rawson Griggs, tethered him to earth with a loving wife and beautiful young daughter.

And then at the age of forty-two, Liliana Griggs was diagnosed with ovarian cancer.

Rawson spent the next four years taking Liliana to the very best doctors and specialists around the world. The most famous photo ever taken of Liliana was on Fifth Avenue, in front of Griggs Tower, near the end of her life yet still carrying Alena in her arms, her head wrapped in a scarf to hide the effects of the radiation.

Liliana Griggs succumbed to her cancer at age forty-six, leaving Rawson a widower and eleven-year-old Alena without a mother.

Rawson never remarried. Not for a lack of suitors. He was the toast of New York: a doting father who could literally buy a woman the world. But work was Rawson's second wife and his only mistress. He coated the pages of every tabloid and glossy magazine, appearing arm-in-arm with the world's most stunning women: models, actresses, heiresses, ingénues, women all hoping to be the one Rawson kept around.

But none of them lasted very long.

Remy found an incredible *New York* magazine story from four years ago about Alena Griggs's wedding. According to the writer, just one week before Alena's wedding to Paul Bracewell, Rawson had torn both the ACL and MCL in his right knee playing tennis in East Hampton. There was grainy paparazzi footage of Griggs hitting a backhand, then planting his foot the wrong way and falling to one knee while his opponent, a well-known celebrity chef, rushed to his side.

It was the kind of injury that would require surgery and months of rehabilitation. Everybody speculated as to whether Alena would be forced to postpone her wedding.

But just one week later, the *New York Post* ran a cover story featuring Alena Grigg's wedding to Paul Bracewell. The reception was at Cipriani and reportedly cost over two million dollars. And rather than print a photo of Alena and Paul at the altar, or the couple's first kiss, the front page featured Alena and Rawson Griggs during the customary father-daughter dance set to *You Look Wonderful Tonight* by Eric Clapton.

Rawson beamed, and the smile on Alena's face was visible from Mars. Sharp-eyed observers pointed to a strange ripple in the tuxedo fabric by Rawson's knee, which many assumed was a brace of some sort.

Witnesses said Rawson danced the entire night. The writer found a source at New York Presbyterian Hospital who claimed Rawson Griggs had been admitted just one week before the wedding, and under great secrecy, to undergo a total knee reconstruction.

One year later, Rawson published a book titled *Never Show Weakness*. It spent six months on the *New York Times* bestseller list. He embarked on a thirty city international tour to promote it. Nobody ever saw him limp.

Once Remy was caught up on Rawson Griggs, he checked his work email. Odds and ends from McCarty which would have to be dealt with. One email from Andrew Pulaski, forty-eight hours after the attack, with the subject line *Feel Better*. The body of the email itself was empty.

Then, on a whim, Remy checked his social media accounts. What he saw made his jaw drop.

There were five hundred new friend requests waiting for him on Facebook, all from complete strangers. There were also about fifty unsolicited messages in his inbox. Most were from strangers, applauding his heroism. Some just wanted to confirm this was the *real* Jeremy Stanton, that guy all over the news. He'd also received half a dozen messages from various women—some of them quite attractive—who *just couldn't help but notice* Remy was alone in his profile picture. And so with that in mind, not to be too forward, but how would he feel about grabbing a drink sometime?

Reflecting on his recent barren dating life, Remy was amused by the sudden influx of prospects. Meeting someone would have been so much easier if he'd just gotten shot earlier. If he ever went through a dry spell again, he'd have to find another famous couple to rescue.

He also checked his seldom-used Twitter account. He'd posted a total of forty-eight tweets in two and a half years, twenty-two of which were angry messages directed at the MTA and various airlines for scheduling delays and lost luggage. But he gasped when he saw his follower count: sometime over the past week, Remy had amassed over fifty thousand new followers. He couldn't remember his last follower count exactly, but he was reasonably sure it was somewhere under a hundred, with a chunk of those being eggs and porn-bots. He scrolled through his list of new followers and was shocked to see they largely appeared to be real people.

And his "at replies" were blowing up. He'd received hundreds of tweets from complete strangers. And not just from random people. There were messages from celebrities. Politicians. Musicians. People whose movies he'd seen, albums he owned.

Then he saw why.

Rawson Griggs had tweeted to the nearly ten million people who followed @RealRawsonGriggs:

Just met American hero @RemyStanton. A great young man with a bright future. My family and I thank him for his selflessness and courage.

Remy decided that he was, for better or worse, in the public eye. So he needed to play the part. He took a thumbs-up selfie and posted it with the tweet:

Just seeing these messages. Overwhelmed and grateful. Glad to be home and recovering. BTW can anyone spare a left arm? (asking for a friend)

He checked his personal email, which was attached to his public LinkedIn profile. There were dozens of requests from media outlets looking for comments, begging for interviews. Emails from CNN. *The New York Times. Vanity Fair. The Guardian. The New York Gazette.* Blogs and websites he'd never heard of. He had an email from a girl he'd dated briefly last year, who'd broken up with him after saying he traveled too much, wondering how he was doing. Another email was from a girl he'd had a drunken yet memorable one-night stand with last winter, who said she didn't even know his name until she recognized his picture on BuzzFeed.

Remy closed his inbox and leaned back in bed. The adulation made him forget, just for a moment, the pain that radiated through his body like a pulse.

Once he was finished marveling at his newfound notoriety, Remy read up on the murder of Dastan Nogoyev. Nogoyev was unconscious when handcuffed and taken to Bellevue for medical observation. He was then transferred from Bellevue and arraigned in Manhattan Criminal Court, then remanded to the Tombs detention center on White Street in downtown Manhattan.

After his arraignment, Nogoyev was being led to a holding cell. There he would stay with several other prisoners who were also awaiting arraignments and grand juries. At around 2 p.m., a prisoner named Domingo Diaz, armed with a homemade shiv carved from the handle of a toothbrush, stabbed Nogoyev over thirty times, perforating his lungs, liver, kidneys, spleen, and both his femoral artery and jugular vein. He bled out in less than a minute, and paramedic attempts to resuscitate him failed.

CNN had complied a profile of Nogoyev. Remy clicked on the link.

Dastan Nogoyev was born in the capital city of Bishkek, Kyrgyzstan in 1990. He spent time as a migrant worker in Russia, earning a little over eight hundred and forty dollars a month as a security guard at a mall in Sirgut, Siberia, and seven hundred and twenty dollars a month stocking boxes at a printing warehouse in Moscow.

Nogoyev had immigrated to the U.S. legally, working menial jobs: janitor at a community college, bar back at a dive in the East Village. Nogoyev had a wife and son who still lived in Bishkek, neither of whom had yet been located.

The gunmen had presumably self-radicalized, and for some reason targeted the Griggs family. So far, no terrorist organizations had claimed responsibility for the attack, and their motive remained a mystery.

The other gunman was still at large. His identity died with Dastan

Nogoyev. Grainy traffic camera footage revealed nothing, just the shape of a man running into the night and then vanishing. Other than the earlobe piercing, Remy hadn't been much help.

Police dragnets had canvassed the entire city. Problem was, they didn't know who they were looking for. Nobody came forward. Jerry Kapinski, a Griggs spokesman, said that even though Mr. Griggs had the utmost respect for the men and women of the FBI and NYPD, he was willing to take matters into his own hands to find the suspect. The mayor condemned Rawson's threat of vigilante justice, but the people seemed to back him up. If the bureaucrats couldn't do it, Rawson would.

Remy could understand Rawson's anger. He'd taken a bullet for Alena and Paul, and the man who fired it could be sitting on a beach halfway around the world sipping a Mai Tai for all anyone knew. The more time the suspect spent in the wind, the smaller the chances were of ever finding him.

Remy clenched his teeth, tensed up, then felt another bolt of pain shoot down his arm.

Ease up. Let yourself heal.

"You alright there, man?"

Trevor was awake.

"Yeah," Remy said. "Couldn't sleep. Between the meds and the pain, I'm a mess."

"Don't push yourself," Trevor said. He stretched, revealing a slab of ab muscles that looked carved from granite. Comparatively, Remy's looked like smoothed-over Play-Doh. "Trust me, one thing I know is that the body needs time to recover. You push yourself too hard after an injury, let alone this kind of trauma, you'll end up doing more damage."

"I know," Remy said. "Just sort of feel helpless. Aimless. By the way, Cheeto-Man, either you went way overboard on the spray tan or you were recently exposed to nuclear radiation."

Trevor laughed. "When you're from New Hampshire with Nordic bloodlines, you need a little artificial coloring."

"No judgments, Orangeade. So how's married life treating you? Chris mind that you're here?"

"Oh, he's thrilled. Seriously. He gets the whole bed to himself and doesn't have to deal with my snoring."

"Go back to sleep," Remy said. "I'm just farting around. Looking into Rawson and this Nogoyev guy. The last few days have been insane. Do you know that I have over fifty thousand Twitter followers? I don't know what to do with that."

"Hey, you get a few more you can start charging for paid posts. You know, 'I'm Jeremy Stanton and when I'm not saving lives, I spend my time in this amazing new breathable underwear.'"

"Always thinking," Remy said. "Get some rest."

"Nah, I'm awake," Trevor said. "I'm up at four thirty most mornings anyway. I teach six a.m. classes three days a week so I have to be up in time for breakfast and a triple espresso."

"Did I ever tell you you're insane?"

"Many times," Trevor said, smiling through bleary eyes. "Still, I love what I do. Even if you still haven't taken my class. So consider me a happy, functional, crazy person."

"I don't know what that's like," Remy said.

"Being a crazy person? What you did the other night I'm pretty sure could be defined as crazy on multiple levels."

Remy laughed. "No. Not that. Loving what you do. Can't say I've ever felt that way."

"You thinking about leaving Pulaski?" Trevor asked.

Remy shrugged. "I've thought about it. Just never really had a viable alternative."

"You think…Griggs? Is that why he wants to see you again?"

"I don't know," Remy said. "Maybe."

"What would you say?"

"I really don't know."

"But you've thought about it."

Remy nodded. "How could you not?"

"He's the kind of guy who changes lives," Trevor said. "And not always in a good way."

"I know," Remy said.

Trevor stood up. "Hey, you got any coffee in this joint?"

Remy pointed in the direction of the kitchenette. "Keurig pods are in the pantry next to the fridge."

Trevor stumbled over to the kitchen and peered inside. "Great. Swamp water in pod form," he said. "Hazelnut. Who drinks hazelnut? Seriously, Remy, I have more food in my gym bag than you have in your whole apartment."

"You want more food options, you're welcome to bring your own pods, you coffee elitist."

"Not an elitist, I just think hazelnut coffee tastes like the inside of a jock strap."

Remy slid off the bed and a bolt of pain shot through his chest. He wanted to stay away from the Oxy unless the pain was unbearable.

"You alright?" Trevor said.

"Yeah. You know, you should have seen Rawson's face when he saw that Nogoyev had been killed. He looked like…I don't know… like nothing. There was something scary about it. Like he was glad the man was dead."

"Can you blame the guy?" Trevor said. "That asshole tried to kill his daughter. You and I both know there's someone out there whose death you in particular wouldn't lose sleep over."

"Don't go there," Remy said.

"Ever think about him?"

"As little as possible."

"Usually the most frightening things I have to deal with are torn yoga pants or brides who want to drop four dress sizes for their wedding in two weeks. This is on a whole different level. Rawson Griggs isn't a normal man, Remy. He exists in a world that is completely unlike anything you or I have ever been in. I've read about him. He doesn't play by anyone's rules. If you're his friend, you're set for life. But if you're his enemy, he'll crush you."

"I know," Remy said. "Thankfully, I'm on his good side. I don't know what he wants from me. But I need to find out."

At eleven o'clock, Alena Griggs entered her father's office. He was hunched over a mountainous pile of paper, a red pencil in his right hand, going through every sheet line by line, his face barely a foot from the page in front of him. The pencil moved slowly. Meticulously. If the devil was in the details, Rawson's pen was his trident.

Though Rawson heard Alena enter, he did not react. Alena stood there for a full three minutes before her father looked up.

She gazed around his office, the way she'd done a thousand times, ever since she was a little girl and Rawson let her in to play while he discussed billion dollar deals. She sat on the floor behind his desk, babbling into a plastic phone, mimicking her dad the best she could. Alena never thought this was strange behavior. It wasn't until she grew older than she learned Rawson got away with things nobody else could.

He worked eighteen-hour days as a matter of routine, and there were times Alena would go weeks without seeing him. And because Rawson expected more from himself, he would push other people to keep up, often beyond their own limits. Often well beyond their breaking point.

Rawson's desk was a massive piece of furniture and the highlight of the office. Six feet long and three feet deep, made from a rich, Victorian mahogany. It had been built in the 1860s, and the wood was rumored to have been carved from the same tree as Abraham Lincoln's desk. It had cost Rawson seventy-five thousand dollars, and he personally polished it weekly with natural beeswax.

The office offered some of the most incredible views of Manhattan Alena had ever seen. The six-foot double-paned bulletproof glass along the back wall overlooked the grandeur of Central Park, its lush canopy of green resembling the top of a thick forest. They were high enough that you could make out the dark blue of the Central Park reservoir to the north. From this perch on the fifty-third floor of the Castle, the entirety of New York City stretched out beyond them, nestled between the towering spires of Central Park West and Fifth Avenue. It was a postcard view.

Other than the mountains of papers and a desktop computer, the only other decor on Rawson's desk was an ornate, handcrafted chess set. The pieces were made from soapstone and the board was a solid chunk of marble. Rawson always challenged business partners to a game. If they didn't know how to play, they declined and promised to learn. More often than not, they did. And they always lost.

On the windowsill sat a bronze bust of Rawson himself. It was turned to face the view outside. Alena always thought the piece was a little odd. She'd asked him: "Who keeps a bust of himself in his office?" It was a gift from a Russian sculptor, he'd said. The bust faced outside so it could keep an eye on the world while he slept, which, given that Rawson slept about four hours a night, meant the bust did not have a very demanding job.

Something about that seemed beautiful and poetic to Alena, and summed her father up perfectly. If Rawson could work twenty-four hours a day, he would.

When she was young, Alena would stand atop the windowsill looking out over the majesty of the city. Rawson always kept one hand on her waist, as though he feared she might fall through the glass. And after Liliana died, Alena noticed Rawson held on to her a little tighter.

She would tell her father, a dreamy look in her eye, that they were floating in heaven. If only the windows weren't there, she could reach out and touch the clouds. Maybe, just maybe, she would find her mother floating among them.

Though Rawson Griggs placated Alena's desire for normalcy, she knew that deep down he didn't want that for her. He wanted Alena to feel special. He wanted her to feel like she was destined for something greater. And once she fully embraced her potential, she would have every resource in the world behind her. Rawson only wanted her to feel normal to the extent that she was able sympathize with others.

"You cannot gain peoples' trust unless you understand them," he'd told her. "How they think. What motivates them. Once you know peoples' desires, necessities, fantasies, you can make them do anything you want. You must act like them. Talk like them. Understand them. Even if in your heart of hearts you know you're not like them. Not in the slightest."

"How's Paul doing?" Rawson asked without looking up from his desk.

"He's rattled. Struggling."

Rawson nodded. "You've always handled things better than him."

"You're too hard on Paul." Alena waited a moment, then said, "I'd like you to invite Paul to attend the strategy meetings again."

"That will never happen," Rawson said.

"Paul is a part of this too. He's going to have to give up his life, just like me. You can't…"

"My decision was not meant to leave room for negotiation," Rawson said. "Paul is not welcome. If he's having difficulty getting over the attack, he has my sympathies and he should see a therapist. But I will not allow any sort of weakness to pollute this. Not when we're so close. Not ever."

"He's not weak," Alena said. "That's my husband."

"Notice your words," Rawson said. "*That's my husband*, you said. Not *he's* my husband."

"You're adding meaning where there isn't any."

"Am I?" Rawson said. He looked up at Alena. "Paul is not my blood. I don't care if he understands the decision. It stands."

"You're putting me in a tough place, Dad. What do I say to him?"

"That's up to you. You're a Griggs. You're my blood. You've faced far tougher decisions. You can handle your husband's fragile ego."

Alena nodded resignedly.

"You're working late," Rawson said.

"Since when is eleven o'clock late?" she said playfully. Her father was still wearing his suit and jacket, his tie cinched. Anyone else would have taken his jacket off. Loosened his tie. Not Rawson. You were either working or you weren't.

Rawson smiled. "It would seem that neither of us wants to go home. But you're the only one who has someone waiting for them."

She changed the subject. "What are you working on?"

Rawson put his pencil down and sat back in his chair. The leather chair squeaked as the large man settled into it.

"The Miami resort," Rawson said. "I want the doors open in twenty-four months. But the local zoning board is giving us a hard time granting us access to the airspace we've requested. We need a helipad on the premises. They're playing hardball, saying it will disrupt air traffic patterns and disrupt local residents. But the whales need to be flown in and land directly on the property. That's a deal breaker."

"Will they budge?" Alena asked.

"Everyone budges. For a price. We're just feeling out what theirs is. It might be a generous contribution to a state senator's reelection campaign. Or, more likely, preferred tee times on the golf course. Local politicians are pettier than purse snatchers."

Alena nodded. Stood there. Her father narrowed his eyes. He knew his daughter better than anyone. Including her best friends. Including her husband.

"Something's on your mind," he said. "Is it Paul?"

Alena shook her head. "He'll be alright. He just needs reassurance."

"It doesn't speak much about the man that he needs such constant reassurance."

"He's a good husband," Alena said. "And a better man than most of the spoiled heirs and trust fund babies you tried to set me up with."

"You make it sound like I was trying to arrange your marriage."

"Weren't you?" Alena said. "You always wanted me to be with a man who could take care of me. Took you a long time to realize I didn't want to be taken care of."

"You were the project that took the longest for me to learn."

"I would like Paul to have your approval at some point. We've been married for four years."

"Then he's had four years to earn it," Rawson said. "Ask your husband what's taking so long."

Alena's scowl let Rawson know she disapproved of that comment. He noticed this and sighed.

"Why don't you sit down." It wasn't phrased as a question.

"I'm never sure whether I'm interrupting you."

"You never interrupt me."

Alena took a seat.

"What's on your mind?" he asked. Rawson leaned forward and steepled his fingers together. To Alena, that posture always made her father look like some sort of Tibetan monk, a soothsayer, some mystic about to share the secrets of the universe to a cynic.

"Do you think he'll come in next week?" Alena said.

"You mean Jeremy Stanton."

Alena nodded. "Yes. Are you sure it's a good idea? How much do you know about him?"

"You'd be very surprised," Rawson said. "I made it my business to know everything about that young man before I set foot in his hospital room. He's smart. He's ambitious. And he has demons. But those demons can be harnessed."

"I understand why you want him. But we could easily let it go. Let him go. We don't need him."

Griggs shook his head. "I have a feeling about Jeremy," he said. "We need young blood to speak for us."

"That's always been my job."

"And you've excelled. But we need someone who is not our blood who can speak for us, who's *not* us."

"But not Paul."

"No," he said. "Not Paul. This young man is a hero. Everyone loves him. Andrew Pulaski might be a mercenary, but he's not an imbecile. Having someone like Jeremy…it appeals to hearts and minds. When an opportunity presents itself, you take it or you regret it."

"Is this an opportunity for him? Or for you?"

"Both. Jeremy Stanton could be an asset. A valuable asset. And he knows what being on our side could do for him. It will change his life."

"I hope you're right," Alena said. "There is something about him. But he could say no."

Rawson smiled. "You know better than that."

She did. Her father had already considered every possibility, every permutation, before he set one foot into Remy Stanton's hospital room. Alena looked at the ornate chess set on her father's desk.

"He won't say no," Alena said.

"No. He won't. When a young man comes from the background Jeremy did, it leaves them with endless ambition, but also lacking the guidance to achieve it. They work themselves to the bone, but only end up enriching other people. If you sell them a different life, a better life, they'll kill for that life. Jeremy Stanton has been waiting for this door to open for a long time. I know it."

"How?" Alena said.

"Because I see some of myself in him. Both diamonds and coal are composed of the same base elements. The only way to know which is which is by applying tremendous pressure. That's what we'll do to Mr. Stanton, and he'll show us which he is."

"It could ruin him," Alena said. "He'll get torn apart. We all will."

"Lions don't get torn apart," Rawson said. "If Jeremy is one."

"You and your obsession with lions," Alena replied. "I still remember the fable you told me when I was a girl."

"The lion and the sheep," Rawson said, smiling. "You remember it."

"Of course I do."

"You know that nobody can judge potential the way I can, Alena," Rawson said. "And the greatest untapped potential lies in those who are ambitious and have been waiting for an opportunity. Remy has been waiting. I'm going to offer him what nobody else in the world can: power. I believe Mr. Stanton would do anything to wield it. And he may wield it well."

"These next few months are going to be different than anything we've done before," Alena said. "I've been by your side my whole life, Dad. And I always will. But this changes everything. Are you ready?"

"I am. Are you?"

"Yes," Alena said. "But I don't know about Paul."

"It is not a wife's job to worry about her husband."

"That's very old-fashioned," Alena said with a note of disapproval. "Attitudes are very different now compared to when you and my mother met."

"Not as much as you think," Rawson replied. "We're going to change the world. I think Jeremy will want to be a part of that. Whether Paul joins us is not my concern."

"I've seen what this can do to families. It can tear people apart."

Rawson paused. "Are you nervous?"

"A little."

"Scared?"

"A bit."

He nodded. "Good. You should be."

CHAPTER 5

Remy had walked by the Castle a hundred times but had never once set foot inside. The Castle, officially known as Griggs Tower, was a sixty-five story behemoth of a skyscraper situated smack in the middle of midtown Manhattan, a gold monolith sparkling amidst the concrete jungle. It towered over the city, attracting hundreds of thousands of visitors a year. And now Remy was standing outside, wearing a freshly pressed suit that was an absolute *bitch* to put on given that his left arm was currently as useful as a rusty can opener. It wasn't too often you were asked to meet with someone at the building that literally bore their name.

The Castle had been erected in 1981, after Rawson Griggs bought the old, decrepit Shearson department store. Obtaining a seventy million dollar investment from half a dozen different banks, Rawson razed the Shearson building to the ground, and in its place built one of the city's enduring monoliths. In order to erect a building of such height, Rawson had to purchase airspace rights from Oliver Mandel, the famous jeweler who owned the building next door. Mandel's Jewelry, at five stories, was a toadstool compared to what Rawson had planned. They had a handshake agreement to sell the rights for five million dollars. But when Mandel took an extended vacation in Greece, Rawson, believing Mandel was getting cold feet, allegedly flew to the island of Santorini, found Mandel sunbathing on Perissa beach, and refused to leave until the contracts were signed.

Construction on the Castle took six years. Over ten thousand workers were said to have had their fingerprints in its creation.

Doormen wore black tuxedos with black top hats and white gloves, welcoming visitors. A horde of tourists stood at the lip of the sidewalk taking pictures, videos, and selfies. The tour guide, a bubbly blonde, enthusiastically recounted the history of Griggs Tower to her rapt audience.

Remy noticed several news vans idling outside of the Castle, well-manicured newscasters doing their hair and makeup while burly cameramen hauled equipment around.

One of the reporters was checking her makeup in a handheld mirror when she stopped primping and turned around. Remy's heart skipped a beat when he realized she was staring at him. She motioned to her cameraman with one finger and said, "Isn't that Jeremy Stanton?"

Remy's eyes went wide and he booked it towards Griggs Tower.

A white-gloved doorman opened the gold-paneled door for him and said, "Welcome, sir."

"Thanks," Remy said, hustling into the lobby. The atrium of Griggs Tower was an incredible sight to behold. The walls were adorned with gorgeous brown tile work, and a waterfall poured delicately down the left side of the atrium that must have been fifty feet high. Four escalators carried professionals and tourists to the second floor, where Remy could see a number of high-end retail shops. Armani. Mont Blanc. Hermés. And, of course, Starbucks.

Remy looked up. He couldn't even see the ceiling.

By the escalator bank, there was a souvenir stand selling all sorts of Griggs-branded merchandise. Hats. Sweatshirts. Coffee table books featuring luscious photos of Griggs properties from all over the world. Inspirational business books authored by Rawson himself. Snow globes. Tie pins. Hats. Sweatshirts. Even a cookbook: *Griggs at the*

Grill, with a cover that featured a marbled steak so mouth-watering it looked carved from a cow fit for Jesus himself. Everything about the Castle screamed over-the-top indulgence, with not a penny spared on opulence.

At the security desk, two uniformed men with guns strapped to their belts logged people in and checked IDs. Remy approached and said, "Yeah, um, hi…I'm here to see Rawson Griggs."

Both guards looked skeptical. The one on the right said with exasperation, "Name and ID."

Remy got the sense a lot of crazy people showed up here asking to see Rawson Griggs. Wasn't too much of a stretch for them to assume he was just another loon.

"Jeremy Stanton. I was, um, invited by Mr. Griggs."

Remy handed the guard his driver's license. The man's eyes perked up. He scanned Remy's ID, then pointed at a touchpad screen atop the security desk. A half dollar-sized circular outline appeared.

"Press your thumb there."

Remy did so. The scanner read his fingerprint. The guard nodded.

"Mr. Stanton, welcome to Griggs Tower. It's a real pleasure to meet you. Thank you for what you did for Alena and Paul."

"Oh, you know. Shit happens."

"Indeed it does. Someone will be with you shortly."

"Great. So I'll just wait here. In the lobby of Griggs Tower. Where I was invited. By Rawson Griggs. Totally normal."

He didn't have to wait long. Less than two minutes later, Remy saw a man approach the security desk. He looked directly at Remy and smiled. He was about six feet tall, thin, mid-fifties, black, with close-cropped salt and pepper hair and a trimmed, gray goatee. He wore a charcoal pinstriped suit and a bold blue tie, held in place by a gold tiepin with a capital G. His calfskin shoes were polished to a high gleam. Remy suddenly felt very self-conscious about his suit, his posture, his sling, everything. He was entering a world unlike any he'd ever known, where first impressions were etched in stone.

"Jeremy Stanton," the man said, holding out his hand. "Damn, it's good to meet you. Kenneth Murphy. CFO of the Griggs Organization. You can call me Ken."

CFO. Christ.

Remy held out his hand, and the man shook it vigorously. Murphy's hand felt smooth, oiled.

"Nice to meet you. Remy Stanton."

Murphy laughed. "We'll see how Mr. Griggs feels about the Remy stuff. He's not a fan of nicknames. Come with me."

Murphy led him towards an unmarked door off to the side of the security desk. He pulled out an ID card and scanned it against a digital reader. Remy heard a lock disengage. Murphy opened the door and gestured for Remy to follow him inside.

They walked down a long corridor with gray walls and soft recessed lighting. At the end of the corridor there was a single elevator. Remy noticed there was no call button.

Murphy pressed his thumb to a keypad. There was a chirping noise and the elevator opened. Murphy entered. Remy stood there.

"Are you coming?"

"Yeah," Remy said, stepping inside. "This just all feels kind of *Mission Impossible.*"

"Oh, you have no idea of the security measures in this building. There are about half a dozen different sets of eyes watching at this very moment."

"Good thing I remembered to zip my fly."

Murphy laughed. "No wonder Rawson likes you."

Rawson Griggs likes me. Remy felt like a nerdy kid getting his first Valentine's Day card.

There were no buttons anywhere inside the elevator. It was programmed to go to one floor, and one floor only. After a minute, Remy's ears popped. He worked his jaw to try and fix it. Murphy smiled.

"Happens to everyone the first time," he says. "Air pressure changes up here. Like an airplane."

Finally, the elevator slid to a halt. The doors opened. Murphy stepped outside, and Remy followed.

A long hallway lay before them, painted in two tones: the top half a light gray, the bottom half a soft blue. Recessed lighting lined the ceiling. The walls were lined with transparent glass office doors. There were no names on the doors, just numbers. The people inside paid no attention to Remy and Murphy as they walked past.

"This is the heart of the Griggs Organization," Murphy said. "There's enough brainpower here to run a country."

"This is like the adult version of Willy Wonka's factory tour," Remy said. He started to whistle *I've Got a Golden Ticket* while silently hoping that the day didn't end with him being turned into a giant blueberry.

"Not many people are permitted up here," Murphy said, as though reading Remy's mind. "Mr. Griggs keeps this floor completely secure at all times."

At the end of the hall, Remy saw three doors. The one in the middle had *Rawson Griggs* etched onto the glass in gold lettering. It was the only office with a name on it. The glass was frosted. It was the only door that wasn't completely transparent.

"This way," Murphy said. He led Remy into the office on the left. Murphy sat down behind the desk. "Have a seat."

Remy looked around Murphy's office. A framed diploma from Harvard Law School hung on the wall. There was a photo of Murphy shaking hands with Rawson Griggs while posing in front of a construction site with a hole large enough to fit a stadium. Another photo showed Murphy and a young woman with their arms around Oprah Winfrey.

"My daughter interns for her," Murphy said.

"Excuse me?"

"Oprah. My daughter is an intern for her magazine. She graduates from Princeton next May and wants to be a journalist."

Remy nodded, as though this explained how a routine journalism major ended up working for Oprah.

"Rawson first went on her show almost twenty years ago," Murphy said. "It was Rawson's first interview after his wife died. The ratings were through the roof. They've been friends ever since. Last year, Rawson asked her to take on my Danielle so she could learn the ropes of working at a magazine. So she did. Rawson repaid the favor by taking out thousands of subscriptions to her magazine which he distributes throughout his properties worldwide."

"That's a pretty nice quid pro quo."

"Rawson is loyal. You'll hear Mr. Griggs talk about loyalty often. If someone is loyal to him, he'll move heaven and earth for them. He likes people to come out on top, because if they do, they're more valuable to him. And Rawson Griggs always repays his debts. Especially if those debts involve people who have shown kindness to Alena."

"Which is presumably why I'm here," Remy said. "So do I actually meet with Mr. Griggs at some point?"

Murphy took a few pieces of paper from a drawer and placed them in front of Remy.

Remy picked them up with his good hand and began to read.

"This is a non-disclosure agreement," Remy said. "If you meet with Mr. Griggs today, you're going to know things that nobody else knows. Things some people would pay a great deal of money to know."

Remy read the papers. Carefully. He'd seen enough NDAs during his work with Pulaski to understand much of the language, but the penalties for violating the Griggs agreement were harsher than anything he'd ever seen before. Essentially, if he violated the agreement in any way, he was subject to lawsuits, penalties, death, dismemberment, purgatory, jihad, fire ants, and tar-and-feathering. Not necessarily in that order. Once he signed, everything he learned while in the proximity of Rawson Griggs, his employees, clients, or consultants, or inside any Griggs-owned property, would have to be sealed within his brain until the earth hit the sun.

"I need to have a lawyer review this," Remy said.

"You could," Murphy said, "but the moment you reenter that elevator, it'll be the last time you set foot on a Griggs property unless you're a paying guest. We'll be generous and offer you a free round of golf if you ever visit the Griggs resort in Palm Springs. But you'll never hear from me or Mr. Griggs again. We'll thank you, sincerely, for everything you've done for Mr. Griggs and his family. But our business communications will end right here. Right now."

"Sounds like you're strong arming me into signing this agreement," Remy said. "And I'll be honest, that really gives me pause."

"Listen, Mr. Stanton. I've worked for Rawson Griggs for two decades. He's the godfather to my children. He paid off my student loans from Harvard. By even extending an NDA to you, Mr. Griggs has made a commitment he rarely makes."

"What kind of commitment?"

Murphy smiled. "Sign, and you'll find out. I won't ask again."

Remy thought about the offer.

He had two options: leave Kenneth Murphy's office, take that weird elevator back down to the lobby, get himself a cappuccino, and return to his boring but not altogether terrible life.

Or he could sign the NDA. It was like that scene in *The Matrix* where Neo and Morpheus sat in massive leather chairs in a crumbling, dilapidated house as rain sheeted down around them. Morpheus opened his hands, revealing one red pill and one blue pill.

"This is your last chance. After this, there is no turning back. You take the blue pill—the story ends, you wake up in your bed and believe whatever you want to believe. You take the red pill—you stay in Wonderland, and I show you how deep the rabbit hole goes."

"One question," Remy said.

"Shoot."

"Do you have a red pen?"

Murphy smiled and opened up his desk drawer. He fished around then handed Remy a red-capped pen. Remy looked at it for a moment, and then signed *Jeremy Stanton* on the final page. He slid the papers back to Kenneth Murphy.

Murphy stood up and walked around to the other side of the desk. He opened the office door and held it for Remy.

"Come on," he said. "They're expecting you."

"They? Wait, who is *they*?"

CHAPTER 6

Murphy led Remy down the corridor past another bank of offices to another blank door with another card reader. Murphy scanned his ID and opened it.

Inside was yet *another* elevator. Remy wondered if the Castle was actually just a massive, billion dollar Rube Goldberg contraption. Murphy pressed his thumb against a touchpad and the elevator opened.

Remy went inside. There were three buttons: 66, 67, and 68. Murphy pressed 68.

"Where are we going?"

"You've seen the brains of the Griggs Organization," Murphy said. "Now you're going to see the heart."

When the elevator door opened, Remy's eyes went wide. He'd never seen anything like this before.

"Please," Murphy said.

Remy stepped out of the elevator. And into Rawson Griggs's apartment.

It was not an apartment so much as a museum to war. The walls were all dark wood paneling, the plush carpets a rich, blood red. The walls were lined with antique sconces, each one with two candle arms jutting from the mouth of a two-headed lion.

Medieval weaponry of all shapes, sizes and time periods hung from the walls. A double-bladed broad sword next to a jeweled scabbard. A bronze-tipped mace hung next to an iron Morningstar. On the opposite wall was a steel war hammer fitted with an ornate wooden handle. In a glass case were numerous metal plates, bent, broken, and pierced, which appeared to be scraps recovered from a shattered suit of armor. Luscious woven tapestries hung from alternating panels. The apartment, if you could call it that, might have been a stronghold for a fifteenth century army.

"Rawson acquired most of these from the Wallace Collection of London," Murphy said. "Some he bought from private collectors and estate sales. He's been collecting for years."

"If New York is ever invaded by marauding tribes or aliens," Remy said, "I'm coming here."

"Get in line," Murphy said.

Floor to ceiling panoramic windows offered a view of the entire city. Remy had to close his mouth and remind himself not to drool. There was no furniture. This was built as a place to admire, not to rest.

"Spectacular, isn't it?" Murphy said.

"That might be the understatement of the century."

"This apartment as it stands took four years to assemble. Every piece of wood, every painting, every carpet, was hand-elected by Mr. Griggs."

"That sounds exhausting."

"Come. Let's meet the team."

Murphy led him further into the apartment. Remy marveled at the weaponry and antiques. Altogether, it must have cost Rawson millions.

Murphy stopped at a wood panel with a bronze doorknob in the shape of a snarling lion. "Welcome to the War Room," he said.

Makes sense, Remy thought. If you were going to have a war room, you might as well have enough weapons on hand to make *Game of*

Thrones feel quaint.

"Ready?" Murphy said.

Remy nodded.

Murphy opened the door to the War Room and they stepped inside.

There were a dozen people seated around a large, oval conference table. The room itself was about twenty feet long and ten feet wide, with none of the ornaments or accouterments of the apartment. Conference phones dotted the table. Two pitchers of water sat in the middle, and each seat had a crystal glass in front of it.

There were no windows. The walls were unadorned other than a few modern sconces. This room was meant for function, not form.

At the far end of the table, seated at the head, was Rawson Griggs. He wore a black suit, a crisp white shirt, and a bright red tie. An American flag pin was fastened to his lapel.

Rawson stood up. The room went quiet.

"Ladies and gentlemen, I'd like you all to meet Jeremy Stanton," Rawson said.

Remy smiled meekly. Then the attendees began to clap. It didn't last more than fifteen seconds, but Remy felt like he'd entered the Twilight Zone.

A woman seated to Rawson's left stood up and said, "Thank you for what you've done." She was elegant and athletic looking, in her late forties or early fifties, with shoulder-length blonde hair, wearing large, impossibly bright diamond earrings and clad in a form-fitting lime green pencil suit. Given how toned her arms and torso were, Remy guessed she could power through a Trevor double session without much trouble.

He wasn't sure what to say. *You're welcome?* That was something you said when thanked for holding a door open. Murphy said, "Jeremy, this is Rebecca Blum. COO of the Griggs Organization."

He went around the table to shake her hand. "Remy...Jeremy Stanton."

"It's a pleasure, Jeremy."

Alena Griggs sat to Rawson's right. She was beaming.

Alena was dressed in a cream-colored blouse with a matching jacket. A thin gold chain dangled from her neck, and she wore a pair of tortoiseshell glasses. She conveyed a rare combination of grace, beauty, and intelligence. Remy was happy to see her again.

A short, bulldog-looking man with thinning gray hair and a creased, oval face walked over, smiling like Remy was a favorite nephew. He wore a pinstriped gray suit with a pink tie. He extended his hand. Remy thought he recognized the man. Then it hit him.

Jesus.

"The city of New York owes you a debt," the man said. He spoke quickly, with a slight lisp. "Everyone here owes you a debt."

"Nobody owes me anything," Remy sputtered. He took the man's hand. His grip was iron. "I'm sorry, I'm…you…"

"Phillip Costanzo," the man said.

"Mr. Mayor," Remy said.

Costanzo laughed. "Not for about ten years, but I'm glad people still remember my old job."

"I would have voted for you," Remy said, "but I was still in college when you ran and wasn't eligible to vote in New York."

"That's no excuse," Costanzo said playfully. "You can always find a way to vote."

Costanzo had sadly squandered some of his legacy over the past decade through questionable consulting gigs on behalf of foreign governments, not to mention a very messy public divorce when he brought his mistress to a taping of *The Tonight Show*.

Remy wondered just why the former mayor was at the Castle.

Murphy pointed to an unoccupied chair. "Sit down. Pay attention."

Remy sat. He grabbed one of the pitchers and managed to pour himself a glass without making a mess. He was confused beyond measure. What exactly was the purpose of this meeting?

Murphy took a seat next to Rawson. The man seated on Remy's left leaned over and whispered, "Jerry Kapinski. Communications director."

Kapinski was in his early forties, spoke quickly, and was lean to the point of starvation. He had a close-cropped head of black and gray hair, sunken eyes, and what seemed like permanent shadows under them. A mist of cologne strong enough to repel mosquitos wafted off of him.

"Jeremy Stanton."

"Good to meet you, Jeremy. We're going to have a lot to talk about."

"We are?" Remy said.

Kapinski just smiled and turned away.

Everyone took turns introducing themselves. Most were Griggs Organization employees, but several introduced themselves as political consultants.

Why would Rawson Griggs be meeting with political consultants?

Remy turned to Rawson Griggs, as did everyone.

Rawson said, "You've all met Jeremy. Now let's get back to work. My announcement is next week. We have a tremendous amount to do before then."

Announcement? Remy thought. He had no idea what this was about. His brain felt like it had been thrown into a blender.

"Rebecca," Griggs said, turning to his COO. "What's the latest polling data on Shaw and Bertrand? Give me some good news."

Remy's eyes went wide. He recognized those names. Now he was starting to understand why he was here, what Rawson's announcement was, and why Murphy insisted he sign the NDA. If Remy was right, this was *huge*. Beyond huge. Game-changing.

"Our latest internal polls show Shaw in her home state with a fifty-seven percent approval rating, forty percent disapproval, eight percent undecided. She's popular in state, but once you look nationwide, her enthusiasm levels are horrid. Only thirty-one percent of registered Democrats list themselves as 'enthusiastic' or 'very enthusiastic' about a Shaw presidency. The Democratic Party is trending younger, and less white, and drifting further to the left. Shaw is a sixty-six-year-old center-left hawk, a five-term senator who voted for the war in Iraq."

"Not as bad as it could be," Griggs said. "But we'll detonate that."

"Bertrand looks worse. Forty-eight percent approval rating, fifty percent disapproval, two percent undecided. His support among Conservative Republicans disintegrated after he announced his support of mandatory background checks on all firearm purchases, and closure of the gun show sale loophole. Plus, as a congressman, he supported the auto bailout."

"This election is all about the lesser of two evils. People feeling like they have no other option," Griggs said. "Bertrand will fall further. Shaw is the bigger threat. But we can neutralize them both. I want to *detonate* both parties."

There were a few nervous chuckles around the room. Remy stayed silent.

Griggs said, "Right now, voters feel their only choices are two of the most unpopular, incompetent candidates in history. There's more excitement for dandruff than Shaw or Bertrand. Folks are angry. You can feel it every day. People know that these candidates are dog shit, but they're being told they're caviar."

Everyone at the table nodded in agreement.

Griggs continued. "And we trust that our internals are accurate? With the amount I'm spending, they'd better be."

"They're solid," Blum replied.

"Good," Rawson said. "I don't want to see any of our polling fall outside the margin of error. When I pay for intelligence, I expect *intelligence.*"

Remy was pretty sure Rawson shot a look at Phillip Costanzo. The former mayor looked down at the floor. *Odd*, Remy thought.

Still, the picture was growing clearer.

Annabelle Shaw was a Democratic senator from Kentucky. Richard Bertrand was the Republican governor of Louisiana. They were currently the frontrunners to be named their respective parties' nominees in the upcoming presidential election, just over seventeen months away. The sitting President, Owen Gladstone, a Democrat, had near-record disapproval ratings. His social positions had left people enraged, his economic policies had left millions unemployed, and his foreign policy had the country on the brink of another Cold War.

Democrats were in a bind because Annabelle Shaw was running to succeed a historically unpopular member of her own party. It would be tricky for her to distance herself from a disastrous administration while also rallying her party's base to the cause.

As for Bertrand, he headed up a Republican Party so fractured that Owen Gladstone was reelected despite a basement-dwelling thirty-three percent approval rating. Bertrand was a thirty-year politician: old, white, patrician, stuffy. A moldy relic and antithesis of the country's shifting demographics. As one GOP strategist had put it, "It's not just that the party trips over its own feet. It trips, and then knocks everyone else off a cliff."

"The bottom line is, people," Rawson said, "I don't just want to win. I want to eradicate everyone else from the playing field."

Remy looked around the table. The entire brain trust of the Griggs organization was assembled. The former mayor of New York offering his guidance. The polls. The consultants. The "announcement" that was clearly a *very* big deal.

All of it coalesced clear as day. Remy realized exactly what was going on.

Rawson Griggs is going to run for President.

And he's going to win.

CHAPTER 7

Remy spent the next four hours getting a crash course in politics. They reviewed polling data, demographics, favorability numbers, Q ratings, and a slew of other factors that had his head spinning. People were broken down by race, ethnicity, religion, background, voting history, everything but boxers or briefs—though Remy wouldn't have been shocked if they'd polled that as well.

The Griggs team had vivisected an entire country with geometric precision. All fifty states, comprised of three thousand one hundred and forty-one counties, mapped out by race, gender, income, age, and more. Thousands of hours of research, all dedicated to answering one simple question:

Could Rawson Griggs be elected President?

Their conclusion? It was possible. *Very* possible.

Remy decided long before the meeting ended that he wanted to be a part of this, *needed* to be a part of this. Rawson Griggs was starting a revolution.

Finally, Rawson stood up and stretched. He did not yawn. He walked around the table, shaking hands, thanking everyone for their efforts. He told the consultants he would let them know whether he'd decide to pay their fees. Remy wasn't sure if he was kidding.

Excitement coursed through Remy. He'd never felt this kind of enthusiasm before. He was given a taste of the greatest drug ever, one he didn't have to inhale or inject. The pain had disappeared. He felt like he could rip the sling off and bench three hundred pounds and then run a marathon.

As people filed out of the War Room, Alena Griggs came up and wrapped her arms around Remy, catching him by surprise. She looked tired but radiant.

He hugged her back with his good arm, wincing slightly as she pressed into his bad shoulder.

"I'm really glad you came," she said. "I was hoping you would, but I wasn't sure."

"You and your dad made me an offer I couldn't refuse," Remy said.

"People have before," she replied. She leaned in closer, until he could feel her breath on his neck. "But not many. And they're all sleeping with the fishes."

Remy laughed. "This is all…I can't even describe it. How long have you known?"

"Things have been getting serious for the last six months. That's when he hired the consultants and pollsters and brought Costanzo on board. But truthfully, I think he's been wanting to do this his entire life."

"I'd hate to be the people who run against him."

Alena laughed. "Me too. And I know him better than anyone. How's your arm?"

"Depends on the day. And time. And the weather."

"Well, take of yourself," she said. "We're going to need you at full strength."

"Full strength for what?" Remy said.

She shrugged and winked at him. Was she flirting? Was he?

"Good to meet you, Jeremy." Rebecca Blum interrupted them. "Will we be seeing you again?"

"Not sure if that's up to me," he said.

"Rawson says you're a fighter. We need more fighters. So I'll cross my fingers."

Blum shook his hand and left.

Remy turned back to Alena. "How's Paul?"

Alena sighed. "Paul is Paul. He's still shaken up. He's normally at these meetings but decided he needed to take a little break. I'm sure he'll be back."

"Well, give him my best. You guys have been through a lot," Remy said. He noticed Murphy looking at him. "I'm being summoned. It was great to see you, Alena."

"You too." She kissed him on the check. "I'm sure we'll see you soon."

Remy watched Alena leave. He could still smell her perfume, feel her hands around his neck. He forced it from his mind. She was gorgeous. Smart. Perfect. And very, very married.

Remy went over to Murphy. "How do you feel?"

"Like my brain has been hooked up to a car battery and driven to ninety."

Rawson walked over. Remy stood at attention. Rawson said, "Time to talk."

Rawson, Murphy, and Remy walked to the private elevator and they went back down to the fifty-third floor. He followed them to Rawson's office. Murphy extended his hand and said, "Good to meet you, Jeremy." Then he left Remy alone with Rawson.

"Come," Rawson said, and led Remy into his office.

Rawson's office was not quite as ominous as Remy expected given his combat-ready apartment. No Iron Throne. No heads of his enemies mounted on pikes. Instead, there was simply an old mahogany desk covered with papers. A few degrees, citations, and awards hung on the walls, but nothing too ostentatious. Function over form. Some sort of bronze head sat on the windowsill. It took Remy a moment to realize it was a bust of Rawson himself. Incredible. Remy wished he could one day be rich and crazy enough to own a bust of his own head.

There were two chairs in front of the desk. No couch. Rawson's office was meant to hold more intimate meetings.

Rawson sat down and motioned for Remy to do the same.

"Do you drink coffee?" he asked.

"I do," Remy said.

Rawson pressed a button on his phone. A minute later, a woman appeared with two steaming cups of coffee on a tray with small pitchers of milk and cream and a tin of sweeteners. She was in her early sixties, hair snowy white and pulled into a bun. Very little makeup. She wore a black suit and demure earrings. She had an elegant, motherly demeanor, and for some reason her presence alone put Remy at ease.

She sat one cup in front of Remy, and another in front of Griggs.

"Cream? Sugar?"

Remy poured a dollop of cream and a packet of Equal into his coffee. Rawson kept his black.

"Thank you," Remy said.

"Jeremy, this is Wanda Lefebvre. Wanda has worked for the organization for, what is it now, eighteen years?"

"Nineteen," Wanda replied with a scolding tone. "Thank you for what you did for Alena and Paul. I've known that girl since she had pigtails and braces." She looked at Griggs. "I believe I've seen that girl almost every day of her life."

"She's grown, my daughter," Rawson said. "One day she'll run this country."

"I don't doubt it. Anyway, it was a pleasure to meet you, Jeremy. Don't let Rawson scare you. He only eats live humans at breakfast, and he's already had his breakfast."

Once Wanda had left, Remy turned back to Rawson.

"I bet you're wondering why I asked you to come here today," he said.

Remy thought for a moment. "Actually, I'm pretty sure I know *exactly* why you asked me here today."

Griggs cocked his head, a faint smile that seemed to say *do tell.*

"You're running for president," Remy said.

"You're perceptive," Rawson said. "But why did I ask *you* to come here?"

"Because you want me to work for you. I'm guessing you want me in some sort of role on your campaign."

"Is that so?"

"Yes," Remy said. "You think I have some sort of value. And you're right. You want to be able to say that the Upper East Side hero supports Rawson Griggs. Endorses him. That this hero, or whatever the media wants to call me upended his life to work for you. You saw the reactions when I walked into that conference room. My support is worth something. I don't know exactly how much, but I know in every campaign, a prominent endorsement is worth something. Right now, my value is pretty high. But you think you're buying low in an effort to later sell high."

"And why do you think that?" Rawson said. He was clearly testing Remy.

"You're a businessman," Remy said. "You know you don't buy an asset at its highest valuation. You buy with the assumption that it will appreciate."

"And you think your value will appreciate."

"I do," Remy said, "and so do you. Having the endorsement of the man who saved your daughter's life says that I trust you. That I *believe* in you."

"You're not wrong," Rawson said. "I do believe your endorsement is worth something. But it's not just your endorsement I'm after. I want you to work for my campaign. Officially."

Remy laughed. "I have a job."

"I know. With Pulaski. A solid firm. At least for someone who wants to hide in the shadows, making just enough money to live but never enough to ever be noticed. *Barely* on the right side of satisfaction. Oh, you'll regale your children one day about all the luxurious Admirals Clubs you got to visit at the greatest airports around the world."

"You're a real sweet talker," Remy said.

"I'm not saying anything you don't already know, Jeremy."

"Maybe so," Remy said.

Griggs continued. "Very few jobs are worth your time and talent. summa cum laude from Yale with a degree in political science. Letterman on the Bulldogs baseball team—shortstop, no less—until Tommy John surgery your junior year ended your sports career with a .277 batting average and twenty-seven RBIs in fifty-nine games. You wouldn't have sniffed the pros. But you did have a three point nine grade point average. Thankfully, you were a better student than you were a hitter. And then you go to work for Pulaski."

"How do you know all this?" Remy said. He felt unnerved, like he was being shown a movie of his life.

"Oh, Jeremy, that's the tip of the iceberg. I know everything. I know that your mother, Margaret, passed away when you were in high school. Breast cancer. A horrible, cruel disease. I lost my wife to cancer as well. And your father…"

Remy shot out of his chair.

"Don't say another word about him. You say his name out loud and I walk out that door right now." Rawson appeared moderately startled. "I'm not just a packet of information to digest. Now look at me. Tell me I'm bluffing."

Griggs put his hand out. An olive branch.

"Please," he said, gesturing to the chair again. Remy sat down. "I didn't mean to flick an exposed nerve. But I need you to know that I'm not coming to you uninformed. There is no cynicism in what I have to offer you. You *could* add tremendous value to my campaign. But I care about my legacy far too much to allow weak-minded people to work for me. I believe you have fortitude. You have tremendous potential that is woefully untapped. You are a race car doing laps at fifty-five on a track to nowhere."

"Again with the sweet talk," Remy said.

"You want flattery, enter a beauty pageant," Rawson said sharply. "Only narcissists care about glitter and tassels. You want *access*. And access is what I have to offer. Whether or not your current value is at its apex depends on how you play the hand you've been dealt. I'm offering a chance to see how high you can rise. With me."

Remy sat there, thinking. A week ago he was at a bar drinking alone, and now he was being courted by one of the most powerful men in the world.

"I understand what you're saying," Remy said. "But you're asking me to uproot my life. Everything I have, I've earned. I've fought for. Nobody gave me anything."

"You think I'm giving you something?" Rawson said, amused. "What surprised me was not just the courage you displayed that night, but it was your carefulness in the days following it. You had every opportunity to cash in. But you haven't done a single interview. You haven't taken any money. Most people would exploit their moment in the sun. But not you. You held back. That speaks of a strategic mind."

Griggs lowered his voice. He leaned forward slightly and placed his hands on his desk. They were wrinkled, rough, calloused. They were not the hands of a man who sat around counting his money and minding an empire.

"This country is broken," Griggs said. "Our leaders are not leaders. I have no interest in letting the status quo remain. I aspire to *do* great things. To *make* great things. To *inspire* people. To change. To lead."

"So where do I fit in?" Remy said.

"Maybe one day you'll be a great leader. But right now, you're a pawn."

"Again with the flattery," Remy said.

"You're twenty-eight years old," Griggs said. "You're smart and you have a spine. More often than not, it's one or the other. But you don't know the world, the complex system of pulleys and levers that keep industries and communities and economies running. Not yet. A pawn must know his limitations. Pawns do not go up against more powerful pieces alone. They pave the way. They create lanes. They make barriers. Occasionally, they must sacrifice themselves for the greater good. A single pawn rarely changes the game, but a phalanx can make a difference. Pawns are soldiers. *You* are a soldier."

"So you want me to be a part of your pawn brigade," Remy said.

Griggs nodded. "Pawns can also become targets. For click-bait driven journalists. Women blinded by celebrity. Zealots who support our enemies. I'm offering you the chance to be a part of something great. And in the process, prepare you for something even greater."

"Alright," Remy said. "Let's cut to the chase. What *exactly* are you offering me?"

"Specifics. Alright. You're currently earning a hundred and ten thousand dollars a year."

"How do you…never mind. That's right."

"My offer is this. One hundred and seventy-five thousand dollars per year. Your title will be communications aide. You will work directly under Jerry Kapinski, my director of communications."

Remy had to take a breath. That was a sixty percent pay increase.

"There's one problem," Remy said. "Even if I'm interested, I'm under contract with Pulaski."

"Yes. For another seven months, which means Pulaski owes you a little over sixty thousand dollars pro-rated. I will offer Andrew Pulaski enough on top of that to convince him to let you out of your contract. I know Andrew. He tends to hire people smarter than he is, which is why you work there. He's also a pragmatist. If he thinks you'll be gone in seven months anyway, he'll take the money. He also has a terrible gambling problem, but that's another issue."

Remy looked around Rawson Griggs's office. He marveled at the lifetime of experiences, of opportunities, of luminaries met and bested, who bowed down to him and sought his counsel, influence, and money.

Rawson Griggs had built himself up from nothing. There were no schools that could teach Remy what Rawson could. No job that could offer the opportunities this one did. And yet, Remy hesitated. If he accepted, his life would never be the same. For better or worse.

He could stay with Pulaski. Get his yearly bonus, eventually buy an apartment in Tribeca, get a hybrid car, summer in the Hamptons, have a mid-life crisis and an affair with some yoga instructor twenty years younger than him. He could live an unremarkable, clichéd life, running along well-paved roads, his footprints unrecognizable.

"Let's say I accept," Remy said, "and you're somehow able to buy out my contract from Pulaski. When do I start?"

"One week from today. I could have your contract bought out in an hour."

"Can I take a vacation before I start?"

Rawson was not amused.

"If you accept, you'll be here next Monday morning at four a.m. Jerry Kapinski will brief you on the details beforehand."

"Four a.m.? Are you serious?"

"If you accept my offer, you will work hours that may seem ungodly now but will become routine. As you learned, we have a rather large announcement to make at nine that morning and I need everyone at the Castle early for a full walkthrough. Showmanship is part of the game. And no good show goes on without preparation and diligence. Having you there, at that announcement, would please me."

"It would help the show."

"Yes," Rawson said. "It would."

"I need night to think," Remy said. "You're not someone who makes potentially life-altering decisions lightly. Neither do I. Give me until tomorrow. I appreciate your offer, and lord knows a week ago this office was the last place in the world I would have ever expected to be. One night won't change anything. But it'll change my world. I think that's a fair request."

Griggs thought for a moment, then said, "I can respect that. I'll expect to hear from you by noon tomorrow. If I don't, I'll be briefly disappointed. But by this time next week, I'll have forgotten your name."

"You'll hear from me either way," Remy said.

Griggs stood up and extended his hand to Remy. Remy shook it. Rawson clamped down as though attempting to crush Remy's knuckles to dust.

"'One secret of success in life is for a man to be ready for his opportunity when it comes,'" Rawson said. "A wise man said that."

Remy replied, "And another wise man once said 'only fools rush in.'"

Remy left. Wanda Lefebvre was waiting for him outside the office.

"Mr. Griggs is quite fond of you," Wanda said as she led Remy away. "I've known him for a long time and I've seen him around thousands of people. I can't say he's taken to anyone as quickly as you."

Remy said, "I'm really not sure what I did to earn that."

"Yes, you do," Wanda said. She led him to the elevator and pressed her thumb against the keypad. The door opened, she said, "I hope we'll see you here again soon."

Remy let the door close without answering.

"I told you. I goddamn told you. He did it. The motherfucker did it."

"Hold on. You don't know that for certain. Rawson has a lot of enemies."

"Yeah. And I'm one of them."

"But you're safe now. Even if he was behind it, which you don't know for sure, there's no way he'd try something again. Especially not with the announcement on Monday. He wouldn't dare divert attention away from himself."

"Maybe. Maybe not. Maybe I get hit by a bus tomorrow."

"Then watch where you're going."

"That's funny. Damn you for getting me into this."

"Me? You came to us, remember? You were the one who offered to work with us. You made that choice."

"Whatever. It's done. I'm done."

"Now hold on. Just hold on. Let's talk. Meet me."

"I don't know."

"In person. I'll pick a spot. Somewhere we'll blend in."

"I don't know."

"Just hear me out."

"Alright. fine."

"*Great. Thank you.. I'll let you know. Oh, and, Paul?*"

"*What?*"

"*Look both ways when you cross the street. Just to be safe.*"

CHAPTER 8

On his way home, Remy bought an expensive six-pack. He took a chilled beer mug from the freezer and filled it with one bottle. Then he gently took his sling off, flopped onto the couch, and put his feet up on the coffee table. His arm was still stiff, but getting better by the day. Thankfully, he'd weaned himself off the Oxy.

He sipped his beer and tried to play out the next year of his life. How would it change working for Rawson Griggs? You didn't work for someone like Rawson Griggs then just leave after six months if it didn't work out. Rawson was notorious for holding on to grudges like family heirlooms. If you got on his bad side, he would make you regret having ever met him.

Remy knew enough about politics to be aware that, once he signed, his life would be torn open. The media would ravage him. Rawson's opponents would upend every stone, open every door. Even the ones he'd nailed shut years ago.

This was the road less traveled. Remy just couldn't see whether it led to greatness or straight off a cliff.

Then the door buzzer rang. Had he ordered food and forgotten about it? He didn't think so...and Trevor would have texted if he planned to come over.

Remy picked up the phone, skeptical.

"Hello?"

"Oh, hi, Jeremy? It's Alena."

Remy's heart began to jackhammer. *Alena? As in Alena Griggs, Alena? Why the hell would she be here?*

"Um, hi?" *Smooth.*

"Can I come up?"

"Um, yeah, sure. One second."

Remy buzzed her upstairs, then hung up the phone and panicked. He surveyed his apartment. The bed was unmade but at least the sheets were clean. He'd thrown out the moldy food, put the dirty dishes in the sink. All in all, the place could have been a *lot* worse.

His heart thumped in his chest. Alena Griggs.

A minute later, the doorbell rang. Remy checked himself out in the mirror. Meh.

He opened the door. Alena looked fantastic. She held a paper bag, and handed it to Remy with a smile.

"My father taught me never to go anywhere emptyhanded. Are you busy?"

"Well, the Sultan of Brunei was planning to stop by at five, but I'm free until then."

Remy took the paper bag and looked inside. A bottle of pinot noir. It looked expensive.

"Um...thank you," he said. "Not to be rude, but *I* was taught you're supposed to call ahead."

"And lose the element of surprise?" Alena said. "Where's the fun in that?" She waited at the door. Finally, she said, "Well, can I come in?"

"Not many people tell you no, do they?"

Alena smiled. "Not many. But that's partly because I spend my time with people who enjoy my company." She paused. "I could leave..."

Please don't.

Remy peeked into the hallway. "Your dad's not coming up too, is he?"

Alena laughed. "No. He likes to make a grand entrance. I'm more subtle."

"Well, then." Remy stepped aside and made a matador wave with his hand. "Welcome to Chez Stanton. It's not exactly the Castle. At a spacious four hundred and fifty square feet, it has all the amenities you need, provided you don't require a separate living room, kitchen, or bedroom. And you're much more likely to find spaghetti al dente than any paintings al fresco."

Shit…when was the last time he cleaned the toilet?

"It's charming," Alena said. "I like it."

"Charming is polite for tiny. I bet your bed is bigger than my apartment."

Alena looked over at Remy's desk, saw the wall calendar from his aunt, cocked her eyebrows, and said, "Corgis?"

"It was a gift from my aunt. I felt bad throwing it out."

"I'm not judging. Well, maybe a little." She pointed at the couch. "May I?"

Remy nodded, as though he could have possibly denied her. Alena moved to the sofa.

"Anyway, you'd be surprised," she said. "We have a two bedroom. It's twelve hundred square feet. I try to live a semi-normal life, but it's not really possible given who my father is and that I work with him. It's like trying to hide a boulder under a raincoat. And let's just say my father and I have different tastes in décor."

"You mean you're not a fan of medieval warfare chic?"

"I told him it was a bit much. He took down the battle axe that used to hang on the wall of his office."

"You're kidding."

"Do I sound like I'm kidding? So, are you going to open the wine?"

Remy opened it successfully, petrified for a moment that he might disintegrate the cork and prove his lack of domesticity. Once the bottle was open, he took his only two wine stems from the cabinet—a Christmas gift from Trevor and Chris—and poured them each a healthy glass. They clinked.

Remy took a sip. "This is good. Really good. How much was this bottle? A grand? Flown in from your dad's Sonoma winery?"

"Fifteen bucks at the liquor store next door," Alena said. "But keep going. Let's see what else you can be wrong about."

"Oh, I can be wrong about a lot. It's one of my most lovable traits."

Alena laughed. "I'm a Griggs, but I'm not my father," she said. "You know a lot less about us—about me—than you think you do."

"You're right. I'm sorry." He took another sip, chastened. "Worth every penny."

"Sit with me," Alena said. She moved over on the couch to make room. He hesitated. She was striking. Poised. The kind of girl he could never meet on his own. But he couldn't think like that. Remy sat down on the couch and pushed himself into the corner.

"So, I need to ask," Remy said. "Why are you here?"

"You don't trust my motives?" Alena said.

"There's a famous saying," Remy replied. "Beware billionaire heiresses bearing good wine."

"Pretty sure the actual saying is 'beware of Greeks bearing gifts.' But I get your point."

Alena sipped her wine. She placed her glass on the coffee table. It was a brown wooden slab covered in notches, stains, and dents. Remy thought the dings added character, but houseguests tended to think it looked salvaged from a dumpster.

"I'm here as a friend," she said, "and, not to put a fine point on it, as a closer."

"A closer?"

"You've seen *Glengarry Glen Ross.*"

"I have. You don't really look like Alec Baldwin."

"Well, I'm guessing you don't own any steak knives."

"Touché."

"No, what I mean is that I know my father offered you a job. And I know you wanted to take a little time to think about it."

Remy nodded. "I asked for one night. Which, considering the fact that you're here right now, means my night is already unproductive."

"So then I'll be quick." Alena shifted in her seat, moving closer to Remy. He didn't move, but felt his blood pump faster as she inched closer. "My father has accomplished just about everything a man can in life."

"That, I know," Remy said.

"And there are wonderful people who work for him. You met some them today. They're loyal beyond reproach. They would fight for my father, kill for him, and he would do the same for them. Kenneth Murphy. Rebecca Blum. Jerry Kapinski. Myself."

"And Phillip Costanzo."

"My father has known Mayor Costanzo since he was a no-name prosecutor in the Bronx. My father supported him when he ran for attorney general. Costanzo came aboard about a year ago as a consultant when my father started seriously considering whether to run. As the former mayor of New York, Phillips wouldn't back my father if he didn't think he would be good at the job. And good for the country."

"So where do I fit into this motley crew?" Remy said. "I'm not a mayor. I've never worked for a company like your father's. The closest I've ever come to working in politics was handing out flyers on a street corner for eight bucks an hour in college for some state senator whose name I can't even remember. Until last week, nobody knew who I was. If I'd had one more drink at that bar, we wouldn't be having this conversation."

"And I might not be here right now," Alena said.

Remy looked down. Sipped his wine. "I'm glad I was there. For you and Paul."

"You see? You *know* the kind of man you are," Alena said. "The kind of man you can be. When I said that people have worked for my father for decades, that's a double-edged sword. My father, well, he doesn't employ a lot of people who tell him no."

"What about family? Friends?"

Alena laughed. "Well, I'm his only family. And you don't get to where my father has by chumming it up at sports bars. He has business partners, and he has enemies. Bottom line: we need fresh blood. We need people who haven't done things the 'Griggs way' their whole life. My father needs clear eyes and a young heart. He needs energy and passion. I think you have that. Maybe it's been hiding away, but it's there."

"You may not be your father. But you sound an awful lot like him."

"I love my father. I would do anything for him. That's why I'm here. You'd be good for him. For us."

Remy said. "So how do you do it?"

Alena looked at him, confused. "Do what?"

"Be Rawson Griggs's daughter and still have a regular life. A regular marriage."

Alena turned away from Remy and took a sip of her wine. He caught a flash of sadness on her face.

"It's never easy. I can't say I really know what a regular life is or what a regular marriage is. This is all I've known, since I was old enough to realize my father wasn't like most dads. He never took me to the zoo. He never pushed me on a swing set. I was never allowed to have slumber parties. But I know my father would start a war for me."

"I hope he never has to," Remy said. "Can I ask a personal question?"

Alena smiled. "Didn't you do that already?"

"Your husband. Paul. Is it hard for him?"

Alena finished her wine and said, "Every day."

Remy nodded.

"Taking this job will change your life," Alena said. "But I don't think you would have come today if that didn't appeal to you. You want to see where this might take you. And so do I."

"Just one more question," Remy said.

"Let me guess. Personal."

"Sort of. What do you do in your spare time? Like, for fun?"

Alena smiled. "You mean do I Netflix and chill? Not really."

"So what do you do, then, when you're not being a Griggs?"

"Well, I try to read for at least an hour a night. I turn my phone to silent, prop myself up against approximately a thousand pillows, and read while my favorite opera music plays in the background."

"I don't know why, but that's not what I expected."

"My family is full of surprises."

"What do you read?"

"Mostly fiction," she said. "When you're knee-deep in multi-million dollar business negotiations fifteen hours a day, you need an escape. I love a good mystery series where I can start the next book as soon as I finish one. And sometimes I'll pour a glass of wine and read a romance novel."

"Saucy," Remy said. "Always with opera on?"

"Always," Alena said. "Maria Callas is my goddess. I cry every time I play her recording of *La Traviata*. Listen to her when you have some spare time."

"I will."

Alena reached into her purse and took out a business card. She put it atop her empty wine glass.

"That's the number for a woman named Grace Rivas. She's a reporter for the *New York Gazette*. She's written pretty extensively about my father and his businesses. She's tough on us, but I trust her to be honest. She's young and hungry and good. If you decide to accept, reach out to Grace. Tell her I suggested you get in touch, and that you're offering her an exclusive—the first interview with you since the attack. She'll do a good job. It's time for you to break your silence, Remy."

Remy nodded. "Thank you. I'll think about all of this."

He stood up and walked Alena to the door. She reached out and wrapped her arms around his neck, pulling him in close for a hug. She smelled like sugar with a hint of lemon. He still wasn't quite sure what to make of Alena.

She leaned in and said, "Say yes."

When she was gone, Remy sat down and finished the rest of the bottle of wine. Then opened his Internet browser and searched for

Maria Callas and *La Traviata*. He sat and listened to several tracks. Then he made three phone calls. And by the time he went to sleep, he'd made his decision.

At eleven o'clock at night, Wanda Lefebvre pushed open the door to Rawson Griggs's office.

"How's your evening?"

Her eyes were red behind her black-rimmed glasses. Her gray hair was pulled up tight into a bun, and her navy suit had faint wrinkle lines. She was tired, but like Rawson would never let on. That was one of the reasons he trusted her—they both knew the importance of hiding weakness. He depended on Wanda for just about everything, and she had access to information about the Griggs Organization nobody else did. Despite all the women who came and went following Liliana's death, Wanda Lefebvre was the closest thing he'd ever had to a second wife.

"Quite good actually," he said. "Today went well."

"The Stanton boy seems like he could be a good fit," she said. "Rebecca and Murphy liked him. And Phillip Costanzo was gushing. Phillip said he senses a little pit bull in Jeremy."

"As long as the pit bull is trained properly," Rawson said.

"Can I get you a coffee? Something to eat?"

He thought about it for a moment, but declined. "I'm going to head out within the hour and get a little sleep."

"I'll have Marco pull the car around at midnight," she said.

"Thank you." Rawson removed his glasses and rubbed his eyes. He'd been poring over speech drafts for the better part of a week. Put together and torn apart and re-stitched. Monday was one of the most important days of his life. Maybe *the* most important. It was the start of something revolutionary. He wished Liliana could have been here for this. The world would have loved her. And god, what that would have meant to Alena.

Rawson had given hundreds of speeches over the years, in front of some of the wealthiest and most powerful people alive. He knew how to hold a room, to feel the pulse of the crowd, how to have them eating from the palm of his hand. Yet he was never nervous. Preparation reduced chance, and chance led to weakness.

Rawson shifted in his chair. He felt the familiar ache in his right knee. The ACL tendon he'd torn right before Alena's wedding had never properly healed. He had waited his whole life to walk his daughter down the aisle, and only cowards limped. Pain was simply an obstacle. And like any obstacle, it could be hurdled or, with enough force, driven through.

That first dance, he'd been in agony. But nobody could tell. Everyone was focused on Alena. Her smile that could have melted steel, her gorgeous dress flowing like a lace waterfall. She was born the Griggs princess, and on that day she truly was, in every way. Each dance step sent a wave of nauseating pain through his body. But Rawson Griggs did not fall. Diamonds *did not crack.*

Wanda opened her purse. She pulled out a small object, a USB drive, which she placed on Rawson's desk.

"It's all set. With Stanton. They had no problems getting access."

"Good. Have they found the father?"

"Yes. He was apparently eyeball-deep in a bottle of Jim Beam, but Phillip's people will have him ready. Just in case."

"I hope it won't be necessary."

"Me either."

"I think Jeremy could be a diamond," Rawson said.

"Someone else seems to think so too. You'll want to see this." She gestured towards the fob.

Rawson picked it up, rolled it over in his fingers.

"I didn't know you sent Alena to see him," she said.

"I didn't."

"Then she went on her own."

Rawson dismissed her. "Thank you, Wanda. Get some rest."

"I will when you do," she said. And then she left.

Rawson waited until the door had closed, then plugged the drive into a USB port. A few seconds later, a folder appeared on his desktop. He opened the video file within.

The file was named *Stanton 01*.

Griggs double-clicked the file.

Rawson pressed play and turned the volume up.

A video appeared. The feed had been recorded directly from a computer's webcam. The image was being broadcast from inside a small studio apartment. The feed sputtered. The image was poor quality, but the technology had not been perfected yet.

At first, there was nothing but static and the sounds of car horns coming from outside the apartment. Two minutes later, the front door opened and Jeremy Stanton entered the apartment.

Jeremy disappeared for a moment, then plopped onto his couch and sipped a beer.

Then, at the twenty-three minute mark, a buzzer rang from inside Stanton's apartment. Stanton answered the intercom, and immediately became flustered. He looked around the apartment as though searching for the cause of a fire. Then the doorbell rang.

Jeremy answered it. Rawson recognized the other voice instantly. His daughter, Alena. She entered Jeremy's apartment.

Rawson watched as Alena handed him a bottle of cheap-looking wine in a paper bag. No Griggs label. Jeremy opened it and poured them each a glass. He listened to their conversation. Then Alena left Jeremy's apartment.

Rawson sat back in his chair. His daughter still had the ability to surprise him.

Rawson let the video run. Jeremy sat on his couch. Then he listened to opera music. For some reason, Rawson enjoyed watching the young man. You could always learn more about a person when they didn't think they were being watched.

Then Rawson's private phone line rang.

"Griggs," he said.

"Mr. Griggs. It's Jeremy Stanton. "I'm in."

"I'm very glad to hear that, Jeremy."

"There's one small condition."

"One condition," Griggs replied. "Alright."

Rawson was still watching the video as Jeremy spoke. It was an odd thing, Rawson thought, speaking to a man while simultaneously watching him on a video that had been recorded the same day with his knowledge.

When they hung up, Rawson had a new employee. He sent an email to Andrew Pulaski. Then his phone rang once more.

"Go secure," Phillip Costanzo said.

Rawson plugged in the code to click over a secure connection.

"What is it?" Rawson said. "Please tell me they've found Alexay."

"I'm sorry, Mr. Griggs. They haven't found him yet."

"God*damnit*, Phillip."

"We know he hasn't left the country. My sources at the FAA tell me his plane ticket was never used and nothing else has been purchased in his name. We have people at the border looking for him, unofficially."

"Have you talked to Brent Scott?"

"Yes. He's reaching out to the Kremlin. He's also put in a word to Kamurzenov. They relocated the family, and we're hoping they might have a lead. But so far, we've come up empty."

Rawson pounded his desk. "So he's out there planning god knows what? We had assurances from these people. You know he skipped that flight for a reason, Phillip. Either he knew we'd be looking for him, or he wanted to stay here."

"I don't know what else to say, Mr. Griggs," Costanzo said. "But we'll find him. One thing to consider: if Jeremy Stanton joins the campaign, Alexay could take that as a personal insult, given Stanton is responsible for Nogoyev's arrest."

"I'm not going to let some mercenary dictate the future of my campaign before it's started. Increase security for Monday's event."

"I understand. With Stanton, sir, it's just something to consider."

"You're using Stanton as an excuse for your failures. Good night, Phillip. Get me answers. *Find him.* Before Monday."

Rawson slammed the phone down. He massaged the bridge of his nose, then turned back to his speech. He needed to concentrate on the factors he had control over. Rawson Griggs could not remember the last time he truly felt fear. But tonight, a cold shiver ran down his spine.

CHAPTER 9

STANTON TO ACCEPT GRIGGS POST

Speculation runs rampant as "Upper East Side Hero" joins the Griggs Organization on eve of major announcement

by Grace Rivas, *New York Gazette*

The Griggs Organization announced today that Jeremy Stanton, hailed as the 'Upper East Side Hero' for his role in foiling the attack that targeted Alena Griggs and Paul Bracewell, would be joining the company in an unspecified role. Stanton, 28, intervened several weeks ago when two assailants attacked Mrs. Griggs and Mr. Bracewell, suffering a life-threatening gunshot wound among other injuries in the meleé. One of the alleged gunmen, Dastan Nogoyev, 26, was murdered in the Tombs by Domingo Diaz, a fellow inmate. Nogoyev's accomplice remains at large, his identity still unknown.

Stanton was previously employed by the consulting firm of Pulaski & Associates, but sources say Rawson Griggs bought out the remainder of Stanton's contract in order to free him up to accept the job.

In a brief statement, the Griggs Organization said:

Rawson Griggs and his family are indebted to Jeremy Stanton for courageously risking his life to do the right thing. As he got to know Mr. Stanton, Mr. Griggs was impressed with the young man's aptitude, acumen, and ambition, and decided to make Mr. Stanton an offer to join the organization. We are happy to say that he accepted. Mr. Stanton will attend Monday's event with Rawson Griggs.

Jeremy Stanton, in his first public comments outside of social media since the incident , said:

I'm thrilled to join an iconic American organization and work beside one of its great leaders and entrepreneurs in Rawson Griggs. I look forward to helping the Griggs Organization build a better future, both here and abroad.

Over the last month, speculation has grown that Rawson Griggs has begun putting together the infrastructure to launch a bid for President of the United States. Monday's event only amplifies that speculation. With sitting President Owen Gladstone's approval ratings at a dismal 29%, and the two projected frontrunners, Governor Richard Bertrand of Louisiana and Senator Annabelle Shaw of Kentucky, having difficulty building enthusiasm within their own parties, a Griggs ticket could add a jolt of excitement currently lacking in the early days of the race.

Spokespeople for both the RNC and DNC declined to comment on the speculation of a Griggs run. And if Griggs does announce, it remains to be seen as to whether he would run on a Republican or Democratic ticket.

But if there's one thing people have learned about Rawson Griggs: always expect the unexpected.

CHAPTER 10

Remy had waited in line for the last *Star Wars* movie. He'd been to concerts, clubs, gallery openings, and parades. But he'd never seen anything like the horde outside of Griggs Tower on Monday morning.

Hundreds of people packed the sidewalks of midtown Manhattan, waiting to get a glimpse of Rawson Griggs. Leading up to the event, the media had speculated wildly, but there was still a palpable buzz, a curiosity, as to just what would happen. Police barriers cordoned off the entrance. Cops searched every purse and backpack. There were enough metal detectors to cover the Super Bowl. Eventually, the lobby of the Castle grew so crowded with media and fans the cops locked down the tower. It was a spectacle like Remy had never witnessed

The Griggs inner circle waited on the second floor of the Castle. The entire section had been closed down for Rawson's use. Eight of them waited. They could hear the crowd buzzing below. Remy looked around. Waiting were Alena Griggs and Paul Bracewell. Kenneth Murphy. Rebecca Blum. Phillip Costanzo. Jerry Kapinski. Rawson Griggs.

And Jeremy Stanton.

In just a few moments, Remy would be on television, broadcast live to millions of people, standing on a stage with a man known the world over. His mundane life of just a few weeks ago had evaporated. Nothing would ever be the same.

Remy rubbed his shoulder, flexed his left hand. He could see the faint surgical scar just above the knuckle on his ring finger. This was his first day without wearing his sling. His shoulder was sore, but the pain was bearable. Today was about showing strength.

Rawson stood in the center. He was silent, head bowed, eyes closed. His black suit shone like armor, his bold red tie like a thick artery down his barrel chest. His beard was neatly trimmed, dark brown hair impeccable, not a strand out of place. He stood tall and looked proud. He looked like a general. Remy pictured the battle gear decorating Rawson's apartment. Maybe Rawson truly thought he *was* a general. Which would presumably make Remy a soldier.

He wanted to earn the man's respect. Reward his faith.

Remy checked his watched. Eight fifty. Ten minutes to show time.

The crowd noise grew. Rawson had instructed the fire marshal to ignore capacity limits. He wanted the event to feel less like a stodgy announcement and more like a rock concert.

He thought about what Rawson said in his office.

Showmanship is part of the game.

"If I can have a moment," Rawson said, stepping forward in front of the group. "I'd like to thank you all for embarking on this journey with me. Some of the people here have worked beside me for years. Some of them I've only just begun to know. The next year will not be easy. We will face obstacles that will test us like we've never been tested. We'll make enemies the likes of which we've never faced. There will be late nights. Hard times. You will spend time away from your homes and your families. There may even be times when you question your resolve. But when all is said and done, you will be proud of what we accomplish. Today begins the revolution. And I wouldn't go into battle with anyone else."

Remy felt a slight tug on his suit jacket. He looked over and saw

Alena standing next to him. She was wearing a form-fitting peach blouse and gorgeous pearl necklace. She mouthed the words *thank you*. Remy smiled back and nodded. Paul Bracewell stood next to her. He looked pale, sweaty. He shifted from foot to foot, anxious. Alena noticed Remy looking at Paul. She sighed. There was nothing to say.

Rawson checked his watch.

"Eight fifty-seven," he said. "Jerry, take us down."

Jerry Kapinski stepped out in front.

"Remember," Kapinski said, "there will be twenty cameras on you at all times. Millions are watching live, and millions more will stream it or see clips. Every move you make will be recorded. Don't speak. Don't cough or sneeze or stumble. If you pick your nose, just leave and never come back. And smile. Look happy. You *want* to be here. Let everybody know. Just keep that in mind and you'll be fine. Okay. Let's go."

Kapinski led the way, followed by Costanzo, Blum, Remy, Kenneth Murphy, Paul Bracewell, Alena Griggs, and then Rawson Griggs. They marched single file towards the escalator bank.

Remy could hear the crowd growing louder. They were restless. They wanted Rawson. They wanted the main event.

Remy was hyper-aware of every nerve in his body. He did a mental scan for any itches, pain, or discomfort. Better to deal with it now. His shoulder felt sore. Remy ignored it. As they approached the escalator bank, Remy finally saw the madness that awaited them. The scene in the Castle lobby took his breath away.

A large podium was erected, flanked by American flags. A swarm of at least a thousand people was packed into the lobby and gathered in front of the podium.

He couldn't count the number of television cameras. It had to be dozens. He couldn't begin to count how many cell phones were out and recording. Easily hundreds. A standing lectern and microphone were set up in the middle of the podium. There was enough room on either side of the lectern for the rest of the group to stand.

Kapinski led them onto the escalator in order. The moment Jerry

Kapinski's feet touched the escalator, the crowd erupted. People were holding homemade signs and cheering.

GRIGGS FOR AMERICA

NO RAW DEAL WITH RAWSON

TIRED OF THE SAME OLD SAME OLD

GET ON THE GRIGGS TRAIN

As Remy stepped onto the escalator, a massive smile spread across his face. He didn't need to fake it. This was a once-in-a-lifetime moment. For the first time in years, he felt a true sense of pride.

People were cheering for *him*.

"Jeremy!"

"We love you, Remy Stanton!"

Remy tried to pinpoint where the cheers were coming from, but there were too many people, too many faces, too many voices. He saw a sign that read:

JEREMY STANTON: HEROES CHOOSE GRIGGS

It made him shiver. It made him feel alive.

One by one, they descended the escalator. The chants and cheers grew progressively louder. When Alena Griggs got on the escalator, she waved to the crowd. It reminded Remy of photos of Princess Diana, Jackie Kennedy. The crowd ate it up. She was the heir to all of it, the best of both worlds. The power and strength of her father, but beauty and grace second to none.

Finally, Rawson Griggs stepped onto the escalator. The crowd rose, thousands clapping, roaring, chanting "Griggs! Griggs! Griggs!" Rawson held his hand up high to welcome the masses gathered in the building that bore his name, the monolith he had built from the crowd up.

The others stepped onto the stage, flanking Rawson. Remy stood between Jerry Kapinski and Phillip Costanzo. Rawson slowly walked towards the podium. He was clapping gently, applauding the crowd for being there. He was a master showman. The crowd was eating it up. Remy scanned the audience. They were transfixed by the show.

A bank of small television monitors, tuned to different stations, was embedded in the floor of the podium, tilted slightly upward, so Rawson and the others could see how they appeared live.

The CNN chyron read: RAWSON GRIGGS EXPECTED TO ANNOUNCE CANDIDACY FOR PRESIDENT.

Fox News showed a beaming, nattily dressed Phillip Costanzo, with the chyron: BELOVED FORMER MAYOR EXPECTED TO SUPPORT GRIGGS BID.

NBC was focused on Remy. His heart sped up. The chyron read: UES HERO STANTON ATTENDS ANNOUNCEMENT IN SUPPORT OF GRIGGS.

Finally, Rawson Griggs reached the podium. He soaked in cheers for another minute. Then he put up his hands, asking the crowd for silence. And when they complied, Rawson turned to face the wall behind him. Suddenly a massive sign unfurled.

It read:

GRIGGS FOR PRESIDENT: THE BEAST WITHIN

The crowd erupted like they'd all just won the lottery.

"Griggs, Griggs, Griggs!"

The chants grew louder. Rawson let them go on. He soaked it in. Not just for him, but for the cameras. He beamed with pride, and made sure to look into each television camera to show it.

Finally, the chants died down.

Once the lobby was quiet, Rawson began.

"Thank you all for being here this morning. This may strike some people as strange, but I've never sought the spotlight. My success has opened my private life to the public, and I have long accepted that. But today, for the first time, I sought out the spotlight. For the first time, I *wanted* to open up my life to the millions of men and women across this great country. Today, I want Americans across this great land to witness history. I want the *world* to witness history. Because today heralds a new dawn. Today we alter our destiny. Today, the long forgotten men and woman of this proud country will be forgotten no more. Because today, I, Rawson Griggs, am proud to announce my candidacy for president of the United States."

The crowd went crazy. Remy had never heard anything like it before, and he hadn't missed a Super Bowl in twenty years. Remy could see people openly weeping, waving American flags, hugging each other like they'd just been raptured.

Another "Griggs! Griggs! Griggs!" chant broke out. This time, Rawson raised his hands quickly, asking people to quiet down.

"Thank you," he said. "Now, you might ask the meaning behind our campaign slogan. The Beast Within. This statement matters to me because, the truth is, America has gone soft. We are overfed and underworked. And sadly, we have gotten used to it. But no more. From this day forward, every man, woman, and child will realize that there is a beast in all of us. And when that beast is strong, when that beast is hungry, nothing can stand in its way. I will unleash the beast in every one of you, and we will make this nation great again!"

The crowd cheered, "Beast! Beast! Beast!"

"You all are," Rawson said. "You're hungry! For far too long, our country has been run by insiders and careerists, politicians who do nothing but spend money to get elected and then reelected, and then when they are expected to do their jobs, they are too busy campaigning. A vicious cycle where nothing gets done and you're forced to swallow it. That system is broken. It is outdated. We will swallow it no more. I pledge to break this cycle. To end the madness. For you." Rawson clenched his fist and drove it down onto the podium to add an exclamation to the last two words.

Rawson paused. He let the words sink in. There was an angry tremble to his voice. Remy looked out into the crowd. They were nodding along with every word.

"Just recently," Rawson said, "there was a terrible attack on my family. An attack perpetrated by two cowards. Criminals who should not have been *in* this country, but were allowed in because the people in Washington turn a blind eye. They claim to relate to you, until the final ballots are cast. They are con artists: breaking your spirit so they can then claim they know how to fix it. Our tolerance for this hypocrisy *ends today*."

As he spoke the last two words, Rawson Griggs's hand sliced through the air like a knife.

Rawson Griggs turned to face Alena Griggs and Paul Bracewell. His lip trembled as he spoke. A righteous anger underlined every word.

"My daughter and her husband might not be here if not for the heroic actions of one good man. One Samaritan made a difference. One decent man. Not much different from you. He stepped up and did what needed to be done, at risk to his life, without any thought of the price he would pay. And in doing this, he nearly paid with his own life. That man, Jeremy Stanton, is here with me today. I am honored to have Jeremy's support, and even more deeply honored to call him my friend."

Griggs turned around to face Remy, clasped his hands together as if in prayer, bowed slightly and said, "Thank you."

The crowd began a long and sustained applause. A "Jeremy! Jeremy! Jeremy!" chant broke out, ringing through the Castle lobby.

Remy had no idea what to do. He hadn't known Rawson would single him out. Should he respond? Ignore it? The chants continued, so Remy raised his left arm—his bad arm—and waved to the crowd. He winced, but this was a signal that he had not been broken. Remy saw Rawson smile.

"Our two-party system is broken," Griggs continued once the applause had died down. "Owen Gladstone will leave office with one of the lowest approval ratings in the history of our country. And the candidates put forward by our two major parties reek like moldy cheese. They have shipped your jobs overseas. Watched as our factories closed. Sat back as our standing in the world diminished. They have authorized sanctions that have smothered nations that could work with us. And yet they still hold out their hands to you, the people they bilk day in and day out. We have embraced failed policies like the Truman Doctrine, which have depleted our resources and turned us from the world's superpower into the world's nanny."

Rawson continued. "Washington is a septic tank. And I am going to drain it."

A massive round of applause echoed through the room, followed by a chant of, "Drain the tank! Drain the tank!"

"I'm telling you, right here and now, that Rawson Griggs will be financing his own campaign. It might cost me a hundred million dollars. It might cost me a billion dollars. But I will not come begging, hat in hand, to the very people I pledge to help. I want to make *you* money. Isn't that a novel idea?"

The crowd laughed.

"Now, you might be wondering. My words are harsh. So which party will I be running for? Well, I'll tell you this: I will not be running for president as a Democrat. But nor will I be running for president as a Republican."

A murmur of confusion broke out.

"I am running for the American people, in order to siphon the poison from our capital. But in order to do that, we need to look back. Look to our history. To what our country once was, and can be again."

Rawson waited a beat. He had the crowd in the palm of his hand. Remy knew where Griggs was going, but he had a thousand people captivated and energized and would draw out the moment.

"Nearly three hundred years ago," Griggs continued, "a ship carrying one hundred and two men, women, and children sailed across the Atlantic Ocean from Southampton on the southern coast of England. They sailed in order to escape persecution. They were searching for hope. They were seeking the new world. It took them two whole months to cross the ocean, all the while braving harsh winds and the pounding of the sea. Their provisions ran perilously low. Many of these souls did not make the journey from Southampton. And those who did survive, to land on the other side of world, were greeted by a harsh winter, unfamiliar territory, and hostile natives. Many more died. But those who survived, escaping oppression and the ruling class who no longer served them, became the backbone for what would later become America.

"That ship was called the Mayflower. It anchored at Cape Cod on

November 11, 1620. And on that day, the survivors signed a document. That document was called *The Mayflower Compact*."

Griggs reached into his pocket and produced a piece of parchment. He unfolded it and held it out to the crowd.

"This is a replica of the Mayflower Compact," Griggs said. "It reads, in part: 'Do by these presents, solemnly and mutually, in the presence of God, and one another, covenant and combine ourselves together into a civil body politic; for our better ordering, and preservation and furtherance of the ends aforesaid; and by virtue hereof to enact, constitute, and frame, such just and equal laws, ordinances, acts, constitutions, and offices, from time to time, as shall be thought most meet and convenient for the general good of the colony; unto which we promise all due submission and obedience.'"

Rawson continued.

"Abraham Lincoln once said, 'America will never be destroyed from the outside. If we falter and lose our freedoms, it will be because we destroyed ourselves.' Today I stand here and state unequivocally that he Republican Party is no longer the party of Lincoln."

Rawson paused again. He scanned the crowd, making eye contact with as many people as he could.

A man in the back yelled, "We love you Rawson!"

Rawson continued.

"Franklin D. Roosevelt once said, 'The test of our progress is not whether we add more to the abundance of those who have much; it is whether we provide enough for those who have too little.'"

Griggs let those words sit for a moment. Then he continued with the words that Remy knew would change the very foundation of the American political system.

"I stand here, Rawson L. Griggs, today, in front of my country and the entire world, to announce that I will be running for president on behalf of a *new* American party. A party for the people. A party that harkens back to the potential we once had, potential that has been stolen from us. But with this new party, we will reclaim a dream long forgotten."

Rawson waited, allowing the suspense to build.

"I have been put on this earth to run for you. The people," Rawson said, "In honor of the purity our nation was founded on, I will be running for president on the newly christened Mayflower Party."

The crowd erupted. Rawson put up his hand. They quieted en masse.

"The Mayflower Party will speak for those who have been left behind, the silent majority, who feel that their interests are no longer cared for, who feel betrayed. Like the document signed by those brave men and women aboard that ship three hundred years ago, this is my compact both with the American people and our allies around the globe. Like our forefathers when they anchored at Cape Cod, today we journey into a new world. This begins right here. Right now. We will not leave anyone behind. We will bring back prosperity. We will bring back hope. We will bring back the America that our predecessors intended. We will take back what is ours. We will unleash the beast within!"

The crowd went bonkers. Griggs campaign staffers walked through the crowd distributing THE BEAST WITHIN hats, flags, buttons, and bumper stickers. Within minutes, half the crowd was wearing bright red BEAST hats. Rawson looked like a proud father at his child's graduation.

As Rawson waited for the applause to die downs, Remy glanced at the bank of television monitors lining the floor. Cameras were panning the crowd for reaction shots. The enthusiasm was overwhelming.

Then Remy noticed something strange on the ABC network feed.

Their camera had panned towards the front of the Castle lobby, near the exit to the street. There appeared to be some sort of skirmish going on outside.

Suddenly, Remy's breath caught in his chest.

The camera was fixated on a police officer, one hand gripping his still-holstered weapon. Another cop had his hand palm-out as if to say *stop*. There was fear in his eyes. Another cop had already taken his Sig Sauer P226 from its holster and was holding it, ready, at his hip.

What the hell was going on?

A woman began to scream. She was pointing at something.

No. She was pointing at someone.

Other network cameras began to swivel around to broadcast the mayhem. Then the crowd turned, curious.

Then, on the NBC feed, Remy saw what the cops were reacting to.

On the camera, Remy could see a young man. Mid-twenties. Short. Dark hair. Dark skin. He wore a black jacket and black pants. There was fury in his eyes. Several police officers were trying to restrain him. The man appeared to be trying to force his way into Griggs Tower.

The man was shouting something. When he turned his head, Remy saw that his earlobes were gouged. And in each hole, Remy could see a shiny, silver ring.

Stani.

A man shouted that word as Remy lay bleeding on the street. A man with silver rings in gouged earlobes.

Then, in one horrible moment, Remy understood what was happening.

The man trying to force his way into the Castle was Dastan Nogoyev's accomplice. The man who'd shot him. The man who'd disappeared.

Then Remy saw what the man was holding, and his blood ran cold.

He was holding a backpack. He had stripped it from his shoulders and was holding it out to the police as if to say *this is for you.*

Then he pulled a device from his pocket. Remy realized that the bag contained some sort of homemade bomb.

Jesus Christ.

Rawson Griggs's eyes widened. He instinctually threw his body around Alena and hurled her to the ground.

Remy shouted, "*Everybody get down!*"

There was a split second between Remy's warning and the moment the man pressed the detonator, the world vanishing in a terrible burst of light.

FALL

"You haven't been returning my calls or emails. Are you okay?"

"Fuck you."

"We still need you, Paul."

"I can't do this anymore. People are dead."

"But not you. You're doing the right thing."

"Every day it's like I'm waiting for a piano to fall on me. I'm done."

"Don't say that. There's so much more. You said it yourself. We need to stop him."

"So figure it out. If you can't, then god help you.

"Give me something. Anything. Come on, Paul.""

"Alright. But I don't know much. Alena mentioned something about Jeremy Stanton meeting with Grace Rivas from the Gazette."

"Did she happen to say where and when?"

CHAPTER 11

GRIGGS CAMPAIGN REGROUPS IN WAKE OF BOMBING

"We will not be intimidated. We will soldier on."

by Grace Rivas and Eric Celsun, *New York Gazette*

The dead have been buried and the wounded tended to following the devastating bombing at Griggs Tower, an act that killed five and wounded dozens on the very morning that Rawson Griggs officially announced his candidacy for president of the United States. Undeterred by the horror and violence, Mr. Griggs vowed that his resolve had never been stronger.

"The American people will not be intimidated by terrorists and radicals who look to upend the will of the people through fear and violence. My heart goes out to victims of this despicable act of cowardice and savagery. And I promise you this: the moment Rawson

Griggs is elected president, we will hunt down these cowards. Words do not prevent evil: actions do. And Rawson Griggs is a man of action. We will work with our current allies, and build bridges with new ones, to create the greatest global safety network the world has ever known."

Medical records have identified the bomber as Alexay Usenov, 28, formerly of Bishkek, Kyrgyzstan. Sources within the FBI confirm Usenov was likely the second man suspected in the attempted murder of Alena Griggs and Paul Bracewell, which was prevented by Jeremy Stanton, the 'Upper East Side Hero,' who has since taken on an active role with the Griggs campaign. Like his accomplice, Dastan Nogoyev, Usenov had spent time as a migrant worker in Moscow, and had come to the United States legally from Bishkek.

Added Mr. Griggs, "The fact that these monsters came to our country legally means we must intensely scrutinize people living both outside of, as well as within, our borders. Radicals do not just come here from abroad. Some are homegrown. Some are here legally. And we will smoke them out."

Mr. Griggs declined to comment on what sort of policy would be enacted to follow through with that statement.

While Griggs himself claims to be self-funding his campaign, a number of pro-Griggs Super PACs have already begun raising money to support his candidacy. One PAC in particular has raised eyebrows: former Mississippi Senator Brent Scott recently submitted paperwork to open a PAC called TEETH OF THE TIGER, and Scott's lobbying firm has already contributed nearly $7,500,000 to its efforts. TEETH

OF THE TIGER has plans to aid the Griggs campaign through direct mail advertisement, robocalls, radio advertising, and phone banking. In the past, however, Senator Scott has come under fire for his employment choices since leaving office, including consulting with the Kremlin-owned, multi-billion dollar natural gas production company, GazProm.

The Griggs campaign had no comment on former Senator Scott, and insisted that, per campaign finance regulations, they do not coordinate with any Super PACs that support Mr. Griggs's candidacy.

Many have also questioned Mr. Griggs's statements critiquing the Truman Doctrine, which many say heralded the start of the Cold War in order to stem Russia's geopolitical influence, eventually leading to the formation of NATO.

On CNN, Rebecca Blum, Griggs's campaign manager, stated, "We will be reevaluating every policy decision made over the last hundred years to determine which ones worked for the American people, and which ones strangled us and our allies with regulations. Nothing is off the table. Nothing."

CHAPTER 12

Remy sipped from his cup, thinking that it was the first time he'd ever met a girl for coffee while three large men with guns waited for him outside.

The armed slabs of beef were part of a massive security force hired by Rawson Griggs in the aftermath of the bombing at the Castle. Remy still hadn't gotten used to them and didn't think he ever would. The night Remy decided to join the Griggs campaign, he'd thought long and hard about the various paths his life could take.

Nearly being killed for the second time in less than a month was definitely *not* one of the options he'd considered.

That was before a man named Alexay Usenov walked up to the lobby of Griggs Tower carrying a pressure cooker bomb in a backpack. Usenov was the unidentified gunman who'd shot Remy and escaped into the night, only to emerge from the shadows to cause unspeakable evil. The only silver lining was that Usenov hadn't managed to worm his way inside the packed Castle lobby. The carnage would have been catastrophic.

The FAA discovered an unused plane ticket in Usenov's name. His flight was scheduled to leave LaGuardia two days after the attack on Alena and Paul via Aeroflot Russian Airlines, with as stopover in Istanbul before landing in Bishkek, Kyrgyzstan. The same final destination as Dastan Nogoyev's unused plane ticket.

Neither man was on a no-fly list. They would not have been flagged leaving the country. There was no evidence of radicalization, no suspicious postings on social media, no trail that would have alerted Homeland Security or the TSA. Both men were invisible until they decided to take lives.

The lobby would be rebuilt. The campaign would push through. And part of that meant Remy making good on his promise to Alena, and meeting with Grace Rivas of the *New York Gazette*.

Remy raised the cup of coffee to his lips. It had taken a solid week for his hands to stop shaking after the bombing. The woman sitting across from him picked up on it.

"Are you sure you're okay?" she asked. "We can do this another time."

"No, I'm good," Remy said. He sipped his dark roast then wiped his mouth with the back of his hand. "Still a little anxious, I guess."

"Given everything that's happened, it'd be strange if you weren't."

Grace Rivas was about five foot seven, with straight black hair that went down slightly past her shoulder blades, and eyes the color of summer grass. She was in her early thirties, with faint lines beginning to creep in around her eyes and forehead. She was young, but spoke confidently, and her eyes betrayed no hint of naiveté. Remy had read her C.V. before their meeting and came away impressed.

Grace was born in Queens to Hector Rivas and Angela Barerra, both Colombian immigrants who had fled Puerto Boyacá as the Medellín cartel was rising to power under Pablo Escobar. Once they settled in Queens, her father got a job driving a taxi. Her mother worked as a hotel maid. Grace had been given no advantages.

She'd earned a B.A. from Stanford and a Master of Science from the Columbia School of Journalism. She took a job on the tech beat at a prominent digital news startup, and when that folded, the *Gazette* came calling. Grace covered Owen Gladstone's campaign during the previous election, and given her experiences in both politics and business, she was the perfect reporter to cover Rawson Griggs. She'd built an impressive portfolio in a short amount of time. Remy could understand why Alena would trust her.

A small digital recorder sat on the table between them. Grace turned it on, and Remy eyed the red light suspiciously.

"I want to start with the day of the attack at Griggs Tower," Grace said. "The bomb set off by Alexay Usenov was a homemade device, a pressure cooker, similar to the ones used by the Tsarnaev brothers at the Boston Marathon. Five people were killed and dozens more wounded. You had just accepted a position with the Griggs campaign as a communications aide. Can you tell me what your thoughts were immediately following Usenov's attack?"

Remy shifted in his seat.

"I remember opening my eyes and not being able to hear," he said. "When the device went off, it was the loudest thing I'd ever heard. It all happened so fast. I had no idea if I was alive, what had happened. I was on the ground, and when I got up, I remember not being able to see the lobby through the smoke. There was glass everywhere. People were screaming. Once it seemed that most people inside were safe, I went outside to see what I could do to help. It was just…chaos. I've never seen anything like it. And I hope I never will again."

"Did you have any idea Usenov might target Rawson Griggs's announcement?"

"I didn't know Usenov's name at the time. I thought I might recognize him from the night he and Dastan Nogoyev attacked Alena and Paul. I think a part of me always worried that the second man was still out there. I didn't think he'd just disappear."

"Neither Nogoyev or Usenov were flagged by the FBI or TSA. In his speech, before the bombing, Mr. Griggs said he would take a much harder line both on immigrants coming into the country, but also people already here who have green cards or work visas. He hasn't elaborated on these plans. Can you speak to those? How exactly does Rawson Griggs plan to keep us safe while upholding the constitution?"

"Well, first and foremost, Mr. Griggs wants to keep us safe. This is a man who, within the last few months, almost lost his daughter and her husband, almost lost his own life in an attack that took the lives of innocent people. So something isn't working when a man can walk into a crowd with a homemade bomb. Rawson's concern isn't just from abroad, but the people already here, working in secret, people who aren't on our radar because we don't know what to look for."

"Rawson Griggs hasn't wasted any time. He's already made campaign stops in Iowa and New Hampshire, and has rallies planned for Colorado, Nevada, Arizona, and Texas in the next few weeks. He drew enormous crowds in Iowa and New Hampshire. You're a political novice. Until recently, you worked at a consulting firm. What does it feel like to be in the middle of all this?"

"It's overwhelming," Remy said. "But at the same time, better than a shot of red bull and a double espresso. Wanting to be a part of something bigger than you has become kind of a cliché, but it's true. Rawson has galvanized the nation. I'm just proud to be a part of this, and honored he thinks I can help."

Grace said, "What is it about Rawson Griggs that you think resonates so much with the American people?"

"He's one of us," Remy said. "Rawson came from nothing. He fought for our country, came home and built an empire from a loan that, today, wouldn't be enough to start a hot dog stand. He feels there's an American spirit that's been lost. He wants to bring that back. And I think the people know they've been let down by their elected officials for years. Rawson Griggs is the kind of man who gets things done. He makes you aspire to be more than you have been."

"Running as a third party candidate is bold, but also risky," Rivas said. "No third party candidate has come close to winning the presidency in the modern era. By eschewing both major parties, Mr. Griggs is forgoing the massive infrastructure and fundraising mechanisms already in place. How can he realistically expect to win?"

"Well, I think the attitude that he can't win is one of the reasons he *will* win," Remy said. "Americans are tired of being told what they can't do. Rawson wants to people to know they can do anything. People are fed up with politicians asking for money. Who needs that money more: the coal miner or the senator? Rawson Griggs is a self-made man. He's employed thousands of people and built some of the most amazing properties around the country. People respond to his spirit. While other politicians are campaigning, Rawson Griggs is working."

"In speeches last week, Mr. Griggs called Governor Richard Bertrand of Louisiana a crook, and Senator Annabelle Shaw of Kentucky a leech who, and I quote, 'has sucked Americans dry like a disgusting leech during her thirty years in office.' Is this the kind of language befitting a man running for president?"

"Rawson isn't a robot. He's saying exactly what other people are thinking. Some politicians spend more time constructing artful phrases than they do governing. Rawson doesn't want time. He works harder than anyone I've ever met."

Grace said, "The strongest performance by a third party candidate in history was Teddy Roosevelt in the 1912 election, when he ran on the Progressive Party and still finished fourteen points behind Woodrow Wilson."

"I'm not sure I heard a question there," Remy said.

"Was this campaign a massive miscalculation? What makes you think Rawson Griggs has a chance?"

"All I can say is this: people can dismiss Rawson's candidacy all they want. But when they go to rallies and see these massive crowds, they understand. Rawson Griggs makes political rallies feel like rock concerts."

"People might buy Bruce Springsteen's albums," Grace parried. "I'm not sure they'd vote Springsteen for president."

"Pretty sure Springsteen would win New Jersey," Remy said.

"It'd be close," Grace said with a smile.

"This is just the beginning," Remy said. "Mr. Griggs has close to twenty million followers on social media. We have unprecedented ability to speak directly to the voters. Governor Bertrand has a forty percent approval rating *in his own state*. Annabelle Shaw is currently in her fifth term in the Senate. These people are political lifers."

"How much did you know about Rawson Griggs before you met him?"

"The same as everyone else: just the Rawson Griggs we read about and see on television. But the truth is, in private, he's just a decent family man. Rawson and I are very different in many ways. I might not have a three-floor penthouse in the sky or my name on properties all over the world, but we want the same thing. A better future for our country."

"We've all heard stories about Mr. Griggs's ruthlessness. He may have nearly as many enemies as he does supporters."

"Rawson does what it takes to win. It's not always pretty. But it's effective. When you go to war, you can't worry about whether you're being polite."

"We still know very little about Mr. Griggs's international ties, including any foreign investments and debts. Will he release that information?"

"If Rawson feels they'll matter to voters, I'm sure he'll consider it."

"Do you have a good relationship personally with Rawson Griggs?"

"Yes, proud to say I do."

"And Mr. Griggs's daughter. Alena. Many people say she's actually his closest advisor. How have you observed their relationship? What do you think of Alena Griggs?"

Remy paused, then said, "Alena Griggs is a phenomenal woman. Strong and smart. She has all of her father's strengths. I think Alena is really just an exceptional, exceptional woman. She keeps her father grounded."

"That's quite laudatory," Grace said.

"Yeah, I suppose so." Remy decided to retreat just a little. He meant what he said about Alena, but for some reason he always felt like he was one step away from crossing a line he shouldn't approach.

"Just a few months ago, people didn't know who you were," Grace said.

"I'd like to think *some* people knew who I was," Remy said, smiling, cutting her off. Grace laughed and blushed.

"You know what I mean. You worked for a consulting firm, Pulaski & Associates. You had a stable, what seems like satisfying, career. But then, overnight, you're a hero. You're on the cover of newspapers. And then, just a short time later, you're on the presidential campaign trail with one of the most recognizable men alive. That's a pretty drastic upheaval, wouldn't you say?"

"Without a doubt. My life has turned upside down. I didn't ask for any attention the night I met Alena and Paul. I just want to turn difficult circumstances into something good, I guess."

"Do you think the attempt on Alena and Paul's life and the attack at the Castle have made Rawson Griggs question his decision to run for president? That his family might be a target?"

"It hasn't changed his mind," Remy said. "If anything, those incidents have firmed his resolve to protect America. It's clear to Rawson that the people in charge right now are letting those duties slip."

"It appears that, barring major upsets, Annabelle Shaw and Richard Bertrand will be the Democratic and Republican nominees for president. Both have long histories of public service. Both have strong fundraising arms and the support of their parties. No third party nominee has won a state during an election since George Wallace in 1968, and no third party candidate has garnered more than five percent of the vote since Ross Perot. Why do you feel Rawson Griggs has a better chance than either of those two?"

"George Wallace ran on a segregationist platform forty years ago. We're a different country now. A better country now. Rawson Griggs's message will appeal to all Americans. And voters across the country feel that Senator Shaw and Governor Bertrand, with all their experience, typify the recycled political class people are fed up with."

"You sound very well briefed," Grace said. There was slight disapproval in her tone, and Remy picked up on it. He wondered if he did sound robotic, coached, a human talking point. But he needed to defend the campaign. Defend Rawson.

"I wouldn't have turned my life upside down if I didn't believe in him."

"Fair enough. You'll be headlining several Griggs events yourself over the coming months. I believe eight events in seven states, including a major event at the Grand Hyatt in Manhattan. You said yourself that your life will never be the same. Do you have any regrets?"

"Not for a moment," Remy said with conviction. "I regret not recognizing Alexay Usenov earlier enough to save people. I don't know, realistically, what more I could have done. It sickens me that people lost their lives. But in a strange way, my getting shot was a blessing. I mean sure, I could have died, but I also wouldn't be talking to you. I wouldn't be able to change hearts and minds like we are. A few months ago, I was consultant, walking around handing out my business card and racking up miles, and nobody cared. But people are paying attention now. That's a responsibility that's both great and terrifying. Because when you have influence, it's up to you to wield it properly. And that's what I want to do, because I think we can do some real good."

"That's a noble goal," Grace said. "Now, talk about you."

"I'm way less interesting than Rawson," Remy said.

Grace laughed. "I don't know about that. Your resumé is impressive. Born and raised in Lancaster, PA. Summa cum laude from Yale, then off to Pulaski & Associates, where you worked with half a dozen Fortune 500 companies. But take me back. Tell me about your family."

Remy exhaled. "Well, my mother, Margaret, was my hero. She passed away when I was in high school. Breast cancer. That's actually one of the issues I want to highlight in on the campaign trail. More access for women to clinics for mammograms and screenings. Less vilification of organizations that offer them."

"You know, I can't really tell if you're a liberal or conservative," Grace said. "What would you call yourself?"

"I wouldn't," Remy responded. "That's why we're running on the Mayflower Party."

"Tell me about your father," Grace said.

Remy's head snapped up with such quickness that Grace flinched. "Let's move on," he said.

"You told me about your mother. Now I want to…"

Remy shook his head. "I'm not going to talk about him."

"This is obviously a wound," she said, not without sympathy. "And I don't want to pour salt in it. But people want to know who you are, Jeremy. Outside the campaign."

"Pouring salt in a wound is your ex-girlfriend inviting you to her wedding. That happened to me once. It sucked. But my father is a wound in the way cancer is a wound."

Grace turned off the tape recorder. Remy looked at her, confused.

"Do you want to talk about it? OTR?"

"OTR?"

"Off the record." Grace's eyes were sympathetic. "You need to understand that even though I've had a very good relationship with the Griggs Organization, and Alena in particular, I need to report this story—your story—honestly. I understand your refusal to talk about your father. And that's your right. But this is *your* story."

Remy rubbed his head. He knew she was doing her job. Few things irritated him more than when he read puff pieces on politicians and celebrities that ignored or whitewashed anything controversial or interesting. He just never thought he would be on the other side, the one having to hold back. He knew working for Rawson Griggs would open up his life to scrutiny, he just didn't think it would be this quick.

"I can't stop you from writing about my father," Remy said. "But I won't comment on him."

"Off the record," Grace said, "I completely understand. My family was no picnic. I haven't said more than one sentence to my mother in six years. I won't bore you with the details. But the only times I hear from her are emails from time to time asking for money. Occasionally, I'll get a voicemail from some new boyfriend of hers, sometimes asking for a little something to help him buy her a birthday present. She hears *New York Gazette* and assumes every reporter makes Matt

Lauer money and lives in a gold penthouse. I live in a studio with a cat."

"I live in a studio too," Remy said. "No cat, though."

"I'm not equating my situation to yours. Just saying I empathize."

"Let me ask you a question," Remy said, noting the recorder was still off. "How often do you think about it? Your mother, I mean. I don't mean to pry...well, I guess you're sort of doing that with me so I'm prying a little bit...but how often?"

Grace's demeanor changed slightly. Her face became softer, more reflective. "Want to know the truth?" she said.

Remy nodded. "Yeah."

"Every damn day. It's affected my life more than anything that's ever happened to me. Ripples don't stop. They just create more ripples."

He let that sink in. Grace didn't take her eyes off of him. She picked up her latte and took a sip.

"Same here," he said. "Not many things can both paralyze you and drive you. It's an angry loneliness."

"Angry loneliness," she said, considering the term. "In what way?"

"Neither of my parents have been a part of my life since I was a kid. My mom passed. My father...wasn't there. You're angry at the world for taking them from you, and that anger grows when you're at school. At college. You see friends' parents come to visit, bringing them food and gifts. When you get your first job—a good job—and you want to call someone to celebrate, but don't know who. It washes over you. The loneliness. You know it's not your fault, but you wonder why you were cursed like this. You wonder why she had to get sick. You wonder why he was who he was."

Remy felt like a massive weight was slowly being lifted off his shoulders. He hadn't spoken about his father, even in such vague terms, in years. Not to Trevor. Not to anyone. Let alone a complete stranger. He'd even threatened to walk out on Rawson Griggs if he pressed the subject. But hearing Grace Rivas say those words—*every damn day*—it was like she was understood Remy in a way the others couldn't.

"You," Remy said. "You're not like I expected."

"Oh really?" Grace said. "How's that?"

"You don't really think of reporters as people. Okay, that came out wrong. But you're like actors. All we see is what you want us to see, on television, in print. I had no idea you owned a cat. Besides, the last time I talked to a reporter, it was in college after I hit a walk-off home run to beat Dartmouth. The whole interview lasted about thirty seconds and they still misquoted me in the *New Haven Register*." He pointed at the recorder. The recording light was still off. "So, I assume we're still OTR?"

"We are. Unless you tell me to turn it back on. Oh, and *for* the record, you're not quite what I expected either."

"In what way?"

"Well," Grace said, "I kind of expected you to be just another fieldbro."

"Fieldbro," Remy said. "What's a fieldbro?"

"Spend a little more time in politics," Grace said, "you'll figure it out. Oh, and don't take it personally if people assume you are one. Just…don't be one."

"I will do my absolute best to avoid fieldbro-ness."

They both laughed, but Remy looked down for a moment, embarrassed for a reason he couldn't quite understand. The last few weeks had been a maelstrom of anger and sadness and rage, endless hours talking to the FBI, NYPD, and Homeland Security and the anti-Terrorism task force. Confronted with all the pain and death, being forced to confront the fact that he was powerless to save those lives. For one day, it was nice to just *talk,* to laugh, to relate to someone else. As much as he enjoyed being around the Griggs organization, Rawson and Alena came from a different world. They did their best to mime understanding true hardship and the fear and uncertainty that came with it.

But theirs wasn't organic. It wasn't their fault. Remy wouldn't wish his pain on anyone. But talking to someone who could hear him, truly *hear* him, felt good.

"Let's get a drink sometime," Remy blurted out. "No tape recorder. No suits with guns. Just good drinks and good conversation."

Grace sat back, surprised.

"See that," Grace said with a smile, "is something a fieldbro would say."

"What? What did I do?"

"You realize this is my job," she said firmly, though Remy detected the slightest hint of hesitation. "I'm always up to have to have a drink with interesting people…but I think we both know what you were getting at."

"Okay. My bad. I shouldn't have asked. Though I'm flattered I might be one of those interesting people."

"I can't allow there even be a hint of impropriety or accusations of favoritism. Another time and another life, maybe."

"Maybe. My fragile fieldbro ego can deal with maybe. I'm still learning, you know. The line. And how not to cross it."

"So we'll chalk it up to inexperience," Grace said. "I'll let you go for now. But I might have some follow up questions. You game?"

"You have my number."

Grace took the digital recorder, slipped it into her purse. She dropped a ten on the table and stood up. Remy could see people taking pictures of them with their cell phones. He still hadn't gotten used to being recognized. Every cup of coffee was a potential photo op. Never before had he taken such precautions to ensure he wore clean shirts and matching socks.

They walked towards the entrance. As they passed the counter, a clerk with thick muttonchops, ear studs, and a septum piercing thrust his fist out at Remy. Remy flinched.

"Hey man," the clerk said. His nametag read *Jim*. "Remy Stanton, right? Just wanted to tell you to give 'em hell. Griggs has my vote."

Remy stuck out his fist and bumped it with Jim.

"I appreciate it. Sorry, still a bit jumpy."

"No worries, my friend. Next time, coffee's on the house."

Remy thanked him.

As they left the shop, Remy heard someone say, "Jeremy Stanton. Hero of the city. Rawson Griggs's monkey boy."

Remy turned to see a stranger standing there with a massive shit-eating grin, the kind of smile that almost begged you to punch him in the face. He wore gray khakis and a navy sport jacket with a bright blue tie. He had a crew cut and a soft chin. He appeared to be about forty and had the look of someone who either got what he wanted, or complained until it was given to him. And he was staring right at Remy.

"Help you?" Remy said. The man stuck out his hand. Remy looked at it like he was holding feces. He turned to Grace. He could instantly tell she knew who he was.

"Mr. Stanton, I'm so sorry for the rude interruption," the man said with complete and utter insincerity. He had a soft Southern accent. "My name is Doug Rimbaud."

Rimbaud waited a beat for Remy to say something. When he didn't, the man continued.

"I'm the campaign manager for Annabelle Shaw."

Remy's eyes widened. Annabelle Shaw was the senior senator from Kentucky, and currently the Democratic frontrunner for president. What in the hell was his campaign manager doing here? And why was he such a dick?

Rimbaud made sure to catch Grace Rivas's eye.

"Ms. Rivas," Rimbaud said. "It's a pleasure to see you again."

"Doug," Grace said, skeptical. Remy wondered what the hell Rimbaud was doing here. It couldn't be a coincidence.

"I just wanted to extend my thanks, and that of Senator Shaw, to Mr. Stanton. You're a true American hero and a patriot. It's just a shame you're working for a clown."

Remy wondered whether it would be worth breaking his hand to punch Rimbaud. He decided it probably was.

"If you're Senator Shaw's campaign manager," Remy said, "then god help her campaign."

Rimbaud reached into his jacket and pulled out a card. He held it out to Remy. "Senator Shaw would very much like to meet with you. Rawson Griggs is a charlatan with no political experience who shouldn't be allowed anywhere near the White House. You should consider working for a candidate who can bring about real change."

Remy took Rimbaud's business card. He looked at it. Then he spat on it and tore it into teeny tiny pieces and let them flutter to the earth.

"That was the patriotic thing to do," Remy said.

Rimbaud smiled, amused. "We both know how unlikely it is for a third party candidate to make any sort of dent in an election. Mr. Griggs's candidacy is a fun distraction from the real race. He's entertainment. You, though, could be a tremendous asset to a real campaign and a real, competitive candidate, Mr. Stanton."

He couldn't help but notice that Grace Rivas had taken out a notepad and was scribbling on it. Remy felt like an idiot. Clearly Rimbaud had wanted to get under Remy's skin, wanted him to lose his cool in front of a reporter.

"When Senator Shaw loses," Remy said, "I'll make sure to look you up if I need to buy a used car."

Rimbaud extended his hand to Remy. "It's been a pleasure to finally meet you, Mr. Stanton."

"Wish I could say the same."

Remy took Rimbaud's hand and pulled it towards him slightly, squeezing just enough so Rimbaud opened his mouth to complain.

"Ow, my ha…." And then Rimbaud shut up. Too bad. Remy would have killed for Grace to include in her story that Doug Rimbaud squealed like a stuck pig due to a firm handshake.

"I just want you to know," Remy said, loud enough so that Grace could hear him, "that this kind of crap is the reason I'm supporting Rawson Griggs. It's the reason we're going to win this election. People are tired of games and cynicism."

Remy let go of Rimbaud's hand. Red fingermarks laced the man's flesh.

"Say hello to the senator for me. I look forward to meeting her at some point down the road. And if she's smart, she'll fire your ass well before then."

Rimbaud rubbed his hand, looked at Grace, then back at Remy.

"He's not what you think he is," Rimbaud said. Then he left.

When he was out of earshot, Grace said, "Well, damn, that was shady."

"He knew what he was doing," Remy said.

"That card ripping was amazing. I have to include that."

Remy laughed. "Go ahead."

He offered Grace his hand. She shook it and smiled.

"It was nice to meet you, Jeremy Stanton."

"Likewise, Ms. Rivas."

"I will. Oh, and OTR, anger and loneliness never go away on their own. It's good to have someone to talk to. You don't want to go through life like that. Trust me. I know."

"Thank you, Grace."

"So if you ever want to talk about that, OTR, I'll have that drink with you."

"I might just take you up on that."

She turned to leave. Then stopped and looked at Remy.

"One more question, actually. On the record."

"Shoot."

"Doug Rimbaud didn't come here by accident. He must have known we were meeting. Senator Shaw has a rally in Portsmouth, New Hampshire tonight. Rimbaud went out of his way to stop by. Which means he knew about our meeting, the time, and the place. How is that?"

"I honestly don't know," Remy said.

"Hmm. Interesting. Take care, Remy."

Grace walked away, leaving Remy asking himself that same question.

How *did* Rimbaud know about the meeting?

CHAPTER 13

Paul Bracewell looked behind him. Then looked again. He stopped on the corner of Bowery and Third, leaned up against a lamp post, and watched passersby, his brow furrowed, waiting to recognize someone, waiting to see if anyone recognized him, making sure he wasn't followed. He wore a pair of loose-fitting jeans, an untucked flannel shirt, and a cracked leather jacket. His brown hair was hidden beneath a trucker cap. He stuck his hands in his pockets. Paul never wore hats. Rarely wore jeans. But he needed to blend in.

He insisted on meeting down here, far away from the madness of midtown. He didn't like being so close to the Castle for fear of being recognized, and over the last year had begun to despise the mere sight of that godforsaken building. Thousands of tourists flocked to the massive metal and gold and steel monstrosity every day to fill up their iPhones with pictures of the Griggs golden calf.

He couldn't walk ten feet from the Castle without being stopped on the street by some tourist group begging for photos. He'd posed for more selfies in the past few months than he ever hoped to in a lifetime. After the incident on the Upper East Side, he felt like a Times Square street performer. A Minion, Captain Jack Sparrow. Miserable beneath a bulky costume. Paul no longer felt like a person. Just a living mannequin to be gawked at.

He should have known better. He should have known that going into the marriage. That wedding was the biggest mistake he'd ever made. Now it was time to figure out how to get out of it without ruining his life.

He twirled the wedding ring on his finger. It slipped on and off so easily. He remembered the day Alena put it on him. Her fingers were so smooth and delicate, like silk on bone. That ruby red smile could have made an army stand down. Once upon a time, he had truly felt like the luckiest man on earth. He *wanted* to marry that woman, *wanted* to be a part of the heralded family. He would have a beautiful, intelligent wife and a father-in-law who could open doors that nobody else on earth could.

Paul thought he would never look back. And he'd spent every day since then doing exactly that.

Paul was an accountant, and a good one. He was also smart, caring, dedicated, prudent. He'd met Alena at a charity ball to raise money for Pencils of Promise, an organization that built schools and offered greater access to education for children all over the world. A great cause.

Paul ended up there by accident.

Oliver Lawton, his college roommate at Wharton, was one of the founders. Oli was a venture capitalist, and like any VC with more money than he knew what to do with, Oli founded a charity and let others run it for him.

Alena Griggs was on the board. She helped run it.

It was luck, really. Paul only went to the ball because his friend Mike O'Brien was in town from Spokane, and the two hadn't had a proper night out since Paul had moved to the big city. Oli comped them the one hundred and fifty dollar tickets, he and Mike dressed like they were going to a James Bond costume party, and hit the town.

The last thing Paul expected was to meet his wife that night.

When he met Alena, Paul was waiting for a drink. Waiting forever.

That was the problem with open bars: people wanted to get their money's worth, and you could grow old before you got served your weak vodka soda.

When Paul finally got the bartender's attention, he noticed a girl standing beside him. He didn't know who she was, only that she was sighing, like many, over the insanely long wait and the dismissive attitude of the bartenders.

"Why is it that every bartender acts like it's a personal affront to them when you order a drink?" Paul said.

The girl laughed. "I could sew my own dress in the time it takes to get a drink."

Finally, the bartender acknowledged him. "What'll it be?"

"I'll order yours with mine," he said to the girl. "What can I get you?"

"Stoli and tonic," she said. A fairly innocuous drink, he remembered thinking. He ordered her drink and got a Makers Mark on the rocks for himself. He left a five dollar tip. More to impress the girl than because the bartender earned it.

When he turned around, he realized that Stoli girl was Alena Griggs. He nearly dropped her drink. She was wearing a white cap sleeve flair dress, and her blonde hair flowed in beachy, sun-kissed waves over her shoulders. She was just a stunning woman. That was the only word that came to mind. *Stunning.*

Alena sipped her drink and sighed. "I think he forgot the Stoli part of the Stoli and tonic."

He saw Mike O'Brien from the corner of his eye, grinning like an idiot. Mike knew who she was and didn't want to interrupt them.

"Next time I'll order two drinks for each of us."

Alena laughed. Laughed at his joke. They spent the night laughing and dancing, then shared a brief, soft kiss before parting ways.

For a long time, Paul made her laugh.

They didn't laugh much anymore.

He never fit into Alena's life. He always felt like Rawson expected more from him. *Demanded* more from him. Wanted him to be a different man with different ambitions.

But the truth was, Paul never changed. He didn't want to change. And Rawson couldn't stand that.

Being a member of the Griggs family was a daily toxic cocktail of anxiety, anger, depression, and near madness. Rawson wanted Paul to alter the very fiber of his being. He was a human metal smith, used to hammering people into the shape he wanted. And if they resisted, they broke.

Paul had resisted at first. And it dawned on him, far too late, that Rawson was the hammer and he was the iron.

Eventually, Paul broke. Which was what led him down this current path. There was no turning back. Not now. He'd done too much, come too far.

When he was certain he wasn't being followed, Paul entered an upscale dive bar off of Bowery called Phebes, pulled a stool out from the bar, and ordered a Makers, straight up. The drinkers didn't pay him a moment's notice. The dark wood décor and low lighting allowed him to keep to himself. He was on his second drink when he felt the tap on his shoulder.

He turned around, petrified for a moment that someone might have recognized him. He breathed easy when he saw who it was.

"I'd buy you a drink," said Doug Rimbaud, "but I see you're already way ahead of me."

Rimbaud took the seat next to Paul and a Grey Goose martini, slightly dirty, with olives. When Rimbaud's drink came, he tipped it back and let out a satisfying moan.

"God, I needed one of those."

Paul said. "You're late."

"I stopped by to say hello to Jeremy Stanton," he said. "They were at that coffee shop forever. Either your boy Stanton likes to talk, or that *Gazette* diva Rivas thinks she's Barbara Walters."

"He's not my boy," Paul said. "And Grace Rivas is a good reporter. Alena likes her." He sipped his drink. "I shouldn't be here. I shouldn't even still be talking to you."

"But you are, and you are. You know you're doing the right thing."

"The right thing is going to get me killed."

"Don't be so dramatic," Rimbaud said. "Rawson has you wound up. There's no way he'd try anything now. Not after what happened at the Castle."

"You don't know him," Paul said. "You think it's a joke. But it's a nightmare."

"That's why you need to keep helping us," Rimbaud said. He placed his hand on Paul's arm. Paul pulled it away.

"I don't even know if I can trust you," Paul said.

"Who else can you trust? Alena? She'll go crying to her daddy the moment she finds out. Stanton? He's bought and paid for. That hero shit has about a one month expiration date."

"I have options," Paul said.

"The feds? Not a chance. You need proof."

Paul finished his Makers and ordered another.

"Maybe I have proof."

"Bullshit," Rimbaud said. "You would have told me."

"Maybe. Maybe not. Maybe I already sent it to someone who I *can* trust. Because after all the info I've sent your way, you haven't changed a damn thing. So maybe I sent it to someone who will."

"Come on, Paul. You know we have to be careful. If we accuse him without proof, it backfires and makes us look like we're spreading unfounded rumors."

"Because everyone knows that nobody spreads rumors in politics."

"We're working on it," Rimbaud said.

"Keep working on it. This is the last time you and I talk."

"Just like that? We're breaking up?"

"You don't get how serious this is. You want to win an election. But you're missing the point. If you lose, you have no idea what's going to happen. This is bigger than Senator Shaw."

"No, I get it," Rimbaud said.

"I don't think you do. Rawson barred me from the strategy meetings. Alena is still in the dark about all of it. She thinks he just doesn't like me, but she doesn't understand the whole picture. She'll refuse to see it. Because he's her father. She'd never turn on him."

"What about Stanton? He's new enough to still have his eyes open."

"He's a wild card. He's smart, but he's naïve. He thinks this is his meal ticket. He won't give that up."

"So work with him. Get him on our side."

"How do I do that?"

"I don't know."

"Stanton doesn't know me," Paul said. "And I doubt he trusts me."

"I think you're overestimating him," Rimbaud said.

"Maybe. But whatever you think of him, Rawson isn't stupid."

Rimbaud sipped his beer. The bravado left his voice.

"You know, when you and I first started talking, I didn't actually think people would support him. This was a precaution. I thought it would be a big joke."

"I took Rawson as seriously as a heart attack. You should have too. Now it might be too late."

"I think people will see through him eventually," Rimbaud said. "Populism has a shelf life."

"And I think your candidate is a sixty-six-year-old career politician who's staler than year-old bread, connects with voters like the wrong puzzle piece, and is going to have to spend half a billion dollars to have any sort of chance. And if she *does* win, people will resent how much money it took to get her there."

Paul swallowed his third Makers in one gulp.

"Take it easy there," Rimbaud said.

"Go to hell," Paul replied.

"If Rawson is as dangerous as you think he is, you're risking everything."

"I already have," Paul said. "Whatever happens to me has already happened."

"What do you mean by that?"

"Nothing."

"So when will I hear from you again?" Rimbaud said. "The first

Democratic debates are coming up and Senator Shaw would love to have some more ammo to fire at Griggs."

"I'm done being your errand boy. It's amazing: Senator Shaw is trying to become the most powerful woman in the world and you're depending on the husband of her opponent's wife."

"We're not depending on you," Rimbaud said.

"Right. Good luck, then. See you on CNN."

Paul slid off the stool. He wobbled, bracing himself on Rimbaud's shoulder.

"Christ, kid, you need to ease up on the drinking."

"This *is* me easing up."

"Once this is over," Rimbaud said, "I know a great divorce lawyer. This guy could get a pearl out of an oyster without opening it. You'll need someone on your side."

Paul didn't respond. He stumbled out of the bar, leaving Rimbaud to pick up the tab. He paused for a moment, waiting to see if he was going to throw up. When the nausea passed, he stepped out into the street and hailed a cab. When a cab pulled up, Paul checked his wallet. He needed to make sure he had enough cash. His credit card receipts all went through the finance department at the Griggs organization. He couldn't risk using his credit card or taking an Uber.

He slid in and gave the driver his address. When the car pulled away, Paul belched.

"Hey, man," the driver said, "you'd better not hurl in my cab. It's only one o'clock anyway. Ain't it a little early to tie one on?"

Paul ignored him. He looked down and saw that both of his hands were shaking. He checked himself in the rearview mirror. He looked haggard, anxious. Paul looked away.

What Paul did not see was Jerry Kapinski, standing one block south of Phebes, watching the cab speed away, holding a cell phone to his ear.

CHAPTER 14

Remy looked out over the audience. Four hundred young men and woman, dressed to the nines, lubricated to the gills, all here to see *him*. He was wearing a fifteen hundred dollar Brioni suit that had been custom-tailored by the same guy who made Rawson's duds. It felt like he was wearing air. He looked like a million—no, a *billion*—bucks. And he needed to. Because tonight was Remy's first time as a headliner. This was his moment.

The Empire ballroom at the Grand Hyatt on 42nd Street had recently undergone a fourteen million dollar renovation, and it showed. Greek-style columns carved from white Italian marble lined the foyer. The ballroom itself sported original tin tiling and metal grillwork, with a recessed ceiling fitted with state-of-the-art digital lighting. Tonight's colors were red, white, and blue. The gorgeous chandeliers dripped with seven thousand pieces of hand-blown glass. Amber lighting spotlighted every table, while the podium itself was bathed in soft white.

A twelve-piece band, all wearing white tuxedos and shimmering dresses, played soft rock and Motown hits as people ate and drank.

Every table was topped with crisp, creamy-white tablecloths and pointed napkins, with sparkling crystal stemware. White-gloved waiters were clearing plates of filet mignon and herb-crusted salmon while refilling glasses of white and red. Two hundred bottles had been flown in from Rawson's own Sonoma vineyard.

This was the ballroom where John F. Kennedy accepted the Democratic nomination for president in 1960. Martin Luther King, Jr. spoke in this very room in 1956, back when it was called the Commodore Ballroom. This was where Hillary Clinton celebrated her election to the Senate. Heads of state from around the world had dined here. Remy was fully aware of the room's history. And tonight, he was the guest of honor.

The invite-only, thousand dollar a plate event had booked up in minutes. Every cent taken in had been earmarked for charity—from wounded veterans to inner city education to reading materials for underprivileged youth. Remy and Jerry Kapinski had put the list together themselves.

Every invitee was handpicked by the campaign due to their influence, be it on social media, on television, in charitable organizations. The money was incidental. The influence was invaluable. This wasn't about asking people to spend a grand for some undercooked meat. This was Rawson proving to the world that he could be the voice of a new generation.

The social media clout alone in the room was astronomical. Remy had tried to calculate the total reach of the attendees, but lost count at a hundred million followers. *That* was what Rawson was after. There were a hundred ways to make money, but very few ways to gain influence.

The room was packed with start-up pioneers. Charity founders. Tech entrepreneurs, dating app CEOs, authors, artists, and, of course, socialites. People who, just a few months ago, couldn't pick Remy out of a lineup. And now they were paying to see him. The Upper East Side Hero.

It was one thing to fight for a cause on Twitter. Remy had taken a bullet. And that was something that even the most cynical tech bros had to respect.

That morning, Grace Rivas's *Gazette* profile of him had gone live. The timing was perfect. Remy's first big PR hit, right before his first event as a Griggs headliner. Just another day in a life that resembled his old one as much as a chicken nugget resembled caviar.

The podium was bookended by two American flags. A placard on the stand read BE THE BEAST and directed people to visit the campaign website.

The room quieted as Rawson Griggs walked to the podium. Remy sat at the head table and quickly checked himself in his phone's camera. He looked good. He smiled.

A round of loud but polite applause greeted Rawson. He wore a Brioni tuxedo with a red bow tie and Armani shirt. An American flag pin sparkled on his lapel.

The microphone stand was about a foot too short. Rawson raised it and smiled mock-sheepishly, as if to say, "Hey, not everyone is this tall."

This was a trick Rawson had taught Remy: ask whoever was in charge of AV to set the microphone about a foot too low. Then, when Rawson raised it, he would appear taller, more impressive.

During one late-night strategy session, Phillip Costanzo had said, "Half of politics is what you say. The other half is how you look while saying it." Remy took the former mayor's words to heart. And thanked his lucky stars and genetic makeup that he and Rawson were only about an inch apart.

"Ladies and gentlemen," Rawson said, his voice slow and purposeful, "thank you all for coming tonight. Now I *know* you're not here to see *me*…" There was a smattering of laughter. He played the audience, pretending to be surprised. "Well, *most* of you aren't here to see me. So I'll be quick."

Remy watched Rawson, but took the time to look around the room. "Make eye contact with as many people as you can," Costanzo had told him. "Even in a room of thousands, it is your job to make every single person feel special, like they have your complete and undivided attention. Like you're there for them as much as they are there for you. Make people jealous. You're a front man. Make them feel special if they get your attention."

Remy looked over at Table 1, the Griggs table. Alena was beaming at Remy. She mouthed the words *good luck*. Remy gave her a thumbs up. Alena wore a green, low cut Roland Mouret dress with crystal drop earrings. She shined, and her smile gave Remy confidence.

Paul Bracewell sat next to her. His tie was askew, his hair mussed, and he'd missed a button on his shirt. Paul was gulping down a glass of brown liquor, his hand shaking as he raised it to his lips. He looked like an absolute mess. They didn't need Paul passing out or barfing at the table. That would dominate the news cycle for days.

Also seated at the Griggs table were Kenneth Murphy, Jerry Kapinski, and Rebecca Blum. Phillips Costanzo was at the Castle doing cable news hits, and Remy knew the former mayor would be talking him up all night.

Rawson continued. "Many of you, I'm sure, have attended fundraisers like these in the past. You've paid a lot of money for the quote unquote *honor* of listening to a boring speech by someone who will then beg you for more money. That is not why you're here tonight. Every cent from every ticket tonight goes directly help those in need. That is the hallmark of my campaign. We want to enrich the lives of people in need, not line the pockets of the wealthy and powerful."

A round of applause started up, and Rawson milked it. As it died down, he said, "Now, some people have said that a third party candidate doesn't stand a chance in a general election. We all know that's a lie. And the man I'm here to introduce tonight is emblematic of that. He's a hero because he stood up to evil at great personal peril. He and I are like you. We fight for *you*."

The crowd applauded politely.

"Tonight, I'm honored to introduce a young man I've gotten to know very well over the last few months. He entered my circle—my family—under some of the worst circumstances imaginable. But the universe works in mysterious ways. He's a great asset to me, a great asset to my organization, and he will be a great friend to you. He's a winner through and through. If I was put on earth to lead this great nation, this man was put here to be my apostle. Please help me welcome Mr. Jeremy Stanton."

The applause grew louder as Remy stood and walked to the podium. His heart thumped. Rawson ceded the podium to Remy with a courteous bow, then took a seat at the table next to Alena. She placed her hand on Rawson's arm and mouthed *good job*. Then they both joined in the applause. Remy made his way to the podium, smiling and waving to the guests. He noticed Paul Bracewell raise his glass at an approaching waiter, signaling for another drink.

Remy's pulse raced. He stood at the podium. Scanned the crowd, making eye contact with as many as he could. He made sure to smile at a few attractive women, because, why not? The microphone was an inch too low for him, but he didn't dare touch it.

"Thank you," Remy said. "Thanks everyone. Really. I appreciate it." When the room quieted down, Remy continued.

"First of all, I hope you'll all call me Remy. Rawson insists on calling me Jeremy, but I'm a little less formal than Mr. Griggs. In fact, this is the first tuxedo I've ever owned." The crowd laughed. Rawson laughed. Remy felt himself relax. "All my friends call me Remy. So tonight, please call me Remy."

A man's voice called out, "You're a beast, Remy!"

Remy smiled and replied, "You know, I told Mr. Griggs not to put plants in the audience." The crowd laughed. Remy felt good.

"As you all know," Remy said, "it's kind of a miracle that I'm standing here tonight. I was in the right place at the very, very worst time. But because of that, I met Alena Griggs and Paul Bracewell. I met Rawson Griggs. Three of the finest people I've ever known. And I'm here tonight to ask for your help to elect Rawson Griggs the next President of the United States."

The applause picked up again. Remy looked around the room, his smile wide and authentic. He caught the eye of a cute brunette who smiled back at him. Remy lost focus for a moment, then regrouped.

"Before we go on, I need to talk about what happened at Griggs Tower. A coward decided to carry out a horrific act of violence. This man, if you can call him that, does not speak for anyone. Not a race, creed, religion, or even the human race. Several people lost their lives. Others will need time, love, and support to recover from their wounds, physical and emotional. Our thoughts are with them and their families. I can promise you that Rawson Griggs will do everything possible to prevent those kinds of atrocities from happening again. When tragedy befalls us as a nation, there are no Democrats or Republicans or Mayflower supporters. There are Americans. We are all family. Families can disagree, and things get messy from time to time. But they always have each other's back."

Remy saw Rawson pat Alena's arm and smile at her. She mouthed *love you, Dad.*

"I want you to know that we will be there for you. Like family. And we will not be frightened, intimidated, or bullied by those who seek to tear us apart. We will not cower in the face of violence. We will not turn shrink. We will fight. We will be the beasts."

Remy looked out over the crowd. He made eye contact with half a dozen people before speaking again. They were all quiet. He had them.

"As Rawson said, we're not here tonight to ask you for money. Rawson has plenty of it, trust me. We'd rather you use your money to build your businesses, to donate to worthwhile charities, to raise your families, to buy that bottle of wine to open at the end of a long day."

Remy waited for the smattering of applause to die down. *People enjoy their wine*, he thought. He also noticed Alena smiling at him.

"What we *are* asking for is your support. I'm not going to lie. You were all invited here because you are influencers. Think about that word. Influencers. This means you wield influence among your peers, your colleagues, the public. Your opinions matter to many people. What you say and do over the next year could very well help influence the results of this election, and the future of our country. Everything you say and do matters. What you post on social media. What you talk about over dinner, at bars, at work, among friends and loved ones.

We are not asking you to give. We are asking you to add. Add to the discussion. I believe you all can agree that this country deserves better. I'm tired of two stale parties squabbling over who gets to sit at the head of the table every four years. We want to bring *new* voices to that table. For good. The Mayflower Party is not just Rawson Griggs, but it's me. It's you. We want to influence the country. And we need your help to do that. I believe we will earn your trust, and earn your support."

Remy felt his pulse quickening as he spoke. The applause halted. Every eye was trained on him. He scanned the room as he read from the speech he'd memorized. No teleprompters. Rawson hated them, and told Remy not to use them unless a gun was held to his head. Teleprompters were the enemy of authenticity and creativity. As Costanzo said, connecting with an audience was less *what* you say, and more *how* you say it.

Alena was watching him. Rawson was watching him. Some of the wealthiest and most influential young men and women in the country were watching him. For a moment, Remy thought about his old cubicle at Pulaski. He could still smell the musty air, the dirty carpets. He remembered how Andrew Pulaski always called him Jerry. The time he was tasked with flying out to Phoenix on two hours' notice to help lay off a hundred workers from an app developer than was going under. Pieces of his soul chipping off, day after day.

Here, now, he felt powerful. Important. And he loved every second of it.

"This is the beginning of a new era. For all of us," Remy said, winding down his speech. "There have been third party candidates before. There have been other men and women who have tried to uproot a system stuck in the muck of the last hundred years. But I promise you this: Rawson Griggs is strong enough to upend that system. We speak for you. Everyone in this room, and everyone outside of it, who demands more. Who expects more," Remy said. "I'm like you. I want my faith rewarded.

"Now, to get Rawson Griggs on the ballot in all fifty states, we need approximately eight hundred and eighty thousand signatures across the country. Each state has different requirements. That may seem like a lot, but when I look around this room, I see at least twenty people who have at least that many followers on Twitter alone. In New York, for example, we only need about fifteen thousand signatures, or less than the capacity of Madison Square Garden. In Florida, we need about a hundred and twenty thousand. If we get everyone in this room to get their grandparents to sign, that's a good start. We need your help in reaching those people, and more. Help us achieve greatness. There is a beast waiting to be unleashed. With your help, we'll remove the chains. Thank you.

"Now, please eat, drink, and enjoy yourselves. Just remember what we talked about tonight. Next round is on me!"

Remy stepped from the podium as the entire ballroom stood and applauded. He felt like his heart could burst from his chest. He went over to the Griggs table, where Rawson was waiting with open arms. The massive man engulfed Remy in bear a hug and whispered in his ear, "That was exceptional."

When he let go, Alena approached him and wrapped her arms tightly around his neck like he was a soldier returning from war.

"You. Are. Amazing," she said. When she let go, Remy saw Paul Bracewell standing with his hand outstretched. He was wobbling, glassy-eyed and unsteady. Paul's breath smelled like the inside of a barrel of bourbon. Remy shook Paul's hand, making sure not to stand too close in case Paul's insides decided they needed fresh air.

"Nice fuckin' job," Paul said.

"Thanks," Remy said, trying to mask his contempt.

Remy went around the table shaking hands. Murphy, Blum, Kapinski, all welcomed him warmly. He looked around the room. He saw dozens of cell phone cameras out, taking pictures, recording him.

From the corner of his eye, Remy saw Grace Rivas leaning against a wall in the back of the room, typing on a cell phone. She was covering the event for the *Gazette* and probably live-tweeting his speech. He hoped she was impressed. Grace was wearing a brown pantsuit. With sneakers. That made Remy smile. Grace looked up and caught Remy's eye. She smiled and went back to her phone.

Alena came over to Remy. She gestured towards the back of the room.

"Grace Rivas, right?"

Remy nodded. "She did a good job on the *Gazette* profile."

"My father wavers between loving her and hating her," Alena replied. "But that's often the way he thinks. Either you're on his good side or his shit list."

"Where am I tonight?" Remy said.

"I think you know the answer to that."

Remy saw a waiter pass by with a tray of white wine glasses. He snagged one and downed half the glass.

"God, I've been waiting for that," he said.

"You deserve it," Alena said, "I've already had two."

"I'll do my best to catch up."

Then Remy saw Paul teetering by the Griggs table. He attempted to sit down, but missed the chair and spilled onto the floor. His glass shattered and a tumble of ice cubes landed on top of him. Jerry Kapinski came around and helped him up, cursing under his breath. Remy heard Rawson whisper to Kenneth Murphy: "Get him the *fuck* out of here."

Alena looked away, either out of embarrassment of disgust.

Kapinski managed to prop Paul onto a chair, but he was rocking back and forth and mumbling to himself. There was a layer of flop sweat on Paul's brow, his hair was unkempt, and the glass had cut his jacket. Remy looked at Alena with concern. The crowd had noticed Paul's display. A few cell phones had come out, snapping pictures of the mess.

"We should get him out of here," Remy said,

Alena nodded. "I don't know what to do. He's been a mess all week. I know he's under a lot of stress. And ever since the attack he's gotten worse. But this is awful. And I can't leave him home. It would look terrible."

"Trust me," Remy said, "if he can't control himself, it'll look a lot worse if he's around."

"I know you're right. But how do you tell your husband that he's an embarrassment?"

"I don't know," Remy said.

"I'd kill to just get out of here, go somewhere quiet and have a drink. Or five. To not have to worry about any of this. You know?"

"You say the word and I'm there."

Alena looked at her husband mournfully. "If only I could click my heels together. But sometimes you have to take care of the kids."

She went over to Paul, who now appeared to be singing something unintelligible in a raspy, high-pitched voice. Remy felt terrible for Alena and wished he could do more. Thankfully, Kapinski and Murphy helped Paul to his feet and led him out of the ballroom before things got worse.

The rest of the Griggs contingent stayed at the Hyatt until the very last guest had drunk their fill and the ballroom was empty. Remy had shaken dozens of hands, been introduced to hundreds of people. Memorizing all those names was a fruitless endeavor. At 11:00, Rawson went up to Remy and said, "I'd have to say tonight was an unqualified success. We raised half a million dollars. And more importantly, I think we—*you*—changed a lot of hearts and minds. Nicely done, Jeremy. Oh, but don't expect me to call you Remy any time soon."

"Thank you, sir." Remy was on a high. He'd never felt such adulation. And from a roomful of people who, not too long ago, wouldn't have considered him twice. Without a doubt, tonight would go down as one of the best nights of his life.

Murphy and Rebecca Blum huddled in a corner. Murphy was nursing a scotch and Blum held a gin and tonic. Their body language suggested they were upbeat about how the night went. Then Remy saw Blum gently rub the sleeve of Murphy's coat, and he wondered what else it suggested.

Remy scanned the room; Grace Rivas appeared to have left. He took out his cell phone and texted her.

Thanks for coming. Sorry we didn't get a chance to talk.

After he pressed send, added:

OTR

Rawson clapped Remy on the back and said, "Get some rest. Tomorrow in the War Room at seven a.m. We have a lot to do."

"I'll be there," Remy said. He was glad he'd cut himself off after two white wines. "You know, I think I'm getting the hang of this."

"Hold on one second," Rawson said. "Rebecca, come here."

When Blum came over, Rawson gave her his cell phone, then put his arm around Remy. "For social media," Rawson said.

They both smiled and Blum took a picture.

"Put that on all our feeds. Caption: 'With the man of the hour.' All appropriate hashtags."

"You got it." Rebecca posted the photo using Rawson's phone, then handed it back to him. "Done."

Remy took out his phone and opened up his social media apps. The post had been up less than a minute and retweets and comments had already begun to pile up. Two minutes later, he had a thousand new followers.

Rawson watched Remy refresh his feed for a few moments and chuckled.

"It's a new world," he said. "We don't even need the media anymore. I have more people watching my feeds than the cable networks combined. Free media. Saves me millions on advertising."

Remy laughed, but he also knew Rawson was right. Shaw and Bertrand were week-old bagels and boring as death on television. Rawson was electricity. The networks covered his every word. He was changing the paradigm.

Remy stuck out his hand. Rawson looked at it and gripped it.

"Thank you," Remy said. "For having faith in me."

Rawson seemed surprised at the sentiment, and unsure of how to react. He shook Remy's hand and said, "You're doing well so far. But don't let sentiment cloud your focus or your judgment."

"It won't."

"In one week, you and Jerry follow up with everyone who attended tonight's event. Make sure we have their support. *Hard* support. If they won't commit to supporting us publicly, let's get them on our side."

"What do you mean, 'get them on our side'?" Remy said.

"There are two ways to persuade people to support you," Rawson said. "The first is by their own free will. The second is by yours. First you give them a carrot. And if that fails, you give them the stick. Tonight was the carrot. I hope the stick isn't necessary."

Rawson walked away before Remy could ask what he meant by that.

They left the Hyatt through the side entrance on Vanderbilt Avenue. Remy said his goodbyes. Rawson got into his car and headed back to the Castle. A crowd waited outside the Hyatt, taxis and Ubers fighting for spots as the scions of the city headed home to their palaces.

He stood there watching them, feeling a stab of jealously, when he heard someone say, "Remy, right?"

Remy turned to see a gorgeous brunette standing on the corner eyeing him. He recognized her from before—she was the girl who all but undressed him with her eyes while he was giving his speech.

He smiled and said, "Hey. I remember you."

"Is that right?" she said. She walked over to him. Her smile was demure, her eyes flirtatious. She wore an emerald blue, single-shoulder ball gown, diamond earrings, and a pearl necklace. Five ten in her strappy heels. Her eyes were large and green and her red lipstick was freshly applied. Her long brown hair curled down around her bare shoulders.

She'd also applied both perfume and lip gloss very recently.

"You were sitting at table three," he said. "You smiled at me. Hard not to notice"

"Well, if you remember every girl who smiles at you, then you *must* have a good memory," she said. "I'm Donna. Donna White."

"Remy Stanton."

Donna held out her hand, and Remy shook it, gently. She had soft skin, delicate fingers.

"*And* you remembered to call me Remy."

"You asked us to. And why would we tell you no?" Remy may have been out of the dating game a while, but even he knew Donna was shamelessly flirting with him. He was happy to go along with it.

"I'm sorry we didn't get to meet properly upstairs," he said.

"I'll forgive you," she said. "You were kind of busy."

He recalled seeing her name on the guest list. Donna White was thirty-two, a prominent activist for clean water charities. She had over seventy-five thousand followers on Twitter. And wasn't wearing a wedding ring.

"It's nice to meet you, Donna. Thanks so much for coming tonight."

"I work at Clean Agua dot Org."

Remy knew that, but pretended he didn't.

"That's wonderful. I've heard of your organization. What do you do again?"

"We raise money to bring clean drinking water to developing countries across the world that don't have access to it. I just wanted to say how inspiring it was to see you speak tonight. I mean, everyone knows Rawson Griggs, but to see a new generation of leaders trying to change the system, I mean…" Donna pretended to shudder. "Just gives a girl goose bumps."

"I believe in what we're going to do," Remy said. "And to have the support of people like yourself who are doing real good, that's exactly why I joined the campaign."

"Do you…" Donna said, hesitating. "Do you have somewhere to be? Like a late-night strategy session or something? I know how important you are, Mr. Guest of Honor."

Remy laughed. "You can still call me Remy. And no, I'm off the clock. Unless Rawson decides to hold a rally at four a.m., which I wouldn't completely put past him. I don't think the man ever sleeps."

"Well, then, Remy, how do you feel about a nightcap? I'd love to hear more about the campaign. I know a great hole in the wall a few blocks from here that has the best selection of top shelf bourbon in the city. Sometimes you can only drink so much wine."

"Thank god, because I only drink top shelf bourbon. I use the stuff on the middle and bottom shelf to polish my Aston Martin."

Donna smiled and without being prompted, looped her arm through his and said, "You have to let me order your first drink. I know the bartender there and he has some specialties that will make your mouth sing."

"You're like a bourbon Beyoncé. I can't wait."

As they walked away, Remy saw Alena Griggs and Paul Bracewell talking animatedly on the corner. Paul was stumbling around, leaning on a lamppost, drunk off his ass. Alena was pushing him, shaking him, trying to get him to wake up or snap out of it. He didn't seem to have any desire or ability to do so. Remy could see tears running down Alena's cheeks. Then Alena pushed him. *Hard.*

Paul nearly fell over a garbage can, but righted himself.

Then Remy heard Paul say, "Go fuck yourself." Then he walked away.

Alena stood there, watching him, a shocked look on her face. She cursed loudly and got into a waiting Lincoln Town Car. Paul stumbled down the block and out of sight.

Remy felt awful for Alena. Paul was falling apart. As much as he wanted to help, it wasn't his place. He hoped they could get Paul the help he needed before something happened. As the campaign expanded and pressures mounted, the stress and pressure would only get worse. If Paul was a mess right now, Remy could only imagine the kind of shape he'd be in come the primaries and general election.

"Hey, you still with me?" Donna said. She was looking up at him with a pair of big, beautiful green eyes.

Remy's heart rate picked up. He placed his hand on hers and said, "I'm all yours."

Remy woke up at three in the morning. He rolled over, saw Donna lying on her side, her brown hair splayed across her bare back, rising and falling with each breath. He traced his finger down her spine and she shuddered slightly.

"One more round?" she said, her voice muffled by the pillow. Remy leaned down and kissed her cheek.

"Go back to sleep."

He slipped out of bed and found his crumpled suit jacket and pants on the floor. He hung them up neatly, then got his iPad and sat down on the couch. His shoulder and hand were sore, but in a good way. A soreness he hadn't felt in a long time.

He opened up his social media feeds, curious to see the early reactions to the Hyatt event. He was closing in on a hundred thousand Twitter followers. The attention was intoxicating. He was still getting the hang of social media, but was now posting dispatches and photos from the campaign several times a day. Each post got several hundred retweeted, and the better ones—breaking news, fun photos, selfies with Rawson himself—hit the thousands.

He was thrilled to see that the hashtag #GriggsBall was trending. And the response to Remy's speech was very, very positive. Many of the attendees posted about the event using laudatory language, singing Remy's praises. Many of them also used the hashtag #TheBeastWithin. Remy figured those were the ones who'd already taken the carrot.

Hari Bhatia, founder of the popular tech website CrunchNet, had recorded Remy's entire speech on his cell phone. Bhatia had posted several clips to Twitter for his 590,000 followers. The posts had already been retweeted over twelve thousand times, and those numbers went up every time Remy refreshed his feed.

The photo of Rawson and Remy had already been picked up by the websites of *Vanity Fair*, *The Hollywood Reporter*, and *E Online*. Rawson was a celebrity. And his star power was rubbing off on Remy. He was loving every moment of it.

After refreshing his feed for another twenty minutes, drunk on the adulation, Remy slipped back into bed.

He checked his text messages for the first time since he left the Hyatt. One in particular made him sit up. It was from Grace Rivas.

You were good tonight. Sure you've only been in politics a few months?

Remy smiled. She was probably asleep, but he wrote back anyway.

I'll take Backhanded Compliments for $800, Alex.

To his surprise, Grace wrote back almost immediately.

Someone is up late.

Working.

Working or "Working"?

Working. Ok, just messing around on social media. This stuff is addictive.

Ha, be careful. It's a time suck. Oh, and I meant that as a compliment. For real. You've picked it up fast. Might as well embrace it.

OTR – it's still weird as hell.

It won't get any less weird. Especially as we get closer to the primaries and general.

Gotta ask. OTR. How did I do tonight?

OTR? Really well. I'd give you a B+.

B+? That's it?

Want to get an A? You need a little more polish. And a better haircut.

Oh, now that's just mean.

You asked.

I did. Night, Grace. Glad you came.

Night, Remy.

Remy plugged his cell in and laid it atop his nightstand. He closed his eyes, but the phone called out to him, begging him to keep checking his feeds to see if more people were talking about the event. Talking about him.

He looked over at Donna. She seemed like a nice girl. They'd gone to the bar, where she'd ordered him the best Old Fashioned he'd ever tasted. It tasted almost as good as their first kiss of the night, a slight hint of bourbon on her breath, their knees touching, her hand moving to his face. He knew right then how the night would end.

He looked at Donna. Smiled. And fell asleep, content. Peaceful.

It would not last long.

Remy's first thought was, *That's not what my alarm sounds like.*

His cell phone was blaring. His alarm clock was programmed to play *Johnny B Goode* when it went off, an old *Back to the Future* joke his ex Nicole had made. She'd said Remy was like her very own Marty McFly. Slowly fading away before disappearing altogether. So she set that song as his alarm music. And it stuck.

Remy picked up his nightstand clock and saw that it was 5:03 a.m. His alarm wasn't scheduled to go off for another forty-five minutes. Who the hell was calling at five in the morning?

The gray of early morning peeked through the shades. The apartment was still mostly dark. The call hadn't woken Donna, thankfully. The caller ID read *Private*. He figured it had to be someone from the campaign. He wondered why anyone would call this early considering they had a meeting at the Castle in less than two hours.

Remy got out of bed, went to the couch, swiped *Accept* to take the call, and quietly said, "Hello?"

"Mr. Stanton? Jeremy Stanton?"

Remy sat up. He didn't recognize the man's voice on the other end, but it sounded serious and urgent. Either some strange guy had found his phone number, or something was wrong.

"Yes, who is this?"

"Mr. Stanton, this is Detective Ferguson with the NYPD. Sorry to wake you, but you're needed at Griggs Tower as soon as you're able."

Whatever remnants of sleep that had still been clinging to Remy vanished at the words NYPD.

"NYPD? Is everything okay?"

"We hope so, Mr. Stanton. Just get here as soon as you can."

"Okay, you've got me concerned. What's going on?"

There was a moment of silence on the other end. Remy's stomach clenched in fear. Then Ferguson asked, "Do you know Paul Bracewell?"

"Of course I do. He's Alena Grigg's husband. I work for his father-in-law's campaign."

"Were you with Mr. Bracewell last night?"

"I was. We had a campaign event at the Grand Hyatt and Paul was there. Can you *please* let me know what's going on?"

"We'll need to talk to you as soon as possible, Mr. Stanton. I'm sorry to say that it appears Mr. Bracewell has gone missing."

CHAPTER 15

Remy showered and changed as quickly as he could. He thought about Alena pushing Paul, then Paul drunkenly stumbling off. Where the hell had he gone after that?

As Remy prepared to leave, he noticed Donna stirring. He knelt down next to her and apologized for his ungentlemanly departure, assuring her it was out of the ordinary, and to help herself to the coffee in the freezer and anything edible in the kitchen.

She smiled, playfully grabbed his shirt, pulled him down, and kissed him deep and long.

"Goodbye, man of the hour," she said.

Remy got the sense she wasn't expecting more.

He took a cab to Griggs Tower. The ride seemed to take eons.

He replayed the previous night in his head, focusing on Paul. He'd never developed much of a relationship with the man, and hadn't gotten a full read on him. He always seemed a little nervous, shaky, the kind of person who was always waiting for the ground to collapse under his feet. Even though Remy and Alena had pressed on from the Nogoyev and Usenov attacks, Paul had seemed to be disintegrating.

Something had been eating at the man, burrowing inside of him, gnawing away. He hoped for Alena's sake that Paul was fine, sleeping off a wicked hangover somewhere. She'd been through so much the last few months. She didn't need more anguish.

When Remy arrived at the Castle, he took the private elevators up to Rawson's apartment and entered the War Room. There were a dozen people gathered around the table, including a man and a woman wearing NYPD badges, and two more men wearing blue slickers with FBI in yellow letters across the back. Remy's heart sank. No way the feds would have come if they didn't fear the worst.

Seated around the table were Alena and Rawson Griggs, Jerry Kapinski, Kenneth Murphy, Rebecca Blum, and Phillip Costanzo. Costanzo was speaking with two men Remy didn't recognize, but the shoulder holsters and earpieces led Remy to believe they were private Griggs security. Murphy went over to Remy. He spoke quietly, urgently.

"Thanks for coming so fast."

"Of course. What's going on? Have they found Paul?"

Murphy shook his head. Remy looked at Alena. Her eyes were streaked with red and her hands were shaking. She and Rawson were speaking to the male NYPD officer, who Remy presumed was the Detective Ferguson who'd called that morning.

"What happened?"

"All I know," Murphy said, "is that Paul never made it home last night."

He looked at Alena, saw the pain etched on her face, and his heart broke for her.

"I don't know the full story," Murphy said, "but I believe Paul and Alena had some sort of falling out after the event last night. She went home. He didn't. He hasn't come back yet and we haven't been able to find him."

"Oh Christ," Remy said.

Murphy nodded. "Yeah. Paul was in bad shape last night."

One of the FBI agents walked to the front of the conference room and said, "Thank you all for being here on such short notice. I'm Special Agent Mason, my partner here is Special Agent D'Antoni, and

I'd like to fill you in on what we do and don't know."

The room went silent.

Mason continued. "Paul Bracewell was last seen at approximately eleven thirty p.m. last night on 43rd Street and Vanderbilt after a charity event at the Grant Hyatt hosted by the Griggs campaign. Jeremy Stanton, over there, was the keynote speaker. Alena Griggs and her chauffeur, Reginald Barnes, were the last to see him before his disappearance. After separating from Mr. Bracewell following the event, Alena Griggs returned home to the apartment she shares with Mr. Bracewell on 89th and York. When Mrs. Griggs woke up at 3:14 a.m. and realized Mr. Bracewell had not returned home, she called his cell phone. When he did not respond to calls or texts, Mrs. Griggs called her father. Wanda Lefebvre from Mr. Griggs's office then called the NYPD and FBI. We have traces running on Mr. Bracewell's cell phone and his credit and debit cards. So far, none of them have registered any hits. We're currently reviewing traffic camera footage from the area surrounding the Hyatt, as well as surveillance video from local banks and businesses around the time in question."

Mason turned to Alena Griggs. "Mrs. Griggs. If you can, tell us what exactly happened last night, and what led to your husband leaving the event on his own."

Alena's eyes were red and her lower lip trembled. She was wearing a sweatshirt and warm-up pants. She nodded at Mason, took a breath, and spoke.

"We had a fight," she said softly. "Paul had been drinking pretty heavily last night. I told him to slow down. I reminded him we were in public and how important it was for my father and Remy, but Paul ignored me. We were at the head table. A lot of people were watching us so I couldn't be as forceful as I should have been. At one point, Paul fell over and broke a glass, and that's when we helped him to leave. Jerry Kapinski waited with him outside until I left. But I didn't go with him. I let my father's people handle it. He resented that. He felt like I was letting them clean up my mess. And he wasn't wrong."

Alena stopped and put her fingers to her eyes, choking back sobs.

Rebecca Blum handed her a packet of tissues and Alena wiped her face. Rawson sat there, stone-faced.

"Please, go on," Mason said with a trace of sympathy. "I know this is difficult, Mrs. Griggs. But we need to hear every detail, no matter how small or seemingly insignificant, that might help us find Paul."

Alena nodded.

"After the event, Paul could barely stand. When I found him outside, he was drinking from a bottle of Jack Daniels he'd stolen from the drink cart. That's when I lost it."

"We found a smashed bottle of Jack Daniels one block north of the side entrance on Vanderbilt and 43rd," Mason said. "We're waiting on fingerprints, but it corroborates Alena's story."

"I asked Paul what was the matter with him. He ignored me and kept drinking. So I…I pushed him."

"Pushed him how?" Mason said.

"Out of anger. Like *get a hold of yourself.* Trust me, I didn't hurt him. He was just shocked. He started yelling at me. I yelled back. And that's when he stormed off."

"What exactly did he say?"

Alena hesitated.

"We can continue this elsewhere, in private, but time is of the essence."

Alena shut her eyes, squeezing out tears.

"He told me I'm not the woman he married," she said. Every word was uttered like a dagger being driven into her heart. "He said he regretted ever saying yes. He said I didn't deserve him."

Remy saw Rawson clench his jaw. He looked like he could punch through the wall.

"Paul had been drinking a lot over the last few months. It started even before the attack near our apartment, where Jeremy intervened. Something happened to him. Something changed him. I don't know what it was, but the attack made it worse. He never really recovered from that night. So when he said that, I told him I never wanted to see him again."

"How did he respond to that?" Mason said.

"He told me to go fuck myself. And then he left. But I was glad he did. I *wanted* him to leave. Then Reginald took me home. Oh god, I hope that's not the last thing I said to Paul."

Rawson was clenching his fists so tight his knuckles had turned white.

"After he dropped me off, Reggie offered to drive back to the Hyatt to see if he could find Paul. I...I told him not to. I thought maybe waking up drunk and covered in crap in a gutter somewhere was exactly what Paul deserved. So Reggie left and I fell asleep. I fell asleep easy. God, it was like a weight had been lifted off my shoulders, like I'd been waiting to say that for I don't know how long."

"When did you realize Mr. Bracewell hadn't returned home?"

"I woke up a little after three to go to the bathroom and get a drink of water. Paul's side of the bed was empty and his coat wasn't in the closet. I called his cell phone. It went right to voicemail. I called again and left a message. Then I texted him a few times. That's when I called my father to see if he'd seen Paul. When he told me he hadn't, we called the police."

Mason jumped in. "Paul's cell phone is either turned off, or the battery ran out. He hasn't used any of his credit or debit cards. At this point, it's safe to say that either Paul Bracewell does not want to be found, or someone else doesn't want him to be found. Now, it's a common misconception that people need to wait twenty-four hours before filing a missing person report. The truth is, when people wait that long, we can lose valuable time. And given the previous attacks and the near-constant threats directed at Rawson and the campaign, we're not taking this lightly."

"Thank you, officer," Rawson said.

Mason continued. "Now, here's where it gets tricky. Paul is an adult. Which means that unless we can confirm he's been the victim of a crime, or has committed a crime himself, he does not legally *need* to be found. Meaning that if we can't prove anything has actually happened to Paul, all we can do is look and hope and file paperwork and wait."

Alena held back tears, but looked like she could crumble. Rawson spoke, his voice laced with a quiet anger.

"Could somebody have taken him?"

"It's on the table, Mr. Griggs," Mason said. "Given your prominence, and that Paul and Alena had been targeted previously, it is a possibility somebody could have taken Paul. Whether that's for political reasons, to hold for ransom, we don't know. And we still don't know whether Dastan Nogoyev and Alexay Usenov acted alone or were part of a domestic terror cell. Nobody has claimed responsibility, which lowers the probably of them being aligned with an actual group. If they were, it's possible that cell could have operatives still working here. But this leads me to believe the two aren't connected. But ransom demands tend to come when the victim's families are at their most desperate."

Just then, Wanda LeFebvre entered the conference room.

"I'm sorry to interrupt," she said, looking at Rawson. "Sir, Governor Richard Bertrand is on the phone. He wanted to extend his sympathies and to offer any assistance he can to find Mr. Bracewell. What would you like me to say to him?"

Rawson thought for a moment. "Tell the governor we appreciate his call, but we're going to keep this private among ourselves and law enforcement. Nothing more. Tell him if he says a word to the press about Paul's disappearance, I'll buy the Louisiana Governor's mansion and turn it into a sewage treatment center."

"Yes, sir," Wanda said. She left the room.

Mason turned back to Alena. "Mrs. Griggs. I know how difficult this must be for you. But can you think of anywhere your husband may have gone after you parted ways last night? Family? Friends? Maybe a favorite bar? The only ingoing or outgoing texts or calls to Paul's cell last night were the ones from you at three a.m., and one outgoing text from Paul to a Michael O'Brien in Spokane, Washington sent a little after midnight. The text itself was gibberish due to Paul's inebriated state. O'Brien responded several times asking if Paul was alright. He did not respond. We've already spoken to Mr. O'Brien who confirms that those texts were his only correspondence with Paul last night."

"Michael O'Brien is Paul's best friend," Alena said. "We don't see him very often. He was actually there the night Paul and I met. There's nobody here he would have gone to I can think of."

"Mrs. Griggs, this is a hard question to ask, but you understand that I have to. Was there anyone else?

"What do you mean, 'anyone else'?" Alena said.

"I won't have you make those insinuations here," Rawson said. "Nobody would ever step out on my daughter if they wanted their limbs to remain attached."

"I understand that," Mason said. "But our number one priority is finding Mr. Bracewell. I don't have time to be polite. You can understand that."

Rawson grunted but stayed silent.

Alena said, "There was nobody else, as far as I know. Paul's parents still live in Spokane. His sister lives in Georgetown with her family. I suppose it's possible he woke up and went to visit them?" Her voice sounded hopeful, but doubtful.

Mason nodded. "We found no records of any flight or train tickets purchased in Paul's name."

"What about bus?"

"We've checked passenger manifests from all major bus lines and come up empty. We currently have agents in Spokane speaking with Paul's parents, Craig and Mary Bracewell, and his sister, Alice Belitnikoff, and her husband, down in Georgetown. So far, none of them claim to have seen or heard from Paul at any point in the last twenty-four hours."

Mason looked at Remy. "Mr. Stanton. Did you go directly home after the event? Did you see Mr. Bracewell at all last night after she parted with Mrs. Griggs? Did you notice anything else?"

"I didn't see him after," Remy said, a little embarrassed. "I saw part of their argument as I was leaving, but that's all."

"And did you go right home?"

Remy hesitated. Then said, "I did not. I went with a…friend for a nightcap.''

"Can that be corroborated?"

Remy felt his face grow red. "I can show you my credit card statement confirming we were at the bar. And if it's absolutely necessary, I can give you the name of the person I was with, but only if it's absolutely necessary. She has nothing to do with the campaign and I met her last night after the event ended."

Mason said, "I might ask you for that information."

"If you need it," he said.

He had trouble looking at Alena as he spoke.

"So what do we do now?" Alena asked. Her voice was shaky. She sounded like a small girl alone on a raft sinking in the middle of a storm. Rawson looked like he could rip a safe right off its hinges. Alena needed comfort, not anger. Remy wasn't sure if Rawson was fully capable of that.

Mason said, "We're coordinating with the NYPD and have alerted hospitals, train and bus stations, and all airports within two hundred miles. If anything comes up on the surveillance footage from the area around the Hyatt from last night, we'll let you know. On the federal front, we've alerted intelligence agencies to see if they've picked up on any threats made towards Mr. Bracewell or Mrs. Griggs. Right now, our hope is that he just had a rough night and is sleeping it off somewhere. Mrs. Griggs, we'll have an officer escort you home."

"No," Alena said, firmly. "I want to stay. Here. With my family."

Mason nodded. He passed his card around the table. Everyone except Rawson Griggs picked it up and looked at it. Rawson let it sit there on the table like a morsel of rancid food.

"Detective Ferguson here will be in contact if the NYPD turns up anything or has any more questions. In the meantime, we won't rest until we find Paul. Let us know if you can think of anything else from last night. Even the smallest details could matter."

"We will," Alena said.

Rawson stood up. "Find my son-in-law."

Mason said, "We'll do our best."

Mason offered no guarantees. Remy knew he couldn't.

"Oh, and on a personal note," Mason said, "Mr. Griggs, I think what you're doing is terrific. This country needs fresh blood. You'll have my vote. But don't go telling people that or I might lose my job."

"I appreciate that, Agent Mason. Thank you all for your efforts. You know your agency and all law enforcement will have the full support of a Griggs administration."

Mason nodded, and then the agents and officers left. The room went silent. Remy looked around, waiting for someone to say something. Alena looked like the slightest touch could cause her to crumble into dust.

"Alena," Rawson said, "if you need to go home, we'll understand."

She turned to her father, a look of steel resolve replacing the sadness on her face. She wiped her eyes and nose and said, "I'm not leaving. This is my family."

Rawson nodded. "Phillip," he said to the ex-mayor. "Anything else we can do to augment the NYPD's effort?"

Costanzo said, "I spoke to Commissioner Ragsdale this morning. They're using all available manpower to try to find Paul."

Rawson seemed sated by that answer. Once again, Wanda Lefebvre entered the room.

"Mr. Griggs," she said, "Doug Rimbaud from Senator Shaw's office is on the line. He says the senator sends her prayers and wants to know if there's anything she can do."

Remy hoped nobody else noticed his scowl.

"So Bertrand and Shaw both know," Rawson said, "which means it's only a matter of time before the press catches wind and this mess goes public."

Remy saw Alena flinch when Rawson used the word *mess*.

"Jerry. Jeremy," Griggs continued. "We need to get ahead of this. I want a press release draft on my desk regarding Paul's disappearance before eight o'clock. Keep it short, vague, and deferential to law enforcement. Make sure people know there will be no further statements on Paul Bracewell until we have more information."

Rawson turned to Alena. "I don't want you leaving the tower today until we know what's going on. If someone took Paul, they could be looking for you as well."

Alena hesitated for a moment, but then nodded her acceptance. Here, she was with her family, and she was safe. And Remy knew Rawson would tear the earth apart to keep her that way.

Rawson said, "There's nothing else we can do right now. But we still have a campaign to run."

Remy's head snapped to attention. Was Rawson really going to hold a strategy session now, with Paul in the wind? He knew Rawson was a focused man, but this seemed heartless, especially with Alena in the room. He surveyed the room. Nobody spoke. They didn't look entirely comfortable holding a meeting. But nobody spoke up against it.

"No time to waste," Rawson said. "Rebecca, have the new polling numbers come in? Where do we stand?"

Rebecca Blum opened up a briefcase and laid out few sheafs of paper. She passed copies to everyone at the table. Alena didn't take one.

"As of right now, we have a lead that's outside the margin of error. But not much. Our internal polling of a three-way matchup between Bertrand, Shaw, and Rawson shows Rawson polling at thirty-one percent, Shaw at twenty-six percent, and Bertrand at twenty-four percent, with the rest undecided or going for small party candidates. CNN's poll of polls gives us a little more cushion. Rawson has a seven-point edge over Shaw. I'm confident our polls are more accurate. We're winning white males without a college degree by twenty points, and we're making headway with white women. Minorities are breaking for Shaw. We need a strategy on how to change that."

"It's all a waste of time," Griggs said. "We need to solidify our base. We can spend months and millions trying to move the needle two points. But even if Shaw pulls eighty percent of blacks and Latinos— which is a reach—we'll pull enough from her base and Bertrand's base to splinter both parties. Focus on whites. I'd rather win eighty percent of the majority than twenty percent of the minority."

"How do we do that?" Blum said.

"I have some ideas," Rawson said. "For another time."

Blum added, "I also think many undecideds will swing our way as the campaign expands and we ramp up our ground game. We currently have campaign headquarters set up in thirty-seven states, and we'll be running in all fifty by the spring. Volunteers are coming in by the busload."

Rawson seemed energized, despite the somber mood. "And we're just getting started." Rawson was smiling like his son-in-law wasn't missing. The casualness unnerved Remy.

"Where else can we improve our numbers?" Rawson said.

"Evangelicals," Blum said. "Bertrand is leading substantially among voters who identify themselves as religious or very religious. He's ahead of you by ten points, and ahead of Shaw by thirty-six. Our polling suggests, though, that enthusiasm for Bertrand is low, meaning evangelicals can be swayed."

"They're voting for Bertrand because the pious are used to voting Republican. But the religious care more about sympathy than empathy. I want to set up a red state church tour. Two full weeks. I want to be in front of every man who wears a white collar you can find, from West Virginia down through Georgia and out to Alabama. Jerry, Jeremy, work with Rebecca. Finalize a schedule within forty-eight hours, get it online and then blast media in each city. Send several cartons of my books to every church as well. Gifts for the parishioners. Rebecca, coordinate with Brent Scott's Super PAC for finance and organization."

Remy looked at Jerry Kapinski, confused by that comment. Brent Scott was a former Senator-turned-influential energy lobbyist, primarily working on behalf of non-OPEC oil producing nations. He had founded a pro-Griggs Super PAC called TEETH OF THE TIGER, which had raised nearly fifty million dollars to support Rawson. FEC laws, however, prevented any sort of coordination between campaigns and their Super PACs, since there was no limit on the amount of money they could raise. It seemed like Rawson was aggressively flaunting that law. And if that was the case, and it went unchecked, it meant Rawson would have an almost unlimited war chest to spend.

Rawson said, "Everyone has their marching orders. Press release draft on my desk by eight. Let's go."

"Consider it done," Blum said. "Jerry, Jeremy, get to work on the release about Paul. Ken and I will work on the tour. I want to kick it off with Joseph Meyer at the Woodlake Church in Texas. Seven million people watch his sermons every week on television and seventeen thousand people go to every service. I want Rawson in the front pew of that church and then a sit-down to get Meyer's endorsement. That'll be the first domino."

Remy and Kapinski left the conference room and went to Kapinski's office.

Kapinski sat down and Remy closed the door. He said, "What was that back there? Are we coordinating with Brent Scott's Super PAC? Isn't that against FEC regulations?"

Kapinski looked at Remy like he was a teenager asking to borrow his dad's car for a road trip.

"You're seriously asking me that?"

"I'm seriously asking you that."

"You can't be so naïve, Remy." Kapinski sat back and put his hands behind his head. "FEC regulation is an oxymoron. It's like saying 'civil war.' We're not 'breaking' the rules. We're just slipping through the cracks that already exist."

"What does that mean?"

"The FEC is a blind guard dog. They sit there barking and hope to scare away the morons. But you walk around the dog quietly, ol' Fido just sits there licking his balls."

"Okay, so how are we evading Fido, exactly?"

"Well, we can't directly coordinate with Brent Scott's PAC. But they have access to any information available to the public, right? So when we announce our scheduling, or post it on the campaign website, it becomes public knowledge. And if we announce, say, we'll be in Des Moines on February 18, then the Super PAC can book the

Iowa Event Center and pay for the space rental and event staff. We're not coordinating *with* them, since the information is public. We're just putting it out there and letting them do the rest."

"That's an awfully large crack."

"We didn't make it," Kapinski said. "Washington is broken, so we use the breaks. Let's say we post a video of a Rawson Griggs speech on YouTube. Any Griggs Super PACs can then use that footage and splice it into their advertising. If they produce an ad Rawson likes, he'll tweet a link to it. If they produce one he doesn't like, he won't. And as long as the FEC has their dicks tied behind their backs, there's no reason we can't use them to our advantage."

"That's not exactly self-financing," Remy said.

"We don't have the fundraising apparatuses of the RNC or DNC or their infrastructure," Kapinski said. "As a third party, we need that money. Rawson is rich, but even I don't think he wants to spend as much money as he says he does. Not when other people can pick up part, or all, of the tab."

"Doesn't that kind of make us hypocrites?"

"Welcome to politics, kid," Kapinski said with a laugh. "Who do you think picked up the tab for your coming out party at the Grand Hyatt?"

Remy felt slightly nauseous. Had he lied to all those people, telling them that Rawson was paying for his campaign when, in reality, he had no idea who was picking up the tab. If Brent Scott had raised that money for his PAC, where had it all come from?

Jerry opened his word processor and pulled up the Griggs press release template. He added the date and began to write. Remy tried to ignore the unease knotting his gut and helped Jerry draft a release about Paul disappearance.

When they had a working draft, Kapinski emailed it to Blum and Rawson.

"Can I ask you a question?" Remy said.

"Shoot," Kapinski said, rubbing his eyes.

"How well do you know Paul?"

Kapinski thought for a moment.

"Not very. To be honest, we were always a little confused by that marriage. They love each other, don't get me wrong. Or they did. But to Rawson, Alena is more valuable that all the money, all the property, all the jewelry in the world. You don't store your valuables in a shoebox."

"So you're saying Paul is the shoebox."

Kapinski shrugged, as if to say *it is what it is.*

"For years," he said, "Rawson tried to fix her up with a who's-who of the world's most prominent heirs and scions. Rawson wanted to create a dynasty. He paraded heirs to half the companies on the *Forbes* 400 to Alena. But she never bit."

"So she went for Paul because he's the regular guy," Remy said. He remembered their conversations in the hospital, Alena's defiance at having full-time security watching over them. Her resistance to being defined as simply Rawson Griggs's daughter. She had power and influence, but seemed to wield it carefully and almost hesitantly, as if part of her had to apologize for having been born into such privilege. Marrying Paul Bracewell proved Alena was her own woman.

"It would never have lasted with Paul," Kapinski said. "Once you go on Rawson's shit list, you never get off."

"So maybe he left," Remy said. "Maybe he realized that and just had to get away for a while."

Kapinski shrugged. "Sure. It's possible."

Just then, there was a knock on the door.

"Come in," Kapinski said.

Wanda Lefebvre opened the door slowly. Her face was downcast. Remy felt his stomach roll. He knew right away.

"Wanda…" Kapinski said. "Is everything…"

He let the sentence trail off. They both knew from the look on her face why she was there. Kapinski looked at the press release on the computer, closed it, and dragged it into the trash.

"It's Paul," Wanda said softly, her voice trembling, eyes reddening. "They found him."

At that moment, Remy heard a horrible, soul-crushing wail come from down the hall. He recognized the voice. It was Alena. Her husband was dead.

CHAPTER 16

THE GRIGGS ORGANIZATION
FOR IMMEDIATE RELEASE
Statement on the passing of Paul Aaron Bracewell

It is with a very heavy heart that we announce the passing of our dear friend, Paul Aaron Bracewell. Paul was the beloved son of Stephen and Elizabeth Bracewell, sister of Alice Belitnikoff, loving husband of Alena Griggs, and cherished son-in-law of Rawson Griggs.

The entire Griggs family extends their heartfelt condolences to the Bracewell family, Paul's friends, and the many, many people who knew and loved him.

At this time, details of Mr. Bracewell's passing have not been made public pending a police and FBI investigation. The Bracewell and Griggs families ask for your sympathy and privacy during this difficult time.

The call came from Detective Ferguson of the NYPD. A woman walking her dog saw Paul's body floating in the East River near Pier 5 in Brooklyn Heights just after seven forty. She called 9-1-1, then flagged down a pair of joggers who jumped in and pulled Paul's body to shore. Paramedics declared him dead at the scene.

He was in the same clothes he'd worn the night before at the event at the Grand Hyatt. His suit was torn, the knees shredded, palms scraped and bloody. The wounds and tears were consistent with someone who'd stumbled and fallen, bloodying himself, before eventually falling into the river, where he drowned. The body showed signs of light trauma, bruising, a few hairline fractures, all of which could be ascribed to objects Paul's body collided with as the current dragged him along.

The amount of fluid in Paul's lungs suggested he'd been in the river for at least six hours. For six hours, Alena's husband floated like a piece of driftwood. Remy couldn't fathom her anguish.

To Remy's surprise and trepidation, Rawson asked him to accompany him and Alena to One Police Plaza to identify the body and speak with detectives. Every fiber of him wanted to decline. He had no place being there, but Rawson insisted. Insisted there was a reason he was asking for such a large favor. Remy knew Alena would need a shoulder during this time, and Rawson's iron countenance did not provide it. So he agreed.

Detective Ferguson led them to small, cold room inside the station. It had lime-green walls and metal-backed chairs. He drew the shades to give them privacy and brought them cups of bitter, lukewarm coffee.

Ferguson led them through the discovery. There were no signs of foul play, and they were awaiting toxicology reports from the lab. The working theory was that after leaving the Hyatt, Paul at some point walked east. He fell, perhaps multiple times, which explained the superficial scrapes and bruises on his hands and knees. Then Paul walked uptown, turned east at some point around 58th Street, and went into the river. It was unclear whether it was on purpose or by accident. And in Paul's inebriated state, he drowned.

Paul's parents were flying in from Spokane. His sister and her husband were driving in from Georgetown. Alena listened, near catatonic, just staring at the coffee. She nodded without hearing. Rawson and Remy listened, knowing it was too soon for her to process it all.

Detective Ferguson said he would leave to give them time to talk. Alena asked where the bathroom was. Ferguson said he would show her. He placed his hand on her back in a friendly gesture. She looked like a puff of wind could knock her over.

Once Ferguson and Alena left, Rawson turned to Remy. Sadness was etched on his face, the lines around his eyes and cheeks seemingly having deepened overnight. For the first time, Remy saw Rawson not as someone striving to be the most powerful human being alive, but as a man. A father.

Rawson placed his left hand on Remy's forearm.

They sat in silence for what felt like hours, but was in reality only a few seconds. The hand on Remy's arm felt both comforting and foreboding at the same time, like Rawson was preparing Remy for some hardship.

"Alena is going to need you," Rawson said. Remy turned his head. Rawson was looking off at the mint-colored wall, unfocused, drifting. "She's never been through anything like this. She was young when her mother died. Young children are easier to console because they don't fully understand."

"I'll be there," Remy said. "Whatever I can do. You know that."

"Alena looks to you more than you know. You're more than her peer. You're her friend. You're her family now. That night you saved her and…Paul…it forged a bond between you two. Forever. It's deeper and stronger than you think."

Remy stayed quiet. There were no words. He just let Rawson speak.

"As a young man, I never believed I was meant to be a father," Rawson said.

Remy looked at Rawson, surprised by the confession.

"I never had that desire for children. Some men do. They want to pass on the family name. They want a legacy. I did too, but not through offspring. I wanted my legacy to literally be my name. My empire. People would know the name Griggs as long as they lived. Children never seemed to be a necessary part of that picture."

Rawson took a sip of his coffee. It was cold and powdery, but he didn't seem to care. Then he continued.

"Liliana wanted a family. She made no secret of it. She made it clear our marriage was contingent on it. And I took convincing. I always felt that if you decided to raise children, you would eventually have to choose between them and your passions. Well, my work was my passion. My legacy was my passion. They were my children before Alena was born. I raised my company from nothing. I planted the seeds with my own hands. I nurtured it, watched it grow into something spectacular. There's nothing I wouldn't do for those children. Nothing. I never thought I needed more. But finally, I relented. Partially because I feared I would lose Liliana if I said no. Partially because, deep down, perhaps I wanted to prove to myself I could be a father. Rise to the challenge. I have never respected people who back down from a challenge. And yet, by refusing Liliana's wish, that's exactly what I was doing."

Rawson's eyes grew red as he spoke. Remy listened, unsure of how to respond.

"I remember the morning Alena was born. It was a torrential downpour like I'd never seen. As we drove to the hospital, visibility near zero, I took it as a sign. I thought God was angry with me for relenting. They were going to make it difficult. But when the nurse put Alena in my arms, her skin so smooth, her body so small, I worried she could just float away…when her tiny fingers wrapped around mine, everything faded away. My empire evaporated. This was legacy. What I passed down to her. That's the love I have for my daughter. She makes everything fade away."

Rawson paused.

"Liliana wanted another child. She hoped for a son. Obviously, there were no guarantees, but she talked about her perfect family being a daughter and a son, and the two of us. I said no. No more. My company was growing. And I knew as long as we had a child together, I would never lose Liliana."

Rawson paused.

"But then I lost her anyway."

"I wish Liliana was here to see what we're accomplishing," Remy said.

"If she was here, Alena would never have married Paul. I was the bad cop. I think she married Paul to defy me. To prove she didn't need the Griggs name. Liliana would have straightened her out."

"Alena is an extraordinary woman," Remy said. "She has your strength. And she has a grounded decency that's beyond admirable. You should be proud of her, and proud of the job you did raising her. Especially on your own."

Rawson said, "I have wondered about you, Jeremy. Whether decency will limit your ambitions. I live to win. There is no other option. And to win, you often have to be vicious. There is no other way. There are times in my life when I wish I had the gentle touch Alena does, but I'm also glad she doesn't see the world the same way I do. That decency you speak of would have served me well when Alena's mother passed. But you have that decency. That is why you helped Alena and Paul that night. I suppose that night showed me you can be strong *and* decent. That is why I wanted you to work for me. You add a valuable element to my campaign. But right now, you are needed in a different way. What Alena needs right now is not in my nature. Man to man. Be there for my daughter."

"I will be," Remy said. Rawson nodded and removed his hand from Remy's arm. It felt to Remy like an electrical current snapping. There was an innate understanding that this was not to be discussed around Alena. And that from that moment on, Remy promised himself he would be there for her.

When Alena came back, she looked as though her soul had left her. Rawson thanked Detective Ferguson and they left the police station. When they walked outside, Remy put his arm around Alena.

She practically fell into him, and he held her up. She was so light, Rey thought. Remy noticed a faint smile on Rawson's face.

He hugged Alena goodbye, felt her shudder as she held back tears. Then he shook Rawson's hand and took a cab back to his apartment. Alena went back to Griggs Tower with Rawson to grieve with what remained of her family.

When Remy got home, he noticed his lapel was damp, and a long blonde hair was stuck to his collar where Alena had wept on him. He would never forget the pain on her face, the agonized wail that seemed ripped from her soul when Paul was found.

Oddly enough, Remy noticed the strain in their marriage the very day he met them in the hospital. They seemed like actors occupying a stage in between takes. Cordial, with little warmth. Alena was like her father in many ways: decisive and shrewd. From what he could tell, Paul was none of that. Alena had seemed to carry him like a cumbersome purse that was too large for the occasion.

After they sent out the release about Paul's death, Remy's inbox had been flooded with media requests. Some producers even had the gall to request interviews with Alena. Respect the grieving widow's privacy, unless it could boost ratings.

Donna was gone when he got back. She'd even made the bed. There was a note on the table with her telephone number inside a heart written in lipstick. Remy looked at the note, then folded it and put it in a drawer.

Remy took a bottle of Dogfish Head from the fridge. He cracked it open and had finished half the bottle before he realized it was barely noon.

He knew working for Rawson would change his life, but he never thought he would have to grieve, to be around death. He felt hollowed out.

And for the first time, unprompted, in months, Remy's thoughts turned to his father. Even though he pushed them away, every so often they would jolt him like a car rear-ended, unwelcome and painful.

He thought about his mother, lying in bed as the cancer that would soon claim her life began to drain the essence of what made her *her*. She was frail, less than ninety pounds at the end. She was only awake sporadically, couldn't focus, and in constantly in pain. Sometimes, on his darkest days, he wished God would take her sooner. If she couldn't recover, then don't let her suffer.

When she was awake, he held her hand, her skin paper-thin, dark blue veins visible underneath. Her hair was gone, her head a mottled mess of dry skin and lesions. Her eyes sunken, cheekbones hollowed out. He forced himself to ignore the horror of death, thought about the good times, the memories he would take with him when she was gone.

And despite his own pain, Remy refused to allow himself to cry around her. Her pain was enough. He couldn't burden her with his sadness. And since he had no outlet for his own pain, his own anguish, it festered.

Two days before Margaret Stanton passed away, Remy's father appeared in the hospital room. Neither of them had seen him in two years. Margaret was asleep, thankfully. Remy was alone with her, skimming a paperback Stephen King novel, but not processing any of the words. And then he looked up and saw his father standing there, and wondered if he was real, or if one of King's horrors had come to life.

Remy's book fell to the floor. His father's mouth was open slightly, as though he wanted to say something but the words had escaped him.

His father had grown deep crows feet around his eyes, mottled veins blotted his nose. His mouth was a stubbled, a dirty little O. His lips were purple, bruised. He wore a scuffed denim jacket, his gray hair in a ponytail tied with a rubber band. His jeans were faded and torn around the hems. He looked like a man the world had tasted, then spat back out.

A pair of aviator sunglasses peeked from his jacket pocket. For some reason, that set Remy off.

Fucking sunglasses.

He wanted to scream. For help. Out of rage. He had no right to be there. He had no right to force one of Margaret Stanton's final memories to be of the man who had broken her from the outside in.

"I just…" Remy's father said. He was looking at the white linoleum floor. He tapped one foot with the toe of other. "I heard from a friend that she was sick. And…um…I known her since I was a kid. She gonna be okay, you think?"

Talking to Remy like he was a drinking buddy and not his son. As though tenure gave him the right to see her. Remy looked at her mother. The faint white scars were still visible on her cheeks, and her nose was still slightly bent. She couldn't raise her right arm above her head because they didn't have health insurance and the bone never set properly. Remy thought about all the times he had to help zip up her dresses. Remy thought about all the times he stood at the entrance to his parents' bedroom.

His father kept a loaded Glock in the bedside drawer. Remy took it out occasionally. Loaded and unloaded it. Figured out how to work the trigger guard. Remy often wondered, if his father refused to stop, if he would have the guts to pull the trigger.

His father. His monster.

"She doesn't want you here," Remy said. He did not stand. Did not approach his father. The man did not deserve any pleasantries. "I don't want you here. Leave before she wakes up."

Remy's father stood there, *tap tap tapping* his shoe. Then he took the sunglasses from his jacket pocket, slipped them onto his face, turned around, and left. That was all. He said nothing to his ex-wife. Nothing else to his son.

That was over ten years ago. It was the last time Remy had seen his father.

Two days later, Margaret Stanton passed away. She fell asleep and never woke up. And then, when his mother's beautiful soul had finally left her disease-riddled body, Remy finally allowed himself to cry.

Things felt like they were spinning out of control. He had relished the possibilities that came with working for Rawson Griggs. But sitting there in the police station, seeing the pain in Alena's face, Remy felt like a fraud. He barely knew Paul. And truthfully, hadn't thought all that much of him when he was alive.

Remy looked down at the floor. He noticed he was tapping his own shoes together. *Like his father.*

Long ago, Remy had promised himself he would not be his father. He would be there when it mattered. He would be there for Alena.

He needed to get his mind off of Paul. Remy opened his campaign scheduling spreadsheet and began to plot out Rawson's travel for the upcoming weeks. He would spend the next ten days crossing the upper Midwest—Wisconsin, Michigan, and Minnesota. He would tour a Ford plant outside of Detroit, a Jelly Belly center in Pleasant Prairie, and a goat cheese manufacturer in Grant County.

Remy was coordinating the details of the Jelly Belly tour when his buzzer rang.

He pressed the intercom and said, "Who is it?"

The voice on the other end was difficult to make out.

"Sorry, can you speak louder?"

The second time, Remy heard the man's voice loud and clear.

Why in the hell is he here? Remy thought. *And why does he sound like he's scared to death?*

"It's Doug Rimbaud. Annabelle Shaw's campaign manager. We met while you were talking with Grace Rivas. I'm here about Paul Bracewell. We really need to talk."

That night, twelve hours after Doug Rimbaud rang Remy Stanton's buzzer, there was a knock on Rawson Griggs's office door.

"Come in," he said.

Wanda Lefebvre entered. Rawson checked his watch. It was after midnight.

"Wanda," he said, "I sent everyone home. You didn't have to keep working."

"It would feel strange going home while you're still here."

Rawson nodded. She was like him. He understood.

Wanda approached the desk. "I know today is…difficult," she said. "But this just happened. I hate to put more on your plate, but you need to see it."

She placed a USB drive on his desk.

"How urgent?" Rawson said.

"Unless there's a general election debate tomorrow," Wanda said, "you'll want to watch it right now."

Rawson picked up the fob and inserted it into his computer. He clicked on the folder that appeared on the desktop, and then opened the video file inside.

He recognized the apartment immediately. He turned the volume up. The buzzer rang, and Jeremy Stanton crossed the room to answer it. He picked up the intercom and said, "Who is it?"

"It's Doug Rimbaud. Annabelle Shaw's campaign manager. We met while you were talking with Grace Rivas. I'm here about Paul Bracewell. We really need to talk."

CHAPTER 17

"What in the hell do *you* want?"

"Not down here. Let me up," Rimbaud said. "And I'll explain."

"Go to hell. And tell the senator she really needs to vet her employees better."

"Senator Shaw doesn't know I'm here. This is about Paul Bracewell."

"What about him?"

Remy was in no mood to speak to Rimbaud. But the way he said that name—*Paul Bracewell*—made Remy think Rimbaud knew something he needed to hear.

"You're on the clock." Remy pressed the button to unlock the front door. When the doorbell rang, Remy opened it. Doug Rimbaud was standing there, looking like he hadn't slept in a year. His eyes were bloodshot, hair askew, and Remy could smell alcohol on his breath.

"Thanks for letting me in," Rimbaud said. He seemed edgy. And the way he kept rubbing his hands together and looking around meant Rimbaud was on coke, or he was very, very nervous.

"Get to it," Remy said. He went to the fridge and took out a beer.

"Can I get one of those?"

Remy looked at Rimbaud. He couldn't believe this asshole's moxie. He grabbed another Dogfish Head, popped the tops on both, and handed one to Rimbaud.

"Thanks," Rimbaud said, taking a long pull. He was sweating. Remy took a seat at his desk. Rimbaud looked around the apartment. "I like the place. Uncluttered."

"What are you, an HGTV publicist?" Remy said.

"I'm serious. At least you live alone. I had roommates until I was thirty. Politics pays a lot less than you'd think. Everyone just dreams of riding it out until you can get one of those cushy job as a talking head on cable news."

"I let you into my home. I gave you a drink. Now tell me why you're here."

Rimbaud took another sip and took a seat on the couch. He leaned forward, elbows on his knees, hands clasped together. Almost penitent.

"Paul Bracewell was working for me," he said. "Well, us. The Shaw campaign."

"Bullshit," Remy said.

"It's true. He'd been feeding us information for about six, maybe nine months. How do you think I knew about your meeting with Grace Rivas? He'd been sending me everything he could. Scheduling information, polling data, FEC violations, internal reports transcribed firsthand from Rawson's War Room."

"That's absurd. He's Alena's husband."

"He might have been Alena's husband, but he was never a Griggs. You know that as well as I do." Rimbaud paused for a moment. "And I can see it in your eyes that you know I'm telling the truth."

"Well, Doug, as much as I'd love to argue about family dynamics, I'm not a psychiatrist and you're not paying me for my time. So you can leave now."

"Alena wasn't the target that night," Rimbaud said.

Remy's eyes narrowed. "What the hell are you talking about?"

"The night you were shot. They weren't looking to kill or kidnap Alena. That's the theory, right? Nogoyev and Usenov were lone wolf radicals looking to send a message by harming the beloved daughter of an American icon. But it's not the truth. Paul Bracewell had been working for us for several months. He knew Rawson was going to run, and he wanted to stop him. Rawson found out. Nogoyev and Usenov were targeting *Paul*. Not Alena. And I believe they did it on orders from Rawson Griggs."

"So now you're telling me my boss is a murderer," Remy said. "I'm guessing he planned the bombing at the Castle too, right?"

"No. I think that was retribution. Rawson had Nogoyev killed in prison so he wouldn't talk. And then, I think, Usenov went after Rawson at the Castle for killing his friend, which was never part of the deal."

"These are some pretty wild theories. Let me ask you a question: do you get an erection while writing your Jason Bourne fan fiction?"

"Wake up!" Rimbaud shouted. "Think about it. How well do you know Rawson? I mean *really* know what a cold-hearted son of a bitch he is."

"Paul may not have been the darling son Rawson always wanted, but he was no idiot. Rawson spends millions of dollars a year on top of the line cyber security systems. Griggs Tower is a fortress. I can count on two hands the people who have access to our servers. If Paul was emailing you from a Griggs account, they would know."

"He emailed us from a private, secure server that we set up for him and burner phones paid for in cash. He never contacted us using Griggs-installed software or from Griggs-purchased hardware."

"So Paul was killed by Rawson because he was a mole for Annabelle Shaw. That's what you're telling me?"

"Yes."

"So I'm guessing Rawson was also responsible for Watergate? Benghazi? Steve Bartman?"

"I'm serious, Jeremy."

"If so, why haven't you gone to the police?"

Rimbaud sighed. "I don't have proof. And, well, if the FBI knew Paul was working for us, it doesn't exactly cast our candidate in the most positive light either."

"You're like a moral and ethical black hole."

"Listen," Rimbaud said. "Politics is a game. Not everyone plays clean. But nobody wants to see people die."

"So you're saying that politics can be dirty, but you're also saying I should believe you, no questions asked? You already tried to fuck with me once. Sorry if you don't get the benefit of the doubt. What you're saying, all this dirt, that's not how real campaigns try to win elections. Real campaigns don't go low."

"Jesus, man, you can't be this naïve," Rimbaud said. "You've been in the game for a few months and you're talking like you were on Lincoln's team of rivals or something. You don't know shit. I'm forty-two. By thirty-three, I'd run successful congressional campaigns for two congressmen, and by forty for two senators. I've been offered jobs by some of the biggest lobbying firms in the country, and I have a standing offer from CNN to be a paid contributor as soon as the election is over if I'm not appointed to Annabelle Shaw's cabinet. I have my pick of any job from K Street to Madison Avenue. If you didn't happen to get in the way of a bullet, you'd be just another suit."

"And if you're telling the truth, you led a man to his death."

"Paul was a big boy. He knew what he was doing and he knew the kind of man Rawson Griggs is. He knew the risks. He was scared, and I didn't believe him. But I never imagined it could end up like this. We both know Paul was a mess the last few months. He knew what was coming. And he kept talking to me. That's how important it was to him to stop Rawson."

Remy stayed silent. He had noticed Paul disintegrating.

"I think you believe me," Rimbaud said. "I'm telling you because you haven't drunk the Griggs Kool-Aid yet. You have clearer eyes than Murphy and Blum, or that stooge Costanzo. Alena is smarter than all of them, but she'd never turn on her old man. Rawson's little girl would never believe the truth about dear old psychotic dad."

"Don't talk about her like you know her," Remy seethed.

"You and Paul Bracewell have something in common," Rimbaud

said. "You're both outsiders. But Rawson likes you. Hell, he might love you, in whatever way a monster can love someone. But you're not his blood. The poison hasn't sunk in yet. It's not too late. That's why I came here. Because you can be reached. Deep down, you know Rawson places loyalty above everything, including honesty and decency. Paul was disloyal. What do *you* think Rawson would do?"

"So if Rawson is the devil incarnate, why did you need Paul Bracewell?"

"Because the devil is smart. If you can't find something on him, it's because he doesn't want it to be found."

"So what exactly did Paul dredge up that Rawson would want him dead?"

"He hated Costanzo. Paul sent us flight manifests from Rawson's private jet that confirmed Mr. Mayor had taken at least half a dozen trips to Kyrgyzstan. These trips started at least a year before Costanzo officially joined the Griggs campaign. Paul hadn't quite figured out why—Kyrgyzstan isn't exactly a superpower—but when we learned that Nogoyev and Usenov were *from* Kyrgyzstan, and had return flights back to Bishkek, it scared us both shitless. He found revenue discrepancies at Griggs properties. Millions and millions of dollars, and Paul couldn't figure out where it was from. A dozen threads that he hadn't woven together yet. But they were there. I know this sounds crazy, but Paul was convinced a Rawson Griggs presidency would lead the country to catastrophe."

Remy sighed. "So we've gone from 'Rawson Griggs had something to do with the death of his son-in-law' to straight up 'End of Days'? Nice chatting with you, Doug. You can leave now."

"Fine."

Rimbaud stood up. He teetered for a second. Remy regretted giving him the beer, in the event Annabelle Shaw's campaign manager yarfed all over his couch. Chalk up one more on the list of things Remy never thought he'd have to worry about.

As he walked to the door, Rimbaud turned back to Remy. There was remorse in his eyes. Rimbaud was taking Paul Bracewell's death hard. Which meant either Rimbaud was a fantastic actor—or he really did have a relationship with Paul.

"Your candidate is not who you think he is," Rimbaud said to Remy, his voice even, sober. "This 'beast' stuff? He's the real beast. You haven't been corrupted yet. Neither was Paul. Don't be blind."

"Says someone who benefits if Rawson Griggs goes down," Remy said.

"Says someone who knows that Paul Bracewell had more integrity in his little finger than you have in your entire body," Rimbaud said. "Take care, Jeremy. Thanks for the time and the beer."

Doug Rimbaud opened the door, left, and eased it closed, leaving Remy sitting there, alone and angry. And just a little bit frightened.

CHAPTER 18

The Griggs motorcade headed to Fairmount Memorial Park, just outside of Spokane, Washington, where Paul Bracewell would be laid to rest. Only four had flown out for the funeral: Rawson and Alena Griggs, Remy, and Kenneth Murphy.

They were in a bulletproof black van, with security detail vehicles flanking them in front and back. Remy felt guilty that such an entourage would bring unwanted attention during such a somber time, but they had no choice.

Remy's black suit hung off him loosely. He'd dropped ten pounds in the last few weeks. Next to him, Alena wore a black dress with a veil hanging over her head. She hadn't said a word since the van departed from the Davenport Tower hotel in downtown Spokane. Rawson wanted Paul to be laid to rest in New York. Paul's family has insisted he be buried back home.

Alena was the tiebreaker. She wanted Paul's final resting place to be near his home. His real home.

Rawson was glued to his phone. The latest polling numbers had come in, and they were a cause for concern. CNN's poll of polls showed Richard Bertrand gaining momentum. Rawson's lead was narrowing.

He was still ahead, but that lead was now within the margin of error. He led Annabelle Shaw thirty-five percent to thirty-two percent, with Bertrand jumping to twenty-seven percent. Rawson was clearly upset, and Remy could tell it was killing him to have to put work aside for Paul's funeral.

Paul's death weighed on Remy heavily. The coroner's toxicology report stated that Paul Bracewell had a BAC of 0.48 the night he died, high enough to slow his breathing and heart rate and likely render him unconscious. It explained why he fell. And why he drowned.

As soon as they'd checked in to the Davenport Tower, Remy raided the minibar. It took two miniature Scotches and a beer to get him to sleep.

He hadn't mentioned Doug Rimbaud's visit to anyone, including Rawson or Alena. It was possible Doug was simply trying to drive a wedge into the campaign. And Remy certainly didn't trust the man. It may have been a dirty, deceitful ruse, but given everything Remy had seen in his short time in politics, it was eminently possible. Doug was a cheap shot artist. Showing up at his interview with Grace Rivas proved that. Yes, claiming Paul was a mole for the Shaw campaign was a step—or ten—beyond that, but once you sold your soul, there were no refunds.

As the motorcade turned into Fairmount, Remy spotted a squadron of photographers gathered at the front gates, snapping pictures of the motorcade as it passed. The intrusion felt ghoulish.

They passed through the Fairmount gates. Hundreds of gravestones were nestled among the rolling green hills and towering fir trees. In the rearview mirror, Remy could see photographers literally climbing the fences, holding their cameras out, hoping to get one last good shot of the mourners.

Remy looked at Alena. She sat across from him, unmoving. Her eyes were closed. He reached out, put his hand on hers. She did not open her eyes, but a whisper of a smile curled at her upper lip, and she said, "Thank you."

He whispered, "I'm so sorry."

Alena nodded, said, "I'm glad you're here."

"Me too."

When the cars stopped, the driver came around and opened the doors. Rawson, Alena, Remy, and Murphy filed out onto the cemetery grounds, heads bowed. There was a chill in the air. Remy buttoned his coat. Alena wrapped a shawl around her shoulders.

Several dozen gathered around the plot where Paul Bracewell would be laid to rest. Remy recognized Paul's mother, father, and sister from photos. The rest appeared to be extended family members and friends. Paul's mother sat in front, weeping behind a black veil. Alena went over to Paul's family and embraced his parents. Paul's mother sobbed loudly, mournfully. His father did not cry, but his trembling lower lip told Remy that tears were not far from the surface. Remy watched them, a sick feeling in his stomach.

Alena stayed with Paul's family. Rawson, Remy, and Murphy stood on the opposite side of the grave from Paul's family and friends. A priest stepped to the front of the casket. He was bald, with a short white beard, heavyset underneath his white robe. He started the service. Remy lowered his head.

"As we lay to rest our son and brother Paul Aaron Bracewell," the priest began, "I would like to read a passage from Wisdom 4:7."

The mourners bowed their heads, and the priest spoke.

"But the just man, though he die early, shall be at rest. For the age that is honorable comes not with the passing of time, nor can it be measured in terms of years. Rather, understanding is the hoary crown for men, and an unsullied life, the attainment of old age. He who pleased God was loved; he who lived among sinners was transported. Snatched away, lest wickedness pervert his mind or deceit beguile his soul; for the witchery of paltry things obscures what is right and the whirl of desire transforms the innocent mind. Having become perfect in a short while, he reached the fullness of a long career; for his soul was pleasing to the Lord, therefore he sped him out of the midst of wickedness. But the people saw and did not understand, nor did they take this into account. Because grace and mercy are with God's holy ones, and God's care is with the elect."

As the priest continued the service, Remy scanned the mourners. Paul was Remy's age. He couldn't imagine the unendurable pain Paul's parents felt, to lose a child that young. He wanted to reach out to them, to say something, to apologize for not having been there for their son. Remy felt like he had let Paul down. He'd never made much of an effort to befriend the man, allowing him to remain adrift.

Now, though, as Paul's body was lowered into the ground, Remy regretted all the times they sat at the same table and never spoke. All the times they'd flown together, driven together, been literally steps from each other, yet had never exchanged a word. He could have reached out. He had failed Paul.

Paul's mother wailed as the casket was lowered into the ground. Paul's father looked like a feather's touch could crack him in half.

There were a dozen mourners who looked to be about Paul's age. Remy figured they were friends from home or school. They were all sullen, weeping, somber.

Except for one man. His eyes burned with anger, his upper lip curled in a sneer. He looked like he wanted to tear something apart.

He was tall and broad-shouldered, with receding black hair and full, red cheeks. A thick, pale scar bisected his right eyebrow. A woman, his wife presumably, stood next to him, crying, holding his hand.

His eyes were not focused on the priest or casket like the rest of the mourners. Rather, he was staring daggers straight at Rawson Griggs.

Remy watched him. He looked like he wanted leap across the grave and strangle Rawson with his bare hands.

Why did this man have such a burning hatred for Rawson? Remy had never seen him before.

The priest blessed the deceased and the interned souls at the cemetery and concluded the service. Mourners filed slowly past Paul Bracewell's family to offer their condolences.

Remy followed the line of mourners to pay his respects to Paul's family. When he reached Paul's mother, she took his hand and said, "Thank you for what you did for my son. Paul admired you greatly. I'm glad there are still men of courage in this world."

Remy simply nodded. It felt like a rope was tightening around his heart, his throat. He began to choke up. He had no idea Paul felt that way. He kept his emotions at bay, but as he passed the immediate family, Remy turned back to look at Paul's group of friends. He found the tall one, the one with the eyebrow scar. He was whispering something to his wife, never taking his eyes off Rawson. Then they turned and left.

Remy needed to know who he was. And why he looked like he wanted to murder Rawson Griggs.

When the Griggs convoy arrived back at the Davenport, they unloaded from the car, drained.

"Did you know Paul's parents?" Remy asked Murphy. Murphy lit a cigarette. Remy didn't even know he smoked. He inhaled deeply, exhaled, and coughed.

"Sorry," he said. "I've quit a dozen times. Rough morning, you know?"

"No judgments." Murphy offered Remy one. He declined.

"I didn't know them well," Murphy said, taking another drag. "I met them at the wedding, maybe once or twice after that, but we really didn't see them often. They didn't live close by. And, well, Rawson isn't exactly the kind of in-law you make Christmas plans with."

Remy said, "We were his family too. We should have acted like it. We should have protected him."

"Every man is responsible for his own life," Murphy said. His lack of sympathy surprised Remy. "Hey, my heart breaks for Alena and the Bracewell family. But Paul was selfish. Bottom line."

Murphy stubbed out his cigarette and went to talk to Rawson.

Remy went over to Alena.

"How are you?"

"I don't know how to answer that. I just buried my husband," Alena replied.

"I can't tell you how sorry I am. I wish there was something I could do or say to make it better."

"I know you do. But you can't. I'm going to go upstairs and rest."

"Text me if you need anything," Remy said. "Anything."

Alena smiled weakly and said, "Thanks, Remy."

She went inside. Remy joined Murphy and Rawson.

"I don't think my daughter has taken a nap since she was a baby," Rawson said. "Even when she was little, she had a motor that would have won the Indy 500." He removed his sunglasses. "Thank you both for coming all the way out here."

"Not even a question," Murphy said.

"Of course," Remy added.

"I trust you saw the latest numbers. This is frankly very disturbing. Take a little time to unwind. Wash the cemetery off of you," Rawson said. "But I want you in my suite at five. Ken, talk to Rebecca and Jerry. I want a total breakdown of where Bertrand's support is coming from. Look at Costanzo's schedule. I may want him involved. Pull him off television if necessary so he's available the rest of the day."

"You got it, sir."

"Five o'clock," Rawson said. "We have a lot of work to do."

Rawson tipped the driver and doorman and went to his suite.

"No rest for the weary," Murphy said.

"Or the grieving," Remy said.

Murphy said, "Do us all a favor. When we meet later, leave the sentiment in your hotel room. This is bad."

"Okay," Remy said.

"See you in a bit."

Murphy left. Remy stood outside the lobby. He was angry about Rawson's and Murphy's callousness. He didn't care about the poll numbers. And he couldn't get the man with the eyebrow scar out of his head. He needed to know where that anger came from.

Remy took the elevator to his floor. At the end of the hallway, Remy could see two of Rawson's private security guards standing outside the suite. Remy went to his room, changed out of his suit, and put on jeans and a sweater.

Then he opened up his Facebook account.

He and Paul were Facebook friends, but Remy had never once bothered to look at Paul's page. He'd never even been curious. But now, he was hoping to find answers.

Remy opened the Photos tab on Paul's feed and clicked on Albums. There weren't many. Pictures from various charity events he'd attended with Alena. Remy scrolled down and opened their honeymoon album. They'd spent three weeks in Croatia. Remy clicked through them. The photos were gorgeous, and wide smiles stretched across their sun-kissed faces. Remy enlarged a photo of the newlyweds standing in front of the bluest sea he had ever seen. The caption said it had been taken on Lokrum Island off the western coast of Dubrovnik. Paul was wearing white linen shorts and a loose-fitting t-shirt, Alena in a yellow spaghetti strap tank top and jean shorts that showed off her bronzed legs. They each wore sunglasses, arms wrapped around each other, wind whipped Alena's long hair about. The caption read: "Love."

Remy closed the photo. He scrolled down and found an album marked "Our Wedding." He opened it.

Inside were dozens of photos, professional and candid, from Alena and Paul's wedding at Cipriani. The event space was packed. There must have been five hundred people there. Each table boasted a gorgeous three-foot high floral centerpiece filled with white orchids. There was a twelve-piece jazz band standing atop a riser. There were mountains of food: lobster tails, buckets of caviar, trays and trays of sushi. There was an ice sculpture in the shape of a heart with "Paul & Alena" carved into it. This was a Rawson Griggs production through and through.

Remy scrolled through the photos. Alena looked absolutely stunning. Her skin shone, her hair a gorgeous cascade of blonde curls. She wore a custom-designed, sleeveless Vera Wang gown that couldn't have cost a penny less than twenty thousand dollars. Her bridesmaids wore pink tulips. The grooms, blue hydrangeas. It looked like a fairy tale come to life.

Remy focused on the shots of young men. There were many: guys doing shots, guys dancing, guys with their girlfriends and wives. Then he found what—or who—he was looking for. The man with the eyebrow scar.

His hair was a little longer, he was a little trimmer, and there he was not wearing a wedding ring. But Remy immediately recognized the scar cutting through the man's right eyebrow. He clicked on the photo to enlarge it. The tag displayed the man's name: Michael O'Brien.

Remy immediately recognized the name. Paul had texted a Michael O'Brien the night he died. Detective Ferguson said the text was gibberish. But O'Brien was the only person Paul reached out to before he died, accident or not.

Remy pulled up Michael O'Brien's Facebook page. His profile picture was taken from his own wedding. Remy recognized O'Brien's wife. She was at the cemetery earlier. Same woman. Same scar. Same guy.

Most of Michael O'Brien's Facebook activity was hidden from Remy's view, but in O'Brien's last post, he'd checked in to a restaurant called Anthony's in Spokane. The post was dated one month ago, and the caption read, "Best sockeye in the state!"

Remy opened the White Pages in another tab, and ran a search for Michael O'Brien in Spokane, WA. The search came back with three hits on Michael O'Brien. One O'Brien was aged fifty-four to sixty-nine. Another other was sixty-five to sixty-nine. The third was listed as being twenty-six to twenty-nine years old. That had to be him.

That Michael O'Brien was listed as the sole proprietor of MOB Real Estate. He'd received a bachelors in economics from the University of Washington, and a masters in finance from Gonzaga. He was listed as having an address on West Indian Trail Road. Remy looked up the directions on Google Maps. O'Brien's house was about seven miles northwest of the Davenport.

Remy checked his watch. It was 12:47. Plenty of time before they were scheduled to meet in Rawson's suite.

Remy cleaned himself up, combed his hair, brushed his teeth, and put on deodorant. He needed to be presentable. He eased open his door and glanced towards Rawson's suite. The guards were still outside. They were in the middle of a conversation. And they weren't looking in Remy's direction.

Remy stepped out and gently closed the door behind him. He walked down the hotel corridor quickly but softly. If anyone asked where he was going, he'd just say he was running downstairs to the café for a bite.

Several taxis idled in front of the entrance to the Davenport. He got into a cab, gave the address to the driver, and they sped off down South Post Street.

The cab took 2nd Avenue west, and then turned onto Maple Street. They crossed the Spokane River, went several miles north, and turned onto Francis Avenue. Remy's cell phone rang. His breath caught in his chest when he saw that the caller was Ken Murphy. Murphy never called him. Texted occasionally. But Remy couldn't remember a single actual phone call.

He didn't know what to do. If he answered, Murphy would know Remy wasn't at the hotel. But what if Murphy had already knocked on Remy's door? This was bad either way. Remy decided to let the phone ring. If Murphy asked him later, Remy would just say he was napping and turned the ringer off. Still, the call made him uneasy.

Twenty-five minutes after they left the Davenport, the cab turned onto West Indian Trail Road. They pulled up to a single-family ranch style home with a two-car garage and a neatly manicured lawn. There was a yellow tricycle with pink ribbons streaming from the handlebars in the driveway, behind a black Ford Taurus.

Remy paid the driver and asked the cabbie for his cell phone number. He would need a ride back. The driver gave him the number for his dispatcher and left.

Remy rang the doorbell, praying Michael O'Brien wasn't the kind of guy who greeted strangers with a double-barrel shotgun. He still wasn't certain Michael O'Brien even lived here, given that the White Pages were as reliable as Wikipedia—Remy had seen how often

Rawson's own entry got defaced. If he'd gone to the wrong house, Remy would just go back to the hotel, return Murphy's call, and let it go.

But then the door opened, and Remy was face to face with the man from the cemetery. He recognized the eyebrow scar immediately. O'Brien was wearing track pants and a Seattle Mariners jersey. He looked exhausted and confused.

"Help you?" he said.

"Mr. O'Brien?" Remy said hesitantly. "Michael O'Brien?"

"That's right," O'Brien said, looking warily at Remy. "Can I help you?"

"My name is Jeremy Stanton. I was at Paul Bracewell's funeral today. I saw you there too."

"I thought I recognized you," O'Brien said. "You're the guy I've seen in the newspaper a bunch. You stopped that terrorist a while back."

"That's me."

"And now you work for Rawson Griggs, isn't that right?"

The question with loaded with venom.

"I do," Remy said.

"Well, then you can go fuck yourself."

O'Brien went to close the door.

"Please, wait, just a second," Remy said. He put his foot into the jamb to prevent the door from latching shut. O'Brien looked at Remy as though he couldn't believe this asshole. "I need to talk to you about Paul. I saw you at Fairmount today. The way you looked at Rawson."

"It was a look, dude. Just a look. My friend is dead. The rest doesn't matter."

"I think it does."

O'Brien eyed Remy, unsure what to make of his intentions.

"Did Griggs send you?"

"No. He doesn't know I'm here. I swear on my mother."

Remy heard a female voice come from inside the house. "Honey, who is it?"

"Hold on, hon," O'Brien said. He turned to Remy. "That's my wife.

We both went to school with Paul. Knew him for almost twenty years."

"I'm just asking for a few minutes of your time. For Paul," Remy said.

O'Brien shuffled his feet, eyed Remy, then opened the door. "You have fifteen minutes. We dropped our daughter off with her grandparents during the funeral. I have to pick her up at three."

"Thank you," Remy said, and stepped inside. "I won't take much of your time."

O'Brien led him to a small living room, with white shag carpeting, an overstuffed blue sofa, and a La-Z-Boy facing a thirty-inch flat screen. A half-finished bottle of Amstel Light sat on the table. O'Brien sunk into the couch and took a swig from the bottle. Remy sat down on a loveseat perpendicular to the couch. He did not expect any hospitality, and O'Brien didn't offer any.

"So what do you want?" O'Brien said.

"How long did you know Paul?" Remy said.

"Oh man. Forever," O'Brien said. He pointed at the scar above his right eye. "Paul was with me when I got this. We were in high school. Senior year, I think, leaving the Northtown Mall on a Saturday night. Coupl'a kids from Shadle Park jumped us. There were four of them and two of us, but we had balls back then. We could have run, but instead we fought like the devil. I ended up with nineteen stitches above my eye and a sprained wrist. Paul got a broken rib and a concussion."

"Sounds like he got the worst of it," Remy said.

"Paul wasn't much to look at, but he'd fight like a goddamn Tasmanian devil. And the more he fought, the more they went at him. Like they needed to prove they could break him. But he never broke. Oh, and he was a biter too," O'Brien said with a laugh. "Heard one of those kids had to get a tetanus shot because Paul broke the skin."

A fighter, Remy thought. *Tasmanian devil.* The man O'Brien described was a very different person than the Paul Bracewell that Remy had known.

"Paul never wanted to stay out here," O'Brien said. "Always dreamed about living in the big city. Making money. *Real* money.

Christine and I—that's my wife—we loved it here. Never had any desire to leave. Paul graduated and went off to Columbia. We knew he was never coming back. But it changed him. We only saw him maybe five, six times since we graduated high school. What's that, ten years? We'd talk or text occasionally, but…hell, life moves on. Once you have a kid, your priorities change. Did you know I was there the night he met Alena?"

"Really?" Remy said.

"Yeah. Christine's sister lives in Brooklyn. She had a baby, so we went to visit for a week. Paul had gotten comped two tickets to some fancy charity ball. You know, the kind of event where you buy a five hundred dollar ticket for free drinks. From getting beat up at malls to getting free tickets to fancy parties. Crazy, huh? So we go. Paul goes up to the bar for a drink, randomly chats up Alena Griggs, and the rest is history. The way he looked at her, he was a goner. Talk about being a good wingman, right?"

"Seriously. And all my friends complain that you can't meet people at bars."

"Who would've thought, you know? Truth is, I always really liked Alena. We all knew who her dad was, and thought she'd be like him. An asshole, I guess. But she was different. She was everything to him. But once they got serious, his life was never the same."

"In what way?" Remy asked.

"I think even though Paul dreamed of working in the big city, he was never a big city guy. Never cared much for glitz and glamour. And, well, you date Alena Griggs, it's like living in a disco ball twenty-four seven. That's not Paul."

"Being around that family, that company, you don't really understand it until you're part of it."

O'Brien nodded, solemn. "Alena loved him. Really did. I never had a problem with her. It's that goddamn father and his sycophants. They're vampires."

"What do you mean?" Remy said.

"Vampires. They drain you of everything that makes you human, and then turn you into one of them. They don't even pretend. Feed the beast, isn't that his slogan or some shit?"

"Close enough," Remy said. "Paul texted you the night he died. Do you know why?"

O'Brien seemed unsure as to whether Remy was on the level. His eyes narrowed. "You gonna leave, go right back to Griggs and tell him about this? And then I end up dead too? No thanks."

"End up dead? You don't really think…"

"That Rawson Griggs killed Paul?" O'Brien sipped his beer, put it down, and wiped his mouth. "I'm not saying that. But I'm not *not* saying that."

"Paul's blood alcohol level the night he died was off the charts. I personally saw him drink enough to stun a horse."

"Maybe so," O'Brien said. "But Paul knew it was only a matter of time."

"What was?"

"He figured one way or another being a Griggs would kill him. Only question was whether it would be Rawson or Paul himself."

"I think we got the answer to that."

"Did we?" O'Brien said. "Paul knew they were coming for him. He knew you getting in the way just pushed the timetable back."

"Come on," Remy said. "That's absurd."

But there was no confidence behind Remy's word. O'Brien was saying the same thing as Doug Rimbaud. And Remy was starting to wonder.

"You spoke to the NYPD the day of Paul's death, right?"

"They called before they found him. Yeah."

"About the text?"

O'Brien nodded. "They wanted to know if I knew where he was, if we'd spoken recently, if he'd said anything that could help the investigation. That text was the first time I'd heard from Paul in a few months."

"Did you tell the NYPD you thought Rawson was involved?"

"Fuck no," O'Brien said. "Griggs has the goddamn former mayor of New York on his payroll. You don't think word would get back to Griggs?"

"The last time you spoke to Paul," Remy said, "what did he say?"

"He was scared. Griggs had banned him from strategy meetings. Paul knew he was being cut out of the loop. He told me he'd been speaking with another campaign. Feeding them info."

"He told you that?"

"Yeah. And whenever he called or texted, it was either from a private number or a strange phone with area codes in, like, Idaho. It was all very weird."

The burner cells Rimbaud had mentioned. Rimbaud was telling the truth.

"He talked about leaving Alena and coming home. I don't think he thought it was realistic. You don't just divorce a Griggs and walk away."

"I believe you about Paul. That he was acting as a mole within the organization. But why did he start? He couldn't have just decided to ruin his life for the fun of it."

O'Brien sat back. "I'd never met anyone in my life who was better with numbers than Paul. About a year ago, we're catching up on the phone. He's telling me that he and Alena have started to talk about having a family. I say that's great, you know, and joke that the kid's grandfather will probably buy him an Aston Martin before he can legally drive. Then Paul goes all quiet."

"Why?"

"He tells me that he and Alena use the same accountant as Rawson. Paul being Paul, he had to be involved in everything finance-related. The Griggs accountant, Benson something, he was one of those 'I'm away from my wife and kids for a night so I'm going to go on a bender' types. Paul met him for drinks one night, and apparently he got bombed on tequila shots and told Paul there were major discrepancies in the accounting for a whole lot of Griggs properties."

"What kind of discrepancies?"

"For example, the Griggs resort in Scottsdale lost money eight straight years, to the tune of something like a hundred and twenty million. But then, two years before Rawson decides to run for President, revenue at that resort suddenly quadruples out of nowhere. Go figure."

"The economy improved," Remy said.

"Not a chance. Paul told me that the Scottsdale resort operated for eighteen months at ninety-eight percent capacity. That's unheard of. The industry average is about seventy-three percent. Not only that, but after eight years of losses, the hotel ADRs *increased*."

"ADR?"

"Average daily rate. It's the average price paid for each room at a given property. Now, normally, when a resort is failing, like the Griggs Scottsdale property, the ADR goes down. You lower the prices to try to attract more customers. But the Scottsdale resort, despite losing buckets of money, actually *raised* their prices."

"Almost like they knew somebody would book at those higher prices," Remy said, "even though they hadn't been previously."

O'Brien nodded. "Exactly. Paul couldn't explain it. But he knew it wasn't on the up and up. And because the Griggs Organization is privately held, they don't need to let anyone know where the money is coming from. Paul had an idea, though."

"Which was?"

"Last winter, the prime minster of some country with a funny name stayed at the Griggs hotel in Washington, D.C. Keergee something."

"Kyrgyzstan."

"That's it. Anyway, the Griggs D.C. hotel had lost eighty million in seven years. The prime minister stayed for four days. But the hotel operated at *one hundred* percent capacity for the two weeks before *and* the two weeks after the prime minister's visit."

"Let me guess: all paid for by the Kyrgyzstan government."

"You take that. The Scottsdale property. And all the Griggs properties domestically, if not internationally. How many hundreds of millions of dollars were getting pumped into Rawson Griggs's bank account by foreign governments?"

"Did he have any documentation of this?" Remy said.

"I don't know," O'Brien replied. "But Paul started to get scared. He stopped calling, stopped texting. He sent me letters in the mail. I mean, who sends actual letters anymore? Funny enough, Paul figured the one way Rawson couldn't track him was by using the good ol' USPS. So when I heard that those thugs who attacked Paul were from Kyrgyzstan, I knew he wasn't paranoid. Somebody really was out to get him."

"Rawson banned Paul from his campaign meetings," Remy said. "He knew something was wrong."

"And that's why, if I had to bet my life on it, Rawson Griggs had something to do with Paul's death."

"Did Paul ever mention someone by the name of Doug Rimbaud?" Remy asked.

"No. Should I know that name?"

"Not necessarily."

Remy heard footsteps approaching, and O'Brien's wife joined them. He recognized her from the cemetery. She was plain yet attractive, with shoulder length red hair tied back in a ponytail. She was also sporting a very noticeable baby bump.

"Hey, hon," O'Brien said. "Chrissie, this is Jeremy Stanton. He was at Paul's funeral today. This is my wife, Christine."

Remy stood up and extended his hand. Christine shook it.

"You're the guy who was on the news a while back," she said.

Remy nodded. "I'm so sorry about Paul. I understand you three were close."

Christine shook her head and started to tear up. "You don't think people you grew up with could be gone so young," she said. Christine looked at her husband, skeptical. "Is he…with Rawson?"

"I am," Remy said, "but I'm here on my own. Mr. Griggs doesn't know."

"Jeremy is here about Paul," O'Brien said. "He's okay. Babe, let me ask you a question. Was Paul the kind of guy who made things up? You know, exaggerated?"

Christine laughed. "I think Paul was the most even-tempered guy

I ever met. I remember when we saw the first *Lord of the Rings* movie in theaters. Oh god, Paul was dating that girl, what was her name... Louisa. You know, the one who always chewed gum loudly. Anyway, when we left the theater, Paul said it was the best movie he'd ever seen. I remember you asked him why, and he said, 'I dunno. It was pretty good.' That kind of sums Paul up. He would describe the best thing ever as 'pretty good,' like you'd talk about hand towels."

O'Brien looked at Remy as though that anecdote proved his point.

"Congratulations, by the way," Remy said. "When are you due?"

"April," Christine said. She patted her stomach. "Can't wait for this little guy to start kicking *outside* of me. I just hope his sister is ready to have some competition for all the attention in our family."

"Paul always wanted a family," O'Brien said. "When they were dating, Paul always talked about wanting kids with Alena. But then as time went on, Paul hesitated. He said he was scared to raise a kid in that family. Photographers everywhere. No privacy. And their kids would never know whether they earned what they got, or whether it was just Alena's name that opened doors for them. That's not a normal childhood."

"Maybe he should have stayed with Louisa," Christine said. "We could have done something about that gum habit. He would have been a terrific dad."

"I'm sorry you never got to see him have a family," Remy said. "I wish I'd known him better. I regret that I didn't."

"I just...don't understand what drove him to this," Christine said. "He was a happy guy. He could be a little introverted, a bit moody, but I can't imagine him letting this happen. You just never know what's really going on with some people."

O'Brien looked at Remy. Obviously his theory about Paul's death and his hatred for Rawson Griggs were unknown to his wife.

Remy stood up. He took out his wallet and removed his Griggs business card. "Do you have a pen?"

"Oh, sure." Christine took a pen from a drawer and handed it to Remy. Remy flipped the card over and wrote on the back. He handed it to Michael.

"That's my personal email. If you can think of anything else, that's how to reach me. You have my word that none of this reaches Rawson."

O'Brien flicked the card between his thumb and finger like he was debating whether to tear it in half. Finally, he nodded and shoved it in his pocket. Then O'Brien took a card out of his wallet and handed it to Remy.

"In case you need anything else. You seem straight. Thank you for caring."

Remy took the card. "One more thing," Remy said.

"Shoot."

"Paul's text. The night he died. Can I see it?"

"Sure," O'Brien said. "It's nonsense."

O'Brien opened his message app, scrolled down, then showed Remy.

The night he died, Paul had texted "TK GZP" to O'Brien.

"See? Nonsense."

"You're probably right. But just in case." Remy scribbled the letters down on the back of O'Brien's business card.

O'Brien walked Remy out.

"Thanks for giving me the time," Remy said. He looked at his watch. It was almost two thirty. "Looks like I went over my fifteen minutes."

"No sweat," O'Brien said. "Appreciate you coming. Sorry we had to meet this way."

O'Brien held out his hand and Remy shook it.

O'Brien closed the door. Remy stood in the driveway, his mind swimming. He called the taxi dispatch number and a cab picked him in ten minutes.

When he arrived back at the Davenport, Remy went to the café and bought a pre-wrapped turkey club and a Dr. Pepper. He wasn't hungry, but it was an alibi in case anyone asked where he'd been.

Remy took the stairs. By the time he got to the sixth floor he was breathing heavily. Trevor would have laughed his ass off.

The hallway was clear. Remy entered his room and wolfed down the food. No new calls. There were no more calls, texts, or emails. His trip had seemingly gone unnoticed. He took a long shower, unable to shake what Michael O'Brien had told him.

Rimbaud had ulterior motives for making Remy doubt Rawson. Shaw was trailing. They needed to make up ground, and driving a wedge into a campaign was solid strategy. Seeds of distrust always grew.

But O'Brien had no motive. And what he said corroborated Rimbaud's story. Remy had no doubt that if Rawson discovered Paul was a Shaw informant, there would be hell to pay. But was he really capable of killing his daughter's husband?

At four thirty, Remy changed into khakis and a button-down and walked to Rawson's suite. Two security guards stood outside. One of them rapped on the door when he saw Remy. A moment later, the door opened from within. Murphy nodded at him, smiling thinly. Remy went inside.

Rawson was seated in a high-backed antique leather chair with gold studs running down the arms. He was still wearing his suit from the funeral. Murphy was dressed casually, like Remy.

The suite was enormous, with a full, ornate living area and a bedroom through a set of French doors. A large pot of coffee sat in the middle of a brass coffee table, along with a few plates of pastries and finger foods. Remy noticed immediately that the two coffee mugs were half empty, and the pastry plate had already been attacked.

Rawson and Murphy had begun the meeting without him. That may have been why Murphy called: to start early. Which meant Remy's absence had not gone unnoticed.

"Jeremy, please sit," Rawson said. He motioned to the couch. Remy took a seat next to Murphy. "How are you?"

"I'm alright. Crashed for a bit and had some lunch. How's Alena?"

"She'll be fine," Rawson said. A strange thing to say, Remy thought, considering her husband had literally been put into the ground just a few hours ago. "She's resting. She might join us for dinner later."

"Good."

Papers were strewn about the table. Remy picked up a pamphlet and reviewed it.

It was the latest *New York Times/Wall Street Journal* poll, and it was worrisome. Rawson's lead was down to just two points over Annabelle Shaw. And Richard Bertrand had broken thirty percent for the first time, on the news that he would commit to upholding the sale of firearms by private dealers and gut so-called entitlement programs to the tune of two billion dollars. Plus, several pro-Bertrand Super PACs had just committed to spend thirty million dollars in advertising over the next month across five swing states. Rawson had reason to be concerned.

"This is…"

"Shit," Rawson said. "It's shit."

"What are we going to do?" Remy said.

"It's already been done," Rawson replied.

Remy was confused.

"What's already been done?

"We've taken care of Bertrand," Murphy said.

Remy's eyes went wide. "How? Wait, not literally, I hope."

Murphy laughed. "They might wish that was the case tomorrow morning."

"What's happening tomorrow morning?" Remy said.

"We wouldn't want to spoil the fun for you," Murphy replied.

Rawson held eye contact with Remy for what seemed like a split second too long, and then took a danish and ate it in one bite.

They spent the next four hours going over Rawson's upcoming schedule, media hits, talking points, and surrogate appearances. Rawson called Alena. She didn't answer her phone, so they ordered room service.

Rawson would hit five swing states in the next two weeks, with rallies lined up in Miami and Denver, as well as bellwether counties like Valencia County in New Mexico, Bexar County in Texas, and Araphoe County in Colorado. Rawson was dying to flip Macomb

County in Michigan. Macomb was a swing county that had voted for Reagan in the '80s, but since then voted consistently blue. Rawson wanted to see BEAST signs in every driveway and hats on every head.

Finally, Rawson called it a night. They would depart Spokane the following morning. A car would them up at 7 a.m. to take them to the private airfield where Rawson's 757 was being held.

The three men shook hands, bleary-eyed and exhausted. Remy and Murphy left the suite.

After Rawson's door had closed, Remy turned to Murphy and said, "Hey, I thought the meeting was scheduled for five. Seems like you guys had been working a while."

"You know Rawson," Murphy said. "The man doesn't rest. You were asleep. We had stuff to do. Don't take it personally."

Murphy clapped Remy on the shoulder. There was a wretched feeling in Remy's gut that he'd been kept out of the loop. He wondered if this was how it started with Paul.

Remy went back to his room, changed, and got into bed. He turned on the television to try to take his mind off of things. News about Bertrand's polling surge blanketed cable news. Remy could picture Rawson in his suite punching holes in the wall.

Finally, he managed to get to sleep.

At 1:14 a.m., Remy was awakened by knock at the door. He shot out of bed, ran to the bathroom and splashed water on his face, then threw on a t-shirt. He knew Rawson was a night owl, but this was absurd.

He looked out the peephole and immediately felt his heart start to thrum in his chest.

It was Alena.

Remy opened the door.

"Alena, are you alright?"

She shook her head. She was wearing white cotton slippers and black sweatpants. Her hair was tied up in a messy ponytail. A loose, light blue t-shirt draped off her shoulders, exposing her collarbone. She'd lost weight. She looked so small, like she'd folded into herself.

"Can I come in?" she said.

"Of course," Remy said. He stepped out of the way and she came in. Alena held her hands in front of her, like she was embarrassed about something. "Is everything okay?"

"I just needed to talk. Being in an empty room after today makes me want to jump out a window. I can't deal with that right now."

"Alena, I…"

She went over to his bed and lay down on her side.

"Sit with me," she said. Remy sat down on the edge of the bed, his pulse quickening.

"Is this my fault?" she said.

"God, no," he said. "Maybe things weren't perfect. But you can't blame yourself. You never wanted this."

"No, I didn't," she said. Alena looked up at Remy. "I met with a divorce attorney. Paul never knew. Neither did my father. A few months ago. I was so unhappy. And so was Paul. We were killing each other. But…I never went through with it. God, I just wanted us both to be happy, and I knew that could never happen as long as we were still together."

"Sometimes the most difficult decisions are the ones you know will hurt like hell, but are still the right decision."

"Maybe. That pain would have been okay. It would have gone away, eventually. But this pain…"

"It will also go away. Eventually."

"God, I hope so," Alena said.

Remy looked at his hands. He couldn't say anything about his suspicions. About O'Brien or Rimbaud or what they thought about her father.

"Do you mind," she said, "if I stay here? I know it sounds weird. But I just need to feel warm tonight."

Remy nodded. "Of course you can."

"Lie down. Here. Next to me."

He pulled the covers down and got into bed. Alena slid in next to him. She smelled like moisturizer. Her eyes and nose were red and raw. She moved closer to Remy. Her body was warm. She laid her head against his chest, draped her arm over him. He could feel her breath on his neck. She closed her eyes. He could feel her heart beating beneath the pale blue shirt.

Alena was asleep within seconds. Remy watched her and felt an ache deep down that he hadn't felt…maybe ever.

Finally, he drifted off to sleep.

And when his alarm went off at 6:00 a.m., Alena was gone.

CHAPTER 19

Rawson Griggs's private airplane was a sight to behold. Affectionately known as Griggs Force One, it was a gleaming 179-foot beast, with custom Rolls Royce RB211 turbo engines that supported a cruising speed of over five hundred and twenty miles per hour. A standard Boeing 757 could seat over two hundred, but Rawson had his jet custom designed to accommodate only a small number of passengers, but provided them unparalleled air travel at the very height of luxury. In the main cabin there were forty plush white top-grain leather chairs, each with its own twenty-four-carat gold-plated seatbelt, along with hand-carved, polished wood tray tables and cushioned armrests.

The adjustable television monitors bracketed to each seat received over five hundred channels via satellite, including cable and premium channels, and the onboard Wi-Fi was better than Remy got in his own apartment. AV hookups allowed passengers to connect tablets or laptops to the television monitors, and each seat pocket came with a pair of white Beats headphones with a gold-plated connector.

There were separate dining and sleeping quarters. A small conference room seated twelve around a large mahogany table. Past the main cabin were two fully appointed guest bedrooms, with wood paneling and mohair couches. The master bedroom had a queen-size bed draped with all-silk linens, as well as a full-size closet and a bathroom with a granite countertop, gold fixtures, and a glass-paneled shower. Each room had a touch screen AV system that controlled that particular room's music, movies, and climate, as well as a made-to-order food and beverage menu delivered right to your door.

Rawson had purchased it for one hundred and twenty-five million dollars in 1997 from a now-defunct British airline that had sold off its fleet during bankruptcy proceedings. Upgrades over the years had cost another fifty million dollars. After Rawson entered the presidential race, he had given the plane a full makeover, including a red, white, and blue exterior, with the name GRIGGS in massive gold lettering across the fuselage.

A van picked the Griggs contingent up at the Davenport Towers at 6:30 a.m. Remy and Alena shared a knowing look, but nothing more. She was wearing jeans and a sweater, her face emotionless.

The four of them rode in silence to the airport. Remy kept refreshing news feeds on his phone, awaiting the Richard Bertrand bombshell. He knew they'd kept him out of the loop. And that scared him.

They boarded the jet inside a private hanger at Spokane International. Half a dozen armed guards escorted them inside, while several more took guard positions outside the hanger. As they boarded the plane, Remy saw Rawson check his phone, then hold it up triumphantly.

"It's live," he said.

Remy opened the *Gazette* app on his phone and waited for it to load. When he saw the headline, he actually gasped. He dove into the first chair in the main cabin and began to read.

LEAKED EMAILS SHOW BERTRAND, RNC, COVERED UP PAY-FOR-PLAY KICKBACKS

"The Governor sold out his constituents." —
Senator Annabelle Shaw

by Peter Drummond, *Daily Wire*

In one of the most extraordinary political hacks in history, the Internet activist group known as PoliSpill last night released thousands of emails obtained from Republican National Committee servers, including dozens sent to and from Louisiana governor and presidential hopeful Richard Bertrand. Included in the email dump were numerous correspondences between Bertrand, his lieutenants, and senior RNC party officials, including RNC chair Bryce Alvin, the most damning of which seem to confirm that Bertrand bestowed numerous perks and even pushed legislature to benefit donors who had contributed large sums of money to Bertrand's election efforts.

Walter Tollefson, CEO of Tollefson Pharmaceuticals, contributed nearly two and a half million dollars to Bertrand's gubernatorial campaign as well as Super PACs supporting Bertrand between 2008 and 2014. Tollefson was then granted at least twelve separate meetings with Bertrand and his staff over that period of time. Six months ago, Bertrand granted an exclusive contract worth in excess of fifty million dollars to Tollefson Pharmaceuticals for drugs to help combat the Zika virus as it spread in Louisiana. To date, there have been over twenty reported cases of Zika in New Orleans. One of the leaked emails also shows correspondence between Bertrand and Florida governor Dick Samuels, in which Bertrand seems to be attempting to convince Samuels to offer Tollefson a similar contract. In the heavily Zika-exposed South Florida region, such a deal could be worth multiples of the one Bertrand signed for Louisiana.

Spokespeople for Richard Bertrand, Bryce Alvin, and Governor Samuels did not respond to requests for comments by press time.

Doug Rimbaud, campaign manager for Senator Annabelle Shaw, the current Democratic frontrunner for president, said in a statement: "It is no secret that pay-to-play schemes have been a toxic part of Washington for years. But now Richard Bertrand and the entire Republican Party seek to bring this kind of explicit and shameful bribery directly to the White House. It is very clear from these emails that, if elected, Richard Bertrand would likely sell the Oval Office to the highest bidder."

When asked about the potential dangers in a foreign collective such as PoliSpill possibly influencing the election, Mr. Rimbaud declined to comment. However, GOP Senate Majority Leader Isaac Connell cautioned the Shaw campaign's exuberance.

"Any attempt by a foreign entity to influence this election should be taken with the utmost sincerity and caution. If PoliSpill is working to undermine the Bertrand campaign, we must ask what their motives are."

Rebecca Blum, campaign manager for billionaire businessman and populist Mayflower Party candidate Rawson Griggs, whose unprecedented campaign has him maintaining a small lead among most national polls, said, "From the moment Mr. Griggs stood inside Griggs Tower and declared his candidacy, he has told the truth. Americans are being sold out, lied to, and kept in the dark by politicians who place their own selfish interests above the nation. Rawson Griggs is not a politician. And any attempt by the Shaw campaign to pretend to be above the muck is laughable. We have no doubt that skeletons in her closet will not stay hidden much longer."

Responding to the concerns about possible foreign intervention in the upcoming election, Blum added, "However this information was obtained does not matter. Everything in them is true. The American people deserve to know the truth, regardless of the messenger."

Remy read the entire article, then remembered to breathe. Ken Murphy turned on the large screen television at the front of the cabin and tuned it to NBC. Alena went into the master bedroom without saying a word, closing the door behind her. A promo spot ran featuring Matt Lauer and Savannah Guthrie.

"At the top of the hour," Lauer said, "we'll be covering the explosive report in today's *Daily Wire* that alleges Pay-for-Play dealings within the Republican Party that could have disastrous consequences for GOP frontrunner Richard Bertrand."

Murphy turned to ABC.

After a few commercials, a promo ran featuring George Stephanopoulos.

"On today's show, we'll dive into the bombshell report that has the GOP in tatters, the Democrats cheering, but seemingly everyone else turning towards the upstart third party Mayflower candidate Rawson Griggs. What this means for the presidential race, on today's *Good Morning America*."

Murphy turned to another cable channel. A heavily made up anchor with shiny, black, immovable Lego hair said, "Can liberalism be linked to autism? Our investigation may shock you."

"Damn. I was hoping for a clean cable news sleep," Murphy said.

"It doesn't matter. Bertrand's poll numbers will be halved by next week," Rawson said. "If he drops out, Bobby Garrett of Wisconsin will become the presumptive nominee. Garrett has been a punching bag for the unions his entire career. And the conservative base likes him as much as they like eczema. Plus, he looks like a flaming doofus. He'll never top eighteen percent in a three-way poll."

"So it's really between us and Annabelle Shaw," Remy said.

Rawson tapped his chin. "I want a rally in Louisville within the next two weeks. Shift things around if need be. I want to go right where Shaw lives and steal her supporters from under her nose. Let the Bertrand campaign swing in the wind. Shaw might stick around. The DNC has a boatload of cash to throw around, and Wall Street loves her. But this will send a message that we will take the fight to her doorstep."

Remy said, "I'll get on with Rebecca and Jerry to plan it as soon as we take off."

"Let Jerry handle it," Rawson said. "You've had a long few days. Take a rest."

The comment caught Remy by surprise. Something was wrong.

Between the early meeting last night, and now being told to *rest*, it was clear Remy was being pushed aside. Could he know about Doug Rimbaud? O'Brien? Alena?

"With all due respect, Mr. Griggs, I'm here to work, and I'm here to win."

Rawson turned to Remy. He acted surprised.

"Is that right? You're here to win?"

"I gave up my life for this campaign. You know the answer to that question."

He seemed to consider this, then said, "Alright, winner. Get on the horn with Jerry. Schedule Louisville. The PoliSpill news throws a massive wrench into the first Republican debate, which is in three weeks. Remy, I want you, Rebecca, and Jerry to set up a policy speech on the night of the first GOP debate. Prepare for a monster."

"Where?" Remy said.

"Los Angeles. I want a large venue. A statement venue. California is a Democratic stronghold. I want to plant a flag there."

"Is a statement venue really appropriate for a policy speech?" Remy said. "Maybe somewhere a little more stately?"

"This won't be just a policy speech. I also want to put on our own pre- and post-debate shows to stream online."

"Most channels have the Republican debate locked on their schedule," Remy said. "Advertisers have paid nearly seventy-five thousand dollars for thirty second spots on the pre- and post-debate analysis shows. Nobody will run our event live."

"I don't want them to run it," Rawson said. "I just want to carve up the network audience. Then we threaten to run events on the nights of every Republican and Democratic debate going forward."

"Their ad rates will plummet," Murphy said.

"Exactly. And then they'll have no choice but to run our events instead of the debates. Maybe not every station, but enough. We hold their feet to the fire. More coverage of the Griggs campaign or we gut their ad revenue to the point where they won't be able to afford a green room."

"The networks will be pissed," Murphy said. "Advertisers will be up in arms when the ratings come in."

"And they will blame the networks, and force them to run what will draw higher ratings. Namely, us."

If Rawson could threaten the networks' bottom line, Remy thought, they'd be at his beck and call.

"Free media," Rawson said. "Ten times more powerful than the money these jokers are wasting on ads. And trust me, Los Angeles won't be a simple policy speech. We're going to give people something to remember."

Remy tried to sleep, and failed. He couldn't stop thinking about the PoliSpill news and Rawson's speech in Los Angeles. He had to admit, Rawson's plan was brilliant. He was gutting the Republican candidates who were already on thin ice after the Bertrand news. And strong-arming the networks, threatening their revenues, would force them to give Griggs even more coverage.

Despite this, it didn't sit well. Paul Bracewell had been buried less than twenty-four hours. Rawson's mourning lasted less than a full news cycle. It all coalesced into a stew that roiled in Remy's gut.

A flight attendant took food and drink orders. Remy wasn't hungry but figured he should eat something. He ordered a western omelet with a cup of strong coffee. The coffee was better than the omelet.

An hour later, Remy noticed Rawson head towards the back of the plane. He entered the bedroom where Alena was resting. Remy heard muffled shouting and ten minutes later they both exited. Alena looked angry, her face puffy, raw. She sat down across the aisle from Remy and closed her eyes.

He leaned towards her and whispered, "Hey, how are you?"

She turned towards him and offered a soft smile.

"I'll be okay," she said.

Remy placed his hand on his empty armrest. Alena did the same on her seat. An unspoken gesture. Then Remy saw Rawson bolt from his seat.

"Put on CNN," Rawson barked. "*Now.*"

Murphy put the television on. Wolf Blitzer was reporting. A chyron at the bottom of the screen read BREAKING NEWS.

"In breaking news this morning, we have learned of developments that promise to shake up not just the presidential race, but potentially the entire Republican party. Well-placed sources tell us that following a bombshell report in the *Daily Wire,* courtesy of leaked emails from the hacker collective PoliSpill, which detailed pay-to-play deals between Governor Richard Bertrand of Louisiana and a large campaign donor, that Richard Bertrand will be tendering his resignation as Governor of Louisiana, as well as suspending his presidential campaign. This comes as federal authorities, including the Department of Justice, are set to begin an official investigation into his dealings that led to tens of millions of dollars in federal contracts Bertrand gave to Walter Tollefson, a Bertrand donor. We also hear that RNC chair Alvin is under heavy pressure from not only the Democrats, but from some within his own party, to resign as well.

"If Bertrand does suspend his campaign, this would leave Senator Annabelle Shaw of Kentucky as the Democratic frontrunner with the GOP in absolute turmoil. In recent polls, Shaw has begun to inch closer to frontrunner Rawson Griggs. Shaw, however, still maintains almost record unpopularity even within her own party. Yet the GOP candidates next in line to take Bertrand's place atop the ticket have all been polling significantly lower than Governor Bertrand.

"This news may benefit third party Mayflower candidate Rawson Griggs the most, as his anti-Washington message gains more fuel. Yet as former New York City Mayor Phillip Costanzo said in an early morning tweet, "This is just the beginning. The Griggs train is going full speed ahead, and anyone in its way is getting run off the track.'

"Needless to say," Blitzer continued, "the mood this morning inside the Castle has to be jubilant."

Remy saw Rawson pump his fist.

"Gretchen," he shouted. A young, nervous-looking flight attendant appeared. "I have a bottle of Krug 1928 on ice in the galley. Break it open. A glass for everyone on board."

Gretchen skittered back towards the galley, and moments later they all had full glasses of ice-cold champagne in their hands.

"To Governor Bertrand," Rawson said. "And this is *before* they see what we have in store for them in L.A."

Remy sipped his glass, knowing full well Rawson was behind the leaks that just destroyed an entire campaign. He looked at Alena, still wearing her wedding ring, wondered how far Rawson Griggs was willing to go.

CHAPTER 20

The Boeing glided through the air, the blue and gold paint shimmering in the early afternoon light. It touched down at LAX, hitting the runway smoothly, bouncing briefly before slowing down. It came to a halt in the middle of the runway in front of several hundred Griggs supporters who had been waiting for the arrival of the frontrunner for president of the United States.

They had been waiting on the tarmac for hours, cordoned off behind velvet ropes like they were awaiting entrance to an exclusive club. A red carpet stretched out like an impossibly long tongue. A phalanx of reporters and camera crews jockeyed for position. Even in a city packed with celebrities, Rawson Griggs drew crowds to rival any of them.

The front door opened and the stairs descended, coming to rest at the foot of the red carpet. Ten campaign volunteers bounded down the steps as baggage handlers opened the cargo hold. They removed dozens of boxes, laid them on the ground, and opened them to reveal several hundred copies of Rawson Griggs's bestselling book *Be Bold, Be Loud, Be a Beast*. Each volunteer grabbed a box of books and handed out copies along the red carpet. The crowd squealed with delight, holding the books in the air like they were winning lottery tickets.

Then Rawson Griggs appeared at the top of the stairwell, and the onlookers erupted in screams and applause. The chants of "Rawson! Rawson!" were loud enough to drown out arriving planes.

Rawson waited at the top of the stairs, smiling, waving, a king surveying his subjects. A slight breeze caused his tie to flutter. Then Rawson held up one finger dramatically and reached back into the cabin.

Wait for it.

He pulled out a fire engine red THE BEAST WITHIN! hat and held it aloft dramatically, like a golfer tipping his cap to the gallery. The crowd cheered as he placed it on his head.

Remy watched Rawson work the crowd from inside Griggs Force One with a sense of awe and detached amusement. Rawson took his time walking the red carpet. He shook hands, signed books, posed for selfies, and kissed babies.

Remy, Murphy, and Alena waited inside the plane. They'd been instructed to wait until Rawson reached the waiting limousine before deplaning, so as not to take attention from the candidate.

"Hail to the king," Murphy said.

"May he live forever," Remy added.

Alena was scheduled to leave the plane second, after her father. Her hair brushed against Remy's cheek as she peered out the window. Remy could tell she'd retouched her makeup before landing, applied a little perfume. She smelled like jasmine. She looked beautiful. Her spirits appeared to have lifted in the weeks since Paul's death. Focusing on the campaign noise allowed her to drown out the sorrow. She and Remy texted day and night, shared mini bar cocktails in hotel rooms to avoid the press—and the loneliness—pinged each other on social media to the point where people grew suspicious.

"You know, I never got a red carpet when I flew Southwest," Remy said.

"My dad knows their CEO," she said. "He can put in a good word. But come on, the movie options suck when you fly commercial."

"Plus you don't get gold toilets."

She laughed. "You mean not all plans have gold toilets?"

"Only the really classy ones."

Alena looked at Remy. "I want you to walk out with me," she said.

Remy was surprised. "But your father said…"

"I know what my father said. I want you to walk out with me. Walking alone just feels depressing. This is a happy occasion. I don't want anyone's sympathy, and I don't want photos with captions calling me a sad widow. I'd like to walk beside a friend."

Remy smiled and put his arm around her.

"I'd be honored," he said.

A black stretch limo waited at the end of the red carpet. Once Rawson finished on the red carpet, he got in. Alena walked to the front of the plane. Remy joined her.

"Ready?" she said.

"After you, my queen."

Alena stepped onto the stairway and Remy followed her. There was a hush, then a gasp, and then the crowd cheered like they were William and Kate. They strolled down the red carpet, arm-in-arm, and the crowd lining the red carpet ate it up. Remy knew this footage would be on all the news broadcasts.

Once they got to the limo, the rest of the contingent exited the plane to far less fanfare and they all headed to their destination.

Rawson said to Alena, "I thought I told you that when you followed me, you were to walk alone."

Alena said, "I changed my mind. I didn't want to walk alone."

"This campaign is not a democracy."

"You might run the campaign, but not me," she replied icily. "I asked Remy to walk with me. And he said yes."

Rawson took out his cell phone. The conversation was over.

At least this will be the most uncomfortable part of the night, Remy thought.

He could not have been more wrong.

The Hollywood Bowl in Los Angeles was a grand outdoor arena that seated nearly twenty thousand people. In its seventy-five-year history, the Bowl had hosted legendary artists such as Louis Armstrong, The Rolling Stones, Ella Fitzgerald, Elton John, and The Beatles. And Rawson Griggs had chosen the Bowl to hold his historic rally, the first in the venue's storied history.

The distinctive and massive semi-circular amphitheater shell sat below the iconic Hollywood Hills. Its architecture drew influence from the famous amphitheaters of ancient Greece and Rome. The shell itself was filled with hollow fiberglass spheres, which were designed by Frank Gehry, giving the Bowl incredible acoustics. They added visual flair to one of the most stunning arenas in the country. Green trees flanked the stage on either side. The hills were flecked with green and brown, the setting sun a gorgeous gold. The air was warm and inviting.

The stage was set for a memorable night.

Attendance were free to the public, available only through the Griggs campaign website. All twenty-thousand tickets had been snapped up in less than two minutes. The resale market was burning up, with eBay and StubHub offering "Griggs Bowl" tickets for upwards five hundred dollars a pop.

Kapinski had sent out a press release touting the overwhelming demand for the event. Rawson had spent the week taunting the "Rancid National Committee" all week on social media. He relished the first RNC debate would take place in a musty college auditorium, while the enormous Hollywood Bowl would be filled to capacity.

"Rawson Griggs wants to unshackle the potential of the American people," the release said, "and tonight, at this historic venue, Rawson Griggs will unleash the beast in all of us."

Rebecca Blum and Phillip Costanzo had stayed behind in New York to run the pre- and post-game show, which would stream live from the Castle. Blum and Costanzo were acting as hosts. Over a dozen guests were scheduled to make appearances, including a Super Bowl champion quarterback, his coach, an Oscar-winning actor—back in 1989, but still—a Grammy-winning country singer, businessman Peter Havana, star of the hit reality show *Money Piranha!*, and the cover girl from the 2003 *Sports Illustrated* swimsuit issue. Rawson wanted the rally and broadcast to resemble a sporting event more than a political event. Even Remy had to admit: you'd have to be a masochist to watch the Republican debate over Griggs TV.

The sky was a gorgeous, molten orange, casting a golden hue over the dome as the event staff prepared for the event. Adorning the stage were, by Remy's count, twenty American flags. A banner hung from speakers that read ALL BEASTS WELCOME! The lettering was as tall as Remy himself.

He stood at the back of Promenade 3, far enough away to be able to view the entire arena. Kapinski and Murphy walked the stage surrounded by technicians and security guards.

With the Griggs TV component, it was imperative everything ran on time. Delays and technical glitches were unacceptable. In just a few hours, the arena would be packed with Griggs supporters from around the country, and millions more would watch from their computers and mobile devices.

Remy had no idea what to expect.

The RNC had half-heartedly asked Rawson to reschedule. But given the turmoil surrounding the Bertrand withdrawal, that was like an umbrella asking a tsunami to help keep it dry.

It was an odd feeling, Remy thought, roaming an empty twenty thousand seat arena. Counting Griggs staff, security, and stagehands from the IATSE Local 33 union, there were fewer than a hundred people inside the Bowl.

Looking out over the Bowl, Remy thought about the early days of the campaign. Back when excitement coursed through his veins, when he woke up every day with a sense of purpose. He relished the attention, the fame, the influence he wielded. It was intoxicating.

Until it wasn't anymore.

The violence that had, months ago, seemed like the isolated plotting of two demented, radicalized young men now felt like it might be part of something far more sinister and calculated. And he was having a very hard time believing, after what Rimbaud and Michael O'Brien told him, that Rawson's hands were clean.

The line waiting to get into the arena was the length of several city blocks. Remy had never seen anything like it. Rawson's rallies had always been well attended, but this was something else. This was political Woodstock. ComicCon for America.

Men and women—and even babies—wore all sorts of colorful costumes. Men came dressed as Lincoln, Washington, JFK. Women dressed as Martha Washington, Jane Adams. And JFK. Babies wore hairpieces that made them look like miniature Ronald Reagans. Thousands brandished signs proclaiming their love for Rawson Griggs and America, usually in that order.

"Incredible, isn't it?"

Remy turned to see Rawson Griggs standing next to him. They watched the endless stream of ticketholders filing in, filling the arena.

"It is," Remy said.

"This country has never seen anything like this," Rawson said. "Reagan. JFK. Obama. They all had ceilings. They were shackled by the limits of their party. We have no ceiling. No limits. My whole life, I've broken down walls and barriers nobody ever thought were breakable."

Remy nodded. When Rawson said things like that, and truly believed it, Remy felt that fire burning in his gut. Seeing thousands of hopeful people marching inside was an awesome sight to behold. Rawson was right. This *was* a movement. But he couldn't shake the notion that there was a dark undercurrent to it. That he still didn't know the full truth. The full scope of what Rawson had done. Or what he could do.

"Do you ever wonder what you're doing here?" Rawson said.

"I'm working the event," Remy said. "Like you asked."

"Not *here* here," Rawson said. "You're being too literal. I mean here. With me. On this journey."

"Oh," Remy said. He considered Rawson's question. "I think about it all the time. I think about the night I met Alena and Paul. That if I'd stayed for one more drink at the bar, maybe met a girl, or just waited ten more minutes, I wouldn't be here right now."

"It's strange how the universe works," Rawson said. "I'm a believer, Jeremy. I believe that things happen for a reason. If you'd had that drink, my daughter might not be here either. Someone up there wanted you on that street at that moment. And now you're here. Just like someone up there wants me to lead this movement. I believe fate had a hand in all of it."

"I've always had a hard time putting stock in fate," Remy said. "I think people should take responsibility for their actions. Fate gives them an excuse not to."

"You're speaking about your mother," Rawson said. "Your father. I know about them both."

"Maybe I am," Remy said.

"You don't want to believe fate was responsible for what your father did to your mother. You want to believe he was capable of stopping it. There's an anger that weighs you down with every step you take."

Remy nodded. He felt his hands shaking.

"I understand that. I used to have that anger. I don't remember the last time I wasn't able to buy whatever I wanted. Persuade whomever I wanted. Have whatever I wanted. I'm on the verge of achieving something that has never taken place in the history of this great nation. And yet, I couldn't have the one thing that can't be bought."

"Liliana," Remy said.

Rawson put his hands on Remy's shoulders and turned him around so they were face to face.

"One day," Rawson said, "you could be a leader of men. Do you ever think about that?"

"I do," Remy said. "I have."

"Let me tell you a story," Rawson said. "A fable, actually."

"A fable?"

"Humor me," Rawson said. "There once was a lioness who lived in the jungle. One day, that lioness gave birth to a healthy baby lion. That small lion was her pride and joy. But one day, on a hunt, the little lion got lost and ended up amongst a herd of sheep. The young lion could not find his mother, so he ended up traveling along with the sheep herd. Months passed. The lion learned to walk with the sheep, eat among the sheep, drink among the sheep. Live among the sheep. Somewhere deep down, the lion knew he was just a little bit different from the sheep. But since he'd been living among them for so long, acting like a sheep was all he knew. In his mind, this lion was a sheep."

Rawson's grip on Remy's shoulders tightened.

"Then one day, an older lion came upon the herd of sheep and decided he'd eat one of them for dinner. But to his surprise, as he approached, he saw a young, strong lion walking among the sheep. As the older lion bounded towards the herd, the younger lion, thinking he was a sheep, ran for his life. The older lion chased the young lion all the way to a riverbank, where the young lion stopped and begged for mercy. 'Don't eat me,' the young lion said, 'I'm just a poor sheep.' But the older lion said, 'Look. There. In the water.' The young lion looked, and he was shocked to see that the reflection in the river looked just like the older lion. The older lion told the young lion to roar. The young lion hesitated. The old lion repeated the order. Finally, the young lion reached deep down and let forth a roar that shook the very ground. And, finally, the lion realized just who, and what, he was."

"You're saying I'm the young lion," Remy said. "And you're the older lion. And you pulled me from the sheep herd and showed me who I was. The beast."

Rawson shrugged. "Every fable is up to interpretation," he said. "When I learned who you were, I made it my job to know everything I could about you. Were you really some random hero? Or was it, perhaps, fate that you were there that night?"

"And what did you learn?"

"There are many similarities between us. Many young men have ambition. Few of them can actually achieve it. With you, I saw the potential for achievement. But you still needed that push. When you joined my campaign, you got it. And your potential grew. You're not yet thirty. Your opportunities are limitless."

"Why do I feel there's a *but* coming."

Rawson smiled. "But you chose not to tell me you met with Doug Rimbaud."

Remy's blood went cold.

"How..."

"Part of the reason I got to where I am is because I know everything about everyone who works for me. I've known about Rimbaud for a long time. And yet I've allowed you to stay here."

"I wasn't sure whether to tell you," Remy said, stammering. "I thought if I told you, then..."

"I might think you were working both sides? Or that Rimbaud told you Paul Bracewell was passing along confidential information to Annabelle Shaw's campaign?"

"I didn't want you to think I even considered that insanity worth your time," Remy said. He was panicked, trying to stay ahead of Rawson's questioning. *How does he know what Rimbaud told me about Paul?*

"And if you really do know everything, you know I spoke with Rimbaud once. Only once, and he came to *me*. And that's last time I speak to him until we get that call from Annabelle Shaw's campaign conceding the election."

"Paul was a complicated man," Rawson said. "Marrying my daughter was the worst thing to ever happen to him. Paul was insecure. Paranoid. At the slightest touch, he shattered like a dropped glass on concrete. Paul and my daughter, they weren't right for each other. It took them too long to realize it. I always saw Alena with someone who had more...ambition. A lion. A lion understands that for his pride to survive, he'll often have to do things that may appear vicious. But when it comes to survival, nothing is vicious. Survival is its own justification. Winning this election, to me, is survival."

"Paul could have survived," Remy said. "We could have helped him."

Rawson smiled, as though humoring Remy's naiveté. "Some people can handle being part of a pride. Some people cannot. They fall behind. You saw Paul with your own eyes, that night at the Hyatt. He was desperate for an escape. He killed himself to find it, and he was sucking the life from my daughter while doing so. As soon as you put yourself in a situation where you need to be saved, you alone are responsible for your fate. I never asked you to save Paul. I asked you to be there for my daughter."

"And I have been," Remy said. "I'd go to the ends of the earth for her."

"Strangely," Rawson said, "I believe you."

"But I still feel guilty about Paul."

"Guilt is a fake emotion," Rawson said. Rawson moved his right hand from Remy's shoulder until it was just underneath his chin. Remy tried to pull away, but Rawson was impossibly strong, his fingers pressing into the flesh of Remy's neck. Hard enough to increase his pulse. "You're still here because I think you still have some value, and because my daughter cares about you. But if you speak to any other campaign, or discuss confidential information with anyone not authorized by me, not only will you be off my campaign, I will destroy you in every way you can imagine. Remember what I said about survival, and if you stand in the way of my pride. Trust me, Jeremy. I will make you wish you'd stayed in that bar."

Remy pulled away, breathing hard. A shiver ran down his spine.

"Now, enjoy the evening. It's almost show time."

Remy watched Rawson walk off, the knot of fear in his gut confirming that Rawson Griggs had just threatened his life.

Remy had seen Bruce Springsteen. Twice. He'd been smothered and nearly trampled at shows at Terminal 5, gotten drunk, once, at the Viper Room, seen Beyoncé at Madison Square Garden with Nicole, the spunky redhead. He'd been smushed among the masses down the

Canyon of Heroes the last time the Yankees won the World Series—also, the last time anyone cheered for Alex Rodriguez. But he'd never seen anything quite like the crowd that was packed into the Hollywood Bowl to see Rawson Griggs.

Twenty thousand souls jammed together to see perhaps the most famous man in the world. This was a policy speech like Woodstock was a poetry slam. The pre-game show began broadcasting from Griggs Tower at precisely the moment the television networks began their coverage. The chyron called it "Castle Cable News." It was streaming live on Rawson's Facebook page, Twitter, and was being carried on the homepage of every major network. A dozen Griggs surrogates live-tweeted the "coverage" using the hashtag #GriggsTV. Rawson was pleased when his show began trending above #GOPDebate.

A half dozen warm-up acts pumped up the crowd before the main event. Thousands of Griggs supporters danced and partied to patriotic rock songs, the night sky lit up by cell phone screens.

Remy worked the crowd, shaking hands, taking selfies, and giving autographs. It felt like he was walking around in someone else's body. And through it all, he could feel Rawson's hand on his throat, those words reverberating in his head.

I will make you wish you'd stayed in that bar.

Remy saw Alena standing among a group of older women. She was wearing a denim jacket with black leggings and gold hoop earrings: full on rock chic. She was the perfect combination of adorable and sexy. One of the women held a cell phone above them. She narrated into the camera, likely taking a video or posting on SnapChat. Remy walked by, careful not to interrupt, but one of the women, wearing a red MAMA BEAST hat, saw him and screamed like she'd won the PowerBall.

"Jeremy Stanton!" she shouted, hands going to her heart. "Oh my goodness. Carol, Rita, look!"

The other women spun around. The woman with the cell phone ran up to Remy, put a meaty arm around his waist, and said into the camera, "Y'all, I don't even know what to say. I'm here with an honest to god American hero. Mr. Jeremy, say hello please."

"Hello please," Remy said, offering a wide smile for the camera.

The woman leaned in close to the camera and whispered, "I'm a little embarrassed to say this but I think I might have accidentally touched this cute boy's butt."

"Careful," Remy said, "I might have to call security."

"Oh, and he's funny too!" Shirley said.

The other women laughed. One said, "Shirley, he's about as old as your son."

The camerawoman, Shirley, shushed her friend and said, "Nobody needs to know that! Mr. Jeremy, can I get a kiss?"

"Absolutely." Remy planted a big smacker on the woman's cheek, and she beamed like it was her wedding day. Remy could see Alena watching them, smiling.

"Well, look at that, I got kissed by a hero," Shirley said.

"Just don't tell Dale!" her friend shouted.

"Shush. Dale wouldn't know a kiss if it came with instructions."

Shirley turned the phone off and put it in her purse. "Thank you from the bottom of our hearts, Mr. Stanton. This night really just…I don't even know what to say. We're just so glad you're going to help Mr. Griggs get elected president. We need to put people back to work and bring our jobs back and get everybody to stop fighting with each other. My husband worked at an air conditioning plant outside Indianapolis for twenty-two years. Well, last April they closed the plant and sent all those jobs to Mexico. I believe Mr. Griggs can bring those jobs back and keep Americans working here."

Remy felt a wave of guilt. This woman had put her hopes and dreams on Rawson. And deep down, Remy had started to wonder if he was exploiting them.

"Ma'am," he said, "that's exactly why I joined Mr. Griggs's campaign. I want that too. Thank you so much for coming tonight, from the bottom of *my* heart. And tell Dale not to worry. There's no competition."

He hugged Shirley, who ran off to gloat to her friends. Remy watched them, conflicted.

"I had no idea you liked older women," Alena said, playfully nudging him with her shoulder.

"Only if they're older and married and know how to use SnapChat better than I do."

"One of Kapinski's people set me up with an account. All I want to do is learn how to use that filter where you get bunny ears," she said. Alena looked out at the massive stadium, the sea of people. All there because they believed in her father. "It's incredible, isn't it?"

"It is. What that woman said, about what she's hoping Rawson can do…that's why I'm joined him. Joined you both."

"It wasn't the money?" she said.

Remy laughed. "The money wasn't bad. You know, it meant a lot to me that you asked me to walk with you today. Especially since you went against your father. Couldn't have been easy."

"Sometimes I need to reaffirm that I have a say in what happens. Even to myself."

"Do you believe in this? In him?"

"I do," she said softly. "And I understand why other people do too." "Why?"

She shrugged. "My father has never failed at anything. He came from nothing. And now look at this. Winning is a drug to him. It's not in his DNA to lose. He'd rip his own heart out before he did."

"Do you ever feel like you've been pulled along? You had no choice but to be Rawson Griggs's daughter. And if he wins…"

"How much different can it get?" Alena said. "My life hasn't really been *my* life since I was old enough to understand."

"Do you think he gets that?"

"I don't know. We don't talk the way we used to. He knows I don't agree with everything he's doing. And he wants to keep me away from it. I don't want to have choose between Rawson the father and Rawson the candidate. But sometimes I look at him and I think he's different. And I'm scared that at some point I'll have to choose between the two."

Remy toed the ground. They stood in silence for several minutes.

Finally, he said, "We haven't talked about Spokane. That night at the Davenport."

"I know we haven't," Alena said. "I haven't really been sure what to say. Easier to just go on as friends."

"You know, you could have at least said thank you," Remy said.

"Ex*cuse* me?" Alena turned to face him, taken aback, but smiling.

"Well, I mean, I had a twin bed in that hotel room. It's kind of small. And you apparently spread out like one of those flying squirrels. Plus, you toss and turn like you're the girl from *The Exorcist* or something. And my ribs *still* hurt from all those elbows. So you *could* have said, 'Hey, Remy, thanks for spending the entire night dangling off the edge of the bed like a lizard.' Something like that."

Alena nudged him playfully. They stood there, arms barely touching. A current seemed to flow between them. Remy's heart was beating like mad. He wasn't sure why, but he put his arm around her. She moved in closer and leaned her head on his shoulder.

"Do you miss him?" he asked. "Paul?"

Alena waited for a moment. Maybe a moment too long. And said, "Sometimes."

"*Ma se tornando non m'hai salvato, a niuno in terra salvarmi è dato*," Remy said.

Alena turned to him. "*La Traviata*," she said.

"I've been listening," Remy replied. "If in returning you have not saved my life, then nothing on earth can save me."

"Remy Stanton. You are full of surprises."

Alena burrowed into him. He held her tighter.

Rocks in a storm, Remy thought.

The last warm-up band finished their set. A stagehand rolled out a red, white, and blue podium to replace the microphone stand. The lead singer, a middle-aged man with a big belly, a long gray beard and a longer gray mullet, wearing a head-to-toe stars-and-stripes jumpsuit with an American flag bandanna, stepped forward. His image was projected onto massive screens for people in the cheap seats.

"Ladies and gentlemen and my fellow kick ass Americans!" he

shouted.

The crowd roared back. A chant of "Griggs! Griggs! Griggs!" echoed throughout the Bowl.

"It is my patriotic pleasure to introduce the man of the hour, the man who was brought here by God himself to unleash the beast in all of us, please welcome *your* next president of the United States, Mr. Rawson Griggs!"

"God Bless the U.S.A." by Lee Greenwood blasted from speakers the size of minivans. Twenty thousand men and women shot to their feet. A deafening roar of applause and approval spread throughout the arena.

Remy and Alena stood together and watched as Rawson took the stage. He was tall, confident, and handsome. He wore a brilliant black suit, a bold red tie, and an American flag pin that appeared five feet tall on the video screens.

Thousands of cell phones immediately went up to record the moment, the night sky illuminated by a sea of bright white rectangles.

Rawson walked slowly. He waved to the crowd, pointing, clapping. He clasped his hands together and mouthed *thank you* over and over. When he stepped to the podium, Rawson grabbed the microphone, leaned into it, and shouted, "Is this a great country or what?"

"Yes!" came the thunderous response.

"And is there anything in the world like a Rawson Griggs rally?"

Twenty thousand people screamed in unison, "No!"

"Are there any beasts in the audience?"

"Yes!"

Rawson waited until the "Griggs!" chants died down. Then he spoke.

"On the other side of the country," Rawson said, "a debate is taking place. Six men and three women who represent a party that has been stealing the American dream for too long. The brilliant lessons about honesty, resilience, hard work, and self-reliance taught by Lincoln and Reagan have been forgotten. And next week, another debate will take place. Four men and two women representing a party that has long pandered to minorities and the downtrodden, promising a better future in exchange for votes. This Trojan Horse Party has played identity politics for decades. But as the American people have suffered, these two parties have remained silent. They hear your cries as they count their ballots."

"I am not here tonight to ask for your support so we can keep the status quo. I'm here tonight so we can bring this movement, this beautiful, unprecedented movement, to the steps of the White House. We will march through the corridors of power and to tell the snakes in charge that they're no longer welcome. The men and women who have put their own interests above those of the American people will no longer be welcome. They have picked your wallets clean and raped your cities and towns for decades. This. Ends. *Now*."

A chant of "This ends now!" reverberated throughout the amphitheater.

Rawson continued.

"The *Lügenpresse*, as they were once known, wants you to believe that our movement should not be taken seriously. They want you to think that an outside-the-box third party candidate has no chance at being elected president. They want to keep you comfortable on the bed of nails that Washington has made for you. They don't want to report the truth because they're bought and paid for. They don't care about the thousands of patriots who stand in this arena today, praying for a better future for themselves and their families. I stand before you tonight, humbly, saying that betting against Rawson Griggs is a losing bet. We will no longer send our jobs overseas. We will not send our troops to die to protect other governments that will not protect us. We will no longer spend blood and treasure propping up countries that offer nothing in return. We will build bridges with nations that have our best interests at heart and create the worldwide superpower we were always meant to be."

More cheers. Rawson waited.

"My first acts as president," Rawson said, "will be to remove all of the useless sanctions that have been strangling our businesses and stunting job growth for decades. For years we have suffocated our great companies and alienated potential trading partners. The days of saber rattling are over. We will extend an economic olive branch to the world. And if they can work with us, then we will work with them to raise our economy to heights never before reached.

"In addition," he said, "we will no longer respect outdated agreements signed years ago, obsolete in a world where these strategies no longer apply. We will immediately be withdrawing from NAFTA."

The crowd cheered.

"The Trans-Pacific Partnership."

The crowd grew louder.

"And the Geneva Conventions."

The crowd boiled over.

"Jesus Christ," Remy said. "Did he say he's pulling out of the Geneva Conventions?"

"You cannot put out an inferno with a bucket of water. And we cannot have a military strategy that handcuffs our brave men and women and prevents them from defending our nation in whatever way necessary. When I am elected, we will rain down a fire on our enemies that will burn hotter than anything they have ever known. If that means considering a nuclear option, so be it."

Remy looked at Alena. *Nuclear option?* He could tell from the look on her face that she was completely unaware of what her father would say tonight.

"Make no mistake," Rawson said. "I do not take these responsibilities lightly. These are tough decisions. But our country depends on them. The rules of war and combat have changed. Wars are waged not just with bullets and bombs, but with computers and smart phones. We must be prepared to adapt to this new form of cyber warfare. Because I promise you, our enemy does not care about treaties. They are planning their next move as we speak. And under a Griggs presidency: we will be ready. We will not treat enemy combatants with kid gloves any longer. People will once again fear us. They will fear the great beast."

A chant of "Beast! Beast! Beast!" broke out.

"A few months ago," Rawson said, "my family and my friends were attacked by two vicious, soulless criminals. I will not repeat their names, because they do not deserve to be recognized."

A loud voice rang out over the silence: "They should burn in hell!"

The crowd cheered their approval, and Rawson allowed a slight smile. "I have no doubt that's exactly where they are. But these two men—and I hesitate to call them that—came to this country legally. They were granted legal status here. They were allowed to work, to play, to live among us. Maybe you crossed their path at some point and never even knew it. Maybe they smiled at your daughters. Maybe they served you coffee. And more of them could be walking our streets right now. They could be in line with you at the grocery store. Giving your children candy at Halloween. Letting us get complacent before they strike."

Rawson took a deep, dramatic breath.

"It is not enough for us to be vigilant against terrorism. We have been on the defensive for too long. We must take the fight to *them*. Not just on the battlefield, but in our own cities and counties."

Rawson's voice grew louder as he spoke the words that would ring throughout the country.

"On day one of the Griggs presidency, I will instruct both Homeland Security and the department of Immigrations and Customs Enforcement to thoroughly vet every man, woman, and child residing in the United States who was not born here. This includes green card residents, illegal aliens, and anyone who intends to travel to this country. We cannot keep our nation safe if we have no idea the quality of people within its borders. If I handed you a box of one hundred crayons and told you ninety-nine of them were safe, but one was an explosive, would you let your child play with it? Evil does not play by normal rules. So neither will we. We will create residential detention centers to house these people while law enforcement vets our citizens properly and thoroughly. It may sound inconvenient. It may sound severe. But I would much rather inconvenience the few for the safety of the many. How many lives would you inconvenience to stop a killer?

Personally, I'd rather keep them off the street than take a chance."

There was applause, but the crowd seemed shocked into silence. Remy thought to himself, *What the hell are residential detention centers?*

"Would you let your child play with something that had even a one percent chance of doing them harm?"

"No!" came the roar from the crowd.

"And neither will we," Rawson said.

Remy looked at Alena. She was watching her father, her face expressionless.

"If you're with me," Rawson bellowed, "stand up! If you place the safety of this country above the cronyism of the elites, above the social justice warriors who put strangers and foreigners above their own neighbors, put your right hand in the air, raise it high, and say, we're with you, Rawson!"

Nearly twenty thousand people leapt from their seats. A sea of hands shot into the air, shouting in unison, "We're with you! We're with you!" at the top of their lungs. Remy stood there, rooted in place. His arm was at his side.

The Hollywood Bowl had turned into a great roiling sea, twenty thousand strong on their feet, pledging allegiance to a man who was promising to keep them safe, to bring back prosperity, to deter evil. By any means necessary.

Despite what Rimbaud and O'Brien had said Rawson was capable of, Remy had retained a sliver of doubt. Now, his doubts were gone.

He had traveled around the country sleeping four hours a night, forsaken his friends, given up his life to try and help this man become leader of the free world.

Suddenly, Remy felt sick to his stomach.

Remy looked at Alena. Hundreds and thousands of people all around them had their hands raised proudly in the air, declaring their love for Rawson Griggs.

Rawson's daughter stared at the ground. Her arms hung limply by her sides.

WINTER

CHAPTER 21

LEAKED DOSSIER ALLEGES SENATOR ANNABELLE SHAW'S HUSBAND WAS LONGTIME CLIENT OF INFAMOUS D.C. MADAM:

Bombshell report drops as Shaw narrows Griggs gap

by Peter Drummond, *Daily Wire*

Photocopies of a ledger purportedly belonging to Kimberly West, a high-profile Washington, D.C. madam, allegedly show that Philippe Shaw, husband of Senator and Democratic presidential frontrunner Annabelle Shaw, was a regular client of West's. The emails were obtained by the hacker collective PoliSpill, which was also responsible for the leaks that led to the resignation of Governor Richard Bertrand. Emails obtained from Mr. Shaw's private server allegedly show that both Senator Shaw and the DNC were aware of Philippe Shaw's dalliances, following a state inquiry into Mr. Shaw's possible illegal use of state credit cards for personal expenses. The emails suggest that both the DNC and Senator Shaw paid West sums totaling nearly $500,000 over the last six years to keep her husband's activities a secret.

West has been long-rumored to "serve" a clientele that includes many D.C. powerbrokers, sports icons, and foreign dignitaries. Yet this is the first time West's infamous "diary" has ever been seen by the public.

In the pages obtained by the *Wire*, Philippe Shaw's name appears no less than eighteen times. Mr. Shaw, who is referred to in the dossier as Mr. Arthur Lee, is listed as having made appointments with various pseudonymous West employees such as Veronika, Jade, Krystal, and DiamonDD.

Ms. West commented via email, "I'm not one to judge peoples' personal behavior, but I'm just not sure I can vote for a woman whose husband was clearly so unhappy at home that he needed to come to me and my girls for comfort."

These emails come at a particularly inopportune time for Senator Shaw. In recent polling, Shaw has consistently been within the margin of error, and is down just three points nationally to frontrunner Rawson Griggs of the Mayflower Party.

Following the suspension of Governor Richard Bertrand's campaign, Wisconsin Senator Bobby Garrett has eked to the front of the GOP field.

However, Garrett has routinely polled far behind Shaw and Griggs. CNN's poll of polls has Garrett behind by double digits in both two- and three-person races, and the analysts widely see the presidential race coming down to Senator Shaw and Mr. Griggs.

Neither Senator Shaw nor the DNC responded for comment before press time.

CHAPTER 22

The crowds grew larger. As did the resistance. The bitter chill of New York winter had settled in. Following Rawson's speech in Los Angeles, both the press and a fairly large swath of the country had turned solidly against Rawson Griggs.

A recent op-ed in the *Wall Street Journal* read:

Rawson Griggs's "speech" in Los Angeles was the most startling display of nativism by a mainstream politician since the infamous "Klanbake," where the resurrected Ku Klux Klan maintained tremendous influence at the 1924 Democratic National Convention and brought shame to our nation. And that a man with no governmental or military experience would suggest the use of nuclear weapons as a legitimate option was both stunning and terrifying.

On CNN, a former presidential press secretary said:

"Rawson Griggs seems to believe that FDR's executive order 9066, which evicted 120,000 Japanese-Americans from the west coast and into internment camps, and remains a blight on the great history of our nation, didn't go far enough in peeling back our civil liberties. Thank about all the progress we've made. Rawson Griggs, by sheer force of ego, cult of personality, and money, wants to literally turn back the clock

seventy years."

In the *New York Times*, a columnist wrote:

It is startling that the so-called "Griggs TV" show would feature a senator-turned-lobbyist like Brent Scott, who has not only raised millions for pro-Griggs Super PACs, but has longstanding ties to the Kremlin. Scott has lobbied for years for the U.S. to ease their sanctions on Russian-imported energy. Mr. Griggs's embrace of Senator Scott, combined with his unwillingness to be transparent about his international debts and conflicts, should shake Americans to their core.

Every morning there was a deluge of stories attempting to eviscerate Rawson Griggs, in every media outlet from Bangor to Seattle, from Austin to Fargo. Every day, Remy expected that the next set of polling numbers would show Rawson cratering amidst the backlash. That Annabelle Shaw would finally overtake him.

But they didn't. Following the leak of the West Dossier, Shaw had begun to lose ground. Rawson's lead was a solid six points nationally.

Remy had lost weight. He was lethargic, moved like an automaton. He was subsisting on buckets of coffee and moist hotel sandwiches that always left his tongue feeling like the underside of a couch. He had turned twenty-nine late in the year, but felt twenty years older. He was pale. The bags under his eyes could have hidden car keys.

And every time Remy appeared on television, Trevor would text him. They were rarely complimentary.

Dude, you look like stuff I scrape off the bottom of my shoe. Are you really going to work yourself to death for this asshole?

Remy could never come up with a response.

Paul Bracewell's death had slowly faded from public consciousness. Remy spent every moment he could with Alena. She was the only person on the team he could speak with, who he could trust. Alena seemed detached from her father. They spoke less and less. Her guidance, once constant and necessary, was non-existent. She rarely came to strategy meetings, and her absence from the campaign trail had not gone unnoticed by the press. Rawson claimed he was limiting Alena's exposure out of safety concerns.

In December, *Time* magazine named outgoing President Owen Gladstone their Person of the Year.

Though the Gladstone presidency will be damned, most likely, with faint praise, it can be looked at as the harbinger of a new era of politics, where decorum and experience play second fiddle to bombast and anarchy. In the wake of President Gladstone, we have witnessed the detonation of the Republican Party, the seamy cronyism of the Democratic Party, and the rise of a man who seems to have the greatest chance at electoral victory from a third party candidate since Teddy Roosevelt formed the Progressive Party in 1912. In 50 years, Owen Gladstone may not be remembered for much. But what he wrought on the country might be felt for generations.

Rawson continued to hold massive rallies that purposefully conflicted with the presidential primaries. Twenty-five thousand people packed the Ladd-Peebles stadium in Mobile, Alabama, which coincided with the second Democratic debate, which had been whittled down to Annabelle Shaw and Herman Levine, an ultra-progressive congressman from Connecticut.

Another thirty-four thousand packed the KI Convention Center in Green Bay, Wisconsin on the night of the GOP primary at Hofstra University. The moderator led off the debate by stating, "Rawson Griggs is currently campaigning in Governor Garrett's home state. At each stop, he has drawn massive crowds. My question is for each of the candidates: why do you think Mr. Griggs's message is appealing to so many Americans?"

When word about the debate questions filtered down to Rawson prior to his event in Green Bay, he took the stage in an arena filled with over thirty thousand supporters and said, "I'm proud to say that, tonight, Rawson Griggs has won a presidential debate he did not even participate in."

Remy went weeks without setting foot in his own apartment. Rawson Griggs appeared to be firmly in the driver's seat. The negative coverage only seemed to embolden Rawson's drive and strengthen his bonds with his supporters, who saw him as a victim of the media.

Remy watched with awe, fascination, and dread. Yet everywhere he went, he couldn't shake what he'd learned from Paul Bracewell, Michael O'Brien, and Doug Rimbaud. He thought about Rawson's barely veiled threat at the Hollywood Bowl. It gnawed at him every time he boarded Griggs Force One, every time he woke up in a hotel bed unsure of what city he was in or why he'd agreed to give up his life for this.

He wanted to leave the campaign. *Needed* to leave, desperately. But if Rawson really was capable of doing to Paul what Rimbaud and O'Brien thought, what would he do to Remy?

Money was pouring into pro-Griggs Super PACs like a busted hydrant. Ben Scott's PAC had spent nearly one hundred million dollars, and every FEC report had them raking in more and more cash.

An investigative report in the *Gazette* by a reporter named Eric Celsun claimed that billionaire Las Vegas mogul Ira Morgenstern would be contributing nearly seventy-five million dollars to Griggs alone. Photos had caught the two having dinner at the St. Regis hotel in Manhattan. Morgenstern had donated nearly fifty million dollars to Republican candidates in the previous election, which was spread over thirty campaigns, including Bobby Garrett of Wisconsin. Between his own campaign war chest and the Super PACs, Rawson had enough money to support three campaigns.

Remy knew that every time the campaign posted their event schedule, every time Rawson tweeted his approval for an ad campaign, it was a sly nod to the fact that he was not beholden to the typical rules of campaign finance. Rawson himself had spent fairly little of his own money. He held campaign events at his own resorts, which he could then reimburse from campaign funds. He held private dinners at his restaurants, wrote off tens of thousands of copies of his own books which were given as gifts. For a billionaire, Rawson was being surprisingly thrifty.

The Griggs train appeared unstoppable. Which was why when

Remy saw Rawson approaching their private airplane hanger at LaGuardia airport one morning, jabbing his finger at Jerry Kapinski and cursing like he was getting paid per swear word, he knew something was very, very wrong.

"Where does that bitch get the nerve?" Rawson shouted, his face as red as the tie on his neck.

Kapinski stammered, "I honestly don't know. We're looking into everyone who has access to our servers. It's very possible she's going on pure speculation."

"It's not speculation," Griggs spat. "I know Rivas. She doesn't print shit unless she steps in it. Somebody leaked information to her. Somebody on *our* side. And if I don't know who within forty-eight hours, I'm firing everyone on my staff and replacing you with the next truckload of illegals that crosses the border. At least if they fuck things, they're only making five bucks an hour."

Jerry began to climb the staircase to board Griggs Force One, but Rawson stopped at the door and said, "Not yet, Jerry. I haven't decided if I'm going to let you on board."

Kapinski stopped and waited for Rawson to disappear inside.

Remy, large coffee in his hand, walked tentatively up to Jerry.

"What the hell is going on?"

Kapinski rubbed his eyes. He looked like he'd aged a year overnight. "The *Gazette* ran a story saying a source from inside our campaign confirms we're coordinating with PoliSpill. That we encouraged the leaks of the Bertrand and Shaw files. So now people are calling for an official investigation into the possibility that we've been working with a foreign entity to undermine the RNC and DNC."

"Jesus. Where did that come from? Who's the source?"

"I have no idea. But now that it's out there, it's a hard bell to un-ring."

"I mean, it's because of PoliSpill that Richard Bertrand dropped out of the race and Annabelle Shaw took a hit in the polls."

"Yeah. It looks bad. But Rawson is denying it emphatically."

"Did we?" Remy asked.

"Did we what?" Kapinski answered, narrowing his eyes.

"Did we coordinate with PoliSpill?"

"Absolutely. Not," Kapinski said, his voice unwavering. "Rawson says we didn't. So we didn't."

Remy thought back to the flight back from Spokane. Bertrand had appeared to be making a move. And the next day, PoliSpill leaked the pay-for-play scandal, nuking Bertrand's campaign and half the GOP.

Remy knew Kapinski was lying.

"Are you two done jabbering?" Rawson shouted from atop the stairway. "Get on board. Conference room. Now. We need to counterpunch."

Kapinski and Remy boarded the plane. Remy checked his *Gazette* app. Grace Rivas's story topped the front page. The headline read:

Inside sources:

GRIGGS CAMPAIGN COORDINATED WITH POLISPILL TO RELEASE BERTRAND/SHAW EMAILS

The article reprinted half a dozen emails sent from a blacked-out email server with a GriggsForAmerica.com address. The PoliSpill reply emails contained a .kg URL, which meant they'd been filtered through a server located in Kyrgyzstan. Though PoliSpill was headquartered in Sweden, several foreign governments were providing them with sanctuary and secure servers, which could then filter the group's communications through global networks to avoid regulation and law enforcement.

This signaled the possibility that the Griggs campaign, and potentially the next president of the United States, was coordinating with an unauthorized intelligence agency to influence the election on his behalf. And if that was the case, it could influence Rawson's future policy positions, allowing foreign governments influence over the leader of the free world.

The speculation was frightening. Damning. And Remy was a thousand percent sure that if those kind of allegations were made against any other presidential campaign, it would signal that candidate's death knell. But Rawson had proven damn near invincible.

The Kyrgyzstan connection bothered him. There were PoliSpill servers based in Kyrgyzstan. And following the failed attack on Paul Bracewell, Dastan Nogoyev and Alexay Usenov were scheduled to fly to Bishkek, Kyrgyzstan's capital.

Remy felt nauseous. But he couldn't let it show. Not just yet. Suddenly, something occurred to him. He took out his wallet and found the business card Michael O'Brien had given him. Written on the back was the text Paul had sent the night of his death. TK GZP.

They joined Rawson in the conference room aboard Griggs Force One. They drafted a response to the *Gazette* piece. By the time Remy finished reading it, he had made up his mind. Things were out of control. It was time to leave the campaign.

GRIGGS FOR PRESIDENT: UNLEASH THE BEAST!

Griggs campaign denies outrageous smears

The *New York Gazette,* which is less a newspaper than a propaganda machine run by the liberal elite, has resorted to spewing flat-out lies in order to see their preferred candidate enter the White House.

Grace Rivas is a parasite on journalism, and should be fired immediately. When Rawson Griggs is elected president, he will create new regulations in order to deal with media outlets that knowingly print false stories in order to defraud the American people. Rawson will make these outlets suffer legally, financially, and forcefully if necessary.

It is time to return this great country to its roots.

Rawson Griggs was placed on this earth to bring back
hope and prosperity, and god help his opponents who
aim to prevent that.

—Rebecca Blum, Griggs Campaign Manager

After the release was out, Remy logged on to social media to see
the reaction. Within minutes, near universal condemnation began to
pour in. It was called dangerous, unconstitutional, totalitarian. Remy
went to Grace Rivas's Twitter feed and checked her replies. He was
horrified. They threatened to cut her. Kill her. Rape her. Find her
family.

Remy stood up from the table. Griggs and the others were
preoccupied watching the cable news reaction. Remy left and went
back to the main cabin. He took a seat, opened up his personal email,
and composed a note to Grace Rivas.

It's Remy Stanton. We need to talk.

CHAPTER 23

The campaign rally at the First Niagara Center in Buffalo drew over twenty thousand ravenous Griggs supporters. Fred Hadley, the bombastic and portly head coach of the NFL's Buffalo Bills, offered an enthusiastic introduction.

"Only one man is capable of bringing back the country we know and love," said Hadley, his jowls shaking. "I know tough men. I spent twenty hours a day working with the toughest sons of bitches alive. And this man I have the honor of introducing today is the toughest son of a bitch I've ever met. We need tough men to take this country back. So let's join Rawson Griggs and unleash the beast!"

Remy worked the press pen, answering questions from reporters, pretending to care about his job, all the while praying the camera didn't pick up the fact that he felt like puking. He refreshed his personal email every thirty seconds, hoping to hear back from Grace Rivas.

Halfway through his speech, Rawson Griggs pointed at the back of the auditorium and said, "I would like everyone here to turn around. Look at the sorry group of men and women who get paid to print lies. After this wonderful event is over, they will print false stories and then go home in their limousines and drink wine from bottles that cost more than your mortgage. They will mock you for supporting Rawson Griggs. So look closely. See what the opposition looks like with your own eyes."

Thousands of attendees turned around and began to boo the reporters penned in behind traffic dividers like cattle. They had nowhere to go, nothing to do but take the abuse. Several attendees walked right up to the press pen, stuck out their middle fingers, and spat on the floor.

Remy refreshed his email again. There was an email from Grace Rivas. It read:

Name the time and place.

Remy checked the campaign schedule. Rawson had a dinner that night with the mayor of Buffalo and some influential county legislators, and in the morning would tour the shipping port on the northeast shore of Lake Erie. Griggs Force One was scheduled for wheels up at 1 p.m., and they'd be back in the city by three. Once they landed, there was a strategy meeting back at the Castle that would last several hours.

Remy wrote Grace back.

Tomorrow night. 10 p.m. Liberty Inn off the Meatpacking District. Room under the name Phil Rawlings.

A minute later, he got a reply.

10 p.m. at a no-tell motel under a fake name? Either you're really forward or you weren't kidding about needing to meet ASAP.

He replied.

Just be there.

He thought about Alena. He had no idea what to tell her, or how. Things were going to get ugly. He didn't care about Rawson, the campaign, or this godforsaken election any longer. But he cared about her. And he had no idea how to go forward without losing her.

The Liberty Inn was one of the few hotels in Manhattan that accepted cash. He needed to limit any electronic records. Given that Rawson knew about his conversation with Doug Rimbaud, he knew there were eyes and ears everywhere. Possibly in his own apartment. He had to take precautions.

Rawson's speech ended, to a round of thunderous applause. He exited the stage to *You Can't Always Get What You Want* by the Rolling Stones. The staff met backstage.

"That went well," he said.

Rebecca Blum pulled out an iPad and opened up their scheduling spreadsheet. "We have surrogates lined up to appear on four different networks this evening. Pushback on the *Gazette* piece is solid, there's a 'cancel the *Gazette*' movement on social media, and Costanzo is looking into Grace Rivas."

"What does that mean?" Remy said.

"It's not important," Blum replied. "If this does dent our polling, it will be minimal and short-lived. On the plus side, nobody on earth is talking about Bobby Garrett or Annabelle Shaw."

Remy said, "What about Grace Rivas? What's Costanzo doing?"

"We need them to know," Remy said, "that there are consequences."

As soon as they got back to their hotel, Remy emailed Grace: *Watch your back.*

She responded: *?*

I don't know exactly. But just be careful.

He spent the next few hours attempting to work, but couldn't take his mind off tomorrow's meeting with Grace. Remy had chosen to step off a cliff. He just prayed he wasn't attached to anyone when he fell.

The following day, after Rawson's tour of the port, complete with photo ops with the mayor and local stevedores' union, the Griggs campaign headed to Buffalo Niagara airport and returned to Manhattan. Remy barely said a word, and thankfully, the rest of the team was duly exhausted.

When they landed, they loaded into a van and a security caravan took them back to the Castle. In the War Room, they buckled down for a four-hour strategy session. Blum ordered half a dozen pizzas from the gourmet kitchen on the second floor. Remy scarfed down six slices of a meat lovers pie on his own.

At eight o'clock, the meeting ended. Rawson would stay to work with Rebecca Blum, but the rest were free to leave. Remy took the private elevator to the lobby and got a double espresso from the café. He noticed several tourists taking his photo. Remy stopped to pose for pictures, struggling to maintain a smile.

He had a small rolling suitcase, but Remy didn't want to go home to drop it off. His meeting with Grace wasn't for another hour and a half. So he withdrew five hundred dollars cash from an ATM, found a liquor store a few blocks from the Castle, got himself a six-pack of a good IPA, and took a cab to the Liberty Inn.

Remy checked in under the name Phil Rawlings, paid cash for one night, and went to his room on the fourth floor. The room was chilly and smelled like mold. He emailed Grace. *Room 412.*

Then Remy popped open a beer and drank. He watched the clock nervously, unaware of just what this night would set in motion.

At nine fifty, Remy heard a knock at the door. He looked out the peephole and opened it. Grace Rivas stood there, along with a man Remy did not recognize. She wore a Burberry pea coat, a smattering of rouge, and a touch of lipstick. She smelled like perfume, and looked like she'd come directly from a nice event. A date, perhaps.

The man was about forty, very thin, with a shaved head, rimless glasses, a bookish demeanor, and wore a *Ghostbusters* t-shirt under his jacket. He stuck out his hand before Grace could introduce him.

"Eric Celsun, *New York Gazette*," he said. "Pleased to meet you, Mr. Stanton."

Remy shook his hand.

Celsun looked around the room. "Any bugs in here?"

"I just checked in," Remy said. "I doubt we're being recorded."

"Not bug," Celsun said. "*Bugs.* Like, the crawly ones. This looks like the kind of hotel that has a lot of bugs."

"I honestly don't know. I can get you some Off if you'd like."

"It's okay for now," Celsun said. "Just…keep your eyes open."

"Thanks for coming," Remy said. "You didn't tell me you were bringing anyone."

"Figured this was important. Eric is a pit bull. Don't let the t-shirt fool you. I thought he should hear whatever you have to say."

"Fair enough," Remy said.

"So, this had better be important," Grace said. "I have to be in Ohio tomorrow morning to cover Rawson's rally in Hamilton County."

"You're going to that?" Remy said. "After I told you to be careful?"

"I'm not letting Rawson Griggs get in the way of my job," she said.

"I'm not worried about your job," Remy said. Grace seemed to understand that Remy was not overreacting.

"I assume you wanted this meeting because of the PoliSpill article."

"Partly," Remy said.

"It must have really struck a nerve with Griggs. That's why you emailed, right? Rawson sent you to ask for a détente?"

"Rawson didn't send me," Remy said. "Rawson doesn't know I'm here. Nobody knows I'm here. Except you two."

Celsun shifted. They looked at each other, starting to understand.

"So why *are* we here?" Grace said.

"Because I think Rawson may have done some terrible things. But I can't prove them. But I think maybe you can."

"Wait, you work for the Griggs campaign."

"Not anymore," Remy said.

"Jesus," Grace replied. "You withdrew?"

"Not officially," Remy said. "I'm out. But I still want access for as long as I can. But he needs to be stopped. And I can't do it alone."

"Alright," Grace said. "Talk."

"Those PoliSpill emails that were routed through the Kyrgyzstan server. I didn't want to believe it before. But now, it's too much of a coincidence to be one."

Grace put down her bag and took out a digital recorder.

"No," Remy said, putting her hand on her arm. "This is off the record."

Grace and Celsun looked at each other. She slid the recorder back into her purse.

"Alright then. This is your meeting."

Grace and Celsun sat on the bed. Remy pulled the desk chair over.

Remy's heart began to pound. This was the moment that would change everything. He could walk out. Say nothing. Go back to the Castle like nothing had happened, help Rawson Griggs get elected president, and see how far the Griggs train could take him.

But he also might never be able to sleep again, or look Alena in the eye again.

Remy took a deep breath and said, "I think Rawson Griggs had Paul Bracewell killed."

Grace's eyes widened and she took a deep breath. He heard Celsun whisper *holy shit*.

"Why?" Grace said.

"Paul was a mole for Annabelle Shaw's campaign. Rawson found out about it and tried to have him killed. The attack by Nogoyev and Usenov, Rawson was behind it. I gummed up the works."

"You think Rawson hired them to kill Paul? Jesus, that's a hell of an accusation."

"After Paul died, Doug Rimbaud came to see me. He told me Paul had been working for Shaw. He told me Paul was convinced Rawson was behind the first attack. That attack failed, and then after Usenov bombed the Castle, Rawson had to wait. The night I spoke at the Hyatt, Paul and Alena got in a fight. Paul was drunk off his ass. That was the final straw for Rawson. Paul was compromised, but also unstable. I think Rawson had somebody murder Paul and make it look like an accidental drowning."

Grace rubbed her eyes. Celsun whistled.

"I don't even know what to say," Grace said. "The fact that Doug Rimbaud came to see you is insane in and of itself. But without any proof or corroboration, there's no way we could print any of this."

"I know," Remy said.

"Do you know what Paul might have been passing to the Shaw campaign?" Celsun said. "If Rawson was really willing to kill his son-in-law, it must have been bad."

"I think it was," Remy said. "After Paul's funeral in Spokane, I spoke to a childhood friend of Paul's. A guy named Michael O'Brien. O'Brien said there were major discrepancies in Rawson's finances. That his properties had been artificially inflating their revenues, and were possibly being kept afloat by foreign governments."

"Griggs is a billionaire," Celsun said. "Why would he need to do that?"

"Paul had found documentation showing Rawson's properties were losing money hand over fist, and had been for years. Then, right before Rawson began exploring his run, the revenues skyrocketed."

Grace said, "As though somebody wanted him flush with cash in order to pay for a campaign. And since Rawson claims he's footing his own bill, he'd need tens of millions, at the very least."

"Presidential candidates are legally forbidden from taking donations from foreign sources," Celsun said. "But private businesses are exempt from that. So it's possible that someone was funneling campaign money to Rawson Griggs through his legal businesses."

"He's also been coordinating with his Super PACS," Remy said, "especially Brent Scott's. The PACs have footed the bill for a ton of Griggs events. It's technically illegal, but…"

"If there's no electronic trail," Grace said, "you can't prove it or prosecute."

"Plus fatcat donors like Ira Morgenstern have been dumping money into those PACS."

"Here's a question," Grace said. "If you blew up the hit on Paul, why on earth would Rawson offer you a job and make you such a prominent part of the campaign?"

Remy said, "He turned chicken shit into chicken salad. I had value to him. I was a hero. I was the guy everyone loved, and I was on Rawson's side. Standing on stage next to him, supporting him, it was a great American story. Rawson turned a giant fuck-up to his advantage. It's kind of brilliant, in a sadistic way."

"And now…what?" Grace said. "You're having a crisis of conscience?"

Remy got a beer from the fridge. He needed to calm his nerves. He took a long pull and wiped his mouth.

"I loved being a part of it. The hero. But if any of this is true, he should be in prison, not the White House. Your article, once I saw that the PoliSpill emails were filtered through a Kyrgyzstan server, I knew. Dastan Nogoyev and Alexay Usenov were scheduled to fly back to Bishkek, Kyrgyzstan after they killed Paul. Remember, they both came from Kyrgyzstan legally. There were no prior records. No red flags. No terrorist organizations claimed responsibility for their attacks. I think there's a connection between Rawson, the PoliSpill servers in Kyrgyzstan, and Nogoyev and Usenov's attacks. Rawson may have used that connection to hire two gunmen who could leave the country without a trace once the job was done."

"Kyrgyzstan itself is not a powerful country," Celsun said. "It has very low natural reserves, and corruption there is rampant. This is not a world superpower. It doesn't make sense for Rawson to risk so much to curry their favor."

"No, but he would risk it for money," Remy said. "The night Paul was killed, he texted Michael O'Brien. The FBI assumed it was gibberish since Paul was intoxicated. But look here."

Remy took out the business card O'Brien had given him in Spokane. He handed it to Grace. She looked at the back.

"TKGZP. I don't get it."

"No, there was a space between TK and GZP. GZP is the stock ticker for GazProm. GazProm is the Russian state-run energy company, which, coincidentally, recently purchased the totality of Kyrgyzstan's natural gas production for one dollar. That's right, *one freaking dollar*. GazProm is a five *trillion* dollar company that's primarily owned by the state. Kyrgyzstan's natural gas production industry was in debt forty billion dollars. They only export about a thousand barrels a day, which is peanuts compared to the monoliths like Saudi Arabia, China, and Russia. But GazProm swallowed up all those debts, and in doing so, claimed exclusive rights to export gas and oil from Kyrgyzstan. Think about that: a five *trillion* dollar Russian monolith buys a country's entire energy supply for one dollar. *That's* what Paul texted his friend. It wasn't gibberish. He was saying that Rawson is connected to GazProm."

"So you think Rawson helped broker an arrangement between Kyrgyzstan and Russia to wipe their debt clean?"

"That's exactly what I'm saying. And he used those connections to find two Kyrgyzstani assassins in the states who had clean records and could return to Bishkek unnoticed. I think Rawson was in debt up to his eyeballs. Maybe to Kyrgyzstan. Maybe to Russia. But someone decided to prop him up to run for president. They could support him with unlimited funds through Rawson's businesses. And then, once he was president, reap the benefits of a friendly administration."

Grace said, "That would explain the part of Rawson's speech where he talked about lessening foreign sanctions."

Celsun tapped a pencil to his lips. "It's also possible that Rawson Griggs has an under-the-table stake in GazProm. That could be where his debts come from. Global oil supply has been significantly higher than demand, which has driven prices down to the point where Russia's entire economy has been destabilized. They need more export partners. The Russian economy has been almost cut in half over the last few years."

Remy said, "I think Rawson bought a stake in GazProm. It would have cost him hundreds of millions, if not billions. And if he's elected president, he could get rid of Russian sanctions, allowing billions and billions of dollars in oil and gas exports to flow here. Rawson stands to make hundreds of billions."

"Look at this," Celsun said. He unzipped his backpack, took out a laptop, and booted it up. He plugged in a 3G SIM card. "Since the beginning of the campaign, I've been documenting every contribution made to the Griggs Foundation over the past twenty years. In 2008, the Griggs Foundation reported a five hundred thousand dollar donation from the LiK, which is an influential annual conference held in the capital of Kyrgyzstan. And in 2008, Rawson Griggs made a speech at the LiK conference in Bishkek, which was attended by about fifteen countries, promoting Kyrgyzstani life, as well as its various industries."

Celsun opened up a spreadsheet filled with hundreds of dates, figures, and names. He did a search and pointed to one line.

"Know what company also had representatives attending this conference?" Celsun asked.

"Let me guess," Remy said. "GazProm."

Celsun nodded. "Winner, winner, chicken dinner. LiK attendees included Vitaly Litvienko, chairman of the board of directors of GazProm. *And* Temur Kamurzenov, head of Kyrgyzgaz, Kyrgyzstan's state energy department, which was sold to GazProm."

"Temur Kamurzenov," Grace said. "That's the TK in TK GZP."

Remy said, "So Rawson speaks at the LiK conference, which hosts the head of Russia's largest energy company, plus the head of Kyrgyzstan's state energy firm, which was then sold to Russia."

"For one dollar," Celsun added. "And check this out," Celsun said. He turned the laptop to face them. He'd pulled up an article from a Kyrgyzstan news site written in 2008. It featured a picture of Rawson Griggs shaking hands with Temur Kamurzenov. And in the background, looking on with a smile, was Phillip Costanzo.

"Maybe the ex-mayor just likes pierogies," Remy said.

Celsun said, "Not to mention that Rawson's biggest Super PAC is run by former Senator Brent Scott, who used to consult for GazProm."

"So why doesn't Alexay Usenov go back to Kyrgyzstan after Nogoyev is arrested?" Grace said. "Instead, he stays in the country and sets off the pressure cooker at the Castle."

"I'm pretty sure Rawson and Costanzo had Dastan Nogoyev killed in prison," Remy said. "But Usenov got away that night. I think the bombing at the Castle was revenge for his friend. Plain and simple."

"Rawson is starting to make Vladimir Putin seem warm and cuddly," Celsun said.

"Here's what I don't get," Grace said. "Paul Bracewell's toxicology report showed that his blood alcohol level was off the charts. The first night, Rawson hires two goons to shoot him. Not exactly subtle. But then to finish him off, they fake his drowning?"

"They might have pulled a *North by Northwest*," Celsun said.

"A what?"

Celsun looked at Remy and Grace, stunned.

"Oh, come on. Seriously? You guys haven't seen *North by Northwest*? Hitchcock? Come on, it's a classic! Anyway, Martin Landau tries to kill Cary Grant by staging a drunk driving accident. They basically pour an entire Jim Beam distillery down his throat and throw him behind the wheel of a car and have him drive down a cliff side. That way, the cops will assume he was just another drunk asshole who didn't have a designated driver. I mean, Cary Grant ends up surviving and Paul Bracewell didn't, but premise is the same. They ply Paul, who's already drunk, with even more. To the point where he's literally incapacitated. He blacks out, gets dumped in the river. No sign of a struggle. And a hundred witnesses can say they saw Paul drinking all night."

"If you're right..." Remy said, shaking his head. "In seventy-two hours, I tender my resignation to the campaign. If I do it before then, he'll know something is up and come down on me hard. Rawson leaves tomorrow for rallies in Pittsburgh and Cincinnati. Once he's back, I'm out."

"Rawson will come after you," Grace said. "This man doesn't just hold grudges. He vaporizes people."

"Yeah. I'm aware. I guess the good thing is that I know he's going to come after me."

Celsun raised his hand like a school kid.

"Yeah?" Remy said.

"Okay, let's say all this is true. We have no proof. The Griggs campaign is a freight train. We're three doofuses. No offense. He's a billionaire supported by other billionaires, and possibly a foreign government. And if he wins, everything changes. So if Griggs has all this ammo, how the hell do you stop him?"

Nobody had an answer.

Remy left the Liberty Inn at midnight. He zipped up his coat, put on a pair of heavy wool gloves, and went to the nearest Chase bank. He withdrew the maximum, five hundred dollars, from his checking account. Then he headed back to his apartment.

Grace Rivas and Eric Celsun left the Liberty Inn half an hour after Remy, staggered ten minutes apart. They went in separate directions: Grace to her Midtown East studio, Celsun to his girlfriend's loft in Tribeca. They had agreed to lay low and regroup following Remy's official departure from the Griggs campaign.

At the Castle, Rawson Griggs sat in his office high above the city, poring over a draft of a speech he would be giving the next day in Ohio. Hamilton was a bellwether county, and if Rawson could swing it to the Mayflower side, he had a damn good chance at winning Ohio.

Rawson scanned the draft with a red pen, circling words that didn't quite fit, crossing out entire paragraphs, writing suggestions in the margins. He would not give the speech verbatim. He would memorize most of it, leaving room for digressions. To Rawson, the key to a good speech *was* the digressions. The way a voice could inflect emotion, the way a hand motion accentuated a point. Like a jazz musician, Rawson allowed himself room to freestyle, to feel the pulse of the crowd, to play the room.

He was pleased with his progress. The speech would be ready. Rawson put down the red pen, rubbed his eyes. Then his landline rang. He picked it up.

"Rawson," he said.

"It's Costanzo. Go private."

Rawson punched in the code to transfer the call to a secure line. "Go on."

"You were right, sir. About Stanton. He met with two reporters from the *Gazette* tonight, including Grace Rivas. We also confirmed that Rivas requested an official press pass for tomorrow. She'll be covering the event in Ohio in person."

Rawson closed his eyes slowly. He felt a deep sadness, just for a moment, before the pragmatism returned. Somehow, he'd hoped it would not come to this. He'd given Stanton a chance. A part of him, a foolish part, saw Stanton in a way that he never saw Paul. But that was over. Stanton was a liability. He was disloyal. And now Rawson had to follow through.

"You know what to do," Rawson said. "You trust the men?"

"With my life."

"Tell them to make it look good. Have you talked to Dennis?"

"I've been in constant contact with him since the beginning. He's ready to go."

"Sober?"

"I gave him a breathalyzer myself."

"Okay. I want him prepared for the morning after tomorrow. Talk to Jerry. Have him handle the details. Make sure Dennis is camera ready. I want someone with him every minute from now until then. I won't permit him showing up smelling like he slept in a bus station."

"We'll have him groomed like a show dog," Costanzo said. "And, sir, I know this isn't easy. We all had hopes for Stanton. But it's necessary."

"Just get it done."

Rawson hung up the phone. The sadness he'd felt a few moments ago was gone. Anger had taken its place. Rawson Griggs was not crossed without severe consequences.

There was work to do. He could not allow himself an iota of sympathy for the pain about to be inflicted on Jeremy Stanton.

Alena got over Paul. Getting over Jeremy would be far simpler.

CHAPTER 24

The next day, Remy went to his local bank branch and withdrew another five thousand dollars from his savings account. He then went home, packed a suitcase, and checked into the Comfort Inn in Times Square. He left his Griggs-issued cell phone at the apartment and took his old cell he hadn't used since joining the campaign. Given that Rawson knew about his meeting with Doug Rimbaud, he wouldn't put it beyond the campaign to have some sort of bug, recording device, or location tracker installed in the apartment. He would be able to access his Griggs email from his old phone, but wanted to remain off the grid until he knew what the fallout from his departure would be.

The hotel room itself was bare bones. The mattress felt like a rough hardwood floor and the carpet fibers probably harbored dust from the 1950s. The Times Square location granted easy access to several transportation hubs, just in case. Remy had no idea if he was being paranoid or properly cautious, but he figured given what Rawson might be capable of, paranoia could be the difference between life and ending up floating in the East River. He hoped he'd given Grace Rivas and Eric Celsun enough thread to weave a story that could derail

Griggs before it was too late.

They still had no proof Rawson was involved in Paul's death. Grace and Celsun had resources and brains, but Rawson had billions of dollars, the former mayor of New York, innumerable domestic and international connections, plus possible foreign agencies willing to bend or even break the law to help him.

Remy lay down on the granite-hard bed and stared at the ceiling. The fan had strands of dust and hair hanging off it. He knew he wouldn't sleep until he officially resigned. All he could do for now was keep his head down, stay put, and hope things remained quiet for the next three days.

Trevor Mayhew and his husband, Chris Lorenzo, left Momoya in Chelsea at 10 p.m. In Trevor's opinion, Momoya served the best sushi North of Tribeca, and it was worth the hour-long wait for their heavenly spicy scallop rolls and chicken katsu don. They split three appetizers, four rolls, a dish of edamame, a kani salad, and two bottles of hot sake. Nothing tasted better than hot sake during the cold winter months. They didn't take reservations, and Trevor enjoyed stuffing his face while watching the line before the maître d' grow longer and longer. Every time he put a piece of fish in his mouth, he could almost hear those poor, shivering souls' rumbling tummies.

When they were both sated, Trevor paid the check and they left the restaurant. Chris was wearing the chunky cable knit sweater Trevor had bought for him last Christmas. It made him look ten pounds heavier, but also made Trevor want to curl up into his arms and fall asleep against the soft wool. If everyone wore chunky sweaters, Trevor thought, there would be peace on earth.

He always felt a little guilty after indulging in a massive meal, but Trevor had worked himself nearly to death over the past six years to become one of the city's most sought-after fitness instructors. He deserved a cheat meal from time to time. CyclePro had upped his salary to a neat hundred and twenty grand last year after Soul Cycle had pursued him aggressively. Combined with private client sessions and brand ambassadorships—what Lululemon paid him to model their tank tops on Instagram was a crime—Trevor was clearing north of a hundred and fifty K. He deserved an extra shrimp tempura roll.

Trevor was well aware that the lifespan of a fitness instructor was short. His opportunities at thirty-nine and forty-nine would be a fraction of what they were at twenty-nine. So Trevor lived frugally. Because once his skin started to sag, once his metabolism began to slow, he didn't want to be like the older instructors who spent their twenties and thirties partying like rock stars and ended up living with their parents once they stopped looking good in Lycra. Trevor was too smart for that.

Chris was a kindergarten teacher, which meant Trevor spent a great deal of time hoping his partner didn't catch whatever germs the little walking petri dishes at school carried around with them. Nothing laid up a fitness pro like a bad cold. Not to mention that clients weren't overly fond of their trainer hawking up a lung during sumo squats.

Chris looped his arm through Trevor's and said, "Nightcap? Flatiron Lounge has live jazz tonight."

Trevor was tempted. He checked his watch, sucked in air through his teeth.

"I have a six a.m. and a seven a.m. tomorrow, and my playlists aren't ready. Unfortunately, those sakés were my nightcap."

"Come on. Just use the same playlist for both classes."

Trevor offered Chris some side-eye as they walked.

"You know, you used to be a lot more fun," Chris said.

"You have a choice," Trevor said. "You can get 'fun' Trevor, who will do sake bombs until the sun comes up, see late-night jazz, and coast through his classes. Or you can have 'six-pack who can afford to pay for sushi and pay seventy percent of our rent' Trevor. Which one will it be?"

"Not fair. It's a Sophie's choice," Chris said.

"That's not at all overly dramatic."

"Okay. Fine. But you owe me one full episode of something crappy on TV before bed. No falling asleep fifteen minutes in and then asking me to fill you in the next day."

"One episode. But it has to be a half hour episode."

"Deal."

"Alright then. Think about what you want to watch."

Momoya was three blocks from their apartment. In fifteen minutes, they'd be home and under the covers. And even though he'd committed to a full episode, Trevor didn't think he'd be able to keep his eyes open once his head hit that goose down pillow.

As they neared 6th Avenue, Trevor heard someone shouting. The voice came from behind them. He assumed the person was speaking to someone else, so he ignored it. But the second time the guy yelled, "Hey, faggots!" Trevor knew he was speaking to them.

"Just ignore him," Chris said.

"I haven't been called that name in a while," Trevor said. "And definitely not in this neighborhood."

"Idiots are like cockroaches," Chris said. "You might not see them, but they're always hiding in the dark."

"And if you approach them, they'll run like bitches," Trevor said.

"Come on. You don't need to start anything."

The man shouted, louder now. "Hey, I'm talking to you, you faggots. What, you can't talk to me 'cause you got each others' dicks in your mouths?"

"Please. Ignore him," Chris said, but Trevor's blood had already begun to boil. It had been far too long since he'd kicked the shit out of a gay basher. He could teach this asshole a lesson and still be in bed in twenty minutes. Plus, the extra adrenaline might actually keep him up for a whole episode.

Trevor heard Chris mumble *oh shit* under his breath. He turned around, and that was when Trevor saw there wasn't one man following them, but three. And two of them were holding metal pipes.

He didn't see the third one raise the can of pepper spray until it was too late.

Grace Rivas took a cab straight from the airport to the U.S. Bank Arena in downtown Cincinnati. It was a chilly day, slightly overcast, and Grace pulled her scarf tight. A massive line wound its way around the arena. Many had been standing in the cold for hours. None of them cared. They would have crossed an ocean to see Rawson Griggs.

Across the road from the ticketholders line was a mass of protestors. Well over a thousand, Grace estimated.

For every action, there is an equal and opposite reaction.

Grace reads some of the signs held by the protestors.

I'M HERE LEGALLY.

MR. GRIGGS, WERE YOUR ANCESTORS NATIVE AMERICANS?

YOUR WIFE WASN'T FROM HERE.

RAWSON GRIGGS = A RAW DEAL FOR AMERICA.

The overwhelming passion, both for and against Rawson Griggs, was something she'd never witnessed in politics. It felt like whether he won or lost, the public reaction would be volatile.

Grace signed in at the press table and waved hello to Jerry Kapinski. Kapinski turned his back on her. He was still pissed about her PoliSpill story, presumably. She entered the press pen and found a spot tucked among the reporters and cameramen.

The press pen was a bit more literal than Grace and her colleagues were used to. The Griggs campaign had barricaded the press corps behind dozens of steel crowd control barriers, as though the crowd had to be protected from the press, or vice versa. Normally they had freedom to roam and report. Here, they were literally penned in.

The U.S. Bank Arena officially seated a shade under eighteen thousand people, but seeing the mass of people already packed in, plus the line outside, Grace was certain the Griggs campaign had overbooked the venue. Probably on purpose.

Hamilton was a hugely important swing county in Ohio. Since

1980, Ohio had voted Republican six times and Democrat four times. It was a true bellwether state, and Hamilton County was a linchpin. Shaw and Garrett had both campaigned here, but had troubled filling VR halls. If enthusiasm was a harbinger of electoral support, Rawson would win Hamilton. Grace knew Rawson wouldn't hold anything back in order to take this county.

Bruce Springsteen's *Born in the U.S.A.* came on the loudspeakers, and Rawson took the stage to a standing ovation. Grace was amused. Politicians loved to play that song. Clearly they didn't actually listen to the lyrics.

This was the third presidential election Grace had covered, and every rally had defined media sections. They were usually areas cordoned-off by ropes or chairs, but this was the first time she'd felt like a prisoner. She had little doubt Rawson Griggs wanted it that way. Rallygoers were by and large hospitable and engaging. But today, Grace felt like Rawson had her and her colleagues dangling on a rope bridge above a piranha pool.

Grace used to have a strong professional relationship with the Griggs Organization, and a particular fondness for Alena. She'd always seemed to be a counterweight to her father's grandiosity, remaining grounded despite being born into the kind of privilege few people in history could understand. Alena was raised with advantages few could dream of, but never seemed to exploit them.

After Paul Bracewell's death, though, Alena had faded from the campaign trail. To Grace, it seemed that Rawson had grown unhinged, bolder. And if what Remy Stanton had said was true, Rawson was capable of truly frightening things.

Rawson clapped as he approached the podium, pointing and waving at the huge crowd.

"It's great to be back in the wonderful state of Ohio!" Rawson shouted. The crowd cheered relentlessly. "I cannot tell you how important your state is. Over the past forty years, the way the county has voted has almost always followed the way Ohio has voted. Think about that. You could say that you, each of you, determine the outcome of this election."

The crowd applauded, and Rawson clapped with them.

"Now, I want to earn your vote. Every one of you. You are each a mighty warrior. Warriors influence the outcome of wars. And make no mistakes, my friends: this is a war. And when that war is over, if you voted for Rawson Griggs, you'll be able to say, proudly, that you were part of something unprecedented. You raised your claws and you fought off the leeches that have sucked this country dry for too long."

The crowd booed. Apparently, they were not fond of leeches. Grace snapped a few photos from her cell phone and tweeted them out.

"Now, in war," Rawson said, lowering his voice, letting people know he was deadly serious, "you have opposition. People who fight against you. They want to stop your way of life. They want you to agree with them, follow them, bow to them."

More boos.

"Millions of Americans are out of work, starving, dying in our streets. They just want a better life. But some people want things to stay the same. They don't care if you can't eat, as long as they come home to a steak. They don't care if you can't pay your rent, as long as they can pay their country club membership."

The booing and jeers grew louder. Rawson was feeding the crowd's anger.

Grace scanned the press pen. She saw her friend Josh Lambert from *The Guardian*. Josh had been on the Griggs beat for months. He'd attended dozens of rallies, and his dispatches were thorough, even, and well reported. They'd shared several late-night dinners post-Griggs rallies, and one chaste kiss that was never spoken of again.

Grace hoped the hotel had a decent bar. She would need a strong cocktail or four after today.

"Now, do any of you read the *New York Gazette*?" Rawson asked. Grace's eyes widened. Her pulse quickened. What was Rawson doing?

Thousands of people replied, "No!"

"In case you pay attention to the news, this terrible newspaper made up a story in an effort to discredit me, and to undermine this great campaign. And by discrediting me, they're discrediting *you*."

The anger was palpable. Grace remembered what Remy had told her: *Be careful.*

Now she knew why.

"There's this one reporter at the *Gazette*," Griggs said. "She's here with us today. Grace Rivas. Little Gracey, are you there in the back?"

Grace froze. Her heart hammered. Rawson was looking right at her.

"There she is," Rawson said. "Can we get a look at this woman? And I use that term very, very loosely."

The event camera swiveled, and suddenly Grace was on every screen in the building.

"Everyone, let Grace back there know *exactly* what you all think of her."

Suddenly thousands of people were looking right at Grace. Hisses and boos rained down, thousands of voices strong. Three words ran through her head.

Oh my god…

The stream of liquid hit Trevor's eyes before he had a chance to see their faces. Within a second, it felt like someone had lit matches under his eyelids. A burning, searing pain flooded Trevor's eyes, and he fell to his knees, gasping. His eyes closed involuntarily. He tried to shield his face with his arms, but it was too late.

Trevor heard a scream and realized they'd sprayed Chris as well.

Anger welled up inside him. Trevor tried to force his eyes open. His nose was running. His face felt like it was on fire. He tried to stand, but felt the metal pipe jabbed end-first into his stomach. He doubled over and retched on the sidewalk.

Trevor couldn't breathe. He couldn't see. His eyes burned, the wind had been driven from him, and he didn't know what they were doing to his husband.

"You like that, you faggot?" one of the men said. "Figured you'd like shit being sprayed against your face, faggot."

Trevor swung his fist wildly, trying to hit someone, anyone, but connected with nothing but air.

Trevor felt the ground around him, eyes still burned shut, looking for something, anything, to use as a weapon. He still couldn't see, but he was desperate. Then Trevor felt a foot stomp on his right hand, pinning it against the ground.

"What do you think you're doing, faggot?"

"I think he needs to be taught a lesson," another man said.

"I think you're right. What do *you* think, faggot?"

Trevor struggled to speak. Snot and tears poured down his face. He managed to open his eyes just a bit, but his vision was hazy, his eyeballs burning.

"Take what you want," he said. "Take it and go."

The men all laughed. "Faggot's trying to buy us off," one said.

"Think we're joking?" another added.

"I'm not," Trevor managed to sputter. "I don't. Please. Take whatever you want."

"Oh, we will," one said. "Sorry, faggot. But you should have stayed in that bar."

Trevor thought *we didn't come from a bar*, right before the metal pipe came down on his right ankle. There was split second between the moment he felt the blow land, and the moment he heard the crack of his ankle breaking.

They were shaking the steel gates of the press pen like it was the cage of a trapped animal. Grace felt rooted in place. She was terrified. They crowd was unhinged. They wanted to hurt someone. And they were all looking at *her*.

Grace took a step back, tripped over a microphone cord, and almost went down. It was payback for the PoliSpill article. Rawson was teaching her a lesson.

"Lying bitch," seethed a heavyset, goateed man wearing a black *Real Women Like It RAWson* t-shirt.

"You should be ashamed of yourself, cunt," said a younger man with a ruddy face and a ponytail wearing combat fatigues.

Grace felt a hand on her shoulder. She whipped around, ready to fight. Josh Lambert was standing there.

"Whoa, whoa, Grace, it's me."

"Jesus. Josh."

"Are you okay? This guy is a lunatic."

"I'm okay," Grace said, even though she definitely did *not* feel okay. Rawson had crossed the line at warp speed. And the scary part was: he knew it, and didn't care.

"Get out of here," Josh said. "Go back to the hotel. Let this blow over."

"No way," Grace said. "This is my job. I'm not going to let Rawson Griggs intimidate me. Fuck him."

Then Grace heard Rawson's voice boom throughout the arena.

"Oh, would you look at little Gracey back there, crying to her friend?" Rawson mimicked rinsing his eyes out. "Folks, this is what journalism has come to. They make up stories to hurt you, but then, like any playground bully, when you confront them, they go off and cry. What do you say to cowards like that? Do we respect them?"

Nearly twenty thousand people shouted, "No!" The jeers and boos surrounded her. More people approached the press pen. The gates were not going to hold.

"They," Rawson said, louder, "are the opposition. This so-called *free press* wants to enslave you. Patriots do not stand for that. *Beasts* do not stand for that."

"Okay, this is getting out of hand," she said to Josh. "Let's go."

Grace put her notebook into her bag. She started to push her way to the exit. It was on the opposite side of the press pen, about thirty feet away.

"Oh, look, she's trying to leave," Rawson said. "Little Gracey, you're in America. If you don't like what people have to say, you don't just get to leave."

Then Rawson held his arms out, like he was inviting twenty thousand people under his wings. "Do you want Little Gracey to leave without being taught a lesson?"

Thousands cried, "No!"

"Then what are we going to do about it?"

"Grace…" Josh said.

"Go. Let's get out of here," Grace said. "God*damn* him."

Suddenly, Grace heard a crashing sound. She looked back and saw that the guardrail surrounding the media pen had been knocked over. People were climbing over the metal gates by the dozens. Anger and malice in their eyes. So many of them were smiling. They were *smiling*.

"What are we going to do about it?" Rawson shouted again.

"Move!" Josh yelled, pushing his way through the pen. He held Grace by her arm and began to drag her through the scrum.

More and more people mounted the gates and headed towards them. Grace felt a hand grab her shoulder. She turned around and saw a strange, leering man holding onto the fabric of her jacket. She tried to pull away, but he held tight.

"Where do you think you're going?" he said.

Grace jerked away, and the sleeve of her jacket ripped.

Josh stepped forward and shoved the man down to the ground.

Rawson shouted into the microphone, "They're leaving! They're too cowardly to face real patriots!"

Grace could see the exit. Reporters and cameramen were trying to clear a path for her while holding back the oncoming rush. Bodies were flailing around. She could hear cursing, shouting, screaming.

Grace felt a hand curl around her ankle and she went down, slamming her knee against a fallen metal gate. She screamed out in pain.

Josh kneeled down and wrapped Grace's arm around his shoulder.

"Ready? One, two, three." He helped her stand, but Grace's knee buckled under her. The crowd kept surging forward. Grace looked over her shoulder. They were still coming.

Her knee killed. Josh half-walked, half-dragged her towards the exit. She looked back again and saw attendees and reporters in an insane melee. She saw punches being thrown, people writhing on the ground in pain. This was a maelstrom unlike anything Grace had ever seen. She was shaking, terrified.

Two security guards pushed their way through the mess and came up to Grace.

"We're going to get you out of here," one said. "Put your arms around our shoulders."

Grace nodded, her knee on fire. She wrapped her arms around each of them and they lifted her up and hustled her away.

Just before they left the arena, Grace turned back. She saw Rawson Griggs's face looming on one of the massive jumbotrons above the parquet floor. His image was fifteen feet tall. Rawson was beaming. As though this was exactly what he wanted to happen.

And what terrified Grace was that she knew it was.

CHAPTER 25

When Remy woke up, it took a moment for him to remember he was in a cheap hotel room. And when he got out of bed, he remembered that when you stay in a cheap hotel, with a cheap mattress, your spine pays the price.

He downed two cups of hotel room coffee—drinkable, barely—and turned on the news. He sipped his coffee with its gross, powdered creamer, scanned his emails, only partly paying attention to the well-coiffed anchors and their too-chipper-for-this-early-in-the-day smiles.

Then the anchors' faces grew serious.

"We have an update from the melee that erupted at the Rawson Griggs rally in Cincinnati last night," the male anchor with Ken doll hair said. "Fifteen people were arrested and four were hospitalized, including *New York Gazette* reporter Grace Rivas, who was singled out by Rawson Griggs during his remarks."

Remy nearly dropped his coffee. *What the fuck?*

He turned the volume up.

The perky blonde anchor said, "The following is video taken on a cell phone by one of the attendees at yesterday's event at the U.S. Bank Arena."

The feed then switched to grainy, shaky, camera footage. Remy heard Rawson Griggs, speaking from a podium:

"Do you want Little Gracey to leave?"

"No!"

"Then what are we going to do about it?"

At that point, whoever was holding the cell phone swiveled to film the press pen. Dozens of people were shaking the metal gates surrounding it. Then, to Remy's horror, the gates came crashing down, and people began to stampede into the pen. In the middle of it all, Remy saw Grace Rivas, her eyes wide, shaken, scared.

Jesus Christ, he thought. *He* wanted *them to hurt her.*

The male anchor continued, "Dozens of media outlets are calling for an apology from Rawson Griggs for what they claim is his instigation of violence towards the reporters covering the rally. The hashtag #WereWithGrace trended on Twitter through the night and into this morning, with some people comparing Rawson Griggs to the leader of a mob. Reporters are calling on Griggs to disavow the violence that many people are saying he provoked".

The other anchor said, "Last night, after the rally, the Griggs campaign issued a short statement in response to the incident.

"The Griggs campaign does not condone any violence that may have taken place at yesterday's rally, which was filled with patriotic Americans. It has become evident throughout this revolutionary campaign that the people are fed up with the status quo, and yesterday they decided to voice their displeasure. While we hope any injuries were not serious, we also believe Rawson Griggs's supporters are patriots who want a better future for themselves and their children. And if people stand in opposition to this movement, Rawson Griggs and his patriotic supporters will have no choice but to fight back."

He had warned Grace. Rawson wasn't going to let her article slide. Why did she have to go to the rally?

Remy grabbed his phone and texted Grace.

Grace: I just heard about yesterday. I hope you're ok. Please write back when you get a chance and let me know how you are. I'm so sorry.

–Remy

This was no longer a campaign. It was something far, far darker.

Remy changed channels. Another morning news show had the rally melee from another angle. This one caught a grinning Rawson Griggs up on stage as chaos swirled around him. Remy felt like throwing up.

"In other news," the anchor said, "police are still looking for three suspects who attacked two men in Manhattan's Flatiron on 21st Street between 6th and 7th, in what appears to be a hate crime. An NYPD spokesman says three men approached the victims, now identified as Trevor Mayhew and Christopher Lorenzo, called them homophobic slurs, pepper sprayed them, and attacked them with some sort of metal bar. Both men are in stable condition at Beth Israel. If anyone has any information that could lead to an arrest, the NYPD asks that you call their tip line immediately."

Had Remy eaten anything, he would have retched it up.

He dropped his cell phone on the floor. His hand trembled as he picked it up and dialed Trevor. The call went right to voicemail.

He cursed and punched the bed. He threw on yesterday's clothes. He didn't bother to shower. Then he went downstairs, hailed a cab, and headed to Beth Israel.

"Trevor Mayhew," Remy said to the guard manning the lobby security station. "He was admitted last night, along with his husband, Christopher Lorenzo."

The guard picked up his phone, spoke a few unintelligible words, then said, "East Wing, room 427."

Remy thanked him and followed signs to the East Wing, walking as fast as he could without drawing attention. The elevator took forever to arrive.

He approached the nursing station on the fourth floor, sweating and winded. A weary, sixty-ish black woman looked up from her computer.

"Help you?" she said.

"Trevor Mayhew," he said, trying to catch his breath. "Room 427."

The woman checked her notes. Then she eyed Remy suspiciously. "You're not press, are you? We've had people from all the networks and papers calling to speak with Mr. Mayhew and Mr. Lorenzo."

"No, ma'am, I'm a friend. We used to be roommates. I give you my word. He has a birthmark in the shape of a donut on his right shoulder blade. You can go check."

Her suspicion turned into a light smile. "Well, alright then. I'll trust you. But if I find out you're lying to me, I'll make sure you end up in the bed next to him."

"Fair enough," Remy replied.

"Down at the end of the hall, on the right. Can't promise he's awake."

Remy thanked her and jogged towards the end of the hall. When he found room 427, he entered cautiously. It was a private room. A curtain was drawn around the bed. He saw a pair of hospital slipper peeking out from underneath the curtain.

"Hello?" he whispered. "It's Remy. Is…is Trevor in there?"

The curtain drew back. Chris Lorenzo was sitting on a plastic chair. His eyes were bloodshot and veiny, but he appeared otherwise unharmed.

"Oh, Jesus, Remy," Chris said. He stood up and they hugged. When Chris let go, Remy saw Trevor lying in the hospital bed. His eyes were closed, his breathing even. His right leg was suspended from the ceiling at a thirty-degree angle. A cast ran from his toes to just below his knee.

"They shattered his ankle to pieces," Chris said. "Fucking monsters. He got out of surgery about three hours ago. Doctors say he'll walk again, but he's got a long recovery ahead of him."

Chris sat down. Remy took a chair from the hallway and brought it into Trevor's room. He looked at his friend, unconscious, and laid his hand on Trevor's arm.

"I'm so sorry, Chris," Remy said. "If there's anything I can do."

"Thanks," he said. "Trev's parents are on their way in from Maine to help out. Hey, the silver lining is that we'll finally get to use our pull out couch. They say he'll have to stay here about a week to make sure he doesn't develop any blood clots."

"He's gonna be alright," Remy said. "What the hell happened last night?"

Chris's lip began to tremble, and he wiped tears from his eyes.

"Sorry, if you don't want to…"

"No, it's okay. Just…it's like a nightmare. I mean, we've been called names before, but for the most part those idiots bark worse than they bite. But this was different. I've never been so sure I was going to die."

"Why?" Remy said. "What happened?"

"We went out to dinner," Chris said. "Momoya. Our favorite sushi place. A lovely night. Nothing out of the ordinary at all. Then on the way home, these guys start following us. Calling us names."

"Names?"

"Faggot, you know, the usual troglodyte slurs. You learn to ignore it. But it always stings a little."

"Then what?"

"They kept going. Kept shouting at us. It was like they *wanted* us to confront them. Trevor was pissed. I thought he was going to kick the shit out of somebody. Then all of a sudden we're both getting pepper sprayed."

"Just like that? No warning? There was no fight first? No warning?"

"None. We turn around and *bam*. Right in our faces."

"Goddamn monsters."

"I've been harassed before. Been called every name in the book. But last night was different. I almost got the feeling that they *wanted* to hurt us."

"What do you mean?"

"They had weapons on them. Crowbars or pipes or something. And pepper spray. They planned to hurt someone. When we get harassed, it doesn't feel that…pre-planned. Sometimes you get into scrapes, but it's usually just drunk assholes at a bar who can't see straight. You don't get followed home in Chelsea by a trio of goons with weapons and pepper spray."

Something started to churn in Remy's stomach.

"So you think they targeted you?" he said.

"Oh, no doubt. But I don't know why they would have targeted us, specifically. I mean, we were coming from dinner. And what that guy said to Trevor just before he broke his ankle…it was just weird."

"What did he say to Trevor? How was it weird?"

Chris paused. Remy knew he was pushing too hard on someone who'd just been through a traumatic event. But he needed to know.

"Right before that asshole smashed Trevor's ankle, he said something like, 'you should have stayed at the bar.'"

Remy felt an icy grip close around his heart. His head swam.

"What's weird is," Chris said, "we weren't even *at* a bar. I wanted to go for a drink, but Trevor wanted to go home. Then we hear 'Hey faggot' behind us. And they didn't stop. Kept calling us names, even when we were on the ground."

"He said 'you should have stayed at the bar'? Those were his exact words?"

"That's right. Exact. I'll never forget them."

"And they kept calling you names?"

"Even after they left," Chris said. "It was almost like they *wanted* us to know it was…"

"They wanted you to know it was a hate crime."

"Yeah."

Nausea swept through Remy. *Just like Rawson wanted people to think Paul's death was an accident. He knows about the meeting at the Liberty Inn. Just like he knew about Doug Rimbaud. He knows I turned against him. He knows everything.*

Grace. Trevor and Chris. It was all Rawson. He's sending a message. That nobody is safe. And if you cross him, he'll hurt you, and everyone you care about.

Remy's phone rang. He didn't recognize the number and declined the call.

"Sorry," he said to Chris. Chris waved it off.

"Hey, do you mind if I go get a cup of coffee from downstairs?" Chris said. "It's been a hell of a night and I want to be awake when Trev wakes up."

"Go ahead," Remy said. "I'll stay with him."

Chris stood up. "Thanks for coming, Remy," he said. "Trev will need you as he recovers. I don't know what this means for his career. He's worked so hard. And for something like this to happen? Just isn't fair."

"He'll be back. I know it. Trevor's a badass. He's gonna fight like hell and come back better than ever," Remy replied. "And when he teaches his first class back at CyclePro, I'll be in the front row."

Chris smiled, and Remy heard him start to choke up. "Sucks it took this to get you into a class. That's one I won't miss for anything. Thanks, Remy. I'll be right back."

Chris left the room just as Remy's phone rang again. Another private number, so again Remy declined it. Then a text message came in.

Jeremy, it's Tracy Lindquist at the New York Times. Wanted to get your comment on the Get Up America! interview airing tomorrow.

Remy figured this was regarding some story about the Griggs campaign. *Get Up America!* was a popular morning news and variety program. Remy figured a Griggs surrogate was scheduled to be on the show.

He responded:

Sorry, Tracy, busy right now, can you ask Jerry Kapinski for comment?

A minute later, he received a reply:

Don't you think you should be the one going on record since it's your father?

Remy stood up. He felt dizzy.

He wrote back:

What are you talking about? My father?

Tracy Lindquist sent over a link. Remy opened it. A video appeared on his cell phone screen. On the video was a man Jeremy Stanton had not seen in over a decade. A face he had tried to forget.

An ominous voiceover ran over a video of a man sitting in a wooden chair, draped in shadow.

"Ever since he saved the lives of Alena Griggs and Paul Bracewell, Jeremy Stanton has become an international hero. He gave up a promising career to join Rawson Griggs's presidential campaign. But there's a side of Jeremy Stanton you haven't seen. A darker side that will shock you to your core. Only one man knows the truth about Jeremy Stanton. And that man is Jeremy's estranged father, Dennis Stanton, who has not seen his son in years. Tomorrow, you will discover the dark side of an American hero."

Remy put his hand to his head. He felt like he was going to pass out.

The program cut to a pre-taped video clip. In it, Dennis Stanton sat on a couch. Dennis looked far older than the last time Remy saw him. Somebody had cleaned him up. He'd never been much for hygiene. His long hair, now fully gray, was combed. His mustache trimmed. He wore a clean button-down shirt, a sport jacket, and black-rimmed glasses. Remy had never seen him wear glasses. He looked gaunt. No amount of makeup could hide his sunken cheeks, dark eye circles. Remy recognized the look in his father's eyes. Shame, and unwarranted anger.

"My wife was dying," Dennis said, with a voice that sounded marinated in whiskey and cigarettes. It was the voice of a liar. "And my son refused to let me see her. I wasn't the best man, but he took my wife away from me. He broke my leg once, and I think he would have killed me. I hear people calling him a hero. I'm ashamed to say it, but my son ain't no hero."

The screen cut away to a somber anchor who said, "Tune in tomorrow morning for my full interview with Dennis Stanton. You won't want to miss it."

When Chris returned from getting his coffee, Remy was crying.

CHAPTER 26

Remy stayed by Trevor's side the rest of the day. His phone rang every thirty seconds. Remy showed Chris the video.

"I don't even know what to say. Who…how…"

"Rawson Griggs," Remy said. He felt drained, hollowed out.

"Rawson? Why? You're like the only sane thing left in his campaign. He's turning into a crazy person."

Remy shook his head. "I can't talk about it now. But I will."

He looked at Trevor. Thought about Grace. Knew all of this was his fault. He remembered the words Rawson had said to him that night at the Hollywood Bowl, after confronting him about the meeting with Doug Rimbaud.

Not only will you be off my campaign, I will destroy you in every way you can imagine. I will make you wish you'd stayed in that bar.

Now Remy knew exactly what he was talking about.

Rawson knew about his meeting with Grace and Eric Celsun. He knew about the Rimbaud meeting. He knew everything. And Remy had been too stupid to realize it. And now Rawson was systematically tearing down Remy and everyone close to him.

How did you get out of the way of an oncoming train when you've tied yourself to the tracks?

There was no question that Rawson was behind his father's reappearance. He had no idea what rock Dennis Stanton had been living under all this time. But Rawson had found him. And it made Remy sick to think about what putrid lies he was going to spill on national television. The notion that Remy forbade his father from seeing his mother was absurd and untrue, especially given the horrific abuse she'd suffered at his hands.

He needed to get the *Get Up America!* interview cancelled somehow. The problem was, *Get Up America!*'s ratings were up twenty-five percent year to date, and it could all be attributed to their near non-stop coverage of Rawson Griggs. He was printing money for them. Remy needed to take a page from the Rawson Griggs playbook. He had to find a way to hit them where it mattered: their wallet.

"Listen," Remy said, "I have something I need to take care of. I'm staying at the Comfort Inn in Times Square in room 411 if you or Trev need anything. I'll be back."

"Why aren't you staying at your place?" Chris asked.

"Bedbugs," Remy said. "Nasty ones."

"That's disgusting," Chris said. "I'll let you know when he wakes up."

They hugged, and Remy left.

When he got outside, Remy called Eric Celsun at the *Gazette*.

"Celsun."

"Eric. This is Jeremy Stanton."

"Remy. Wow. Well, I guess tomorrow can't be any worse for you, can it? Unless, you know, you get that weird tree bark disease or something."

"Trust me, I'd rather have that. Diseases are curable. Lineage, not so much. How's Grace?"

"She's doing alright. Spoke to her a little while ago. Sprained MCL, bruised kneecap, needed a few stitches, but she's tough. She's mad as hell."

"It's retribution," Remy said. "For the PoliSpill article, and our meeting the other night. My best friend had his ankle broken the same night Rawson sicced twenty thousand people on Grace. *Now* do you believe me that Rawson is dangerous?"

"Dangerous? Eating street meat is dangerous. Rawson threw twenty thousand people on Grace like a pack of dogs. That's another level dangerous, man. Good thing I know Jiu Jitsu."

"You do?"

"No…but Keanu Reeves learned it in, like, ten minutes in *The Matrix*. Can't be that hard. Listen, will you go on the record about the *Get Up America!* interview? Give your side of the allegations?"

"Actually," Remy said, "I will. And that's what I wanted to talk to you about."

"Okay. What do you have in mind?"

"How hard is it for you to get police reports from other cities and states?"

"Not very," he said, "unless the records have been sealed."

"These wouldn't be. I need you to get police records for Dennis James Stanton. Date of birth March 30, 1955. He lived in Lancaster, Pennsylvania until at least ten years ago, and the records would be kept there. I don't know where he's been living the last ten years. I haven't spoken to him in a decade. But there will be police reports from Lancaster. I need you to find them. And I need you to publish them."

"Okay, but I have to ask. Is this, like, a favor? Because you know I have an actual job and it doesn't entail digging into peoples' personal lives just for kicks."

"I understand. And no, it's not just for kicks. A major network is planning to run an interview with a man who has numerous domestic violence charges against him, and the network completely neglected to mention that. I think *Gazette* readers will want to know *Get Up America!* is promoting a domestic abuser like he's some courageous whistleblower. I know Rawson orchestrated it, but that doesn't matter. People deserve to know the truth about my father."

"Okay, my editors might be interested if there's really smoke where you say there is," Celsun said. "But they'd be even more interested if you went on the record to accompany the story."

"You get the police reports, I'll go on the record. But the article needs to go live before the interview airs."

"Christ, Jeremy, it airs in less than twenty-four hours and I haven't even run this by my editors yet."

"Well, then stop wasting your time talking to me and talk to whoever you need to talk to. Then call me back once you have the reports."

"You got it," Celsun said. "I'm sure I don't need to even ask this, but I have the exclusive on this, right?"

"You do."

"Blammo. Awesome. Be in touch."

Remy ended the call. He prayed Celsun was as good at his job as Grace.

Then he saw that he had three new text messages. They were from Alena.

Remy, I saw this thing with your dad. Please call me.

I heard about Trevor. Can we talk? I don't know what's going on. I asked my father if he's heard from you and he refused to speak to me. Something is wrong. Please get back to me.

I don't know what's going on. But I need to see you.

Remy stared at the texts. He felt an ache in his heart. He wanted to talk to Alena desperately. He wanted to see her. To go somewhere, just the two of them, away from this madness.

But what could he say? He couldn't tell her that her father was a monster.

So Remy turned his phone off without responding to her.

The next order of business was a little trickier: he needed to get a weapon.

Buying a gun in New York City required a four-month waiting

period to get a license approved. Remy didn't have four months. And, sadly, he didn't know any shady characters who could get him one off the books—not to mention the possible legal repercussions if he was found with an unlicensed firearm. And if he ended up in prison, Remy could expect to receive the Dastan Nogoyev shiv special, courtesy of Rawson and Phillip Costanzo

But he couldn't walk around emptyhanded. Not after what happened to Trevor and Grace. A knife would be too cumbersome, too butcher-y. And besides, he wasn't Rambo. Brass knuckles wouldn't do a thing if someone actually *did* have a gun or a knife. Unfortunately, it was illegal in New York State to own a taser or stun gun. Still, he wouldn't have to worry about getting killed in prison if he was already dead. Sometimes you had to make the decision that seemed to be the least terrible.

Remy walked to an Internet café. He ran a quick search for legal online stun gun and taser sales. Dozens of people sold them legally through sites like eBay. He narrowed down his search to sellers in the TriState area. He found six dealers.

Remy created a dummy Gmail account registered under the name Phil Rawlings. He emailed all six of the dealers. He claimed to be in immediate need of a stun gun for self-defense purposes due to a series of break-ins in his neighborhood.

Then he sat. And waited.

He refreshed his email constantly. There was no word from any of the dealers, Eric Celsun, or Grace Rivas. Media requests were pouring in, hoping to get Remy to comment on his father's *Get Up America!* interview. It was a strange feeling, after months of being part of the Griggs rapid response team, to be ignoring media requests.

He drank four cups of coffee. His tongue felt like a sofa cushion. An hour later, Remy refreshed his inbox and found an email waiting for him from a dealer named Max420XXXX. He opened it.

Phil – I sell various types of stun guns and tasers, legally. I cannot illegally sell them within the state of New York. I only ship merchandise to states where carrying such weapons for self-defense purposes are legal.

However, if you would like to come by for a cup of coffee, I live in Kew Gardens. Stop by any time. I only brew the expensive stuff.

Max, or whatever his real name was, gave his full address. Remy replied and said he'd come by that afternoon. He left the café, went to the bank, and withdrew another thousand dollars from his savings account. Then he bought a gray winter hat, a pair of cheapo sunglasses, and ear buds.

He walked west to 8th Avenue and got on the E train. He took a seat, slipped the glasses on, put the buds in his ears, and prayed he looked more like a guy who didn't want to be bothered than a guy who had something to hide.

Remy walked west off the E train from Jamaica Avenue. Nobody had recognized him on the subway. He'd spent the entire ride in nervous anticipation. Had someone recognized him, posted a photo to Twitter or Instagram, Rawson would know where he was. He'd never been so relieved to be left alone.

Remy walked south on 126th Street towards a row of single-family homes. He opened the gate to number 36, a detached colonial style home with a one-car garage. A brown Volvo was parked in the driveway. There was a note in a child's handwriting taped to the mailbox that read *Welcom Mistr Mailman.*

Remy rang the doorbell. He heard someone approach, and a man opened it.

"You must be Phil Rawlings," he said.

"Yup. And you're…Max?"

"You can call me Max. Come in."

Remy stepped inside the house. Max was youngish, late thirties or early forties, wearing a red and black flannel over a blue t-shirt, with loose-fitting jeans, floppy brown hair, and two days of beard stubble. The apartment was neat, except for a desk in the corner piled high with papers. Dozens of Legos were strewn about. The desk was bracketed by two shelves that were filled with financial texts and investment books by celebrity financial gurus. Remy guessed that Max was a day trader.

Family photos lined the walls. Remy looked at the one hanging over the desk. Max stood in the middle, next to an attractive woman, his wife, presumably. A young girl of about seven stood in front, smiling. The girl wore a shirt featuring Rey from the new *Star Wars* trilogy. Max and his wife's hands rested on the girl's shoulders. They were all beaming. Max's family looked kind and normal.

"Give me a second," Max said. "Can I get you something? Water? Snapple?"

"I'm good, thanks."

Max nodded and went upstairs. He returned a minute later with a large duffel bag. He unzipped it and pulled back the folds. Remy's jaw dropped.

Inside were dozens of tasers and stun guns of every shape and size. Tasers that looked like handguns. Flashlights. Even what appeared to be cell phone cases. And they came in different colors: black, blue, red, pink.

"Ladies like 'em pink," Max said. "Who says self-defense can't be fashionable? Now, first things first. Take off your shirt and pants."

"Excuse me?" Remy said.

"You heard me. You refuse, I'm gonna have to ask you to leave."

Remy sighed, then removed his shirt and pants. He contemplated the life decisions that had led to him standing half naked in a strange man's house in Queens staring at a duffel bag of illegal weaponry.

Max picked up the pile of clothes and searched them. Then he circled Remy. He patted Remy's butt, ran his hands over his socks, then smoothed Remy's underwear over his thighs.

"Alright," Max said. "Put your clothes on."

Remy did. "Thank you for being gentle."

"Service with a smile," Max said. "So what're you in the market for?"

Remy answered, "Something for protection. Small enough that I can conceal it, but powerful enough to only need to use it once."

"Protection, huh?" Max said. "But you need to be able to conceal it." He nodded, as if to say *you're full of shit*.

"Can you help me or not?"

"Do you even need to ask that? Here. Try this."

Max pulled out a rectangular object the size of a garage door opener and handed it to Remy. It was light. Remy turned it over in his hands.

"This is the Stun Master, Lil Guy model," Max said. "I call it the Napoleon. This baby is small, like the name implies, but this sucker packs twelve million volts."

"Holy crap. In this little thing?"

"You can put down a water buffalo with this bad boy," Max said. "And here. Complimentary holster. You can strap that to your leg, arm, wherever."

"It's perfect. And it definitely works?"

"You want me to test it on you?"

"That's really alright," Remy said. "So what's it cost?"

"This model here retails for about thirty bucks. It's yours for five hundred."

"Five hundred? Are you serious? That's like a two thousand percent markup."

"And you wouldn't be here if you had the time or ability to get yourself one at retail price," Max said.

Remy sighed. "Five hundred. You're a thief. Show me how it works."

"No problem. Those metal probes on top are the business end. See that switch on the side? Down position is off. Middle position is the flashlight. Top position means the bugger is on. When it's in the top position, all you have to do is just hold down the trigger button on the front and bop them with the probes to give someone a twelve million volt tickle. Just make sure not to keep the switch in the top position or you'll accidentally fry your nut hair off."

Remy flicked the switch to the on position and put his finger on the trigger. "Just press that?"

"That'll do it. Try it."

Remy pressed the button and a blue flash sparked across the tips.

"Gnarly. What's that one?" Remy said, pointing to another object in the bag.

"Oh, now this one is really cool," Max said. "It's called a Yellowjacket. Looks like a cell phone case, right?"

Remy nodded.

"Well, it's actually a taser that *looks* like a cell phone case. You slip it over your cell phone, and then put this around your wrist." Max held up a thin black bracelet with two small buttons on either side of the band.

"It looks like a FitBit," Remy said.

"That's the idea. It's designed to look like a fitness tracker. Someone robs you and nabs your phone, you just depress both buttons simultaneously, and *blam*. They're dropping your wallet, your phone, and probably a load down their pants."

"How much is that one?"

"Retails for a shade under two hundred. Tell you what. I'll give you them both for eight fifty."

"Done."

Remy counted out the bills and gave them to Max. "Now, if you go through a metal detector and they catch you carrying either of these, we never met. And if you give me up," Max said, pointing to a small glass orb above his computer. *A camera. Shit.* Remy hadn't seen it. "I give you up. But don't sweat it. I'm not looking to get anyone in trouble. You gotta do what you gotta do to defend yourself these days. Right, Mr. Stanton?"

Remy's head snapped up. He opened his mouth. "Wait..."

"Don't worry. Like I said, I have a business to run here. But I recognized you the second I opened the door. But if you need these babies for protection, then politics is a much dirtier business than I thought."

"You have no idea," Remy said.

Remy felt the Lil Guy taser snug against his ankle. He spent the entire ride hoping it didn't go off accidentally and set his leg hair on fire. He'd slipped the Yellowjacket cover on his phone. It added considerable bulk to the device, but it was worth it. He wondered if the bulge on his ankle was visible, making him look like some bootleg secret agent. Either way, he felt a little better with some protection, even if the odds were fifty-fifty that he accidentally used them on himself first.

When he got off the E train Port Authority, Remy saw he had a voicemail waiting from Eric Celsun, plus a text that read: *Call me ASAP. Prepare to be happy.*

Remy returned to his hotel room and called Celsun.

Celsun picked up and said, "Hey, Remy. Holy crap, your dad was a giant dick."

"Tell me something I don't know."

"Okay, well, you might not know this. I found three police reports pertaining to a Mr. Dennis James Stanton. Born in Lancaster County, DOB of March 30, 1955. All domestic violence situations."

"That's him."

"Let's see…the first police report I found was filed on September 17, 1979."

"That's before my parents were married," Remy said. "Before I was born."

"Okay, here we go. This is directly from the report. At two in the morning," Celsun said, "after receiving a 9-1-1 call, Lancaster police arrived at the home of a Ms. Elaine Steadman on suspicion of domestic violence. The investigating officer wrote: 'During an argument involving caller's boyfriend, identified as a Mr. Dennis Stanton of Lancaster, PA, the suspect grabbed victim by throat and punched wall next to her head. He then threw her down violently onto couch. Victim states she was thrown with such force that she hit a nightstand on the side of the couch and struck her shoulder. Marks on victim's throat and shoulder and damage to property are consistent with report. Steadman claims Mr. Stanton left the scene prior to her 911 call.

"Misdemeanor charges were filed against Dennis," Celsun said, "but dropped when Ms. Steadman refused to cooperate."

"Do they say why she refused to cooperate?"

"This might explain it," Celsun said. "I rang up the Lancaster courthouse and found a marriage certificate filed in Lancaster County for Elaine Steadman and Dennis Stanton, dated October 22, 1980."

"He was married before my mother?" Remy said. "I didn't know that. So she declined to press charges and then married him?"

"Well, briefly," Celsun said. "The marriage was annulled four months later."

"Unreal," Remy said. "I never knew that."

"The second report is from April 3, 1985."

"Okay, that's after he married my mother, but still a few years before I was born."

"Similar scenario," Celsun continued. "Police respond to a 9-1-1 hang up, find a Mrs. Margaret Stanton neé Twomey locked in a bathroom. Dennis Stanton is not on the premises. When an officer picks the lock on the bathroom door, they find Margaret Stanton on the floor holding a kitchen knife. She has bruises on both arms and a superficial scalp wound. Mrs. Stanton claimed Dennis Stanton attacked her with a phone. The arm bruises were defensive wounds. Stanton gets charged with domestic assault. Margaret Stanton refuses to cooperate."

Remy shook his head. The only thing that terrified these women more than Dennis Stanton's abuse was what he might do if they cooperated with police.

"The last report on record is from February 8, 2002."

"I remember that one," Remy said.

"You should. You were the one who called the cops."

"That's right. Go on."

"Police responded to a 9-1-1 call from Jeremy Stanton, the fourteen-year-old son of Margaret and Dennis Stanton of Lancaster, PA. Police arrived to find Dennis Stanton incapacitated on the floor of the family's home. Upon receiving a medical evaluation, Mr. Stanton was determined to have a compound tibia fracture. Margaret Stanton had locked herself in her bedroom. She was suffering from severe arm and facial wounds, which were later determined to be a fractured eye socket and a dislocated elbow. Mrs. Stanton said the injuries were obtained when Dennis Stanton grabbed her violently by the throat, punched her in the face, and twisted her arm behind her back. Both Jeremy and Margaret Stanton confirm that Jeremy pulled Mr. Stanton off of his mother and pushed him, at which point Mr. Stanton tripped on a nearby floor lamp, which is how he received his injury. Both Mr. and Mrs. Stanton were taken to Lancaster General Hospital for treatment. Jeremy Stanton was questioned and released by Lancaster PD. Dennis Stanton was arrested and charged with domestic assault."

Remy felt his hands start to shake. He remembered that day. He was in his room, reading a Piers Anthony novel, when he heard a loud crack come from downstairs. It was the sound of his mother's cheekbone being broken. Remy remembered the next crack, when his father's leg broke. The feeling of euphoria when he saw Dennis writhing in pain on the floor. Finally, he was old enough and strong enough to fight back. To protect her.

That day was the second to last time I saw him, Remy thought. *The last time before my mother died.*

You deserved it, you asshole.

"That charge stuck," Celsun said. "Dennis Stanton pled guilty to two counts of second degree simple domestic assault and was sentenced to three years at the Lancaster County Correctional Facility. His sentence was reduced to fifteen months because of, get a load of this, good behavior."

"There were other instances," Remy said. "Of violence. A lot of them."

"Maybe so, but these are the only police reports on record. Still, it's more than enough to call into question *Get Up America!* airing an interview without disclosing that the subject is a convicted domestic abuser. You said you'll go on the record. Can I still count on you for that?"

"There's nothing I'd rather do," Remy said. "But I have one small request."

Two hours later, Remy sent an email to Rawson Griggs, CC'd to Kenneth Murphy, Jerry Kapinski, and Rebecca Blum.

Subject: *Griggs campaign – Stanton Employment*

Body: *To the Griggs campaign staff – I am officially tendering my resignation from the presidential campaign of Rawson Griggs effective immediately.*

Sincerely, Jeremy P. Stanton

Two hours after Remy's email went out to the Griggs campaign, the *New York Gazette* ran a story by Eric Celsun:

CONVICTED DOMESTIC ABUSER TO BE FEATURED ON GET UP AMERICA!

Griggs campaign denies coordination of interview featuring Dennis Stanton, father of former staffer Jeremy Stanton

by Eric Celsun

Dennis James Stanton, father of former Griggs communications aide and 'Upper East Side Hero' Jeremy Stanton, is scheduled to appear on tomorrow morning's *Get Up America!* The network has been heavily promoting what it calls an "exclusive" interview. The promotional material for the interview alleges that the younger

Stanton committed violent acts against his father, compounded with emotional abuse centering around the care of the elder Stanton's now-deceased wife, Margaret.

However, police reports from Lancaster County confirm that Dennis Stanton, 62, has been charged no less than three times with at least four counts of domestic violence, towards Margaret Stanton and a Ms. Elaine Steadman, whom he was married to briefly before their union was annulled. Following his conviction on the latter of the three charges, the elder Stanton spent fifteen months in a correctional facility in his hometown of Lancaster, PA, and was released in 2004.

When reached for comment, Jeremy Stanton, who has officially resigned from Rawson Griggs's presidential campaign, said, "My father terrorized my mother and me for years. That anyone would give a convicted abuser airtime and publicity after his legally documented history of violent behavior is appalling and pathetic. Dennis Stanton's voice should be shunned, not amplified. If you know Dennis Stanton as well as I do, you know he's lying because his mouth is open. I'm sorry the folks at the *Get Up America!* didn't bother to learn the truth before taking the word of a convicted abuser and promoting him to millions of people."

Producers at *Get Up America!* did not respond for comment by press time, but sources close to the network claim they are seriously considering pulling the interview. Another source claims that the Griggs campaign may have paid Dennis Stanton to take part in the interview in an effort to discredit Jeremy Stanton, who resigned under hostile terms.

Reached for comment, Rebecca Blum, Griggs's campaign manager, said, "Jeremy Stanton was window dressing for our campaign. Nothing more. He reaped the fruits of his allegedly selfless act for months, and over that time he became both unreliable and unstable. Despite this, the Griggs campaign paid him handsomely for his time. Jeremy Stanton had no more knowledge of our campaign than does a model hired to appear in an advertisement for a car dealership. Rawson Griggs barely knew Jeremy, and the American public will forget about him in due time."

Said Jeremy Stanton, "When I joined Rawson Griggs's campaign, I did so because I believed in him and what he stood for: reform, individuality, strength, and responsibility. But those tenets have taken a backseat to nihilism and violence that I believe will drive us apart more than pull us together. I have come to fear the potential of a Rawson Griggs presidency, and I can no longer continue to support the candidate."

When Remy saw that the article was live, he took out his iPad and found the file he needed: the guest list from the event at the Hyatt the night Paul Bracewell died.

Remy then blasted out an email to the entire guest list, linking to Eric Celsun's article. It read:

Dear friends –

It's been months since I stood before you and asked you to support Rawson Griggs for president of the United States. As many of you know, that is no longer the case. I do not support Mr. Griggs, and I hope that given his actions and words over the last few months, you have reconsidered your support as well.

I'm writing today for personal reasons as well. Tomorrow, my father is scheduled to appear on a popular morning show to discredit me. Though I cannot prove it, I am certain this charade was orchestrated by the Griggs campaign.

Below is a link to an article just published in the New York Gazette. My father, whom I have not spoken to in over a decade, is a convicted domestic abuser. This news program withheld this information from their promotion, and the public, likely due to the ad revenue Rawson Griggs had brought their network.

It is not enough to condemn the network for these actions: we must literally take it to the bank. As I said that night at the Hyatt months ago, you all have influence. I hope that you will spread the word about your disapproval for what Get Up America! plans to do. I will be boycotting the network until this happens. I hope you will consider joining me, and encouraging those who follow and trust you to do the same.

    Sincerely,

    Jeremy Stanton

Rem sat back in bed in his hotel room and took a deep breath. He had just waged war on Rawson Griggs. Remy's army was online. The Hyatt guest list alone could reach a hundred million people. Now he just prayed it worked.

Fifteen minutes later, Remy checked his social media feeds. Dozens of people from the email list had posted the link to Celsun's article, along with the hashtag #WeSupportRemy, promising to boycott not only *Get Up America!* but the entire network. Influential reporters and even other campaign surrogates joined in. Within an hour, #WeSupportRemy was trending.

One of the re-posts came from Doug Rimbaud:

Campaigns may have their differences in policy, but giving this "man" airtime is shameful. #WeSupportRemy

Every time Remy refreshed his feed, he had dozens of new replies. Of course there was a fair amount of backlash; Griggs supporters threatening to put his dick in a blender, saying his father had wasted the sperm, saying that they hoped, once elected, Rawson Griggs would send Remy to Guantanamo.

At least the haters were creative.

Two hours after Remy blasted the Hyatt guest list, *Get Up America!* issued a statement on their Facebook page:

Due to the release of incendiary information previously not seen by Get Up America! that directly contradicts statements given by Dennis Stanton, tomorrow's interview will not be airing. There is no scheduled run date at this point.

Remy jumped off the bed and pumped his fist in the air. He called Eric Celsun.

"I had a feeling you'd be calling," Celsun said.

"What's your favorite drink?" Remy said. "Because I'm buying you a lifetime supply of whatever it is."

"I don't accept gifts from subjects, but if you sent a six-pack of hard cider to the office, I wouldn't turn it down."

"Hard cider? Really?"

"Heaven in a bottle, my friend."

"I've never tried it. I don't think they served hard cider on Griggs Force One. Seriously, Eric, great work. Thank you."

"You don't need to thank me," Celsun said. "I didn't do it to curry favors. I did it because it was a legitimate story. It just so happened that it was also the right thing to do. Always nice when those two things line up."

"Well, thank you anyway. Part of me wishes I could see my father's face when he hears he's off the air. I just hope the bars in Lancaster have enough Wild Turkey."

"I think the Griggs campaign had your father on standby," Celsun said. "They were able to get him on air crazy quick. I'm guessing the Griggs people approached your father well before approaching *Get Up America!* In fact, I wouldn't be surprised if they got to him not too long after they hired you. Maybe even *before* they hired you. As an insurance policy, a 'break glass in case of emergency' just in case you went rogue. Which, well, you kind of did."

"In the meantime," Remy said, "I'm reasonably sure that Rawson Griggs killed the last guy who was disloyal to him."

"Well, I hope you can sleep tonight knowing you've pissed off Keyser Söze."

There was a knock at the door. Remy bolted up from bed. He looked at the taser sitting on the nightstand. The little piece of plastic and metal suddenly looked grossly inadequate.

"You know, Keyser Söze?" Celsun said. "From the movie with Kevin Spacey and the lighter and...hey, Remy, you still there?"

Remy grabbed the taser from the nightstand and crept to the door. What if he peeked through the peephole and someone shot him in the eye? Had he seen too many movies? Or was this his life now?

"Remy? Remy, you there?" Celsun was still on the line.

"I'm here. Just hold on a second."

Remy figured if someone shot him, at least Celsun would hear it.

"I know you're in there," came the voice from the other side of the door.

It was Alena. Remy almost fell to the ground in relief.

"I'll call you back," he said to Celsun, and ended the call. He opened the door. Alena was standing there in jeans and an overcoat.

"What the hell is that thing?" she said, pointing at Remy's hand. He was still holding the taser. He tossed it onto the chair in the corner.

"The last few days," he said, "bad things seem to keep happening to people I care about. Thought I might be next."

"I know about Trevor," Alena replied. "Can I come in?"

Remy nodded. She entered and hung her coat on a chair. She was wearing a white turtleneck and her hair was done up in a bun. She was dressed simply, but as always she made the clothes look better than they were.

"How did you know where to find me?" Remy said.

"I heard about Trevor. I met him when you were in the hospital. God, that seems like ages ago. You weren't returning my texts, so I thought you might be with him. So I went to Beth Israel. You were gone, but Chris told me where you were staying. Does your place really have bedbugs?"

"I sure hope not," Remy said.

He couldn't tell her the real reason he was staying there. What he believed her father had done.

"You know I left the campaign."

Alena nodded. She sat down on the bed. Remy pulled out the desk chair and sat across from her.

"I'm sorry but I'm not," she said. "You've been different recently. We've all seen it. You used to have this, I don't know, *lightness* to you. It's killed me to see that dim."

"I've watched the same thing happen to you," Remy said. "And it eats away at me."

"I know," Alena said. "I miss how it was before. How are you?"

"Considering I spent the whole day trying to submarine a tell-all interview with my own father after visiting my best friend in the hospital—I'd say I've had better days."

"I'm sorry," she said.

"Why are you sorry?"

"Because I know what it's like to feel like the world is crashing down around you," she said. "But you were there when I needed you, when I hurt. And I know you well enough to know that you'd need someone too, when you were in pain."

"Sometimes I can't believe I've only known you a few months," Remy said.

"I know," she said. "Come here."

Remy hesitated, just for a moment, then moved to the bed. His heart was jackhammering. He could feel the blood rushing in his temples.

"Lie down," she said.

He did. She curled up next to him. Her perfume was light, crisp. He could feel her breath on his neck. He thought about the night in Spokane, Alena curled up next to him, the slight tickle as she breathed in and out.

"So we go to sleep, and when I wake up, you'll be gone, right?" Remy said. "That's how this works?"

"Not this time."

Alena leaned over Remy and kissed him softly on the lips. At first, he was frozen by the shock of it. He didn't move. But then he felt Alena's hand burrow under his neck, pushing his head up, and he pressed back into her, kissing her deeply.

Remy shifted onto his side until he was face to face with Alena, running his hand down her neck, her shoulders, her back, resting it on her hip. She slid her hand around his back and pressed him towards her until they were touching, moving against each other. She wrapped her leg around his, pulled him closer.

Even though this was the first time they'd been this close, Remy felt like he knew her touch, her body, every inch of her.

They kissed for what seemed like hours. Then, slowly, they slipped off their clothes. He ran his finger down the curve of her spine and felt her shudder, heard her moan softly. Remy took the time to look at her body, head to toe. He wanted to remember this, remember every inch of skin, every curve, because he had no idea what would happen next.

"I've wanted this," he said to her. "You have no idea how much I've wanted this."

Alena stopped kissing him and looked him in the eye.

"Yes, I do," she said.

Remy began to kiss her neck, learning her body's rhythms as he touched her, outside and in. She gave him a condom and when he was ready, she pulled him on top of her gently. Remy took his time, discovering what made her shiver, what made her moan. And then she took him inside of her, and he stared into her eyes as they moved together, knowing she would be there in the morning.

And she was.

CHAPTER 27

Remy looked at the woman lying naked in bed, and wondered if, just for a while, they could disappear somewhere. Somewhere nobody knew them. Where she wasn't Alena Griggs and he wasn't Jeremy Stanton, and they could wear loose fabrics and lie on a warm beach and drink sugary cocktails, then retreat to a sun-dappled cabin with a ceiling fan and a soft bed and make love for hours on end.

Somewhere that wasn't a cheap hotel room in midtown Manhattan, where they'd wake up and still be who they were the day before.

While Alena slept, Remy showered. He took his time. When he got out, she was sitting up in bed, the bed sheets wrapped around her shoulders, his cell phone in her hand.

"You got a text," she said, "from Grace Rivas. She wants to meet with you, apparently."

Remy walked over and took the phone. Alena looked at him, clearly expecting some sort of explanation.

"What are you two meeting about?"

"Alena," he said. "It's complicated."

"Coming here last night was complicated too," she said.

"I know."

Remy took a deep breath. He didn't know what to say. But he couldn't keep it from her any longer.

"Your father," he said. "I think he's done some terrible things. And I've been working with Grace to find out whether they're true."

Alena held the sheet closer, eyes narrowing. "What kind of *things*?"

"Alena, we don't have to talk…"

"Yes. We do. What kind of things do you think my father has done?"

"I really don't want to go into it now. There's too much we don't know."

"*What kind of things?*" Alena stood up, taking the sheets with her. She pushed Remy backwards. He stumbled, surprised.

"I think he may have had something to do with Paul…with Paul's…"

"With Paul's what?"

"With Paul's death."

Alena looked like she'd been punched in the stomach. "You… what?"

Remy nodded.

"You think my father had something to do with my husband's death?"

He nodded again.

"Oh, fuck you, Jeremy," Alena said. She tossed the sheets back on the bed and grabbed her clothes. She marched into the bathroom and locked the door. Remy stood there, shaking. What the hell could he have done?

"Alena," he said, shouting through the door. "Please. Let's talk."

She came out a minute later. Clothes on, hair a mess.

"Stay. Sit down."

"Not a chance," she said. "I know my father never liked Paul. But he would never do something like that. Why would he risk his campaign, risk *me*? Just because he disapproved of the man I married?"

"No," Remy said. "He did it because Paul was working for Annabelle Shaw's campaign."

Alena's mouth hung open. Remy felt wretched. There was no easy way to say any of it. And there was never a way he could have told her.

"I shouldn't have come here last night," Alena said softly. "You're lying."

"God, trust me, I wish I was," Remy said. "He was feeding them information. Paul found out your father was being propped up by foreign money. Tens of millions, maybe more. Your father was near broke. He was being used. And when he was elected, your father could direct government policy to make millions, if not billions. For them and for him."

Alena stood there, shaking her head. "That's insane. *You're* insane."

"It's not just me," Remy said. "You know Michael O'Brien? Paul's friend from Spokane? Paul told O'Brien all of this."

"And you decide to loop me in *now*? After I sleep with you?"

Remy looked at the floor, shame burning through him.

"I didn't know how to tell you. There was never time, and I couldn't say anything while I wasn't sure. But now, I'm sure. I've seen you dragged through hell. I didn't want to pull you further down."

"If this isn't further down," Alena said, "then you tell me: what is it?"

He said nothing.

"Go to hell, Remy. I should have never come here last night."

Alena took her coat and purse and left the room, slamming the door behind her. Remy felt his face grow hot. He sat down. Looked at his hands. Felt a tear drop into his palm. He punched the mattress, holding in the kind of rage than only came when you got exactly what you dreamed of, only to lose it the next moment.

He bit his lip. Sat there, unmoving, for an hour. Then Remy wiped the tears away, picked up his phone, and texted Grace Rivas.

Tell me when and I'll be there.

The *Gazette* offices were three blocks west of his hotel.

So Remy walked east. He had no idea if anyone was following him, but better to be safe than dead. Plus, he knew the *Gazette* would have tight security, so, unfortunately, the tasers had to be left in the hotel.

He took the 6 train down to Union Square, then transferred to the N, which he took to 34th. He then hopped on the uptown B train, which he rode to 81st.

At 81st, Remy walked around the Museum of Natural History, over to Columbus, down to 80th, and then west where he got on the downtown 1 train at 79th and Broadway. At Columbus Circle, he transferred to the downtown C train, which he took to 42nd and 8th. Which was literally one block from the *New York Gazette*, and just two blocks from where he was staying. The whole route took nearly an hour and a half to complete.

When he arrived at the *Gazette* offices, Remy approached the polished granite security desk with his ID ready. There were two metal detectors screening visitors and their bags. Two guards manned the desk, with another guard at each metal detector. And they all looked like they could break Remy in half.

"Hi, I have a meeting with Grace Rivas at the *Gazette*."

"Photo ID. Please place your briefcase flat on the belt."

Remy did so, and handed his license to the guard. When the guard took Remy's ID, he did a double take.

"Mr. Stanton. You've had a hell of a week," the man said. "Look into the camera."

Remy offered a weak smile to the orb affixed to the desk.

"Twelfth floor."

He got his bag and took the elevator to the twelfth floor. When the door opened, Grace Rivas was standing there, waiting for him. Remy smiled, and she returned it. She had a bulky brace on her right knee and held a cane. Remy stepped out and gave her a gentle hug.

"Damn, it's good to see you," he said.

"You too. Last time we talked, you were only a minor celebrity. I'm shocked you don't have a personal TMZ crew following you around by this point."

"And your knee didn't look like someone had taken a sledgehammer to it."

"It feels worse than it looks," she said.

"How are you doing?"

"I'm angry," Grace replied. "Pissed. I want to nail Rawson Griggs more than anything in this world."

"*If I only had a hammer,*" Remy sang, "*I'd hammer in the morning. I'd hammer in the evening.*"

"God, you're a dork. Come on, Eric is waiting for us."

The twelfth floor of the *Gazette* newsroom was a massive open floor plan, lined with rows and rows of cubicle after cubicle, with a perimeter of single executive offices. There was a wide red staircase in the middle of the floor plan.

Grace led him through the newsroom, walking gingerly with her cane. He'd never been inside a newsroom this large before. It was a constant blur of activity: dozens of reporters talking and typing and yelling. As they walked, Remy noticed a few reporters stare at him as they passed.

Grace led him to an office in the back. Eric Celsun sat at a conference table leafing through a stack of papers. Grace closed the door behind them. Remy shook Eric's hand.

"Good to see you," Remy said. "Thanks again for everything with Dennis."

"Don't you mean Dad?" Celsun said.

"No. I mean Dennis."

Celsun smiled. "Don't sweat it." He was jittery and talked like a record played at double speed. "Sorry. Too much coffee today. Do you want a cup? Of coffee? How do you like it? Your coffee? Strong? I like it strong."

"I'm good," Remy said, hoping Celsun's heart didn't explode from a caffeine overdose before they had a chance to talk. Remy looked over the mountain of papers on the table. "You've been busy."

"Sleep is for losers. I was able to get the 990 forms from the Griggs Foundation dating back twenty years. They're mandatory tax filings for charitable organizations. And they're simply fascinating."

"How so?"

"Look at this," Celsun said. He handed a piece of paper to Remy. "These are the top ten donors in terms of total contributions to the Griggs Foundation over the last twenty years. Recognize any of them?"

Remy scanned the list, then stopped at one name.

"Temur Kamurzenov. He ran Kyrgyzstan's energy program."

Grace added, "He also owns a U.S. shell company that contributed millions to Brent Scott's Super PAC."

"Kamurzenov donated a hundred thousand dollars every year like clockwork to the Griggs Foundation."

"So Rawson had a relationship with Kyrgyzstan energy chief going back two decades," Remy said. "That's how he was able to broker the deal with GazProm to sell Kyrgyzstan's energy supply to Russia."

"It would also explain why PoliSpill would run communications through Kyrgyzstan," Grace added. "If PoliSpill was coordinating with the Griggs campaign, they would need secure transmissions through a friendly country with a government that would turn a blind eye."

"I think Rawson plans to lessen sanctions on Russian energy exports," Remy said. "That kind of policy change would be worth billions, if not trillions. Spending a few hundred million to help Rawson get elected would be a drop in the bucket."

"For the last thirty years, Saudi Arabia has been our largest oil supplier," Celsun said. "We currently import over a million barrels of Saudi crude a day, and thirty-eight thousand a day from Russia. That's a *lot* of revenue the Kremlin is missing out on. And when the U.S. started exporting oil and LNG, or liquefied natural gas, to Europe, it broke Russia's stranglehold on European energy exports. Russia is the world's largest oil exporter. If the sanctions are gone, it would severely cut down on our gas exports to Europe while expanding Russia's to us."

"Rawson must have a stake in GazProm," Remy said. "You know what every insanely rich man has in common? They all want to be *more* rich. It's not just about the presidency. If this policy changes like we think it will, Rawson will own part of the largest global exporter of natural gas in the world. Problem is, nobody can prove it."

"It sounds like Paul Bracewell had proof," Grace said. "Too bad he never got to share it."

Remy tapped his chin. "When I met with Michael O'Brien in Spokane, he said Paul was scared. He knew Rawson was tapping his electronic communications. O'Brien said that Paul would only correspond via snail mail, that even Rawson couldn't track something just dropped in a mailbox."

"Do people even still use snail mail?" Celsun said.

"O'Brien said the same thing. But what if Paul *had* proof? He just didn't trust the electronic files wouldn't get traced."

"My actual physical inbox is a wasteland," Celsun said. "Ninety-nine percent of the mail I get is from crazy people who literally cut my articles out of the paper and doodle things on them like *Celsun is Stoooopid*. I haven't checked it in months. Grace?"

"Me either." They looked at each other. "You don't think…"

Grace and Celsun looked at each other and bolted from their chairs. Celsun ran out of the conference room and Grace followed him, limping. Remy sat there wondering what the hell had just happened. A few minutes later, they returned with a manila envelope that looked like it had been dragged through a sewage system.

Celsun slammed it on the table like it was some sort of trophy.

"Yahtzee," he said.

Remy looked at the sad, tattered envelope. "What is that?"

"Check the return address," Grace said.

Remy looked. "Holy shit," he said.

"Griggs Tower," Grace replied. "It's a message."

"It was Paul," Remy said. "And look at the date of the postmark. Paul sent this the day he died."

CHAPTER 28

The three of them stood around the table in stunned silence. Piles of papers, printouts, folders, and briefings had been shuffled to the edges of the table, months of research treated like detritus. They'd been shunted aside for this, the few pages that before them. They were a game changer.

Five pages. Laid out in a row horizontally.

"Is this really what I think it is?" Remy said.

"I believe so," Celsun replied. "God love the USPS."

"From now on, I'm going to check my mailbox every five minutes," Grace said.

Spread before them were five pages from Rawson Griggs's official tax returns from 2008. They included his salary, debts, schedules, and forms. Paul had mailed these to Grace the day of the event at the Hyatt. Just hours before he was found floating in the East River.

"We need to confirm the authenticity of these pages before we can even think about running them," Grace said. "Remy, you mentioned there was an accounting firm that handled work for Rawson Griggs. They would be able to verify these documents." She used her finger to underline the accounting firm listed on the top sheet: Benson, Hawes, and Seligmann.

"Benson," Remy said. "That's the guy. O'Brien told me about an accountant named 'Benson something' who'd worked on Griggs's tax returns. Paul knew him. That's how he got these."

Grace turned her laptop around for them to see. She'd pulled up the Benson, Hawes, and Seligmann website and found Benson's bio page. "Here he is. Hayes Benson. Founder and senior partner. It says here, 'Mr. Benson has worked with some of the most prominent citizens and corporations in the country, including Comcast, NewsCorp, Exxon, and the Griggs Organization.'"

"And look here," Celsun said, pointing to a line on the third page of the returns. "Look at the losses Rawson Griggs claimed in 2008."

"Jesus," Grace said. "Can that be right? One point eight *billion* dollars? How is that even possible?"

"I'm willing to bet that's Rawson's stake in GazProm," Eric said. "He spent nearly two billion dollars to go into business with the Russian energy department."

"That's the year Rawson made his speech at the LiK conference in Bishkek, Kyrgyzstan," Remy said. "Which was attended by Temur Kamurzenov and the head of GazProm."

"So, if Rawson spends two billion to buy into GazProm, and his properties are losing money hand over fist, it's entirely possible Rawson was essentially bankrupt prior to launching his campaign. Which is why all that foreign money started flooding into his properties."

Remy added, "Paul said that Rawson's properties were running at an unheard of capacity rate. They needed to keep Rawson solvent. Make him appear wealthy. And the money they spent to do it, even if it's hundreds of millions, is incidental. Because if he wins, if Russia can start exporting energy here, it's a new global economy."

Celsun said, "And then there might as well be an invisible pipeline running from Moscow to Washington, D.C."

"I'm going to the Benson, Hawes, and Seligmann office," Grace said. "I need Hayes Benson to confirm these documents in person."

She took the pages, left the room, and came back with two sets of copies. She placed one in a manila folder and put it in her briefcase and laid the others on the table. "If Hayes Benson confirms the authenticity of these documents, we have enough here for one hell of a story."

"Agreed," Remy said, "but is it enough to stop Rawson?"

"That's not our job," she said.

"You're kidding me, right?" Remy said, incredulous. "After what that monster did to you in Cincinnati? What he did to Paul? What he's capable of doing if he's elected?"

"We still don't have proof that Rawson did anything to Paul Bracewell," Grace said. "There's been no investigation. No proof of foul play. For us to even *touch* that story, we'd need something hard to go on. Financial ties to the Russian energy federation are a big deal. We have enough here to tie him to all of that. But you don't accuse the frontrunner for president of the United States of murder unless you have proof."

"Or you have a confession," Celsun said. "And good luck getting *that.*"

Remy felt heat rising up from his chest to his neck, anger starting to coil and burn. Grace could have been killed and she was still pretending that this was all about the story, all about plastering some article on the front page of the *Gazette* in the foolish belief it could do anything to even dent the hide of the Griggs battleship. Maybe the ties to Russia and links to PoliSpill could pierce his skin, but the wounds would heal.

"You have proof, *proof*, that this man is using his power to enrich himself and put our country at risk. What the hell else do you need to take a stand against him?"

"We don't do our jobs based on taking a stand," Grace said. "I want Rawson to go down. *Hard.* But lawfully."

"You have an obligation," Remy said.

"To who? To you?"

"To people. To tell them the truth."

"Which is exactly what we're doing. But if you want me to allege capital crimes based on conjecture or your gut, you're in the wrong place."

"I'm sorry," Remy said. "I thought you were a fighter."

Grace approached Remy until they stood toe to toe. She looked him right in the eye. She was nearly a head shorter than him, but didn't stop until their toes were touching. Remy felt something slip. The anger coursed through him, but he couldn't fully understand why. It wasn't Grace. He was angry about Alena, about how he'd kept this from her, how she had every right to leave him that morning.

He'd wanted to be with her for months, and now it was tarnished. So he was lashing out. He knew it. Grace knew it.

"I have fought battles you cannot fathom. You've had hardships? Well, so have I. I have fought my whole *life*. And I'll be damned if you'll question any of it."

Grace grabbed her briefcase and walked out of the conference room, her cane clacking on the linoleum. Remy watched her go, silent. He turned to look at Eric Celsun.

"Whoa," he said. "That was intense."

"Thanks for the analysis."

"She's right, you know," he said. "The second you let people know you have an agenda, your credibility is shot. If these documents check out, we'll print the story. Then people can judge for themselves."

"And if they still vote for Rawson Griggs? Who might be acting as a puppet for a foreign nation?"

Celsun sighed, shrugged. "That's their choice."

"I'm don't want to leave that up to chance. There's too much at stake."

"We're not your enemy, Remy. If Rawson had a hand in Paul's death, and if Dastan Nogoyev and Alexay Usenov are linked to Rawson's ties in Kyrgyzstan, we'll want people to know. But we can't prove that yet."

"I'll prove it," Remy said. And then he left the *Gazette* without any idea of just how he was going to live up to that promise.

CHAPTER 29

The apartment felt damp. Like a steam room left alone for days. Alena wasn't quite sure when it started to feel that way, but everywhere she went, she felt like she was walking in a swamp. She knelt down, ran her hands over the hardwood floor, but the boards were as dry as the day they were installed. She checked the air ducts, the bathroom ceiling, the spaces underneath the dishwasher and refrigerator. They were all as dry as a bone.

Alena picked up the phone and called the front desk.

"Yes, Mrs. Griggs?"

That dagger. Mrs. Griggs. She didn't know how long people would keep calling her missus, if there was a statute of limitations on how long you kept your married status after your husband died. But every time that word—missus—escaped someone's lips, it felt like a blade slipping through her ribcage.

"Hi, Don. I think there's a leak in my apartment."

"Ah, so sorry. I'll have maintenance up right away to take a look. Where's the leak coming from?"

"I…um…I'm not sure."

"Bathroom? Kitchen?"

"No, neither one."

"Bedroom?"

"Nope. That's fine."

"I…uh…what should I tell maintenance?"

"Just…forget it. I'm mistaken. Thanks, Don, sorry about this."

"Should I have them come just in case?"

"No, that's alright. I'm sure they're busy."

"Not a problem. Call back if you find the leak."

Alena hung up the phone, then found herself sliding down the wall until she was seated next to the fridge. She took deep breaths. Being the daughter of Rawson Griggs meant Alena had a life most people would never understand, a life most people only dreamed of. Because that was what they believed it was: a dream. Being a Griggs meant you were surrounded by glitz and glamour twenty-four seven, your days full of charity lunches, your nights full of parties and balls. You were one of the beautiful people, your every desire catered to, never wanting for anything.

But there was also a devastating loneliness, a hollowness, knowing she woke up every single day with a life that did not fully belong to her. For the last fifteen years, Alena received an email from Wanda LeFebvre containing her father's itinerary, which, more often than not, was also her itinerary. There were always dinners to attend, pols and businessmen to wine and dine, wealthy and influential people to impress. And she would dress exquisitely, act politely, fake modesty when appropriate, laugh like she meant it, and always have a good-looking man by her side.

She'd had no shortage of those men throughout her life. Placeholders. Paperweights. Men who looked dashing in photographs, men who made other women envy her like mad. European shipping heirs and well-coiffed movie stars and scions who still used the phrase "old money" without a sense of irony.

They came and they went and sometimes they left impressions, but most of the time those impressions lasted as long as an impression in a pillow. Once in a very long while one would leave a small crack in her heart, but never anything large enough that it couldn't be healed with a bottle of Malbec and a movie marathon.

And then Paul came along. He was different. Funny and smart and charming, and it happened totally by accident. There was no artifice, no pretension. Paul didn't carry himself like the other men, that slow, deliberate walk most of her suitors had, the unhurried gait that suggested the world would come to them. Paul was fun and funny and sexy, and he was hers.

And that was the Paul she tried to remember. The man she could lie in bed with all day, laughing and kissing. Not the man who'd faded away, who'd come to resent her and her family and everything she'd ever loved.

Alena had hoped Paul's personality would rub off on her father. Lord knew he needed some more levity in his life. Instead, Paul's personality was dissolved like powder in a glass of water.

And now she was a widow.

Widow.

That word, always spoken with a mouthful of glass. Barely thirty and tasked with starting over again. At night, when she couldn't sleep, Alena thought about the horror of having to date while one, a Griggs, two, a young widow, and three, very potentially the next First Daughter. Alena figured she might as well sail off into the Atlantic Ocean on a small raft and never return.

And then there was Remy. There had been something between them from the start. But she stemmed it, pretended it wasn't there until it killed her to do so. She'd wanted him before last night, wanted to feel naked in his arms, but couldn't face the aftermath. What would happen next?

And then, when it finally did happen, when she went to sleep, his bare chest beside her, she woke up with everything changed. She was foolish to think she could just start a new romance with Remy. Maybe another time, another life. But not this one.

Her father had made passing attempts to get her back on the campaign trail. He had practically begged her to accompany him to

Salt Lake City to woo prominent Mormons. Utah voters tended to place extra emphasis on morality at the voting booths, and Rawson wanted to showcase his daughter as proof of his commitment to the nuclear family. Alena declined.

Alena knew her father would offer Remy a job. Rawson could see the value in everything, people especially. Remy had value to him, to the campaign. He couldn't have foreseen how it would end. Maybe Alena wanted him to hire Remy. Maybe she needed something—someone—new.

But she couldn't hide her fear at what the campaign had become. Who her father had become.

What Remy had said about Paul was insane. Insulting. Horrifying.

But she couldn't get it out of her mind. Maybe that was why she enjoyed her time with Remy. With him, she could just be Alena.

She couldn't ignore it. She couldn't forget him.

So she sent Remy a text.

I need to see you. Tell me when and where.

And then she waited.

She was convinced he wouldn't write back. When she left the hotel, that would be the end of it. And she would have to live with that. They both would.

And then her cell phone rang. Alena answered it. Immediately, her hand went to her mouth.

The conversation lasted less than thirty seconds. Her hand shook so much the phone clattered to the floor. And when Alena picked it back up, she was crying.

Jeremy. Oh god, Jeremy.

She grabbed her coat and ran out the door. She had no idea if he was still alive.

CHAPTER 30

Remy tried to let go of the anger, but it rubbed against him like a stone in his shoe. How dare Grace lecture him on responsibility. Was he the only one who saw the danger of a Rawson Griggs presidency?

He was tired, fed up, angry with himself over Alena, and decided to hell with it all. He was tired of the cloak and dagger nonsense.

It was bitterly cold outside. When he got back to his hotel, Remy took a hot shower, threw on a Comfort Inn bathrobe—which was about comfortable as a straitjacket—sat in bed, and watched the news. Every network followed Rawson Griggs around the country like groupies, broadcasting every moment of every speech. Remy remembered what Rawson had said about the value of free media, and felt a white hot rage when he thought about the millions of dollars in free publicity networks were basically throwing at Rawson by broadcasting him nonstop. He owned the airwaves.

Remy watched a solid five hours of cable news before starting to feel sick. He thought about texting Alena, but didn't know what to say. How did you come back from accusing someone's father of murder? Remy needed a drink, and not one that came out of a bottle the size of his thumb.

He cleaned himself up, threw on a pair of jeans and a V-neck sweater over a button-down, put on a hat, strapped the tasers back on, and left the hotel. There were a dozen bars within walking distance of his hotel, but Times Square was all tourist traps serving crummy frozen burger patties and charging nine dollars for a domestic draft. He needed something a little more familiar.

Remy took the 6 train uptown to 86th, then walked east towards the river until he got to Bailey's. The bar he'd been drinking at the night he met Alena Griggs and Paul Bracewell.

Ian was behind the bar. Remy slid in and ordered an IPA.

"Well, lookie here. By Abraham Lincoln's ghost. Thought we'd seen the last of you, Remy."

"Still here," Remy said, "for better or worse."

Ian poured two shots of Jameson and put them on the bar along with Remy's beer.

"Let's see if we can't make it more better than worse," Ian said.

They clinked glasses and downed the shots.

A basketball game was on. Remy sipped his beer and tuned out. Nobody approached him. Nobody noticed him. He ordered a plate of nachos and wolfed them down.

"Beast this, motherfucker," he said, shoving four goopy chips into his mouth.

Remy felt his phone buzz. He took it out and saw a text from Grace Rivas.

He read it and a smile spread across his face.

Confirmed with Hayes Benson that the Griggs tax return pages are authentic. Eric and I will be writing the story tonight. Should go up tomorrow or the day after. Thank you for all your help, Remy. I can't say whether this will have the effect you want, but it's the truth, and that's all we can do.

Grace

That was worth another drink.

After he finished his second beer, Remy paid and left a ten dollar tip. It was a gorgeous evening, a cool wind coming off the East River. Sometimes the city took his breath away. Part of him missed being just another guy living amongst the concrete jungle. Before he had to worry about matters of national security, before he knew anyone named Griggs.

Ten more minutes either way that night and Paul would have died and nobody would have been any wiser and Remy's life would have continued just the way it was. Instead, he was living in budget hotel in the middle of a tourist mecca, trying to stay hidden from some of the most powerful people in the world. If Remy had a chance to go back, choose the other path, maybe he would have been better off.

He headed towards the subway. It was a nice night out and he needed the air. He was tired of it all. He walked slowly west down 85th Street. He saw a teenage girl walking her dog, a young couple necking in a doorway.

Remy smiled.

He did not notice the man come up from behind him holding a metal bar. All he heard was a faint *whoosh* before the bar cracked across his shoulder blades, driving the wind out of him and forcing him to his knees. The second blow glanced off the side of his head, knocking him unconscious before the pain even had a chance to register.

And he felt nothing when they picked him up and tossed him into the back of a waiting van.

CHAPTER 31

When Remy opened his eyes, he had the headache to end all headaches and his upper back screamed in pain. It took a minute for him to focus, and as soon as he realized where he was, the terror set in.

He was lying on his side on the floor of a van. The floor was covered in clear plastic sheeting. A black curtain cordoned off the rear of the van from the driver. On the sheeting, next to his head, Remy noticed a few drops of blood. It was red and fresh. His blood.

Electrical tape was fastened over his mouth. His hands were bound behind him with what felt like a plastic tie.

Remy managed to pull himself into a seated position. His breathing was ragged, and his heart jackhammered in his chest. The tape forced him to breathe through his nose, but the clotted blood forced the breaths to come in quick gasps. He felt like he might hyperventilate.

Two men sat on the floor of the van across from him. Their faces were hidden under ski masks. Their eyes were fixed on Remy. They said nothing. He tried to reach his left pocket, but could feel that it was empty. They'd taken his phone. He looked down at his ankle. They'd taken the taser. His trigger bracelet was still on, though. They probably assumed it was a fitness tracker.

Remy tried to speak, but his words were unintelligible through the tape. The men did not move. The windows were covered in black tape. He couldn't see where they were or where they were going. Counting the driver, there were three people in the van. And Remy didn't get the sense that they were taking him to a hospital.

One of the men held a metal pipe in his gloved hand. In the other hand, he held the taser than had been strapped to Remy's ankle.

Remy wondered if that pipe was the same weapon that was used to break Trevor's ankle. There was a good chance they were the same men. The fewer people in the loop, the fewer fuck-ups. And wherever the four of them were going, it was very likely only three would be coming back.

Remy tried to speak again. He struggled against his bonds. The men didn't react. They weren't concerned about him escaping and didn't seem to be in a conversational mood.

Every bump in the road sent a jolt of pain through him. The van bumped along, every pothole jarring his head, causing him to yelp into the tape covering his mouth. His head pounded. Panic was setting in, adrenaline coursing through his veins. He was being driven to his death.

Then Remy saw a light flash. It was his cell phone. Someone had texted him.

One of the men picked up the phone and looked at the screen. Remy saw the man's eyes widen.

He leaned over to his partner and whispered something in his ear. Remy couldn't be sure, but he swore the second man said something that sounded like *shit*. Remy figured anything bad for them had to be good for him.

The second man crawled over to Remy and flicked open a switchblade. Remy forced himself back against the wall of the van. He struggled, tried to scream, tried to twist away. The man grabbed Remy by the neck. Remy closed his eyes, sure his throat was about to be cut.

But instead, he felt the knife slip between his hands and cut the plastic tie.

Then the man sat back against the opposite wall. He folded the knife and put it in his pocket.

Remy brought his hands forward. He rubbed them together to get the blood flowing, get his circulation back. The tape was still on his mouth. He reached up to remove it, but the man closer to the door said, "Don't touch it. If you do, I'll cut one of your eyes out."

Remy stopped. The man held out Remy's phone.

"You got a text from Alena Griggs."

He mouthed *Alena?* through the tape.

"She said she needs to see you. Now, obviously, that's not going to happen." The man had a slight accent. Hispanic? Remy couldn't be sure. "Problem is, it's Mr. Griggs's daughter. So if she gets suspicious, she tells her father, she starts asking around, and that's a problem. And so it's in all of our best interest that little Miss Griggs doesn't get suspicious. Hear what I'm saying?"

Remy nodded.

"So what you're going to do," he said, "is write back. You're going respond so she doesn't get suspicious. That's it. No signals. No calls. I'm going to watch you type it out. You type anything else, or try to call or text anyone other than Alena, after I cut your eye out, I'm going to find that reporter friend of yours and cut her tits off. You get me?"

Remy nodded.

The man handed Remy the phone. He smelled like sweat and cotton. As Remy opened the text area, the man looked over his shoulder like a suspicious spouse.

Remy figured he could probably type and send the word *help* before they could stop him. But he also believed them that they would harm Grace if he did. He had one chance. He had to time it perfectly. And if he didn't, he was dead.

Remy wrung out his wrists and began to type.

Hey Alena. No can do. Busy. Rain check?

The man took the phone from Remy and deleted the text.

"Don't be so casual," he said. "Asking for a rain check would make her suspicious. Don't be stupid. You want to play with your friend's life?"

Remy shook his head. He took the phone back and wrote: *Hey Alena. I'm busy right now, but I'll drop you a line later.*

The man nodded and pressed send. Then he showed the phone to his partner.

The moment the man held the phone up for his partner to see, Remy pressed the buttons on his trigger bracelet.

Bright blue sparks shot out of the cell phone case. The man holding the phone shrieked and fell backward, his body convulsing on the dirty van floor. The second man, his face just inches from the taser when it went off, was knocked back against the door.

"What the fuck is going on back there?" the driver shouted. "Diaz? McGuire? The hell?"

Remy launched himself at the second man and knocked him off balance. He straddled the man and punched him in the face. He heard a crunch and a spurt of blood jetted from the man's broken nose. But when Remy raised his fist once more, the man blocked it with his forearm and backhanded Remy across the head.

Remy's head spun as he fell over. He was dizzy, unbalanced. The van sped along.

The man with the busted nose pushed Remy off of him and reached down towards his ankle. Remy saw a glint of metal. The man had a gun tucked into an ankle holster.

Remy grabbed the armed man's hand. He tried to push Remy off, but the lurching vehicle sent Remy sprawling to the far side of the van. Remy saw the man unstrapping the gun from its holster. Remy had mere seconds before he would die. Then he saw the reflection of another piece of metal. The pipe. It was trapped under the downed man's leg.

Remy yanked it out just as the second man freed his gun. As he raised the weapon, Remy cracked the pipe across his forearm. He heard a snapping sound and a scream as the man's arm broke. The gun clattered to the floor.

While the gunman howled, Remy went back to the man who'd been debilitated by the Yellowjacket. He grabbed the Lil Guy taser from the floor. The gunman man was holding his broken right arm, gingerly reaching for the gun with his left.

Remy went over to him, said, "Fuck you," charged the taser, and jabbed it into the man's sternum. He let out a shriek, convulsed, then lay still.

Remy picked up the man's gun. It was as a Glock G19. He grabbed his cell phone from the floor. He found his wallet in the man with the broken nose's jacket. Remy turned on his cell phone and opened the camera app. He went over to each man, lifted their mask, took a picture of their faces and texted them to Grace Rivas with the message:

Find out who these assholes are.

The driver yelled, "Diaz? Talk to me! McGuire?"

Remy ripped the electrical tape from his mouth and took a long gulp of air. Then, holding the gun, he climbed through the curtain into the front passenger seat. There was a shovel on the floor. Remy knew exactly why they'd brought it along.

"Hey there," Remy said, holding the gun to the driver's head. The driver was a white man, mid-thirties, dressed in cargo pants, a flannel work shirt, and a down jacket. He was not wearing a mask.

"What the fuck is going on?" the driver yelled.

"Sorry. Diaz and McGuire aren't available to take your call right now. But you're going to stop this van, right now, before I blow a second hole in your dick."

"The hell I am," the driver said. "You see where we are?"

Remy looked out the window. They were driving across a bridge. Traffic was sparse. The speedometer read forty-five miles an hour. Remy recognized where they were headed. They were taking him across the George Washington Bridge on the upper roadway towards New Jersey, where he would be killed and buried. He only had moments before Diaz and McGuire came around, and at that point, unless he wanted to figure out how to incapacitate three very angry men, he was as good as dead.

"Stop the car *now*," Remy yelled, jamming the gun against the driver's head.

The driver laughed, kept going. "You ever fire a gun before, kid? Careful before you shoot your balls off."

Remy looked at the gun and said, "Good thing my Dad kept a Glock in the house and never bothered to lock his drawer." Then Remy deftly released the three internal safety mechanisms and fired a round right between the driver's legs.

"Jesus Christ!" The flash from the gun blinded them both, lighting the entire van up like a firecracker. The noise from the round discharging made Remy's ears ring. A trail of smoke wafted out from the bullet hole in the seat cushion.

"Ow, that fucking burns!" the driver yelled.

He jammed on the brake, bringing the van to a screeching halt. Remy had to brace himself to avoid being flung into the windshield.

Once the van had come to a complete stop, Remy put the gearshift into park, then turned the ignition off and grabbed the key.

"Hey, you little shit, you can't just…"

Remy jabbed the charged taser into the driver's shoulder. He saw a cell phone in the man's pocket. Remy took it.

He unlocked the passenger side door and stepped out into the middle of the upper roadway of the George Washington Bridge. Between the cold, fright, and adrenaline, Remy was shivering uncontrollably.

Two cars stopped short, horns blaring in the night. Remy cut through the traffic to the eastern side of the bridge, where he tossed the gun, the car keys, and the driver's cell into the Hudson River.

Then Remy ran as fast as he could towards the Manhattan end of the bridge. As he neared the exit ramp, he took out his cell phone and dialed Alena.

She picked up on the third ring.

"Alena," he said, breathless and petrified. "They tried to kill me."

CHAPTER 32

The crowd outside of Griggs Tower had grown to at least a thousand. Cops, supporters, protestors, reporters. The whole block was cordoned off by metal gates, and inside those gates stood a dozen dump trucks, parked bumper-to-bumper to prevent anyone from driving up with a car bomb.

With the presidential frontrunner living right smack in the middle of midtown Manhattan, half the city was closed off. Traffic was a mess. One of the city's most visited landmarks was being guarded like Fort Knox.

Which was why, as they pushed through the maelstrom around the Castle, Alena Griggs and Remy Stanton went almost unnoticed until they approached the lobby. That was when someone yelled, "That's Alena Griggs! Oh my god, and she's with Jeremy Stanton!"

The crowd began to surge forward to get a better look. Camera phones came out. The crowd clearly realized that Remy entering the Castle with the daughter of the man whose campaign he had resigned from was a pretty big deal.

Everyone could tell something was very wrong. Stanton looked angry. Alena looked scared. Remy appeared to be pushing Alena

Griggs, forcing her to enter the Castle. People began to speculate that he had kidnapped her, that maybe this kid was really unstable like Rawson Griggs had said.

"Something's wrong with the Griggs gal," one man remarked. "I get the feeling she really didn't want to be with that Stanton kid. I hope he doesn't hurt her."

It took less than ten seconds before everything on the 53rd floor went haywire. Alena Griggs stepped out of the private elevator, Remy Stanton at her back. The first person to see them was Jerry Kapinski.

"Alena…it's so good to see you, how have…Jeremy, what the fuck are you doing here?"

"We're here to see Rawson," Remy said. His hand was at Alena's back. He was pushing her down the corridor.

"Just let us in to see my father," Alena said, her voice trembling. "Just do what Jeremy says."

Kapinski took out his cell phone. Remy only had moments before security arrived.

They continued down the hallway. Dozens of staffers came out of their offices to see what was going on. As they approached Rawson Griggs's office, Kenneth Murphy stepped into the hall.

"Can't let you in there, Jeremy," he said. "You need to leave. Now."

"I'm not going anywhere," Remy said, not even trying to hide the rage in his voice. "You tell that son of a bitch he has to answer to me. Now. Step aside, Ken, or someone's getting hurt."

Murphy saw that Remy was holding onto Alena. He looked like he might be dangerous. Murphy stepped aside. Remy opened the door to Rawson's office. He pushed Alena forward and closed it behind them. Rawson was sitting behind his desk. He stood up, calm. He looked from his daughter, over to Remy, and back.

"Speak, before I tear your head from your neck," he said. "Alena, are you alright?"

Alena nodded. "I'm okay."

Remy laughed. "Decapitation? That's a little messier than burying me somewhere near Fort Lee."

"You're a sick, demented little man," Rawson spat. "You betrayed me and you disgraced yourself. And now you bring my daughter here as, what, some cowardly show of force?"

"You told me once that I was a lion," Remy said.

Rawson laughed. "You're a sheep, Jeremy. You always were."

Rawson came around the corner of his desk faster than Remy believed a man his size could. And before he knew what was happening, Rawson's massive hands were around Remy's throat. He heard Alena gasp. Rawson pushed Remy backwards until he hit the wall with a thud.

Rawson's fingers dug into the soft flesh under Remy's chin, cutting into his throat.

"Dad, stop!" Alena cried.

"You would stand up for him, this misfit?" Rawson said, looking at Alena, confused.

Rawson's grip was like iron. Less like someone who pushed paper and signed checks than someone who hoisted the very marble and concrete into the buildings adorned with his name. His strength again surprised Remy. Painfully so.

"Just in case you get any ideas like your friends in the van," Remy said, struggling to speak, "fifteen minutes ago I posted on social media that I'd be coming here to see you. Oh, and a whole lot of people outside snapped our picture when we entered the Castle. So if your security guards decide to get frisky, it's public knowledge that this is the last place I was seen. So be careful, Mr. President."

Rawson released his grip and shoved Remy back against the door. Then he returned to his desk and sat down.

Remy massaged his throat.

"If you're done with your sad little power trip," Rawson said, "get the fuck out of my building."

"Not before you answer for Paul Bracewell," Remy said.

Rawson narrowed his eyes and said, with just a split second hesitation, "What in god's name are you talking about?"

"You murdered Paul," Remy said. "You tried to have Nogoyev and Usenov do it for you, but I got in the way. Sorry about that. Everyone assumed they were terrorists or radicals. But really, they were just getting rid of Paul after he found out that you're the Manchurian fucking Candidate. Paul was feeding info to Doug Rimbaud. About your properties. About GazProm. He knew you were practically bankrupt. Paul was a loose cannon. And big dick Rawson Griggs couldn't have that. So you had Costanzo's goons dump him in the river. Maybe Costanzo even did it himself, so the old dog could prove he still had some fight left in him."

"You're insane," Rawson said. "Alena, this man is demented."

"Paul was your daughter's *husband*," Remy said. "And you threw him away like a candy wrapper."

"Dad," Alena said, her voice soft, fragile, "what is he talking about?"

"Absolutely nothing. Jeremy is clearly a sick man. I should have left you in that dead-end job to have a dead-end life to be a nothing just like you were always meant to be. I gave you purpose, I saved you from mediocrity, and you spat in my family's face."

"And you're a murderer," Remy seethed. "Because Paul found out the truth. You're going to turn Washington into the Kremlin West. You stand to make billions and billions from Eastern oil exports. You would have been one rich bastard."

"I already am," Rawson said coolly.

"But there's always more," Remy replied. "Right?"

"Alena," Rawson said, "I'm sorry for allowing this man to poison our lives. He should have never been allowed near you. It ends today. I'm having you thrown in prison, and I promise you won't leave standing up."

"Just like Dastan Nogoyev," Remy said. "We both know you had him killed. But you couldn't find Alexay Usenov to shut him up too, right? And then he bombed your building in retribution for your killing his friend. Your daughter was a hundred feet away when that bomb went off."

"This is beyond ludicrous."

The office door opened and three burly men wearing suits and earpieces came in. They averaged about six foot two, two hundred forty pounds, and looked to get the most out of their gym memberships.

"Your private Mr. Olympia team doesn't change anything," Remy said. He reached into his pocket and tossed a piece of paper on the floor in front of Alena. "She'll want to see that."

Alena knelt down, picked up the paper, and began to read.

"Get him out of here," Rawson said, smiling politely. "But do it *gently*. We don't want to harm this special little snowflake. At least not yet."

"Go to hell, Rawson," Remy said as the guards dragged him out of the office. Remy looked at Alena. He mouthed the words *I'm sorry*.

Once Remy was gone, Murphy entered the office, tentatively, and shut the door.

"You okay, boss?" he said. He noticed Alena standing in the corner. She was reading the paper that Remy had dropped. "Boss?"

"Yes? What? I'm fine. Everything is fine. Brief interruption. We're still planning to fly out to Colorado later today."

"The Denver Coliseum is ready for us, sir," Murphy said. "Eleven thousand people waiting. Kapinski says the line started forming yesterday."

"Good," Rawson said. He looked over at his daughter, noticed she was engrossed in the paper Remy had dropped. Murphy took the hint.

"Let me know if you need anything," Murphy said, and he left.

"Alena?" Rawson said. He stood up slowly. "Are you alright? Did he hurt you?"

She did not respond. Her eyes were glued to the paper.

"Alena? What is that?"

Rawson came around the desk. He took the paper from Alena's hands. She let him have it.

"What is…"

"Is it true?" Alena said.

"Is what true?"

"Did you kill my husband?"

"Alena, that's absurd," Rawson said. "Jeremy is a crazy person. You heard those ravings. He's a lunatic."

"Read that," she said. "It's the draft of a story that Grace Rivas is running tomorrow in the *Gazette*. It says you spent two billion dollars buying a stake in GazProm. That you were worth nothing on paper. They claim to have a copy of your tax returns and that your accountant confirmed its authenticity. It also says Paul was funneling information to Annabelle Shaw's campaign because he found out about this and wanted to stop you. Is that true?"

"Alena, I love you with all my heart. This is madness. I won't discuss it."

"Is it true, *Dad*?" she shouted. Alena pushed her father, who teetered back on his heels, shocked. His daughter had never laid a hand on him. He stammered.

"My business is large and complicated and has been for years, you know that," Rawson said. "I won't discuss these matters with you."

"They have *proof* you've been dealing with Kyrgyzstani officials for twenty years. That you were paid half a million dollars for a speech there. The men who tried to kill Paul and me, the man who *bombed your building when I was there to support you*, were from that country. So please don't stand there and tell me this is none of my business. The Griggs name has been my business from the moment I was born. You made it my business. I never had a choice. Are we broke, Dad? Where is all the money for this campaign coming from?"

"Trust me, Alena, you want no part of this," Rawson said. "Go home. Mourn your husband, and then move on. Like I mourned your mother. I did so and then moved on. In a few months, you and I will have the world and none of this will matter."

"Answer me," Alena said. "Did you kill Paul?"

"Alena, please."

"All this, this campaign, for what? More money? Power? You were working with murderers while I had to sleep in the bed where my husband used to be? You chose this over your *family*?"

"You are my family," Rawson said. "Since your mother died, you have been my only family. Paul was never a part of our family. You and I both know that. He may have been your husband, but he was never one of us."

"That was a choice *you* made," she said. "You never let Paul in. You never wanted him."

"When your child makes a mistake," Rawson said, "it is a father's duty to correct that mistake."

"Fathers don't talk like that," Alena said. "You don't get to direct my life. I don't care how many millions and billions you make. I don't care whether you win this election. You are not god. You do not decide life and death."

"I decide what is best for me. For us. I always have. And I've always been right. Every time. Your husband was a snake," Rawson said. "He sided against us."

"What did you do, Dad?" Alena said, pleading. She shouted, "*What did you do?*"

"I did what I had to do to save us. To save this campaign. To save you."

"That's bullshit," Alena said. "This was never about the campaign or about me. It's always been about you. I never cared about all the people you burned over the years because they weren't my family. I looked away. I always took your side. I defended you at your worst. But Paul saw something I didn't. And so you decided he was dangerous. You didn't want him coming to those meetings because you knew he was working for Shaw. Jeremy messed up your plan the first time. But you got a second shot. And you took it."

"Alena..."

"I want to hear you say it. As my father. As the man who gave me away at my wedding. As the man who heard me say 'til death do us part,' and then decided it was up to him to decide when that would be. I need to hear you say it."

"Alena…"

"*Say it!*"

Rawson nodded. Tears formed at the corners of his eyes. Alena began to tremble. She had never seen her father cry.

"Say it," she said again, softly, pleading.

"Paul was going to destroy everything," Rawson said. "I couldn't let that happen."

"So you tried to have him killed that night near our apartment. And when that went bad, you had Costanzo's goons pick him up when he was drunk outside the Hyatt. And, what, they made him keep drinking until he blacked out? Then they dumped him in the water like garbage? Is that what happened? Is that what you did?"

"Yes," Rawson said.

Alena's mouth opened, but nothing came out. She choked back a sob, tears flowing down her cheeks.

"I need to hear you say it," she said. "I need to hear you say that's what you did."

"That's what I did," Rawson said, his voice shaking. "But it was all for you."

Alena seemed to sink inward, her body folding into itself as she doubled over. Sobs wracked her body.

"I did it for you," he said. "For our family. Our future."

"You destroyed my family," Alena said. "You did it for you. You ruined my future."

Rawson shook his head violently. "Paul would have destroyed our family's future."

"So your solution was to *kill* him?" Alena cried. "I buried my husband thinking I'd done something wrong, that'd I'd driven him away. Our last words to each other were hateful and angry. I never had a chance to tell him I was sorry because you took him away before I could. You would have let me live with that my whole life. Seeing me in pain was better than admitting the truth. Why? What could possibly be more important?"

"I'm going to change the world," Rawson said. "Once I'm in the

White House, I can usher in a new era for this country. I have a plan in place to create a global economy like the world has never seen."

"Save your stump speech for the road," Alena said.

"There are a million men like Paul. He could have brought all of this down, and you know better than anyone I couldn't allow him to do that. I love you. But think about all the people whose lives will get better. We will break down walls that have been in place for decades. *Centuries.*"

"None of that is worth killing for," Alena said.

"It's *all* worth killing for. Nobody ever changed the world without doing things that other people wouldn't," Rawson said. "And yes, once my term is up, and I'm an old man, you will be set for life. You will find love again. You will marry again and have children, and those children and their children will live in a better world. They will have more money than they can dream of. What I'm doing now—I will give people a gift that will resonate for generations."

"The only gift I wanted, you stole from me."

"It can be replaced," Rawson said. "Everything can be replaced."

Alena shook her head. Rawson went to his daughter. He held out his arms. She pressed her hand against his chest, holding him back.

"Please," Rawson said. "You are my child. You are part of me."

With each sob, Rawson seemed to shrink. Alena let her hands drop. Rawson wrapped his arms around her, engulfing her in his bear-like frame. He held her close, this woman, this girl. His baby girl. Now and always.

"I'm sorry, Alena," he whispered. "This will all be fine in time. I promise."

Alena pushed her father away gently and looked into his eyes. She had never seen him cry. Not when she graduated high school or college. Not when Liliana died. Not at her wedding. For a moment, it broke her.

"I'm sorry too, Dad."

Rawson managed a smile. "Alena, what could you possibly be sorry for?"

She looked down, at her suit jacket, at the gorgeous circular gold brooch with the gemstone in the center.

Rawson looked at it, seemed to admire its beauty and craftsmanship. Then his eyes narrowed. He reached out and took the piece in his hand. It was not real gold. He pulled it gently.

And that was when Rawson saw that the gemstone was not a stone at all. A thin wire protruded from the back of the piece, trailing down into the inseam of Alena's jacket. He saw his own reflection in the dark gloss of the stone, which he now saw was a small camera. And then, too late, he realized what Alena and Jeremy had done.

"I'm sorry, Dad," she said, weeping. "I'm so sorry."

Rawson stood up, extending his full height and girth. He took a step back.

"Alena," he said.

"Dad…"

And he said simply, "I understand."

The office door burst open and half a dozen men and women wearing FBI jackets entered. They surrounded Rawson Griggs. Alena stepped back, plastered herself against the wall. One of the agents stepped forward.

"Rawson Griggs," he said. "Agent D'Antoni. We met before. When your son-in-law—*cough*—died. It is my absolute pleasure to say that you are under arrest for conspiracy to commit murder. And something tells me that'll be far from the last charge."

Two agents pushed Rawson against his desk and handcuffed him behind his back.

"Dad, I'm so sorry," Alena said.

As Rawson was led out of his office, he looked at his daughter and said, "I was wrong. You were the lion."

Then Rawson Griggs was led away.

Alena sank to her knees, alone in her father's office, with its spectacular views overlooking the grandeur of the city he helped build, and cried.

FALL

CHAPTER 33

RAWSON GRIGGS SENTENCED, MAYFLOWER PARTY COLLAPSES

**Country looks to repair its wounds
behind leadership of
President-Elect Annabelle Shaw**

By Grace Rivas and Eric Celsun

The stunning collapse of an American empire was complete today as iconic businessman and former presidential candidate Rawson Griggs was sentenced to life in prison after being found guilty of six felony charges, including conspiracy to commit murder in the death of Mr. Griggs's son-in-law, Paul Bracewell, and treason for Griggs's partnership with the foreign activist group PoliSpill, which coordinated with the Griggs campaign to kneecap both of Mr. Griggs's Republican and Democratic opponents. A jury found unanimously that Mr. Griggs knowingly orchestrated an effort by foreign bodies to influence the United States presidential election by working with PoliSpill to first target Republican Richard Bertrand, who dropped out of the race, and then Annabelle Shaw, who weathered the storm and went on to win the recent election despite the lowest voter turnout in decades, defeating Wisconsin governor Bobby Garrett by a narrow electoral college margin of 279-259.

Despite facing charges that could land him in prison for the rest of his life, and being removed from the national ballot in the wake of his indictment, Rawson Griggs received nearly two million write-in votes from supporters who were convinced Griggs had been set up by his political opponents, or who felt his alleged crimes were not severe enough to swing their vote.

Griggs's daughter, Alena, at the center of the investigation, was hailed as a whistleblower for getting a confession of her father's crimes. Yet Ms. Griggs was called a pariah: many felt that their dreams of a Griggs presidency were dashed when his crimes came to light. Ms. Griggs, long seen as the heir apparent to an iconic American empire, has not spoken publicly since her father's indictment. And with the Griggs Organization's assets frozen, it remains to be seen how she intends to carry on her family's business, if at all.

The Griggs trial featured testimony from Jeremy Stanton, the so-called "Upper East Side Hero," who had been hired by Griggs after he prevented the assumed attempted murder of Alena Griggs and Paul Bracewell. But after thousands of emails and phone logs were subpoenaed from Griggs servers, the Department of Justice uncovered proof Bracewell had been targeted by Griggs himself after learning that Bracewell had been acting as an informant for Annabelle Shaw's campaign.

Amidst his suspicion of Rawson's crimes, Jeremy Stanton had resigned from the Griggs campaign. Following the controversy surrounding a never-aired interview with his estranged father, Stanton was later assaulted by men who were then identified as employees of Phillip Costanzo's security firm. One of the assailants, Fernando Diaz, has been identified as the brother of Domingo Diaz, the inmate who killed suspected assassin Dastan Nogoyev in prison as he awaited arraignment.

The Griggs Organization, once a hallmark of American industry, money, power, ambition, and success, lies in shambles.

Following Rawson Griggs's arrest, thousands of pro-Griggs supporters organized demonstrations around the country. In Pleasant Prairie, Michigan, hundreds of unemployed men and women held a vigil for Mr. Griggs outside of a now-shuttered Jelly Belly plant. Griggs had drawn thousands to his rally in Prairie last year, and residents, facing a devastated local economy, believed a Griggs presidency would bring this derelict town back to greatness.

"I don't care what he did or who he had to go through to do it," said Ann-Marie Butler, 56. "You don't make an omelet without breaking some eggs. Rawson found some bad eggs, broke them, and we should be praising him for it, not jailing him for it. Whatever Rawson Griggs did, he did for the good of the country. But I know Rawson will pull through. Beasts survive."

The result of the Griggs incarceration is a nation that is as divided as ever, with an unpopular president-elect presiding over an electorate whose majority did not vote her into office, whose party does not control the House or Senate, and who will find many of her proposals blocked by an admittedly obstructionist Republican Party.

President-elect Shaw, in a press conference following her victory, said of the Griggs scandal, "Rawson Griggs tapped into a very real anger felt by many Americans. I do not condone his horrific actions, and I am thankful his presidency did not come to pass. America as we know it would have ceased to exist. But I do want to tell the many people who believed in Rawson Griggs that we feel their pain. That we will not stand by while our cities and towns crumble. That we will not forget them. Rest assured that the common man and woman will be remembered and play a role, a significant one, in the future of this great country. I am proud to be a president for all of us."

Following her press conference, President-elect Shaw sped to a $25,000 a plate fundraiser at the Mandarin Oriental Hotel in Manhattan to help pay down her millions of dollars in campaign debts and to raise money to aid her transition team.

CHAPTER 34

I'm going to die. This time, for real. There's nothing I can do to stop it. *My luck has run out. Please bury me next to my loved ones.*

Those words ran through Remy's mind as he straddled the bicycle seat, hooked his shoes into the clips, and prepared to take Trevor's spin class for the very first time. The studio was filled to capacity: fifty trim and toned "students," all clad in colorful spandex and polyester outfits, waiting to sweat off half their body weight over the next forty-five minutes. Remy looked around, terrified. He hadn't seen this much muscle and sinew since he went on an ill-advised first date to the *Bodies* exhibit. Remy wondered if anyone ever had the misfortune of passing out before the class actually started.

He was sitting front row center, as promised. Chris sat on the bike to his right. To his left was a girl in her mid-twenties wearing a neon green sports bra with abs that looked like the underside of an egg carton. Generic dance music was playing as everyone clipped in and adjusted their bikes.

"This was a very bad idea," Remy said to Chris. "Any advice?"

"Just don't fart during class," Chris said. "That's a big no-no."

"Got it. Do they have paramedics here? You know, just in case?"

"Quit whining," Chris said. "I've only seen three people die during Trevor's classes."

"Are you serious?"

"Of course not, you big ninny. You'll love it. Trust me."

A side door opened and Trevor walked up to the podium. A single bike sat atop the mount. The class cheered and clapped as Trevor clipped in. He plugged his iPhone into the speaker setup, which was about the size of a small SUV. Trevor wore a large brace on his ankle, but otherwise looked no worse for wear. He had on a gray, sleeveless CyclePro t-shit, black spandex pants, and a blue headband. Trevor looked like he'd just escaped a 1980s fitness video, but it worked.

Trevor clasped his hands together and leaned forward.

"Thanks, everyone," Trevor said, beaming. He choked up as he spoke. "It feels so, so great to finally be back. It's been a long, tough road to get to this point. But now I'm back and I can't wait to kick all your asses."

Forty-nine people clapped. They were fired up. Remy couldn't understand why so many people were this excited to get their asses kicked.

"Now, I said I wouldn't embarrass them," Trevor said, "but this is *my* class, so tough shit. I want to thank my loving and patient husband, Chris, who put up with my cabin fever the last few months and finally learned how to make the bed. I love you, babe."

Chris blew Trevor a kiss and waved to the class.

"And my good friend, Remy Stanton. Some of you might know Remy from this little election thing over the past year, it wasn't really *that* big of a deal, and we won't hold it against him that he worked for Voldemort before finally wising up. Seriously, though, Remy's the best friend a guy could have and I'm glad he's here. And this is his first class, so I'm going to make it special."

Remy didn't want special. He was just fine with not falling off the bike.

"Now," Trevor said, flicking a switch that turned the studio into a dark cave. "Let's ride!"

Trevor turned the music on, Remy prayed to God, and the class began.

He was still alive. He felt like a human puddle and looked like a drowned rat, but Remy had survived. For forty-five minutes, Remy pedaled, sprinted, climbed hills, and occasionally had to remind himself to breathe. Chris was right, though. He felt like he might throw up, but the adrenaline rush was fantastic. It was the best workout he'd gotten in, well, forever.

When the class ended, Trevor thanked everyone again, dismounted his bike, and gave Chris and Remy a slimy hug.

"So," Trevor said to Remy as he toweled off. "What'd you think?"

"You played too much Beyoncé," Remy said.

"My classes are usually ninety percent women. They like Beyoncé. People don't get pumped listening to Barry Manilow, or whatever the hell you keep on your iPhone."

"Barry Manilow is a little too gangster for me."

"Seriously," Chris said. "How'd you do?"

"Weirdly enough, I loved it. I'm shocked to say that. So am I invited back?"

"You'd better come back," Trevor said. "But from now on you have to book on Sundays at five p.m. just like everyone else. My classes fill up in less than one minute. No joke."

"You're like the pied piper of gross, sweaty insanity."

"I take that as a wonderful compliment. So, on to brunch next?"

"I'll go shower," Remy said. "Meet you out front."

"Go ahead. Oh, and bring your friend."

"My friend?" Remy said. Trevor pointed towards the back of the studio. Remy's jaw dropped. Alena Griggs was standing there, wearing a white tank top and green Lululemon pants. She was sweaty, her ponytail askew, and breathing like she'd just climbed a mountain. Remy wondered if his beating heart was visible through his shirt.

Alena waved at Remy, and he went over to her.

"Hey," she said.

"Hey. So…can I hug you, or would you prefer to wait until I'm no longer a sweaty mess?"

"Give me a hug, you sweaty mess."

Remy wrapped his arms around Alena. He felt like crying. They hadn't seen each other in months. God, he'd missed her.

"Alena emailed me last week asking if she could come to my first class back," Trevor said, putting his arms around them both. "As you can see, I put her in the back row. Now don't get me wrong, I like this gal, but I don't need all you celebrities taking away my spotlight."

"Totally understandable," Alena said. "Consider me a regular from now on."

"We're going for brunch after this," Trevor said. "Care to join us?"

"Only if where you're going makes a good Bloody Mary," she said.

"Ooh, I like this girl," Trevor said. "Go get ready. Everyone meet outside in fifteen."

Remy touched her hand, felt her fingers curl around his. "I missed you."

"I missed you too."

"I'm glad you came. Maybe at some point we can catch up. Just the two of us."

"I'd like that."

"Hey, oh my god, I love you two. Can I get a selfie?"

One of Trevor's "students" had noticed Remy and Alena, and was holding out her cell phone eagerly. Her trapezius muscles were bigger than Remy's head.

"Sure," Alena said.

The girl posed in front of them and they all smiled as she took the picture. "My boyfriend is gonna *freak*," she said. "Thanks! So are you two, like, a couple?"

"Alright, move along," Alena said.

The girl left, and Remy laughed.

"I thought I was done with those," Remy said.

"You'll never be done with them," Alena replied. "Now go get cleaned up."

Remy showered and changed and met Trevor, Chris, and Alena outside the studio. Their faces were all bright red and sweat-sheened from the workout. Remy was starving. Forget Bloody Marys, he didn't care about drinks as long as they served food. Preferably something carb-related and smothered in cheese.

Trevor and Chris walked ahead, holding hands. Remy felt awkward. He wanted to touch her hand, see if she was receptive or recoiled. The choice was taken from him when he felt Alena take his hand, gently. He folded his hand around hers and smiled.

"Should we…talk about everything?"

"Not yet. Sometime. Right now, I just want to be Alena and Remy. No last names."

"That sounds wonderful."

They walked towards the restaurant. Then Remy heard someone call out from behind them: "Mr. Stanton! Ms. Griggs!"

Alena whispered, "Ugh, not another one."

Remy turned around. A man was jogging hurriedly up to them. By the time he arrived he was out of breath. He was in his mid-forties, slightly pudgy, with wispy black hair. He was wearing gray slacks and a brown sport jacket.

"Peter Drummond, *Daily Wire*," the man said, heaving. "Somebody…hoo, give me a second…posted on Twitter…that they saw you both in at CyclePro. Really glad I caught you. Mr. Stanton, mind if I ask you a few questions?"

"Sorry," Remy said, "we're on our way to eat. You can email me."

"Mr. Stanton, please. Just quickly. How do you feel about President elect Shaw?"

"I'm sure she's a very nice woman," Remy said.

"Did you vote for her?"

"It is the constitutional right of all Americans to keep their ballots private," Remy replied.

"What are your plans now that the election over? Will you go back to Pulaski & Associates?"

"Not at the moment," Remy said. "I'm kind of happy being a free agent for a little while. Now, excuse us."

They continued to walk, leaving Drummond standing behind them.

"Just one more question," Drummed shouted. "Mr. Stanton, would you ever consider running for office yourself?"

Remy stopped. He looked at Alena. She smiled. Shrugged.

He said, "Give me a minute."

Then Remy turned back around.

ACKNOWLEDGMENTS

To my hearts: Dana and Ava. The word love is inadequate for you. Being your husband and father fills me with pride like nothing else I've ever experienced.

To mom, dad, and Ali: for your unending love and unconditional support.

To Scott Miller: for your advice, and for going along with this crazy idea.

To the many people I spoke to in various branches of government, journalism, and political consulting in the research for this book (none of whom I have been permitted to name). Thank you for your fascinating stories, your candor, and for essentially doing the trapeze above a swimming pool filled with piranhas in the three-ring circus that is politics.

A few of the books I read in researching this book that are well worth your time:

Game Change by John Heilemann and Mark Halperin
Fear and Loathing on the Campaign Trail '72 by Hunter S. Thompson
Dark Money by Jane Mayer
It Can't Happen Here by Sinclair Lewis
All the President's Men by Carl Bersntein and Bob Woodward
Nixonland by Rick Perlstein
The Selling of the President by Joe McGinniss
The Golden Kazoo by John G. Schneider
Trump Revealed by Michael Kranish & Marc Fisher

Thank you above all to the readers: those who have waited patiently for a new book, and to those just joining the party.

Welcome.

ABOUT THE AUTHOR

Jason Pinter is the bestselling author of five thrillers with over one million copies in print worldwide in over a dozen languages, as well as the Middle Grade adventure novel *Zeke Bartholomew: SuperSpy*. He has been nominated for the Thriller Award, Strand Critics Award, Barry Award, RT Reviewers Choice Award, Shamus Award and CrimeSpree Award. Two of his books—*The Fury* and *The Darkness*—were chosen as Indie Next selections, and *The Mark*, *The Stolen* and *The Fury*, were named to The Strand's Best Books of the Year list. *The Mark* and *The Stolen* both appeared on the 'Heatseekers' bestseller list in The Bookseller (UK). *The Mark* was optioned to be a feature film.

He is the Founder and Publisher of Polis Books, an independent publishing company he founded in 2013. He was recently named one of *Publisher Weekly*'s inaugural Star Watch honorees, which "recognizes young publishing professionals who have distinguished themselves as future leaders of the industry."

He has written for *The New Republic, Entrepreneur, The Daily Beast, Medium* and *The Huffington Post*, and has been featured in *Library Journal, Publishers Weekly*, MediaBistro, *Mystery Scene* and more. He lives in Northern New Jersey with his wife, their daughter, and their dog.

Visit him at www.JasonPinter.com and follow him at @JasonPinter.